RIVENLAND

By the same author

Cross Cut

Out of Time

Wake Us Tomorrow

t published 2012 by Time Link Publications
Warneford Gardens, Exmouth. EX8 4EN
elink@btinternet.com

opyright Lee Ellis 2012

Rivenland is a work of fiction. Any similarity to real persons, living or dead is entirely coincidental.

ISBN 978-0-9557928-4-7

A CIP catalogue record for this book is available from the British Library.

Cover design based on an original painting by Carole Ellis

Prepared and printed by:

York Publishing Services Ltd
64 Hallfield Road
Layerthorpe
York YO31 7ZQ

Tel: 01904 431213

Website: www.yps-publishing.co.uk

RIVENLAND

Lee Ellis

Time Link

Firs
12
tin

C

A

1

MATTHEW tries to move, but the pain sears up his leg. He eases it carefully and the pain gradually subsides. He shuts his eyes. This is the worst part. More men die after the battle than during it. Better it comes quickly than lying here beneath that mocking sky, listening to the cries, smelling the gore, tasting the bitter bile, wondering if you'll choke in your own blood or go out in breathless agony...The same uncaring sky looked down as we fought...Blank it out. He opens his eyes, but all he sees are the wooden boards of the cart. He stretches his arm down to his leg, fingers the slash in his clothes and feels oozing liquid. He slides his thumb further down. It's sticky. Congealed blood. Not the outcome he expected. In the full flush of reckless adventure young men live forever. Others would be cut and shot, sliced and slain. For luck is all in parrying sword thrusts or avoiding musket balls. Luck, a cool head and sharp reactions. But luck has run out. A life gone before it's really begun.

A sudden image of a farmyard. He's chasing a running piglet, his little legs struggling to keep up. His father races ahead and catches the animal. Then he's in the house. He's come in early from the field and talks to his mother as she prepares dinner. He banters with his sister. Now he's in London, marching out of the city. His first taste of the war. Edmund, his brother in law is speaking.

"Prince Rupert's force comes! The Royalists have sacked Brentford, the soldiers taking food and drink from tables, stealing from houses, throwing furniture and bedclothes out of broken windows. Whole families are driven into poverty by the looting, while plundered townsmen were put in irons or tied with ropes to be led away like dogs."

Harrowing, wild days! We were afraid, but determined. For the war began in the streets before King or Parliament had any armies and we believed ordinary people might change everything. That madman had to be stopped entering London.

And he was stopped as the whole city mobilised against him. Then on the farm again. Now back on the barricades at Turnham Green, men, women, even older children working all day and night to put up the defences, his sister pulling cannon and digging ditches, driving a cart so fast, almost forcing others off the road. If anyone shirked or complained of tiredness someone shouts 'He shall not pass' and the task was soon completed.

His own fresh voice punches from those heady days.

"We'll string him up if we capture him, but he'll not venture this way again."

1642. It could be yesterday. So much packed into these two years, more than likely for the rest of his life. Easy enough if the rest is to be lived only on this cart. You only think about the past when you have no future. Regrets pile up, polluting remembrance. So little time left. Don't sully precious minutes with remorse.

Now he's drilling with the trained bands at Billingsgate. He'd been working in the cloth trade only a few years when the quarrel between King and Parliament erupted into open warfare in the Summer of 1642. Vital, reckless glorious days! The Royalist lord mayor refused to summon the companies of armed citizens, but that didn't stop men mustering and training and during the crisis in January the force soon enlarged to six thousand.

Matthew urging on his friends.

"The King will come to his senses, it'll soon be over."

Soon be over. If only he'd known then...A sudden thunderous bang followed by a rush of explosive air and searing timber. The battle is still close. Better this way, the next assault carrying him off so he doesn't have time to think...but terror grips him. Running and shouting. They'll not leave him here in the blood and smoke to die wretched and alone? He tries to shout, but manages only a poor wearied groan. He tries to move, but feels nothing, not even pain. He felt it before. He can't feel anything. Does that mean his leg is no more? Has he already gone? He shuts his eyes. It won't be long now. Drift, drift into nothingness. No he won't go!

"Now then, my lad what have we got here?"

Matthew tries to turn to the gruff, low voice, but nothing happens and he sees only vague shapes and indistinct flickering light. His whole body is paralysed!

"Turn him," the voice says, "I need to see that leg."

If they turn him they'll kill him! He tries to speak, but there's no sound except the clattering wagons and marching men. All movement around him, but he cannot move! Then stout arms grip him and he's turned half onto his side.

"That's enough," the gruff voice comes again, "Not too far. Now let me see."

The pain returns. Dull at first, then stronger. He grits his teeth. It's a good sign. If he can feel there is hope. His eyes clear slightly and one dull shape becomes a hazy man.

"Who are...who are...?" Matthew says, weak and falteringly

"A surgeon lad," the gruff voice announces, "come to see what can be done with..."

He breaks off, his firm hand pawing at Matthew's leg as he mutters to his assistant, the words as indistinct as the man's features. Then he's firmly held as the surgeon pushes and pulls. Matthew feels as if his leg will be thrown right out of the cart.

"There lad," the surgeon says, finishing his fearsome manipulations, "That'll ease it a bit."

"Will I...will I...?" Matthew bleats.

"Lose it?"

The surgeon smacks his lips, shakes his head and exchanges further incoherent remarks with his assistant. Then the pain, stimulated by the surgeon's rough handed prodding and poking erupts once more, stabbing right up his body as if burning torches scorch his flesh and sharp needles are thrust into his bones.

"Not much hope," the surgeon says, "even taking off would do no good. He's as comfortable as he can be, but..."

"No, no," Matthew screams, the pain devouring his bowels, shooting up his arm and over his chest, then shouting with his last vestige of energy, "I'm not done yet! You'll not take it off!"

"No, no, lad, I'll not take it off. What I'll do is..."

The pain is in his head. He can't take any more, the words trail away. How did he get here, what desperate mistake or random accident brings him to the brink of death? He means harm to no particular man and scarce anyone means any harm to him. Yet who was the man who did this thing, where is he now...riding away in glory...or also struck down, now lying on the cold ground so ready to take him too...what then...how will he fare...what is he like...?

...then oblivion, dark, comforting, slithering nothingness... and is it hours or days before he sees that spiteful sky, hears the rumbling of the wheels and feels each pitch and roll of this damnable cart? Images come and go, memories slink across only to slide away, jump back, mixed and mangled before being wrenched away once more.

Now he's with the trained bands again...then hearing the terrible news of Brentford...now on the lines before Turnham Green...then where is this place...he's riding...it can only be... Cropredy Bridge...fateful awful place where his leg...

"...I can patch him up as best I can. It's a rudimentary dressing, I must get on, there are others"

...that cursed surgeon! Damn him!...

"He'll not last more than a few days..."

I will, I will!

"We're off to London"...another voice...the carman...

"Don't leave me here! I'll stay in the cart," Matthew insists, "I'll take my chances on the road. If I'm to die, I'll die in London"

4

"You'll not survive the journey. I give you a few days at most"

...damnable surgeon again. I will, I will stay...

...then the trained bands again, the Blue regiment. Matthew adapts well to the military environment and is promoted...

Clattering on the rough ground, unsprung wheels hammering the stony ground through every bone and muscle!

...now his sister's house ...dreadful news from Brentford... "Just one regiment taken by surprise...they fought bravely, but were driven back, many captured, many drowned in the river..." Brentford so close to London, Skippon's trained bands head west to unite with the Earl of Essex's soldiers. They must prevent the Royalists getting nearer to London!

Bump, thud, into the hole! No smooth road to London, the infernal wheels pummelling his frail and shaky leg, battering right through his back!

...at Turnham Green they meet and Puritan preachers spur the people to their duty.

"When you hear the drums beat, say not I am not of the Trained Band, nor this, nor that, but doubt not to go to work and fight courageously and this shall be the day of your deliverance."

...thousands of citizen soldiers block the road, thousands more in hedges, ditches, orchards, gardens, stables, barns and taverns. All the way to Westminster and the City are barricades and more men, cannon at every gate and street, fieldworks quickly dug across the suburbs and armed ships patrol the river...

...if the King wins here the road to London is open and any chance of securing liberty will be lost, all they hold dear trampled under the hooves of Prince Rupert's cavalry...they shall not pass...twenty four thousand stand in their way...

...the Earl of Essex rides from regiment to regiment to shouts of "Hey for old Robin." Then Phillip Skippon calls to his soldiers...

"Come on, my boys, my brave boys, let us pray heartily and fight heartily. I will run the same fortunes and hazards

with you. Remember the cause is for God and for the defence of yourselves, your wives and your children. Come, my honest, brave boys, pray heartily and God will bless us..."

Seventy rickety rackety miles, his mind beaten as much as his body, days and nights in the rattling cart, remembering the rough gloomy voice and those cold heavy hands. Was it days the surgeon gave him or only hours? Rattle, crunch, bump, bash...if the wounds don't kill him the road surely will...

...will he ever see Jane again...but that was before...when he was young and the world was new...when everything was possible...if only he could see her one last time before...

He wakes stiff and cold. It's just dawn, but the cart clatters and clanks along the rutty potholed road. How far now? No one says and he hasn't the energy to ask. Will he ever reach London, ever see his sister again?

...she comes with a cart stacked high with victuals and drink and this afternoon the troops will be well fed...

Clunk, bang, into the hole, his leg seemingly torn from its socket! As if he was still in that battle...

...battles cannot be won by steel and pike alone. Victory needs right words to harness beliefs...oh how heartily they cheered Skippon at Turnham Green, the general's invigoration infusing them with the elixir of freedom...

Crash! The cart stops. Something has fallen off. A brief respite, but Matthew has so little time. If he's to prove that wretched doctor wrong he must get to London soon...

...The hours pass slowly and quietly. Rumours spread of an imminent attack, but the King's army, outnumbered, tired and hungry, turn and retreat. The capital is saved without a shot being fired. The spirit of the people prevails...

He feels a sudden upsurge of strength and tries to lift himself, pulling up slightly on his elbow, but the pain shoots up his leg and is too much and he drops back down. The cart moves off again, but rest...he needs to sleep...his eyes close...

...Cropredy Bridge... Now at last they will triumph! For the war was not won two years ago at Turnham Green. Trained Bands were not enough and he wanted to become a professional soldier. From his life on the farm he could ride and was determined to join the cavalry. He learnt fast

and he learnt well, receiving a commission and promoted to Captain after the battle of Newbury in 1643...then came Cropredy Bridge and that fateful awful charge...

The respite was short. He wakes with a start. Oh come sleep again, he's so wearied, so worn...but sleep may bring a longer never ending rest just like the never ending rumbling of this damned cart! While he's awake there's hope he'll make it to London, to his sister's house, there to rest, not here on this foul clattering carrier to Hell!

...to London, Elizabeth...Jane...now is not the time...not the past...but now...now and life...

By the time the cart arrives in London Matthew is in a bad state, but despite the doctor's gloomy prognosis, still alive. His sister Elizabeth runs from the house. She's in her late twenties, a couple of years older than Matthew.

"What's this, what's this?" she cries as Matthew is unceremoniously dumped at her door.

"Survivor of the battle at Cropredy Bridge," the carman says, "Is he yours, missis?"

"Of course he's mine," Elizabeth says, "Help me get him inside."

The back breaking journey has exhausted Matthew, his injuries serious and his troubles only just beginning. A doctor is called, his prognosis almost as dismal as his gruff colleague on the battlefield.

"Look after him well. It's his only hope and a slim one at that."

"I will nurse him as best I can," Elizabeth says, "At least he'll die in peace."

Matthew is barely conscious as Elizabeth and her husband Edmund Culshaw carry him upstairs.

"I'm done for," he mutters as they settle him in bed.

"You certainly are," Elizabeth says, "Done with soldiering and putting the world to rights!"

Matthew is too weak to argue and slips into a deep sleep, which continues for the next three days, interspersed with erratic wakefulness and troubled dreams. Dreams of riding hard under attack and falling, falling, falling...of men lying on the ground, injured, dead...why should he survive when so many other men sturdy and true have gone?

With oscillating hope and despair Elizabeth and Edmund watch as he declines and rallies, rallies and declines, but he holds on by his fingertips. Summer becomes autumn and autumn becomes winter, but this fortune of war smiles a little. His leg heals with careful tendering, his mobility gradually returning and he retains both his life and his leg, but his military career at least for a time comes to a sudden end, leaving him with a permanent limp. But he is recovered and in the spring is summoned to General Skippon's headquarters, hoping it will bring news of his imminent return to the army.

Phillip Skippon, a respected professional soldier rose through the ranks of the Dutch army in the Continental wars. Though he has not served under him for over two years, Matthew has great respect for the general. He does not have long to wait and is soon ushered into the general's room. Skippon looks older than a couple of years should have aged him. Maybe Matthew is the same. War is no respecter of youth and beauty.

"It's been a long winter," Skippon says, "You've been staying with your sister, I believe?"

"Yes, I've been in London since...my injury."

"Sit down, captain."

"I'd prefer to stand, general, just give me my orders."

"It's not quite that simple. There are matters to discuss. Besides I'm sure your leg..."

"I'm perfectly capable of standing."

"Sit down, captain...Matthew, please."

Skippon speaks firmly, but not harshly. Reluctantly Matthew sits, carefully placing his left leg at the side of the table. Skippon watches the manoeuvre carefully.

"It's nine months since Cropredy Bridge. You served with distinction, but your injury was serious. A long recuperation, but it seems you are much improved."

"I get about very well," Matthew says.

"Your sister looks after you."

"She's very attentive. Sir, about my return to the army..."

Skippon lifts his hand.

"In God's time, captain, you must be patient."

"It's not God I'm impatient with. If I could just..."

"You are a valuable officer, Matthew. I have heard fine reports. But this war has to be fought in many ways. The army does not get into the field on its own, it needs support... Parliament needs supporters."

"Sir, I do not see..."

"Patience, captain, please. There are matters other than fighting demanding a soldier's attention. I have to consider all persons of repute in this city and throughout the whole county of Middlesex. Joseph Manning is the local Justice in the village of Harringstead in the north of the county. A pleasant enough place I understand, but there have been a number of disturbances."

"There have been disturbances in many places," Matthew says dubiously, "In times of war..."

"Yes, but Joseph Manning is...influential."

Skippon pronounces the last word with slight distaste. He and Matthew's eyes meet in a look of mutual solidarity, but then he moves on.

"What do you know about witchcraft?"

"Nothing."

"Good. You have an open mind. Justice Manning is concerned that witchcraft is at the root of recent disturbances in the area. Such an affliction so close to London will need to be dealt with...if the allegations are true."

If Skippon doubts the veracity of these allegations, why is he so keen to get involved? Unless he is under pressure and has no choice? Matthew probes.

"Surely sir, these are not matters for soldiers."

"I shall be the judge of what soldiers should be concerned with!" Skippon snaps.

"I'm sorry, I meant no..."

"Of course you didn't, Matthew," Skippon says gently, "but you must understand we can't let such a thing take root. It would sap the strength of the people and thereby undermine the cause. Think if it spread to London."

"I doubt that very much."

Skippon looks at him as if to ask how Matthew can possibly know, grimaces and then continues

"Manning has asked for a thorough investigation by reliable officers. He has no wish for disreputable persons to be involved. I cannot quarrel with that, but in these difficult times I cannot release experienced officers, needed elsewhere. Obviously inexperienced men are a different matter. Therefore I have arranged for lieutenant Hugh Crittenden to be spared for a short while. However, while Justice Manning is grateful for him, he is insistent a more senior and *experienced* officer is also involved. I can see the advantage of two officers. It's likely to be investigated more thoroughly and concluded more quickly. As you are not yet fully recovered for active service, I naturally thought of you. Lieutenant Crittenden has his orders to report to you tomorrow. You will then proceed to Harringstead, contact Manning and commence your investigations."

Matthew finds the prospect of investigating witchcraft almost insulting, but restrains his first explosive reaction. He must concentrate on his main priority.

"I know my injured leg has debarred me from immediately rejoining the regiment, general, but I am greatly recovered. As you will see, I came here without assistance. I had hoped therefore I might return to active service very soon."

Skippon sighs, then smiles benignly.

"I've explained the difficulties, Matthew. If I don't use you, how am I to meet Manning's concerns? Take a capable officer out of the line? No, nor can I delegate this to a civilian with let us say doubtful motives. We must not fall prey to those too subject to suggestion and wild talk. Times are bad enough. I don't want the citizenry of this city deflected from the godliness of our cause by a frenzied terror. If there is a genuine infection it has to be properly identified and dealt with accordingly."

"This...task," Matthew says, "once completed, will be followed by my return to the army?"

Skippon hesitates, glances at Matthew's leg and pulls himself up.

"We are in God's hands in everything we do. If it is His wish, then it will be."

Matthew stares into Skippon's kindly eyes. He doesn't doubt the general's sincerity and he cannot pose to such a devout man the question of what if it is not His wish?

"And my orders. I assume I will be operating under your authority not those of Manning."

"You are commissioned by Parliament. You operate as I do under its authority."

Matthew's profound disappointment stuns him into silence.

"Any other questions?" Skippon says.

"No...no, sir."

Matthew stands and is dismissed. The return walk seems longer and he tires, his leg aching a little. He may have overdone it on his outward journey, but stubbornly refuses to rest and trudges on in a daze, only gradually comprehending the full import of these new orders. He has heard of witches, but not given them much attention. It's the spring of 1645. The war is at a crucial stage. Witches are about as far removed from soldiering as he could get. He's not even been in that part of the country where they've been reported. Witchcraft doesn't shock or frighten him. Neither does he feel any strong need to investigate and stamp it out. In these troubled times witches are peripheral to winning the war and bringing the King to his senses. He is a soldier again, but not yet considered fit for soldiering. It galls him and he strikes the wall angrily, making several people turn in alarm.

Edmund opens the door. Matthew steps slowly over the threshold.

"You are tired, Matthew," Edmund says, drawing up a chair into which Matthew gratefully slumps.

Elizabeth comes hurrying from the back. She immediately notices her brother's fatigue.

"Is it a malady of the mind or the body that ails you, Matthew? The debility of your leg or the summons to the general not to your liking?"

"Both," he says despondently.

She sits down opposite him.

"A long walk for your leg. I said you should take it steadily. You need to..."

"My leg is alright!" Matthew thunders, striking the table with his fist.

"Aye, aye, but not so sound as your temper, brother."

"I'm sorry," Matthew says, "I am disappointed."

"Not yet returning to the army?" Edmund says.

"I have other orders from General Skippon. He wants me to play the constable."

He briefly tells of his mission.

"Do you know the nature of these disturbances?" Edmund says.

Matthew has omitted any reference to witchcraft.

"I will discover that when I meet Joseph Manning," he says and then with some bitterness, "If I'm fit to ride across a whole county why not fit to mount a horse in the cavalry?"

"Mounting is one thing," Elizabeth says, "But what if you were to fall off?"

"Good riders don't fall off!"

"Not on any ordinary ride, but in the army..."

"Do you choose to instruct me now in the arts of war, madam?"

Elizabeth is about to react, but Edmund puts his hand on hers.

"Enough, wife...and brother. Are there not battles enough in this land without starting new ones in this house? Come, let us eat."

Over their meal present troubles are forgotten and they play out recent misfortunes and distant memories with the repetitive torment for which they never tire. Edmund talks of the wharves where he works, the distressing shortages and privations the war has brought. Elizabeth repeats the war's gossip of losses and cruelties. Matthew talks of the 'final victory' which must come.

"Some say this civil war is a war without an enemy," Edmund says.

"There is an enemy," Matthew says, "The enemy is the mote in men's eyes, the curse on their minds that denies freedom."

"Not the King then?"

"Aye, of course the King if he'll not see sense."

"How far we've come," Elizabeth says, "from those simple days on the farm. Who would have known then we'd be fighting our own King."

"We can't go back," Matthew says, "the world has moved on and we must move with it."

He subsides into a doleful silence, but unable to lift his depression, goes out to clear his head and regain some evenness of spirit. He feels better, but the evening is chillier and his leg drags a little, slowing him. This disability irritates him. He has rested for some hours. His strength should have restored. He puts it down to the long convalescence. He's not given it enough exercise over the winter. A good walk will soon restore the suppleness and he'll have to maintain such a regime every day. But he tires and steps into a tavern, fully intending to continue his walk after a short rest.

The 'Phoenix' is a lively convivial place and Matthew submerges his brooding disappointment in the boisterous excitement of others. He's been too long out of company and realises how much he's missed the comradeship of the army. He laughs at the jokes, exchanges stories and shares in the songs. Yet he's not part of the merriment. He joins their world for an hour or so of innocent amusement, but remains apart. His world is in the army where the real conflict is being fought. The war is like a parasitic weed. It can be pulled away or covered up, but it always comes back. It's always there. They talk of what the war takes away, but also of what it gives back. There are the shortages, the things that have to be done without, but there's also the opportunity of the times, the beginning of a new age, the ferment of new ideas. In every tavern in every town someone is ready to talk about ideas. It reminds Matthew of Edmund, reading the latest pamphlet, debating how church and the country should be reformed. Matthew doesn't share his enthusiasm. He needs to know where he stands, who he stands for. Bandying ideas only gets you more confused. Inevitably his thoughts drift back to the army and his dismal conversation with Skippon. He feels guilty at not doing a proper soldier's job and as his detachment increases the congenial atmosphere dissolves. His only concern is to leave.

"Could I trouble you, sir. Are you resident in these parts?"

A man in his late forties stoops from the other side of the table.

"Yes, I am sir," Matthew says, "at least for the last few months."

"Then you may be able to help me. May I join you?"

Matthew nods assent and the man sits at the table.

"I am looking for my daughter. She has been gone these two days from her employment in the country. I believe she is in London."

He speaks with a desperate earnestness and stares almost imploringly. Matthew is eager to get away. He senses this man will detain him and now regrets allowing him to sit.

"London is a big place," he says unhelpfully.

"Indeed so sir, which is why I have started my enquiries without delay."

"Many young people come to London every day and in these times..."

"She's just twenty, a slight girl with distinctive red hair, bright blue eyes and a happy disposition."

"I have not seen her."

"Then I am sorry to have troubled you. However if you do see her, please inform the lady of this house. I will be back regularly."

The man leaves his name, then goes, accosting others around the tavern with the same distressed intensity. There are many shaking heads. No one has seen his daughter. With a final word to the landlady he leaves. Matthew wonders how many more fathers seek their children and children their parents. He thinks of his own brother. How many more poor souls up and down the land displaced by this war, never to return?

Elizabeth is his only family. They were brought up on a farm along with their elder brother and two younger sisters. Life was good when they were very young, but bad harvests were the first of those reversals that would end the happy time. Increasing debt forced the family to sell off more land until what had once been a good holding became a puny one and they had to lease more land. He's not heard of his brother, John. He left the farm after their father died. Edmund asked if Matthew had heard anything from the army, even from the other side. Elizabeth protested.

"Surely John would not fight for the King against his own brother!"

"The war divides more than the nation," Edmund said.

Matthew had not responded and the subject was dropped, but he remembered John's words.

The King is the tree that holds our country together. This Parliament hacks at the roots. They seek to bring him down. It is not right.

Edmund had clashed with him, saying the King can only rule in partnership with Parliament for it represents the people, but was inflexible and bent on confrontation. *He must be resisted.* John and Edmund never spoke again.

It's time to go. For a few steps his leg has little feeling, but it gets better and he's soon striding away quite rapidly. He's relieved. He may have a limp, but the weariness has gone. When he gets to the house he's glad to see Elizabeth and Edmund have retired. He's in no mood for conversation. Up in his room he pulls off his boots, but sits for some time on the edge of the bed musing on this strangest of days that began with so much hope and ends with profound disappointment and sorrowful thoughts.

He lies down, but sleep eludes him until he tires of the discussion with Skippon and the endless repetition of the same phrases. He sleeps and dreams. Cropredy Bridge again, the horse galloping wildly under him, but now a different army faces him, composed entirely of women, running headlong and screaming incessantly. An army of witches with long unkempt hair, wielding long sticks and coming straight at him!

He wakes suddenly, sitting up, sweating and shaking. The fearful images gradually recede and wakefulness drives out sleep. Yet still he's tormented by scraps of recent discussions with Elizabeth, Edmund, Skippon, even the man in the tavern looking for his daughter. His orders are clear. Once Crittenden has made contact they must leave for Harringstead in search

15

of...He shifts position and turns to the wall. Witches. He repeats the word, relegating it to the mundane innocence of other words less charged with meaning like saucepan or hose or doorknob. Ridiculous!

He gets up. Edmund has already left for his work. Elizabeth rakes and rekindles the fire. Despite his shortened sleep he feels better and resigned to the new task, restless to begin. After breakfast he fetches his horse. When he returns Hugh Crittenden has arrived. He looks older than his twenty years, matured in military affairs, having seen action in minor skirmishes with Royalists.

"Now you're on the staff," Matthew says with slight derision.

"Temporarily attached," Hugh says, "this is not my normal duty...like yourself," he adds, glancing at Matthew's leg.

Until Matthew briefs him, Hugh assumed the 'investigation' would have a purely military dimension. He's surprised to hear of Manning's fears, but is less fazed than Matthew about possible witchcraft.

"If it's Parliament's business, then it's our duty."

Matthew can see why Hugh has been transferred to special duties. He's competent and well motivated. Whatever awaits them at Harringstead, Matthew will be ably assisted. They journey along the west road, avoiding Westminster and then at Tyburn turn north along Watling Street. They ride at a steady, unhurried pace. They can easily reach Harringstead within the day and Matthew wants to spare the horses. So close to London this is not dangerous country, but tired mounts will be of no use in an emergency. Matthew is in no talkative mood and they say little except to exchange information on their respective experiences, surprisingly discovering a common link with Cropredy Bridge the year before.

"You were an officer of Foot," Matthew says, "serving under General Skippon?"

"We attacked, but were repulsed. We lost a colonel and eight other men."

"Aye, we also lost some good men that day."

"Is that where you were injured?"

Matthew nods, slapping his left leg.

"But it's mended well, too tough for the King's musket ball!"

They arrive in early afternoon. Harringstead is a medium sized village, with most of the houses and two inns along the two streets. More houses, the smithy and the church are grouped around the green where there's also a third inn. Here they take a room, stable their horses and get a meal.

"Soldiers?" the landlord says with slight apprehension.

"Here to see Joseph Manning, the local Justice," Matthew says, "Can you direct us?"

"Syme House, a little way out of the village, close to the river."

"Is it far?"

"Do you go today?"

"Yes."

"It's shorter on foot through the fields, but depending on how long your business is...?"

Matthew doesn't respond.

"...if you need time then it may be better to ride, taking the road along the river."

"He's inordinately inquiring," Hugh says disapprovingly when the landlord is out of earshot.

"We may need some time with Manning," Matthew says," We will ride. On the way we can get our bearings, get a feel for the place."

They saddle up, but walk the horses through the village, sizing up the villagers as much as they are sized up in return. Before they reach the road, Matthew takes a deliberately circuitous route around the fields, stopping several times to stare towards the houses of the village. It's a pleasant ride alongside the river with the sun on their backs. Matthew breaks their silence,

"Have you formed any impression of the place?"

Hugh thinks for a moment

"It broods," he says.

"Aye, a good description, something hanging over the village," Matthew says, laughing, "Maybe it's a great big hen, brooding over the country!"

Matthew looks at him expectantly, but Hugh is quiet.

"But what sort of hen? A community gripped by witchcraft? What sort of egg has the hen laid?"

Matthew laughs again. Hugh hesitates, unsure of Matthew's seriousness.

"Maybe we will find out at Syme House," he says at last.

"Well said, lieutenant! Then let us get quickly now to the Justice!"

Hugh laughs too, though still unsure. Matthew rides on quickly and Hugh follows. Syme House is a substantial property, some sixty years old, with extensive grounds on all sides. At the front door a servant comes out and takes their horses.

"Captain Fletcher and lieutenant Crittenden to see Mr. Manning," Matthew says.

A second man leads them through a spacious hall into a light and airy room. A man in his forties rises as they enter and are announced. Joseph Manning introduces his wife, Constance and his daughter, Olivia. Matthew and Hugh stand near the door. Manning invites them to the table, where they sit at the far end, opposite him. He smiles broadly.

"You are settled, I trust?"

"We are comfortable at the inn, I thank you, sir," Matthew says.

"Do you have any experience of witchcraft, captain?"

"Fortunately no, sir."

"Fortunately for you maybe, but less so for us. I'm sorry, captain, I meant no disrespect."

"None taken, sir."

"When we are faced with the utterly inexplicable, any knowledge of the dark agencies would be welcome."

"We are soldiers, sir. We are used to dealing with implacable forces. If there is wrong doing here we will root it out."

Matthew sits with his hands, palms down on the table, staring resolutely at Manning.

"I fear we are up against something stronger than wrong doing as you put it."

"I'm sure, Joseph, what captain Fletcher and lieutenant Crittenden may lack in experience, they will amply make up for in vigour and determination," Constance Manning says, smiling at the officers.

Matthew nods in acknowledgement, but continues to stare with the same intent at the Justice. Manning leans back and then pulls himself up in his chair, as if rearranging his body in parallel with his thoughts.

"It began with complaints of the corn being trampled in several fields. I put it down to excessive sensitivities by certain villagers, but they said it was witchcraft."

"Stray animals perhaps," Matthew says, "Negligence in leaving gates open."

"Precisely, captain. That was exactly my comment. Witchcraft was a step too far. Things remained quiet for a time. I am not one to leap to the most extreme explanation. Then dead animals were found in the fields."

Matthew raises his eyebrows.

"Oh I know, captain, surely such things are not that unusual, but both cattle and sheep and it was not just in the fields. Some carcasses were discovered in trees, in hedge bottoms, even on fences. That you will agree is not usual."

"Even so..."

"Some of the creatures discovered were wasted away as if they'd been starved or subjected to some horrible disease."

"Can we see these animals?"

"Such fearful things could not be left. They have all been destroyed."

"So we only have the word of those..."

Matthew's scepticism irritates Manning.

"Reliable persons were involved."

"Did you see these things yourself, sir?"

"My steward, Lexden, a most reliable man, he saw them."

"Then we will see Mr. Lexden."

Manning hesitates.

"Unfortunately he's not here to assist you."

Matthew grimaces. Manning changes tack.

"Lexden found notes left near some of the animals. I will show you."

He produces some scraps of paper. Each has a phrase such as 'This is the beginning,' 'Take warning' and 'Take heed of the curse,' in a scrawling hand.

"Then accusations were made that this was the work of a witch."

"Or witches," Matthew says.

"Witches?"

"These notes, they are not by the same hand."

Manning studies the papers.

"They could be the work of more than one person," he says reluctantly, "but definitely the work of a person...or persons without learning."

"Enough learning to write," Matthew says, "they might also have been deliberately written in the appearance of someone ill educated."

"Hmm...yes...that is a possibility. Then there have been difficulties with some of my servants. Plates dropped, a fire in the scullery, a cupboard crashing from the wall, mysterious injuries."

"Serious injuries?"

"Cut fingers, scraped shins, not serious, but inexplicable."

"Carelessness by servants is not..."

"Captain, they say they were bewitched!"

"By whom?"

Manning grimaces.

"They were insensible to my questioning. Perhaps you will be able to ascertain the cause of these afflictions."

"If they are genuine afflictions."

"They cannot be discounted. In my view..."

"You mentioned your steward, I would like to see him."

Manning grimaces and shuffles his feet uneasily.

"So would I captain. Samuel Lexden has been missing for several days."

"Away on your business, sir?"

"Away certainly, but not on my business. No one has seen nor heard of him. I'm getting concerned."

"An estate without its steward, that is inconvenient."

"Inconvenient be damned! Lexden was convinced witches were at the root of all these disturbances. He has been one of the most outspoken declarers against witchcraft. I fear his disappearance is connected."

"You believe a witch or witches has abducted him?"

"Spirited him away. It's not unknown elsewhere."

"Has Mr. Lexden any enemies?"

Manning laughs.

"Lexden undertakes his duties with diligence and rigour. That doesn't always endear him to tenants. A steward's job is not to court popularity. He's a hard man, but a fair one."

"You mean he's hard to everyone?" Matthew says cheekily.

"I mean he's a man on whom I can put absolute trust."

"When he's here."

"Is there anything else I can help you with, captain?"

"A list of individuals who may have wished Mr. Lexden harm."

Manning laughs again.

"That is your task, captain, to identify particular individuals. Any list I give you would include more than half the village. Even I don't believe they are all witches."

Matthew shift uneasily, unsure of Manning's seriousness and slightly irritated at what sounds like an instruction.

"Now sir," he says, "I would like to see your servants. Alone if you don't mind, in their own quarters."

They exchange steely looks. Then Manning loosens up, conscious Matthew will remain insistent. The servants are assembled, standing in line in the kitchen with Matthew and Hugh on the opposite side of the long table. If Manning were present, they would be unlikely to reveal anything useful. There are two absentees, Martha the scullery maid who is out collecting eggs and Ned Frattersham, a young lad who helps in the grounds.

"He's been missing for days," Cotter, Manning's principal manservant says critically, "He's gone before, but always comes back...though..." he twists his forefinger at the side of his forehead "...not always sure where he's been."

Matthew invites them all to sit and briefly explains the purpose of his enquiries, emphasising his commission from Parliament rather than their master. He hopes it will make them speak more freely, but he's not sure they understand the distinction. In Harringstead Manning is Parliament. After asking some preliminary questions about their duties he's about to move on to specific incidents when the back door is flung open and a young girl runs into the kitchen.

"Mrs. Shaw, Mr. Cotter, I've just heard, I had to run back and tell you, it's so..."

It's Martha, the scullery maid.

"Sit down, girl and get your breath," Mrs. Shaw, the cook says.

Martha slumps into a chair at the end of the table, catching her breath, unaware of the two soldiers.

"Whatever is wrong," Cotter says.

"It's Mr. Lexden. They've found him out on the West Field."

"About time he turned up."

"But he's dead."

2

"CUT up and hanging out. Just like those animals!"

After Martha's garbled account Matthew abruptly terminates the interview with the servants. He reports the news immediately to Joseph Manning, who accompanies him and Hugh to the fields. A few men are gathered around some bushes a quarter mile from the house. These have been cut back to reveal the body, otherwise partially concealed by the hedge.

"Who found him?" Matthew asks as they come up.

"I, sir," says a small man, holding a sickle, "I saw a rabbit run this way. I didn't take much heed, but then I thought it was still here so I came over. Thought I might bag him," he shakes the sickle, "then I saw... (he points to the outstretched right arm) ...it was no rabbit."

"Did you touch the body?"

"Not then, sir. I called the others (he motions to three other men standing beside him) and they came over."

"The body has been moved," Matthew says, crouching down and peering over the prone form.

No one speaks.

"Well?" Matthew says, looking up belligerently.

"Yes, sir," the man says nervously, "we didna' mean no harm. We had to see who it was. We only turned him over onto his back so we could see his face. Then we saw it was Mr. Lexden."

"How many of you, where did you hold him?"

"Two of us, me and Joshua," the man says, nodding to one of the others who stares fearfully at Matthew, "We held him here."

He points to two places on Lexden's right side.

"And no one has touched him since?"

"No, sir. We sent young Edward to the house. He come back saying he'd met Martha, the scullery maid and..."

"Who is that?" Hugh says.

A thin youth, around sixteen is pointed out. Hugh looks across to him.

"You saw fit to entrust this awful discovery to a young girl?" Hugh says.

"Begging your pardon, sir," the youth says, "but I thought it best for Mr. Manning to hear from one of his own servants."

Hugh is ready to upbraid him, but Matthew, noticing the peculiar mixture of fear and impertinence in the youth's manner, waves for him to say nothing. Neither the youth nor any of the other men look Manning in the eye. Martha's description of the state of Lexden's body, though luridly exaggerated in the telling through several tongues, retains a rough accuracy. The right arm and left leg have deep gashes and there's also a wound to his chest. Matthew glances at the sickle, but while these injuries are startling, they are superficial and there is no congealed blood. After examining these carefully Matthew turns his attention to the victim's head and discovers heavy bruising and some blood at the rear. He then examines the bushes and looks up at the labourers.

"You men, how much have you disturbed this hedge?"

"We pulled it aside to get at him," the man with the sickle says.

"What about up here," Matthew says, pointing to where stout twigs have been pushed far back.

"No sir, we didn't do that."

"If you've finished, captain," Manning says, "I would like him taken to the house."

"By all means, sir."

The men ease the body from the hedge bottom and carry it across the fields to Syme House.

"A dead man doesn't bleed," Matthew says to Hugh as they walk behind.

"Those cuts were real enough," Hugh says,

"Yes, but they didn't kill him. Wounds like that would have bled profusely and there was hardly any blood around them. They were inflicted after death. The blow to his head is what killed him."

"Then why cut him after death, there would be no point?"

"Did you notice the hedge?"

"The men said they'd only disturbed it slightly, but the branches have been pulled apart and some twigs are broken away."

"Not consistent with the men discovering the body and turning it over?"

"It wouldn't have needed that much disturbance."

"So, unless we have an exceptionally large rabbit in these parts, somebody pulled that hedge apart for a purpose."

"It could have been Lexden himself, crashing into the hedge as he fell from the blow."

Matthew considers this for a few moments.

"No. A man falling into a hedge, even from a heavy blow would not have caused that damage. It's a stout hedge. It would largely break his fall."

"Unless he was pushed by the murderer after he was struck."

"It would still need a lot of pressure and would be bound to leave scratches on his hands and face and there are none. It would also have left a large hole in the hedge. The men who found the body would have had no need to pull it apart. Remember the first man on the scene said all he could see at first was the right arm. It was only when he and the others opened up the hedge they saw the whole body. If Lexden had fallen or been pushed into the hedge the body would have been seen from the other end of the field."

"So the men did open up the hedge, that's the explanation."

"No, no," Matthew is adamant, "it doesn't relate. They turned the body over to see who it was. That would have caused some of the damage, especially at the bottom, but not all of it. The branches were newly broken, but some, nearer the outside had been pulled back to their original positions."

"Someone broke the hedge and then pulled it back."

"Why would they do that?"

"To hide the original disturbance."

"Precisely."

"But why, to hide the body?"

"Yes. They knew it would be found before long, but they might delay the discovery. My guess is Lexden has been dead several days. He was probably killed around the time he disappeared."

"But if he didn't fall and wasn't pushed, he was... put there."

"Which accounts for the large disturbance."

"So he wasn't killed in the field?"

"I don't believe so."

The grim procession is nearing the house. They walk on in silence for a few moments. Hugh looks around, then motions to the men carrying the body.

"None of them like Mr. Manning and Lexden wasn't popular. You can do a lot of damage with a sickle."

Matthew shakes his head.

"The knock on the head killed him and that must have been from a blunt weapon of some kind."

"A hammer perhaps?"

"Hmm...could be anything...even a heavy saucepan."

"But the cuts on the body. Maybe they didn't kill him, but a sickle could have done them."

"Not unless it was a very blunt tool or had been used with incredible delicacy – hardly necessary after the murder – otherwise the cuts would have been much deeper. No, my guess is those wounds were done with a small knife."

"A kitchen knife?"

"Could be."

"So the murderer could have been a woman. Bashed him on the head with a heavy pan, then cut him up with a kitchen knife."

"And moved the body?"

"Could have been two of them."

Matthew cogitates this for a time.

"A couple of..." Hugh begins.

"Don't say it," Matthew cuts him off.

"There are plenty of others who *will* say it," Hugh says, "if you're right about the cutting, then it smacks of some sort of ritual and the body in a hedge is similar to the animals in trees and so on. That means witchcraft."

Matthew grimaces, but says nothing. At the house everyone is assembled. Matthew briefly examines the body again, satisfying himself of the conclusions already reached. Then he excuses himself and returns to the kitchen. The news of Lexden's death has struck the servants into shocked silence and incoherence. Those that say anything are convinced his death is a result of witchcraft, but despite his repeated questioning no one is able or willing to suggest any particular culprit. Young Ned Frattersham is still absent. The others exchange nervous glances as if to say he may be the next victim.

"There's a curse on this house," Martha says.

"Be silent, girl," the cook reprimands her.

"But it's true, Mrs. Shaw, the family is cursed."

Mrs. Shaw tries to shut her up again, but Matthew intervenes.

"Who has cursed the family?"

Martha glances at Mrs. Shaw and then at Cotter. Their stern silence is enough.

"Oh, I don't know, sir, I just heard."

"From whom did you hear these things?"

"Everybody, everybody says it."

Matthew is unable to break the blank silence that follows. Neither does he get much response from anyone about Lexden. Other than repeating vague gossip (Matthew suspecting at least some of it probably manufactured on the spot) no one has seen or heard anything specific concerning the steward's disappearance or murder.

"He was a hard...working man," Cotter says, the only response to Matthew's requests for how well they knew him, though with a certain emphasis on 'hard.'

No one has any view on potential enemies or who might wish him harm, which Matthew takes as passive endorsement of Manning's comment that most of the village probably disliked him.

"Are they afraid of witches?" Hugh says later.

Matthew is doubtful

"They are afraid of something," Hugh persists.

"Or caught up in the a frenzy that may soon sweep through the whole village."

Joseph Manning and Constance await him in the main room. Lexden's body has been laid in an ante room next door.

"I have sent for Reverend Stradsey," Manning says, "I am unaware of any relatives of Mr. Lexden. The least I can do is arrange for a good Christian burial. This is a terrible business. You can confer with the vicar when he comes. Were the servants able to assist you?"

"Unfortunately not. None of them saw the steward at any time after you noticed his absence yourself."

"They are probably utterly terrified as will be most of the village by now. It's witchcraft, captain, I'm absolutely convinced of it," Manning pulls himself up sharply. No longer just the local landowner, suddenly he is very much the Justice, "There is a particular woman, Prudie Westrup. I fear I may have been a little lax in my dealings with her in the past. The vicar has upbraided me in that matter though I took it disfavourably from him at the time. She has been somewhat forthright in her views and has chosen to express them with a degree of forcefulness."

"Directed against yourself, sir?"

"I fear so."

"One of the papers that were found refers to a curse."

"Local legend, idle talk by tipsy men and gossipy women…" Manning says dismissively.

"If you wish me to take such talk seriously."

Manning sighs and waves his hand.

"Very well. A hundred years ago the largest landowner in these parts was Larkhall Priory. At the dissolution of the monasteries those holdings were sold to a number of local families. Not long afterwards certain scurrilous persons, intent on mischief, said such land was cursed because of its origin and by extension so were the families themselves."

"What families were involved?"

"Most of the land was taken up by two families. The Collvers and ourselves."

"So you believe your two families have been the focus of the recent ... peculiar events?"

"Only my family. Nothing has occurred to the detriment of the Collvers," Manning says acidly, "The disturbances have been primarily directed against myself or my tenants."

"You feel Prudie Westrup is behind these disturbances?"

"She has cursed me," Manning says, "She is an evil woman."

Constance suddenly and surprisingly intervenes.

"Really Joseph, evil is a very strong word."

"I must speak as I find Constance," Manning says, glancing at her with slight disapproval and then a little nervously at Matthew, "for many years she has opposed me with a succession of obstructions."

"What sort of obstructions?" Matthew says.

"We have had our vexations in the past. There were the usual troubles in the thirties. Necessary reorganisation of the land, everyone was properly compensated when the commons were enclosed."

Matthew remembers well such 'reorganisation' in his own village. His family and many others were not 'properly compensated,' reducing their fuel and pasturage. It's a biting reminder of his younger days. His instinctive sympathies are with the dispossessed, but he remains open minded.

"...unruly elements sought to exploit the situation. We had periodic outbreaks of tearing down fences and driving animals over crops. It got worse with the Scots war. None of us wanted to fight fellow Protestants, but disorderly soldiers making their way north stirred up our people, asking them what grievances they had, encouraging them to take back the enclosed land."

"That was five years ago," Matthew says doubtfully.

"Simmering discontent by lowly people, captain. If the meanest rise out of their station, where are we then?"

Where indeed, Matthew thinks, but remains silent.

"There have been many such disputes over the years..." he says.

"Indeed so, captain, but few others I submit have been accompanied by curses and threats."

"She is a difficult woman," Constance says to Matthew, smiling indulgently at her husband, "and unfortunately she is behind with her rent."

"I will need to speak to her."

"I will give you directions," Manning says, "Though you would do well to confer with the minister. It is a matter closer to his calling."

"You might do better to speak to John Collver," Constance says.

"Constance!" Manning says sharply.

"I too must speak as I find, Joseph. The Collvers too are no friends to this family."

"Even so, to attack Lexden..."

"Say what you mean, Joseph, tell Mr. Fletcher."

Manning hesitates, then turns to Matthew.

"Constance is right. I cannot know for sure, you understand, but for some time I have suspected...and now this latest business...in the past John Collver or those connected with him have encouraged disreputable persons in the disturbances for his own ends."

"Encouraging disruption among your tenants?"

"Common people couldn't have the wit for all the disturbances. Lexden was convinced Collver was behind some of them."

"You think John Collver is connected to Lexden's death?"

"It's difficult to believe, but..."

"And is John Collver connected to the witchcraft, sir?" Hugh says.

"Oh no!" Constance says.

"No," Manning agrees, "I cannot believe that, but Collver's irresponsible machinations may have contributed to an instability in the community in which women of that sort can thrive."

Matthew rises.

"I will proceed with my enquiries and probably return tomorrow. Lieutenant Crittenden will remain and speak again with your staff."

He speaks to Hugh in the hall.

"What do you make of Justice Manning?"

"The gentleman treats us with respect and courtesy. He keeps an orderly household."

"These disturbances...animals straying, idiot villagers, stupid servants...did not warrant our involvement," Matthew says disdainfuly.

"But now we have the murder of the steward and the threatening notes need to be investigated."

Matthew nods unonvincingly.

"It might be easier with just one of us. See if you can get more out of the servants. They are holding back."

"Manning is convinced Prudie Westrup is a witch."

"But it seems his wife is not."

Hugh return to the Mannings, then Matthew leaves Syme House. He finds the household a peculiar and frustrating mixture of revelation and obfuscation. Information, albeit speculative appears to flow, but then stops or runs away. Hopefully he'll make better progress in the village. On his way he gets to the church. It's a squat structure with a short nave, making the layout almost square rather than rectangular. The communion table is not quite in the centre of the church, but slightly east towards the altar. At the east end there are signs of damage in the walls and still roughly sawn stubs on the floor where the original altar rails have been torn away. While Matthew examines these he hears footsteps and turns to see a tall man standing at the west end beside the south door.

"You must be one of the officers come to investigate our disturbances."

The last word is pronounced slowly and deliberately, each syllable stretched out emphatically.

"Captain Matthew Fletcher and you are, sir?"

"Jeremiah Stradsey, vicar of this parish."

They walk towards the centre of the church, stopping a few yards apart, carefully scrutinising each other. Stradsey, a man of thirty five has large bushy eyebrows and deep set eyes, now intently focused on Matthew.

"Justice Manning has advised me of your visit. I wish you well with your investigation. It is not the usual occupation of a soldier."

"I agree with you there, sir, but I must serve the Parliament in whatever way I can."

"And evil must be driven out wherever and however it arises."

Matthew is used to stern and stirring sermons from adamantine even fiery ministers in the army, but the tone of this man unsettles him.

"I see you were examining the remains of the altar rails," Stradsey says, walking towards the altar.

Matthew follows him.

"They were destroyed one day five years ago by soldiers on the way to the war with the Scots. Rough, coarse fellows, bent on destruction for its own sake."

"Perhaps they were opposed to the separation of the community and their minister."

"So they cried at the time, 'Papist idolatry, put nothing in the way of the people and their God!'"

"It happened everywhere," Matthew says resignedly.

"But wanton destruction, captain, so many statues and images destroyed too."

"In the passion of war..." Matthew begins.

"There was no war then, at least not in England."

"But there is a war now, sir and I am commissioned by Parliament to investigate your disturbances. If we could..."

"Your are commissioned by the army, captain."

"It is the same."

"I fear it is."

Stradsey looks into Matthew's face with an accusatory glare as if he alone is responsible for all the ills that have befallen the country since that day when zealous soldiers removed his altar rails.

"I understand from Mr. Manning that you may be able to assist me..."

"Stripped me of my surplice. Rabble, sir, rabble from the dregs of the county. Said I was 'wearing the rags of Rome!'"

"Rabble who are fighting for our liberties, sir, never forget that," Matthew says curtly.

"But the liberties for whom and for what ends?"

With a look of intense annoyance, part aversion, part unease, Stradsey retires to one of the pews.

"You are very young, sir," he says as if youth is an affliction.

Matthew sits at a nearby, but not the nearest pew.

"Old enough to appreciate what is important and young enough to fight for it."

Stradsey grunts.

"Witchcraft is at the root of these troubles. I told Manning, but he tarried. He's a good man, upright, godly, but not always sufficiently vigorous in prosecuting the Lord's work. If this evil boil had been lanced from the first there would have been no need for...anyway that is past. We must deal with the world as it is. Evidence has to be *discovered*, captain. It won't show itself naturally. Have you any previous experience in these matters?"

Matthew sighs irritably. The same question again, impugning his integrity. He shakes his head.

"Allow me to lend you a most efficacious volume. It will greatly assist you in your work."

Stradsey hands a book to Matthew.

"One must have the right tools for the job, captain. You will find *The Discovery of Witches* an absolutely essential adjunct to your enquiries."

Matthew thumbs the book briefly before putting it in his pocket.

"I am grateful to you, sir. I will study it carefully. You are familiar with the contents?"

"I have given it a smattering of attention. My other duties, you understand, time presses. Now, I assume you will be seeing the relevant women. They need to be questioned *closely*, you understand me?"

"My questioning of such persons, if it takes place, will be *thorough*, sir, of that you can be in no doubt."

Stradsey puckers his lips.

"Some of the recent abominations have been directed against Justice Manning."

"So I have been informed."

"There were others of course, but Prudence Westrup and Alice Sandon need to be examined. Prudence Westrup has long been a disorderly woman and has always shown an unwarranted hostility to her betters, Joseph Manning in particular."

"Has she had any cause for this antagonism?"

Stradsey starts at the word 'cause.'

"Mr. Manning is blameless. Evil is cause in itself. Mark, what I say, captain, you would do well to question this woman at the earliest opportunity."

"I mark what you say, sir."

Matthew is glad to get away. Stradsey unsettles and angers him. It's only after he leaves the church he realises he's not informed him of Lexden's murder. It would probably have brought even more intemperate language and he'll find out soon enough. He has no wish to quarrel with the vicar, but the sanctimonious arrogance annoys him intensely. Stradsey may be conscientious, guarding his flock against evil, but Matthew senses intolerance and a liability to condemn on flimsy evidence. Yet he must remain neutral. The man may be right and it's unwise to discount any source of information.

Matthew disapproved of the ritualistic changes attempted by the late Archbishop Laud. He's therefore reluctant to denounce the removal of images and statues, taking down altar rails and positioning the altar table back in the centre of the church. Yet he cannot condone excessiveness and so long as the vicar doesn't interfere with the freedom of others' consciences he is entitled to his views. Unlike Edmund Matthew is not tempted to seek God among the many new sects that have sprung up in London. His religion is simple, but traditional and he has no need to embrace newfangled faiths anymore than he approved of returning to the unreformed ways of the past.

By the time he returns to the inn not just the news, but every conceivable explanation for Lexden's murder is on everyone's lips. Suddenly Matthew is no longer the suspicious stranger to whom people speak only when spoken to. The witchcraft fever has taken hold and they are keen to make the first move and share their views with him. Unfortunately views are not facts.

After being accosted by a dozen assorted commentators he retires to the back room, only to be trapped in the corner and given the benefit of the landlord's take on the situation. He stops short of saying Lexden's murder is the work of witches, but advises Matthew to 'heed the feelings of the people.' Matthew reminds him he can hardly heed anything else for as a soldier he is engaged in a mighty conflict concerning the feelings of the people.

"There are people and people," the landlord says, "and some might say it's not their feelings that have been properly taken into account."

"And do any of these *people* who might have wished Samuel Lexden harm, have names?"

"Oh they all have names. You can easily get a list. Go to the church, it's called the parish roll!"

The steward was evidently not a popular man. The landlord laughs, much as Manning did before Lexden's body was found, but despite the grim jocularity makes a serious observation, reinforced by all others. The village is a hotbed of continuing strife. Most are petty, inter neighbour disputes that flare up brightly only to die down just as quickly. A few are the flames from long slow burning embers, though not serious when stripped of bombast and bluster. John took Robert's sheep just as he did last year, though then it was Robert taking it from John. Mary rowed with Peg and struck her with a ladle. Last time it was a bucket and Peg struck Mary. Yet beneath and beyond these perennial upsets there's a deeper convulsion to which Manning alluded and Matthew finds more disturbing. For nearly twenty years a sustained conflict has been slugging out between the local landowners, their tenants and labourers. There have been victories for both sides, but more land has been successively enclosed, cutting off ancient rights so the people have periodically retaliated by destroying fences. Both sides have even resorted to violence, though until the recent events it has been fairly quiet. Lexden, as the representative of the largest landowner has been at the forefront of these battles and is seen by all as interpreting his duties rigorously and unwaveringly. The generally fraught situation explains a great deal, but it is also unhelpful because there could be so many potential suspects.

"Some say 'tis witches," the landlord says, though as Matthew detects without too much conviction.

He waits for a response, but Matthew says nothing.

"It's easy to accuse," the landlord says at last, "Certain women were taken by the constable, but later released. You've probably heard."

Matthew confirms he has, 'from various sources.'

"Will you be seeing them?" the landlord asks pointedly.

"I'll probably see everybody," Matthew says resignedly, "Everybody seems to have a view on events."

The landlord waits again. He wants to talk, but Matthew won't oblige. Eventually he can hold back no longer.

"I'm not accusing her, (Matthew nods with a slight smirk) but Prudie Westrup is not the easiest of women. She's a widow, husband gone ten years or more, whether that makes her like she is, having to shoulder her burdens alone, I don't know."

"She's an older woman?"

"About forty. She owns a portion of land by the North Field and has a small cottage."

"Land originally part of Larkhall Priory?"

The landlord smiles.

"The priory owned most of the land round here, but not Prudie's, at least not her original holding. She inherited it from her father. When her husband died it reverted to her. They say even in the old days the Priory tried to take it from her great grandfather, but they were unsuccessful. It's small, but it's always been a neat little parcel."

"You said her original holding, what did you mean?"

"That's the point. Hers was a wedge between lands owned by the Priory. When these were sold off at the Dissolution, the Mannings and the Collvers bought those two larger holdings from the Crown. So she still has the same strip between the two. Her grandfather acquired more land next to the original holding as a tenant of the Mannings. Both them and the Collvers have tried to consolidate their own estates by getting her own land. She's refused to sell, but with times so hard she can't afford the hired labour so she's had to give up some of the leased land from Manning. Even for what's left she's behind with her rent, but then so are others."

"And Lexden was assiduous in trying to collect the arrears?"

"You could put it that way."

The following morning Matthew makes an early start, but doesn't get far from the inn. Near the church Stradsey approaches. He could cut across the fields, but Stradsey waves and hails him. Reluctantly Matthew walks on, though at a slower pace, then notices Joseph Manning beside him. Matthew stops a few paces before them and lifts his hat with a cheery 'Good morning, gentlemen,' hoping that will suffice, then moves to the side, but Stradsey bars his way.

"Captain Fletcher, a word if we may."

Stradsey emphasises 'we' though Manning seems distracted and almost stands behind the minister.

"We are concerned with the conduct of your investigation."

"Indeed, sir?" Matthew says, only barely suppressing his anger at Stradsey's tone of impertinent interference.

"When we talked yesterday, I was unaware and you saw fit not to enlighten me, of the death of Lexden," Stradsey says with undisguised annoyance, continuing after a short disgusted pause, "Unnecessary tardiness is being exhibited in your enquiries with regard to the local witch covern. In fact, those enquiries are so delayed they have not yet begun!"

Matthew stands back, staring at Stradsey grimly. He glances at Mannng, who avoids eye contact.

"The conduct of my enquires is a matter for myself alone, sir. If it is ... tardy as you put it, it will be for a purpose."

"I see no purpose in unnecessary delay," Stradsey says, pouting his lips and drawing himself like a determined bullfrog, preparing to snap up some unsuspecting insect.

"What appears to you as delay may be to a purpose, it may indeed be *necessary?*"

"This witch covern and cult is..."

"There is no evidence of a witch covern!"

"In my view..."

"You views, sir, are no doubt of inestimable value in the context of your calling, but they are of no consequence in the context of mine. I will brook no interference – howsoever high may be its source (Matthew glances at Manning who makes no response by word or gesture) – into my investigations. I remind you, *sirs* (another glance at Manning as if forcing him to choose between him and Stradsey) this is a military investigation and I am therefore answerable only to the army."

Manning tries to speak with a plaintive 'Perhaps,' but Stradsey comes in again, determined Matthew will not have the last word.

"This is a most unusual way of conducting affairs. In other areas where similar difficulties have been encountered professional witchfinders have been employed."

"I have heard of such people," Matthew says coldly.

"In those areas, I speak of Essex and..."

"This is not Essex and I will decide what assistance I may or may not require."

"I find your attitude decidedly unhelpful, sir."

"And I am becoming decidedly less patient with your interference, sir!"

Fuming like two boiling kettles, Matthew and Stradsey move aggressively towards each other. Manning suddenly steps between them.

"Gentlemen, please, there is another more pressing issue to be addressed first."

Matthew and Stradsey step back, thereby avoiding the embarrassment of the Justice having to prise them apart.

"Young Richard Collver has gone. I fear his absence can have only one explanation."

"Richard is John's son?" Matthew says, "I was on my way to..."

"Young men come and young men go," Stradsey says

irritably and then with a slightly disdainful glance at Manning, "Family disputes are secondary to the enclosing threat of evil," now turning to Matthew again, "Your dilatory approach may mean Prudie Westrup will be allowed to get away."

Matthew puffs angrily and draws up again.

"At this stage I have no ev..."

"She has to be seen!"

"Lieutenant Crittenden is dealing with it."

"You have delegated..."

"Gentlemen!" Manning intervenes again, "I really must insist that you listen to me!"

He waits a few seconds until sure both are not only quiet, but also really attentive.

"I have long suspected that John Collver, his brother Henry and his son Richard, are of doubtful loyalty to the Parliament."

"Disloyal, in what way?" Matthew says.

"Such a view is not...should not...be lightly raised, though I have expressed concerns in the past, but I am now surer than ever. The Collvers are Royalists, their first duty is to serve the King!"

"Such is the duty of us all," Mathew says, "If...when...he returns to a true course advised by Parliament rather than by the false counsel of those around him."

"I mean the Collvers harbour more immediate considerations."

"They are spies?"

Manning shuffles his feet, shakes his head slowly, searching unsuccessfully for an appropriate expression.

"Come sir," Matthew says, "These are not matters for trivial jest."

"I don't jest, sir," Manning thunders angrily, "I can only speak true to the stirrings of my inner self. Lexden warned me to be careful of them, I should have listened to him."

"And was his warning specifically concerned with these matters?"

Manning shakes his head again, pouting his lips and grimacing.

"He advised me to be careful in dealing with them and

said as Justice I should know more of those with which they were in contact."

"He had solid evidence?"

"Not as such, but he was a man of observation and integrity. His death...coming so soon after he said these things..."

"You believe the Collvers to be responsible?"

"Lexden may have been ready to disclose the evidence."

"And John or Richard Collver were determined to silence him?"

"It is not something you should discount."

"I will bear it in mind."

"Without delay, captain, without delay. Richard Collver may be on his way to join the Royalist armies. I demand you organise a force for his immediate recapture."

"A man cannot be recaptured when he has not been captured in the first place."

"Precisely. Which is why you must take action immediately."

"I was on my way to see John Collver when you accosted me, slowing down the performance of my duty," Mathew says sarcastically, "So now, sir, if I may..."

"No, captain, no," Stradsey intervenes, "The first priority must be the discovery of the witch. Prudie Westrup's apprehension is the first priority."

Matthew's ignores him and steps aside.

"I am speaking to you, sir," Stradsey says.

Mathew turns to him, glaring ominously for a second in which no one, including himself is sure what he will do.

"And I have already informed you that High Crittenden has the matter in hand."

Matthew turns again to go. Stradsey steps towards him, intent on physical restraint, even putting out his hand, but thinks better of it and pulls back.

"Giving her time to get away! I really must insist!"

"No! You must not insist."

Manning now intervenes, strongly disagreeing with Stradsey, upbraiding him for daring to 'give instruction to the officer' without even consulting himself. Stradsey is just as adamant, repeating his tirade about witches in general and the need to 'take hold' of Prudie Westrup in particular. They argue vigorously, each trying to outdo the other in how long and how strongly they have been warning of their respective concerns, Manning about the Collvers' 'Royalism' and Stradsey about Prudie Westrup and her 'demonic associates.' The more vociferous they become the less they notice Matthew edging away, quickening his pace, slipping around the church and across the adjoining fields.

Several times he stops and glances back. The raised voices are soon lost when he gets to the other side of the church. He expects to hear Stradsey's footsteps, but he hears only the sighing of the breeze, the call of the ever busy birds and the buzzing of the industrious insects. They are not concerned with witches and Royalists, civil strife and political dispute, and will still be singing and bustling when those that do are long gone.

Matthew determines to visit the Collvers or failing that Prudie Westrup or Alice Sandon, but then sees Hugh returning from Syme House and they go back to the inn together. Over the meal they exchange their meagre findings, Matthew quickly summarising the input from the villagers, high in quantity, less in quality.

"There's a pervasive ungodliness about this place," Hugh says.

"Their debilitation is perhaps not just waywardness in faith," Matthew says, remembering the altercation with Stradsey.

"I tell people they must put their trust in God and be steadfast."

Matthew leans back and sighs. Hugh is well intentioned, but inexperienced.

"We are conducting an enquiry, not bandying sermons. You will need to be a little more precise."

Hugh swallows hard. He's too used to vague observations being accepted almost without question, though he's already learning that won't satisfy Matthew.

"You're beginning to sound more like the constable than a soldier," he says sulkily, immediately regretting it.

Matthew glares, such a label is not to his liking. Then he laughs.

"Well said, lieutenant, but innuendo, speculation, idle gossip and alarmist imagination isn't enough!"

Hugh swallows again. Mathew watches him wryly, wondering if he might swallow his own tongue.

"There's a general discontent, reflecting particular local grievances...land problems, tenants' complaints, they have a strong antipathy to landowners..."

"All landowners?"

"To Manning in particular. Certain radicals were mentioned..."

"What about witchcraft, has there been a long standing problem?"

Hugh twists his hand back and forth and pulls a face. This is a subject on which he knows Matthew will be especially critical.

"The area has avoided the worst of the witch disturbances as in Essex and Suffolk."

"And what do the people feel?"

"They seemed indifferent...until recently. Now some are beginning to wonder whether witches have caused the recent troubles."

"They all feel this?"

Hugh hesitates.

"There are others – usually of the baser sort – they are unconcerned, especially if Manning's land is involved."

"So, there's no evidence of witchcraft."

"Some say certain women have made alarming predictions. Isn't that evidence?"

"These women have been questioned and then released. One's word to another, no corroboration, no evidence. What about the servants at Syme House?"

"They all believe they've been bewitched. That's how they explain the disappearances of Ned Frattersham and Sarah Radbourne."

"And Lexden's murder?"

"They didn't say."

"Who has bewitched them?"

Hugh shrugs.

"More half accounts and dribbling hints! Damn them!" Matthew thunders.

"Prudie Westrup could be behind it. Such women need to be questioned."

"Aye indeed. I suppose we must, though I don't care to be shoved in a certain direction simply because the whole village, including its betters are deranged that way," Matthew says, then as Hugh looks at him questioningly, "Yes, alright. Tomorrow you can go and see her. I shall stay with the gentry and go to the Collvers. Did the servants say anything more about young Ned Frattersham?"

"He's still not been seen."

"How does he fit into the Manning household?"

"Not very well. He does a bit of everything, a lot of nothing if you listen to Cotter. He's about seventeen, but appears much younger, a bit simple. Cotter implied he's only kept on because of Manning's softness for the boy."

"Probably harmless."

"Perhaps, but Lexden mocked him so much even the lad himself realised he was making a fool of him. Ned resented it."

"Have they any idea where he is?"

"No. Nor why he left though the cook overheard some sharp words the day before. Lexden said he was lazy and stupid."

"And what did Ned do?"

"Nothing. It was all over in a couple of minutes."

"But that doesn't mean Ned accepted it. He might have slipped away, brooded over it, come across Lexden and felled him."

"But where, if Lexden wasn't killed out in the field?"

"We don't know that yet. Big lad is he, this Ned?"

"Big enough by all accounts."

"So, we have a clear suspect – if he can be found."

"Perhaps, but he's not the only one missing. There's also a maid, Sarah Radbourne, she's also disappeared."

"Not very good at keeping his staff is he, Manning?" Matthew says sceptically, "When you say 'disappeared' it could mean she was discharged."

"It seems not. She left the same day as Ned Frattersham."

"Odd Manning didn't tell us all this before. Even now after the death of his steward, he's more concerned with this witchcraft obsession and his rivalry with the Collvers than problems in his own house. Did you mention any of this to him?"

"He couldn't add anything more than I already knew."

"Why didn't he tell us about Ned and Sarah?"

"Said it didn't seem important and when Lexden's body was found he was too shocked."

"Not too shocked to tell us about Prudie Westrup and reverend Stradsey's views."

Matthew pronounces the last three words slowly and contemptuously, then says, "Was Sarah on bad terms with Lexden too?"

"No one had much to say about her, but Manning doesn't like her father. Thomas Radbourne is a leader of one of the 'local radicals' as Manning calls them."

"Meaning people pulling down fences and reoccupying common land."

Matthew considers for a moment, repeating the name 'Radbourne.'

"What is it?" Hugh says.

"Nothing...at least...there's something about...no, never mind. We'll have to talk to this Thomas Radbourne."

Hugh grimaces.

"Not so easy."

"Don't tell me?" Matthew says whimsically.

"Afraid so. He's also disappeared."

3

AS determined as Jeremiah Stradsey to find Prudie Westrup, Hugh leaves the inn earlier than Matthew and tries to follow the landlord's directions to her cottage, but quickly loses his way. He should have listened more carefully and established some identifiable landmarks. Finding his way by named fields is utterly confusing.

"Left at Broad Oak and right at Great Harring after taking the line of Drensell for two hundred yards."

Away from people and habitations the easier it is to believe witchcraft is involved in the steward's murder. In the country nature holds its dubious sway, unrestrained by human fellowship and God's order. Unbounded nature with its sinister beings and 'powers' frightens him. Even in the army, on those rare occasions he's away from the camp or the closeness of other soldiers, he finds the country threatening. He's comfortable with the openness around London, so long as the country is confined and the fields are within sight and sound of the city.

He's only a day's ride from London and less than a mile from the village, while the army has fought in Yorkshire and Cornwall, but now he feels a thousand miles from its righteous cause. The further he tramps the more he stops, turning behind anxiously. He sees nothing, hears nothing, at least nothing recognisable, for even birdsong and scurrying rabbits assume an eerie devilry. He imagines fearsome creatures with scary screech and trembling flurry. An abominable creature like Prudie Westrup perhaps? He chides himself. He has a job to do and someone to find.

In his haste he's taken a short cut along a track with fields belonging to Manning on one side and Collver on the other. Prudie's place has to be near, but he can't find it. He must have travelled a good two miles now from the village. He should have brought his horse. It was foolish to come on foot. Should he go on or turn back to the village and take the 'longer' route? A man is walking slowly towards him. Hugh grips his sword instinctively, but then relaxes. He is alone and carries a scythe on his shoulder. Only a labourer, he should be no threat, but like all men he probably carries a knife on his belt. It's open country. If there are others, Hugh should see them.

The man speaks first as if he knows him. Perhaps not surprising, everyone in the village knows of the two soldiers at the inn.

"Are you lost, sir?"

"I am looking for Prudie Westrup."

"Then you have passed her place."

"I saw no cottage."

"That's because it's beyond Drensell Wood."

He looks at Hugh as if he's just reminded him of his own birthday. Hugh stares questioningly as the man continues.

"Go back about three hundred yards, turn left by Long Baulk, then..."

"Long Baulk is a field?" Hugh says irritably.

"It is, sir."

Hugh has had enough of fields with names.

"How will I know one field from another?

"You can't miss it, you'll see the wood beyond."

"I've already come that way, I saw no wood."

"Can't see what you're not looking for, come, I'll show you."

They walk together the short way. Hugh asks about Prudie, but the man either doesn't know her or is unwilling to say. Hugh sees the trees.

"Long Baulk?" he says with mock certainty to his companion.

The man nods and points to the side of the field.

"Through the wood, her place is on the other side. It's not far."

The man walks back towards the village. Hugh is reluctant to take the path through the field. He now realises he would have been wrong to have brought the horse, but it might still have been better to have gone the other way. The man is out of sight. Woods are notorious places of devilishness. Alone again the irrational fears return.

By the time he leaves the village Matthew has almost forgotten the interfering clergyman, but though he's sceptical of reliance on 'feelings' or personal antipathy, Manning's image of John Collver as a closet Royalist persists. Is Justice Manning's righteous concern based on the true cause or the old dispute over land? He may not be alone. Three years of war has wearied many true souls. Persistent shortage of materials and foodstuffs make them wonder how real are the distinctions between King and Parliament when they are trying to make a living. Yet Manning is not at that level. He doesn't need to sacrifice his ideals to make ends meet. If his accusation against the Collvers is groundless, he was never an honourable man when he took Parliament's side three years ago. Matthew has never questioned his stance. The objective remains unchanged. Not King or Parliament, but King and Parliament. They have to be balanced and the King upset that balance. When the King comes to his senses the war will be over.

He has to slow. He's not yet used to his injury. His limp is more pronounced when he's tired and he must learn to pace himself properly for long walks. He stops to rest at a stile. Perhaps he should have ridden. No, he's allowed the confrontation with the minister to unnerve him, walking too fast too soon. In a moment he will be alright. His gammy leg is a frustration, but he must trust the unknowable desires of Providence. If his future part in the struggle is confined to interviewing prickly and suspicious landowners, gossipy landlords, not to mention meddlesome vicars, then he must accept his lot. Though that last burden is not so easily accepted!

He walks on, though at a slower, less jolting pace. Stradsey is in his mind. His large, gaping eyes, the irises almost wholly surrounded by white, giving him a constantly alarmed expression as if he continually witnesses some infernal apparition. His obsession with witchcraft and his intemperate outbursts trouble Matthew, but is he right? Should he have gone to see Prudie Westrup and left Hugh to see the Collvers? Should he ignore the vicar's bombast and pay more attention to what he actually says? Not easy. The vicar's very presence repels him. He won't be coerced. As responsible local leaders neither he nor the Justice has shown much perspicacity, instead preaching intolerance or peddling personal spite.

It's difficult to believe Collver is a Royalist. Why did he not join the King at the outbreak of war? Some did, even from predominantly Parliamentary Middlesex. Is there a greater dispute than avaricious intents on Prudie Westrup's land that divides the two families, going right back to the original parcelling out of the priory's holdings? But if Manning is right and Lexden discovered Collver at the centre of a Royalist conspiracy it would be a strong motive for his murder.

'Aspenfield,' the Collver house contrasts starkly with Syme House. Squat and not particularly large, more like ears of corn in a field than the grand residence of a local magnate. From a distance it could even be the home of a yeoman or substantial tenant. Then as he gets nearer Matthew notices its length. Closer still, its impressiveness is not in size, but the delicacy of its ornamentation with the decorated parapets and carved figures around the entrance porch.

There's a long delay before the door is answered. He's not expected, but in such a large household he assumes someone will be around. An elderly man eventually appears, staring vacantly, almost disdainfully. Is it arrogance or ignorance or both? Does this old retainer represent the head of the house?

"Your business, sir?" he says slowly, dismally.

What damn business is it of this geriatric buffoon, surely they've already heard of the disturbances?

"Parliament's business...sir."

"Indeed sir, and what is..."

"I am captain Matthew Fletcher. I wish to speak to Mr. Collver about certain unexplained events and in particular the murder of Samuel Lexden, his neighbour's steward."

For one moment the old eyebrows are raised slightly.

"I assume you wish to see Mr. Collver senior, sir?"

"You assume correctly."

"One moment, sir."

The door is snapped shut, not even leaving a slight opening to indicate eventual entry. Matthew is left out until the master deigns he should enter. Until then his servant cannot take any chances. The wait is only a few moments, but seems longer. He hears no voices, no concentrated discussion, no querying of his identity, no sudden resigned acceptance he will have to be admitted, only the reopened door, the same impassive eyes and the dull, "Step this way, sir."

He's led across a dark, narrow hallway, past several closed doors until a final one is opened and he is unceremonially ushered into a room only slightly lighter. The servant doesn't precede him and Matthew instinctively moves a few steps away from the door before turning to find the old man has already left without a word.

"Come in, sir."

The voice, soft, high pitched seems to come from the window. Through the glaring sunlight Matthew discerns only a vague, dark shape until his eyes adjust and he sees a lone man staring at him from behind the table. Matthew introduces himself.

"I have been expecting you," John Collver says, standing, "Please be seated."

Matthew hesitates. Collver beckons and then resumes his own seat. Matthew puts his hat on the table, looking intently before sitting down. Collver is a small man, but stature as well as initial impressions can be deceptive.

"This is a simple house," Collver says, then perhaps conscious of Matthew's unspoken distaste for his abrupt reception, "There are few servants and I have few visitors. We have only old Jacob."

Old Jacob's role is not defined, nor is the 'we' explained. No assembled family here. Matthew takes the initiative.

"I understand your son Richard is not here."

"No. Is it him you wish to see?"

"Perhaps."

Collver stares expectantly, but Matthew doesn't oblige and he is forced to break the silence himself.

"I'll help you all I can, captain, though I suspect that may not be much."

Is this modesty genuine or put on for Matthew's benefit?

"I assume you know why I am here, sir?" Matthew begins.

"Most unfortunate about Mr. Lexden."

His voice is grave, but his eyes have lost none of their spark. 'Unfortunate' is as far as he goes to express the loss of his neighbour's steward.

"You knew him?" Matthew says.

"I knew of him of course, but saw him seldom. I understand he went about his duties most assiduously."

Collver doesn't flinch from Matthew's stare, his expression unchanging.

"You did not speak?"

"I don't believe I can have exchanged more than a dozen words with him in the last ten years," Collver says dispassionately then, catching Matthew's inquiring look, "Our paths did not cross."

"Mr. Manning had been experiencing certain difficulties prior to the untimely death of his steward."

"So I hear."

Matthew goes through the various unusual occurrences without mentioning them being attributed to witchcraft. Collver listens carefully, nodding silently.

"Mr. Manning is of the view..." Matthew begins.

"That I have some involvement? Yes, captain, I am aware of the views of the local Justice of the Peace," Collver pauses and then answers Matthew's unspoken question, "but I assure you, whatever...whoever is behind these events, it has nothing to do with me."

Collver's face never varies, no twitch, no flinch, nothing to show he's in any way unsettled. Time to switch tack.

"Where is your son Richard?"

Only now does Collver's expression change.

"I have no idea," he says, looking directly at Matthew, but immediately turning away.

"I have been informed your son's loyalty to the cause is questionable."

Collver turns back, his eyes angry and desperate. He's about to speak, but holds back.

"I have even been advised..." Matthew continues.

"There's no truth in it," Collver thunders, "It's a damned lie!"

"What is a lie?"

Collver has been leaning forward aggressively, getting as close as he can to Matthew across the table, the more forcefully to make his denial. Now he leans back.

"I...Richard...the whole family...we are as loyal as anyone else."

"Your family has no Royalist sympathies?"

"Most certainly not!"

Collver stands and goes to the window, turning away from Matthew as if to emphasise his displeasure. Matthew fully expects an accusation of disreputable behaviour. Why should he, a mere army captain, see fit to impugn the reputation of a local worthy, albeit one fingered by an equally worthy neighbour? But Matthew's patience has worn very thin since the earlier confrontation with Manning and Stradsey and he won't endure another tirade. Collver remains silent, but immovable, his displeased back still firmly facing Matthew. If Manning is right, could this be the rear end of a traitor? Now is the time to open up the real relations between him and Manning.

"You are not on good terms with Mr. Manning and I am told this has been the position for several generations?"

It shakes Collver from his petulance.

"Who told you such a thing!"

"Please sit down, sir."

With his equanimity already unsettled and now utterly broken, Collver's mouth quivers slightly, his hand shakes, but Matthew stares him out, sweeping his arm across the table. Collver sits.

"The relations between your two families is well known, sir, it is unimportant who informed me."

Collver is ready to argue, but slinks back in his chair, only speaking after a considered pause.

"It is unwise to believe everything you are told, captain."

"Indeed so, but between you there have been certain... concerns... regarding the land of a woman called..."

Collver laughs.

"Is that it, is that the substance of my disagreement with Manning, Prudie Westrup's strip of land?"

"That and..."

"Oh yes, of course, my so called allegiance to the King!"

"And why should I believe you rather than others, sir?"

"Because Manning won't admit why he is really so antagonistic towards my family, why he casts this slur of disloyalty on us and above all why he makes so much of my son's absence."

His hands and face shaking, he suddenly stops, gradually calming. Matthew waits patiently.

"There is a matter between us," he continues, "or rather linking us. Joseph Manning sees fit to draw shameful and wholly unjustified conclusions from my son's absence, but that is not the view of all his family."

"Lady Constance said..."

"I do not refer to Manning's wife!"

"You said linking between the families."

Collver swallows hard, puts both hands on the table and looks defiantly at Matthew.

"Just before he left...left abruptly without advising me that he was going...my son informed me that for some time – at least several months – he'd been seeing Manning's daughter, Olivia in secret. I can only assume his long rides – well away from my lands or the village or so far as I know Manning's estates – had been to meet up with her. I need hardly say this is a matter of which I strongly disapprove, not just because of a liaison with a family with which we are not, as you so rightly put it, on good terms, but also because of the blatant deception. I would have preferred him to have faced me as a man and stated his intentions."

"He was perhaps only too well aware of your disapproval..."

"Yes, indeed."

"Is Manning aware of this?"

"Lexden made the discovery and naturally informed Manning. He saw them together one day, from a distance. He was unsure it was Richard, but when she returned he asked Olivia and she admitted it was him. Manning tried to stop her going out, but she managed to get a message to Richard who then informed me. The next day he was gone."

"Mr. Manning did not advise me of this when he said your son had disappeared."

"No, exactly. He only saw fit to slur my son and myself."

"But it means your son..."

"Could have killed Samuel Lexden?"

"He has left very suddenly."

"He did not kill Lexden. He left because of his relationship with Olivia."

"Yet Justice Manning has not approached you on this matter?"

"No he has not, but then he wouldn't."

"Surely in the circumstances, despite your differences..."

"That he would want to confront me and demand an explanation for my son's dishonourable behaviour?"

"Something like that."

"He doesn't need to come here to do that. The silent blade is often the sharpest. It cuts deeper. Manning will know that I know. He will have great pleasure in imagining my disquiet."

"And his own."

"He will blame me for everything. My pain is only the latest and he knows it."

"Why then did he advise me?"

"So that you would do as he desired and come here, ready to accuse me."

"I came of my own volition. It was always my intention and any accusations I make will not be at the behest of anyone else."

"No doubt, but I'm sure he was still very concerned you were not delayed."

Matthew's silence is enough as he remembers Manning's earlier insistence, even despite Stradsey's objection. Collver nods knowingly.

"My family is already humbled captain."

He pauses, perhaps wondering if he's said too much. Matthew waits.

"As you know my family has been here since the dissolution more than a hundred year ago. You could say if we are gentry, we are new gentry."

Matthew is surprised by the *if*. Those regarded, however unkindly, as upstarts from the previous century are usually reticent about the soonness of their elevation.

"We should therefore have been contented or at least prudent, but the estate was not enough. My father was keen to invest in more than land. He became acquainted with London cloth merchants, no one you will have heard of... Edward Amberley and Jonathon Ellerton."

Collver is looking away. It's fortunate. He might otherwise have noticed the recognition of Ellerton in Matthew's face. By the time Collver does look towards him, Matthew has recovered his inscrutability.

"It was not a wise investment or...as it can be more accurately described with the wisdom of hindsight... speculation. Ellerton on the other hand, being wiser or in receipt of better information pulled out before the crash. My father lost substantially. Joseph Manning became a later investor when the losses, but not those of our family had been recovered. We have never been the same. Sacrifices had to be made. To this day my brother Henry has to work as a mere clerk in the same firm our father once partly owned. So you see, captain, Joseph Manning does not need to visit this house to witness our misfortune."

Collver's voice gradually trails away until the last word is almost inaudible. They are silent for a time. Matthew unsure what to say and Collver having said it all. Matthew asks about Lexden and the Manning's other staff.

"I hear one of them has gone missing too, the young servant girl, Sarah Radbourne," Collver says.

"You know her?"

"No, only her father. Troublesome fellow even when he's in a good mood, which isn't often."

"You've not been involved in his agitation?"

"Another foul accusation by Manning?"

Matthew grimaces ambivalently.

"I've had nothing to do with him."

Matthew asks a few final, mundane questions, impresses on Collver the importance of advising him if he hears any news of his son and then leaves. He rides quickly from Aspenfield, only slowing when the house is out of sight. The only sound is his horse's hooves on the hard grass and track, the occasional bird call and the soft babble of the river. In the silence he can think more clearly. Burdened by his family's peculiar 'misfortune' Collver is a man of saddened candour. Or is it more a repressed anger? Rightly or wrongly he blames Manning for the failed business adventures. Far from uniting them, young love seems to have increased their enmity, Richard's relationship with Olivia yet another reason for him to hate the Manning family. The two men denigrate each other at every opportunity, even dragging in the leader of the discontented labourers. That at least Matthew doesn't take seriously, but Collver has a motive for attacking Joseph Manning's interests, while his son may have killed Lexden as the revealer of his secret affair.

Hugh assumed it was a small wood, which he would quickly pass through, but blundering in too quickly he loses his bearings in the half light. Still believing it's only a small place he wanders around for a track or obvious exit, but nothing is visible. The man said Prudie's place was not far. Did he mean the cottage is not far *from* the wood? Just like the landlord with his named fields. Are these people deliberately obscure in their directions? He should have gone the other way! He walks aimlessly, gradually realising when he recognises the same trees and undergrowth that he's traversed a wide circle. This only increases his tension. He stops and kneels down. An instinctive reaction, make yourself smaller in the face of an enemy, but this is no battle lieutenant! He looks round despondently. Then he hears the rustling, someone near, behind the trees.

He crouches even further down, hands on the ground to keep his balance. He hears it again, the creeping rustle slower, but louder and getting closer. Is Prudie prowling for her next victim? It stops. Maybe it's seen or heard him. Down on his haunches Hugh can see nothing beyond the undergrowth, increasing his vulnerability.

"A soldier and afraid of a witch," he thinks, "Stand up and face the fiend!"

He lifts himself slowly, at the same time easing along the ground towards the shelter of a tree, trying to make as little noise as possible. He gets up behind the tree and listens. He hears only his own breathing, loud as a giant on a drunken spree. Then the rustling comes again, sudden, intermittent like a bird's tentative hopping across a lawn. He edges around the tree. Some five yards away is a dull, thin shape, hovering beside another tree, brazenly without cover. It seems to be alone.

"Show yourself," Hugh barks, stepping into the open.

The shape turns to face him.

"Who are you?" Hugh shouts.

The shape stares back, but in the shadows Hugh cannot make out the face. Then it turns and runs into the trees. Hugh runs in pursuit, careering into trees, becoming snagged in gorse, continually calling "Come back, come back!" but the figure knows the woods better and gradually increases the distance between them. Hugh emerges into open ground. At least the mysterious stranger has shown the way out the wood. He stands for a time, surveying the fields in every direction, but the figure, witch or otherwise is not to be seen. Hugh is quite alone except for the circling crows who seem to be calling jeeringly, "Goooone awaaaay, Goooone awaaaay!"

For a few moments his anger stops him clearly seeing into the mocking and empty country. Then as his frustration subsides he spies the mean cottage. It's only a couple of hundred yards. His instinct is to run quickly towards it, but what if the elusive figure is Prudie and she lies in wait? He walks along the edge of the wood. A low hedge running between two fields is the only cover. He walks beside this slowly, keeping his head down, hoping he's not been seen.

The hedge finishes at a narrow track. Beyond is a low fence, enclosing a small vegetable plot, surrounding the cottage. The field at the rear is not separated by any enclosure, so Hugh assumes this is part of Prudie's own property, with Manning and Collver holdings on the other three sides. The thatched, single storey cottage is small with a stout door and two firmly shut windows. He waits and watches. No one comes out or runs over the field. She must be inside or close at the back. The light is failing, but he will be clearly visible. He walks on, no point now in hesitation or hiding.

Matthew is in deep thought. He'd not wanted this assignment, but having been forced on him he was determined to bring it to a rapid conclusion. Even after Lexden's murder he didn't feel the investigation would be too onerous so long as he was able to keep Stradsey at bay. Now he's not so sure. Even so close to the centre of Parliamentary power people feel insecure and fearful. What if the war should go badly wrong with the Royalist armies sweeping through the Home Counties on their way to London, wreaking terrible vengeance on those who dared to stand up for their freedoms and defy the king?

The meeting with John Collver has exacerbated his misgivings. He's being pulled down into more intricate levels. The suspiciously absent Richard Collver and a possible London dimension in of all places his own cloth trade. Harringstead is a cauldron of conflicting pressures – political with the allegations of Royalist conspiracy, witchcraft connected to the elusive Prude Westrup and social unrest against both Manning and – so he would have Matthew believe – Collver, led by...what was his name...Matthew forgets.

They might at least be able to concentrate on the wretched witchcraft allegation or get it out of the way once Hugh has seen Prudie Westrup. Then they can decide what next to do.

He's inclined to return to London. Richard Collver may be there. Besides he may reluctantly have to follow up the cloth trade connection. He hurries on to the inn, anxious to discuss matters with Hugh. The place is crowded, full of beery and pipe smoking labourers.

"Have you seen him?" the landlord says as Matthew comes up to the bar.

Matthew looks at him derisively. Does this man always speak as if he continues an earlier conversation that never took place?

"Many have seen the stranger wandering about in the fields. Should have thought you would want to know, with your... investigation..."

"I don't know what you're talking about," Matthew says exasperatedly.

"So you've not seen him?"

"Who?"

"Ah, now there's a question," the landlord says, tapping his nose, "some say one thing, some say another, but..."

Matthew moves away.

"He's been seen before...if it's the same man..."

Matthew stops and shrugs. The landlord beckons him to come closer and leans down to face Matthew squarely.

"Amberley...Edward Amberley."

A familiar name, the cloth merchant.

"He's here now?" Matthew says.

"No, long gone I reckon, just like before."

Matthew turns away again.

"Just thought you'd like to know," the landlord calls after him, suitably affronted.

Matthew is hungry. He turns back.

"I'd like to order some food, but I'll go up and get lieutenant Crittenden first."

"He's not in."

Matthew is surprised.

"Not back yet. In that case I'll wait."

He goes to a quiet corner and tries to ignore the noise around him. It's gets quieter as the men go home, but Matthew continues to wait.

Hugh stops before the door. If she's seen him, she'll be at the back, waiting for a chance to escape while he goes in. He circles the cottage, but sees nothing as the shutters are up. As he suspects there is a rear door. He leans against it and listens. Nothing. This has to be secured. There are several large flints, buttressed against the cabbage patch. He takes some of these, wedges them against the door and then returns to the front, listening carefully as he goes. Still nothing. She's run, probably barricaded the house after trying to scare him in the wood. Stupid woman! He'll be no more frightened here than he was in the wood! There'll be no holding back now.

He hammers the door repeatedly. There's no reply and no sound from within. He pushes against the door and it gives easily, swinging open with a shrill squeak. It's dark as there's no light from the windows. He calls out and leaves the door open. Even before his eyes adjust to the dimness he can tell the place is bare and no one is there. He searches the three small rooms. There's a pail, cutlery, pans and some tools, but no clothes or food except for two small bottles on the table. The remains of a dark brown liquid are in the bottom of one. He picks it up and immediately reels back, assailed by the pungent and foul odour. The bottle sips from his hand and smashes loudly on the floor. His head swims momentarily. He grips the back of the chair and gradually recovers. What is this stuff? He looks down, the floor smeared by the contents of the broken glass. He kneels down, but has to get back up as the smell hits him again. He edges away and resumes his inspection. Like the floors and walls, the bed is stripped bare. The ash in the fire is not only cold, but also damp from the recent rain in the chimney. Prudie has gone. If she was in the wood, she's not been home for at least several days.

Why no lock on the door? Another devil's trick? Perhaps she's spirited away her possessions as well as herself. Or had she to leave so quickly there was no time for locks? Yet the windows are shuttered. Maybe they should have come earlier, but then the ash in the fire...she would have gone anyway. He goes out, closing the door slowly with a distinct finality as if is a no one will see this place again for a long time. Outside it's darker than he expects, the afternoon light almost extinguished in the creeping twilight. Deep in thought he walks back, head down, staring at the vegetables. Then he sees them. Feet. Or rather shoes, common, rough, dirty.

"What are you doing here?"

He looks up to face his interrogator.

4

THERE'S no pain at first, only a rapid scraping scratching as if in his haste he's brushed his leg against an overhanging branch. Now a draining, searing emptiness as if all life has been wrenched from it, but still no pain. And an eerie, hollow silence as if he's been lifted out of the field, away from the noise and smell of battle. Yet he's still here, riding disorderly, desperately like the others. Though not so, for he sees them quicken and spur away, faster, faster. He tries to follow, but the horse will not, cannot...what's wrong with the nag! Is it lame, has it been hit? Then the pain comes at last. A first faint, almost gentle warming, then burning, hotter, stronger, longer. It's not the horse. Then he remembers. Those last musket shots seemed so close, so near, all around. He looks down. The scarlet stain grows wider. There can be no mistake now. One musket ball too many. It's not the horse that's hit. It's his leg.

So far, so quick, too soon. Just after the clock struck one they'd charged, yelling those curdling field words 'Victory without quarter!' Chasing the enemy maybe a mile. Then in the heady carelessness they'd pursued them further. On and on and on to break and open the Royalist rear, so far, so very far. Then the foot soldiers turned at Hays Bridge made a stand behind hastily overturned carts. We've come too far! No Foot of our own in pursuit. They're too far back! Then they planted their musketeers. We must turn!

He feels it now as if he's scraped not the branch of a tree, but coals and still the musket fire. His eyes glaze and he slumps in the saddle. Where are the others? Away, way ahead, returning to secure the bridge and the soldiers at Cropredy. He glances round. The Royalist barricade remains. Musketeers loading, aiming, firing and he a sitting duck. He must get back with the others, but he can't move. With any slight turn he's pierced as if by many daggers and an unbearable stabbing creases from his leg through his whole body. Then his leg, now oozing an awful, creeping redness, cracks like spitting twigs on a hot fire. Fire! More musket shots. He's slowed now to a dismal trot and slowing more by the second. The pain subsides, replaced by a twisting of his body right up to his head until he'll explode with the pressure. His eyes well over. He can see nothing. His head floats. Even the unrelenting musket fire subsides as he slumps forward. As the horse jerks he slithers to one side, loses his hold and falls to the ground...

...Matthew wakes up cold. The window has blown wide open and in his sleep he's pulled the blanket onto the floor. He leans down to pull it up, almost slipping out the bed and plunging his hand into the pisspot before grabbing the blanket. He turns over and buries his head. He rode yesterday afternoon from Harringstead, stabling his horse late, then hurrying through the dark streets past drunken louts and brazen prostitutes, before reaching his sister's house. In his tiredness he'd been in no mood to tolerate fools. Hugging the sides of the houses for some time, deep in thought, he was accosted by a young inebriated popinjay coming the opposite way.

"Give way, sir!" he shouted.

Matthew looked up disconsolately, mumbling, "No, sir, step aside into the street. I was here first."

"Indeed you were not sir, give way."

The younger man with his red rimmed hat, which could be a size too large for him and his bright boots, stood astride, blocking the narrow path. It had been a tiring ride. Matthew's boots were mud spattered and tight. He desperately needed a drink and his bed. His sister's house was close. He'd no time to waste bandying words with the wastrel. He glared defiantly, drew his sword and lunged it at the man.

"Out of the way, sir or by Jesu I'll run you through!"

With the tip of the quivering blade only inches from his face and a rueful glance upwards, the young man stepped aside.

"Have a care with that piece, sir!"

"Have a care with your tongue," Matthew said, hurrying on.

In the chilly morning air his mood has not softened He gets up and closes the window, painfully banging his toe into the pisspot as he returns. Cursing, he climbs back under the covers, but is almost immediately disturbed by Elizabeth's strident voice.

"Matthew! Get your breakfast now or it goes to the pigs!"

His rolls over and groans. Mornings are always the worst. Accumulated worries, ambivalent memories and concerns for the future sapping confidence and exacerbating doubts. A nervous rumble in the pit of his stomach grows. Maybe he just needs his breakfast. These unsettlements usually clear up as the sun advances. He gets up again and peers disconsolately at the lightening sky, then down at the narrow, enclosed street. He rubs his chin and ruffles his hair. A woman in the house opposite shakes a rug from her window and stares back at him. He turns away.

"Matthew!"

He staggers for his clothes. They are on the corner chair where he threw them last night. He struggles to dress, his feet seemingly too big for his hose and hops around the room as he gradually steers it up his leg. Exhausted with one leg in, one leg out he lands back on the bed and stretches back. He counts the cracks between the beams in the ceiling. A slight twinge makes him half sit up and massage his leg. It will go. Swinging his legs over the edge of the bed, he sits up, looks at his leg and strokes it. The pain has gone. He recalls the dream again. Cropredy. He shrugs, gets up and takes a few steps. The stiffness eases and he returns to the window. The woman opposite throws out the pisspot. He turns away as it splashes on the stone. He finishes dressing and slaps his leg. Lucky leg, he thought at the time he would lose it. They said as much, but it wasn't to be. Now it fools everyone. That drunk last night probably thought, a man with a limp, he's no match for me. Matthew smiles. Everybody fooled. Except the army.

"The pigs get it now!"

He grabs his coat and runs to the landing.

"Nay sister, leave it there, I am coming!"

He bounds down the stairs, tripping over his own feet at the bottom, almost falling before he catches the banister, which shakes under the pressure. He staggers to the empty table.

"You've not thrown it out?" he mumbles.

Elizabeth bangs a large, laden plate on the table.

"Just in time, those hungry pigs will be disappointed."

"Their loss is my reward," he says, tucking in.

Elizabeth sits opposite.

"At least the long night ride didn't rob you of your appetite."

"Only a little sleep. I got back quite late."

"You woke me up. You must be careful at night. You might have run across a cutpurse or worse."

"Not quite," he says, remembering the young doltish drunk again.

"Why did you leave Harringstead so late?

"There were things to attend to."

"Must have been important to hold you back so long."

He changes the subject.

"Edmund working?"

"He'll be down at the wharf all day. There's a large consignment expected..."

Matthew isn't listening. He's on his horse, speeding through the evening for the ambivalent security of the capital. The blackness of the cloud covered sky plays tricks with his eyes, but the horse follows the road, as if it knows only by keeping going can they avoid the unknowable threats of the night. He remembers nothing of the journey until reaching the outskirts of the great city, for then as now, his mind is still in Harringstead.

Has Hugh an over eagerness to draw attention and make his mark, holding back his report hoping it'll bring him later commendation to expand an arrogant self worth? Their minor disagreements swell in his recollection. Has he allowed him too long a leash? He's young and has to learn. The best lessons are learnt from mistakes, but some mistakes aren't reversible. He's fired with the godly flames of enquiry, determined to unearth the truth without fear of upsetting the over mighty or seeking the favour of ascending influentials, but would he deliberately keep Matthew unaware of a significant development? No. Hugh's disappearance is too sudden. It could be sinister.

Matthew waited at the inn for over three hours. He contemplated scouring the village, but by then he'd consumed far too much ale and was in no fit condition, so retired to bed. He assumed Hugh would arrive back late and he would see him in the morning, but it was not to be. Hugh was not in his room and the landlord had not seen him. Matthew waited until ten and then walked around the village. No one had seen Hugh. As he tramped the fields Matthew was annoyed with him for getting lost in some idiosyncratic enquiry, yet dark concerns took over and grew. Had Hugh found out too much, strayed into a trap to be attacked by the same assailant who cut down Lexden?

He reached the church and went inside. It was unlikely Hugh would want to spend time there, but Matthew had to cover all eventualities. It was late morning and the church was empty. It had been a long walk. Matthew sat at the back to rest awhile and watched the drifting motes caught in the narrow shafts of sunlight piercing the nave from the south windows. Increasing anxieties, the after effects of the previous night's drink and the morning exercise dulled his mind and made his eyes heavy. He leaned forward slightly and closed them. He could have been in prayer.

"Seeking the Lord to aid your enquiries, captain?"

Stradsey was standing in the side aisle, a slight smirk at the corner of his mouth, his steely eyes mocking. He must have been lurking at the east end. Matthew had not seen or heard him before sitting down.

"I always seek the Lord's help in the pursuit of truth and the prosecution of justice," Matthew said.

"The Lord helps those that help themselves. I trust your lieutenant is pursuing his enquiries into those evil women rigorously."

"He was when I last saw him," Matthew said stiffly and with the slightest inclination of his head, picked up his hat, "I will bid you good day, sir."

He didn't turn at the door. He felt the church's tranquillity transgressed by the minister's presence. It was not a comforting thought. He returned to the inn. Hugh had still not appeared. He ordered a meal and sat alone at one of the outside tables, staring across the green.

"Still looking for your friend?" the landlord said when he brought the food.

"Have you seen him?" Matthew said.

"I asked around after you left this morning. Dick, the blacksmith saw him yesterday. He was walking towards Narrow Baulk field, but he didn't see him come back."

"Narrow Baulk field?"

The landlord pointed to a track, passing a small coppice to a field about half a mile towards the north east. Matthew had gone that way in the morning, but had turned west towards the river. When a few locals arrived, he enquired again, but no one had seen Hugh. He checked with the blacksmith, but he couldn't add anything to the landlord's account. Short of any other indication of Hugh's whereabouts Matthew followed the track. He felt invigorated after the meal and struck out quickly in the warm afternoon sun. As he neared the trees he was besieged by swarms of gnats, so veered into the adjoining grassland. When he reached the field, full with ripening barley, there was no sign of Hugh. He peered into the shimmering haze in all directions and was about to return to the inn, then realised the track continued towards Syme House. Matthew had no enthusiasm for seeing the master of the house again, but there was the remote possibility he might shed some light on Hugh's movement. Besides he could not leave Harringstead without seeing the JP.

The track petered out, so he had to force his way through some scrubland, another coppice and then over the fence. As he dropped down onto the soft grass two large dogs came snarling out of the bushes. Matthew drew his sword and waved it menacingly at the nearest one. He'd no wish to injure them, but wouldn't hesitate if they got closer. The first dog stopped out of sword thrust distance and started barking loudly. The second joined in. The three chimneys, poking imperiously above the steep roof, made the house unmistakable and Matthew stepped out for it. The dogs followed at a discreet distance, barking incessantly. He must be seen soon. He should have made his presence known at the front, not creeping round the back like a burglar or footpad. A servant emerged from a rear door and came to meet him. One of the dogs got nearer, baring its teeth, saliva dripping from its mouth. Matthew swished with his sword, just missing its ear. The servant called off the dogs. Matthew put back his sword, not wishing to appear hostile. The man stopped as he drew level, seeming to recognise Matthew, but casting a condescending glance at the sweaty beads on his forehead and the dust on his boots.

"Your master at home?" Matthew said aggressively.

The servant hesitated.

"Captain Fletcher wishes to see him."

Mathew elbowed past the man and entered the house.

"What shall I say sir?" the servant said, skipping beside him.

"Parliament's business...he'll understand."

Matthew tramped past, startling the cook and maid in the kitchen.

"Your pardon, ladies," he said, doffing his hat, "I am here to see your master."

The manservant ran in front, leading the way upstairs to the main hall. All was as before, the beautifully carved staircase, the elegant heavy cabinets and immaculately polished floor. Yet it seemed wider, lighter, but strangely less imposing. All strength and stability and broad backed security, yet Matthew felt a detachment, a lack of connection between the house and its inhabitants. It could have been because he'd come from the servants' quarters. He heard women's voices from the upper floor then the servant ushered him into one of the front rooms. Manning sat alone, smoking his pipe with two more large dogs at his feet. One growled threateningly as Matthew entered. Manning slapped it down and beckoned him to a chair.

"Sounds like you've already stirred up my dogs."

"My apologies, sir. I came through the fields."

"No matter, captain," Manning said, proffering a pipe and tobacco, "Any progress?"

"No sir," Matthew said, turning it down, "I'm hampered by the disappearance of lieutenant Crittenden."

"I've not seen him. I assumed he was with you."

"He's not returned after I sent him in search of Prudie Westrup."

"Aha!"

Manning tapped the arm of the chair with his fist.

"You were warned, captain, of that woman! The reverend Stradsey advised you yesterday."

Matthew bridled at the mention of the minister.

"Indeed he did, sir, but as I explained, the course of my enquiries is a matter…"

"What about Richard Collver," Manning intervened gruffly, "any news of that Royalist?"

Matthew sighed deeply.

"No sir, there is not."

"You have seen his father."

"He does not know of his son's whereabouts."

"So he says."

"He also says that Richard has had a relationship with your daughter, Olivia."

Manning looked away.

"A matter on which you chose not to advise me."

"I did not think it important. It is not relevant to the Collver's Royalist sympathies."

"But it could be relevant to Richard's disappearance."

Manning grimaced, then turned back quickly.

"Has the lieutenant found Prudie Westrup?"

"I've already told you I've not seen him," Matthew said, irritated.

"Oh, yes of course," Manning said distractedly, but anxious to change the subject, "Your young assistant may be involving himself in matters beyond his understanding, indeed beyond the understanding of many older and wiser than himself. There are dark powers abroad, sir and that woman..."

"I take it you have no knowledge of mistress Westrup?"

"I do not. If I had you would be the first to know."

Manning inhaled deeply, exhaling a long plume of blue smoke as if to further emphasise, as it curled towards the ceiling the gravity of his message. Matthew was sure Stradsey would be the first to be informed rather than himself.

"In the meantime I must go back to London..."

"Indeed," Manning said with a quizzical forcing of his eyebrows.

"...but will return if you become aware of any significant intelligence. I shall be obliged if you would inform me immediately of information concerning lieutenant Crittenden."

"Be assured of my best attention."

"And you of mine."

Matthew turned to him at the front door.

"One last thing, sir. Did you once have a servant in the house, called Sarah Radbourne?"

"Yes, I did."

"Why did she leave?"

"I have no idea, she left very suddenly."

"Do you know where she is now?"

"No."

Manning offered to lend him a horse to return to the inn, but Matthew declined. He'd no desire to be beholden in any way and was upset by Manning's implied criticism of his investigations. The walk back had none of the light airiness of his earlier amble to the house. The wind was up and murmured through the trees. The sun was low in the sky and it was a weary trudge as the orange tinted clouds turned grey, reflecting his dismal mood. Some of the clouds got darker, almost black, though the threatened rain did not come. By the time he reached the inn he was cold and tired and wondered whether it would be better to stay in the village that night, but by then he was resolved. Whatever the weather he would not remain another night in the village...

"*Matthew?*"

...It was not just the disappearance of Hugh. After all they had only recently met. There was an undercurrent of hostility. When the landlord brought his horse from the stable he spoke in a surly tone, no doubt disappointed Matthew wasn't staying another night, but it could be more. As he rode to London Matthew felt he'd left a place where he could trust no one. Only when he approached his sister's house did he realise the significance of the local labourer's leader – Thomas Radbourne...

"*Matthew*, are you listening to me!"

Elizabeth is glaring at him across the table. He mumbles incoherently.

"I've asked you three times if you've had enough."

He looks down at his almost empty plate.

"What? Oh, yes, I've had enough."

He pushes the plate to the side.

"Matthew," she says gently, "What is on your mind?"

He tells her of Hugh's disappearance.

"What will you do?"

Matthew stares back vacantly, unwilling to acknowledge Elizabeth voicing his own thoughts.

"There's nothing I can do until there's more news. Meanwhile other matters need my attention. I must carry on with other enquiries away from Harringstead."

"You believe his disappearance is connected to this murder?"

"When I was last in London I met a man called Thomas Radbourne. He was looking for his daughter. I thought nothing if it at the time. Then the other day I was informed of a servant girl, working for the Mannings called Sarah Radbourne. "

"Not that uncommon a name. Is it the same girl?"

"I didn't ask this Thomas Radbourne where he came from. If it was Harringstead, then it has to be her. I saw him in the 'Phoenix.' I will return there."

Matthew spends the rest of the morning lounging about the house until Elizabeth tires of him under her feet and grabbing a broom almost sweeps him out of the house. After wandering around he arrives back at the 'Phoenix.' A band of light from the street catches the empty tables and chairs. Only a couple of old men huddle in a dark corner, well away from the noise and clatter outside. A waitress emerges from the back and looks expectantly at Matthew. He makes sure no one he knows is lurking in any shadowy crooks.

"There was a man in here a couple of weeks ago, looking for his daughter, Thomas Radbourne."

"Never heard of him."

"In his forties, a dark, small man. Have you seen him?"

"We get everybody in here. Anyway, if he's still around he's more likely to be back at night. Now, do you want a drink?"

"No...thank you."

He steps back into the street. The sun is high. A few men enter. The waitress will be pleased the midday trade begins. He follows the street towards the river. The nearer he gets the busier it is and he has to dodge the heavy carts and wagons. It's not always possible to keep close to the buildings and the streets are littered with horse shit. As he turns into a narrow lane he looks up to spy any pot emptiers. The sky darkens. It starts to rain, slowly at first and then heavier. Soon the drains flush and the eaves splatter onto the stones, the water collecting in pools to lift accumulated filth in a dirty stream down to the river. He steps into a shop doorway. Others join him to escape the rain until six are cramped into the narrow space. The later arrivals, water dripping from their hats drubbing their boots, nudge closer to avoid the water cascading from the roof. Their bodies so close together, steam rises from their clothes with a pungency of dampness and sweat. A man jostles Matthew as he comes out of the shop, pushing him into the street. The man apologises. The rain eases. Now is a good time to continue his journey and keeping close to the side he reaches the bottom of the lane and turns onto the wharf.

The river is crammed with boats and ships, their lumbering cargoes heaved and swung by an army of swarthy dockers and stevedores. A continual file of vehicles filters forward to set down their loads or to be quickly filled again. The array of waiting wagons never diminishes. As soon as one leaves it's replaced by another, the queuing line perpetually replenished. Foremen bustle constantly, checking what comes in, what goes out. Matthew looks for Edmund from vessel to vessel, but doesn't see him. He walks on until he reaches a noisy tavern close by London Bridge, the 'Anchor.' By now parched and a little hungry he ignores the mid afternoon revelry and goes inside. He finds a stool by the window and orders ale and a pie.

The man sitting opposite is tucking into a huge plate of pork and vegetables. In between mouthfuls he grins amicably, displaying an unusually white and straight set of teeth, which reminds Matthew of some kind of wild cat. The smile is broad, yet menacing though the man seems friendly enough. He refers to Matthew (as well as to anyone else) as 'pilgrim' and asks about the war.

"You look like a soldier, pilgrim, I should say cavalry. Am I right?"

Matthew nods. The man devours another hunk of pork and continues, waving a cabbage laden fork.

"Thought so, I'm usually right. At Marston Moor, were you in the charge?"

Matthew shakes his head. He's about to explain, but after another slurp of beans, the man interrupts him.

"Terrible business, so I hear. Glorious, but terrible, maybe you were lucky not to be there, but then..."

"You seem very well informed," Matthew says, "Are you in the army yourself?"

"Connected," the man says, polishing off the last of his meal before emitting an enormous belch, "Supplies for Parliament, that's my business."

"I see. You are regularly in here?"

"Most days. They serve a good chop."

He exhibits the immaculate teeth and proceeds to pick bits of pork from them.

"You may have come across the man I'm looking for."

The man has no knowledge of Radbourne, but offers to keep an eye out and make immediate enquiries. After completing his tooth picking and swilling down a long draught of ale he moves from table to table asking if anyone has seen Radbourne. He even interrupts an animated group singing loudly near the rear door. He receives some bellicose comments, but they calm down when he agrees to accompany them in their next rendition and fill up their empty glasses. They could be soldiers. After completing his circuit of all parties he returns to Matthew. No one has seen or heard of a man looking for his daughter.

Matthew is ready to go, but the man, well provisioned and even better lubricated, insists on further discussion about 'how the struggle goes.' As more ale slides down his throat Matthew wonders about commissariat profits, then decides it's time he left.

"But you've not told me your story," the man says, grabbing his arm.

Matthew pulls it away and is about to get up when he notices three of the erstwhile singers standing over him. They are stout, heavy fellows.

"I'm sure these pilgrims would like to hear too," the man says, with a wave of his hand and a wide toothy smile.

They sit and listen impassively as Matthew explains his injury before returning to their corner and launch into a new bawdy ballad with gusto. Matthew gets up.

"Sorry I wasn't able to help you find your friend, pilgrim," the man says, "Come again and we can talk some more."

Matthew walks back along the riverside into the setting sun. Halfway back to the house he reaches the 'Coal Heaver's Inn,' much smaller than the 'Anchor,' but even more crowded. He's determined not to get stationed too close to anyone so circulates, or more accurately is circulated through the carousing throng, as he looks for Radbourne or anyone who might have seen him. The exercise takes over twenty minutes. As he returns to the door he's accosted by a colourful woman with leering eyes, luridly painted cheeks and a well exposed cleavage.

"I always like to please a soldier," she says as he sidles past.

"No doubt, madam," Matthew says, glaring at her forcefully as he grabs the door, "but I am not that soldier."

Relieved at having survived both the delectations and dangers of the 'Coal Heaver's Inn' he inhales several deep breaths of the evening air and walks west to where the Fleet enters the Thames. Here the riverside's assorted fragrances reach their most challenging, but it's more refreshing than the stifling suffocation of the tavern. He looks into the Fleet and sees no dead dogs as the city's perennial myth espouses though there are many other items of rubbish and effluent. He walks along the wharves turning close to the north line of forts and defensive trenches constructed some two years ago. As the last daylight is lost, he stops and gazes for a few minutes wondering how long before such things can be relegated to the past. He turns up his collar in the cool evening breeze. He'll try a few more places in pursuit of Radbourne, so turns back towards the city.

The wind stirs up and by the time he reaches the bridge across the Fleet, he's thoroughly chilled and glad to reach 'Fenner's' tavern, less raucous, more reputable than the alehouses by the river. He intends only staying a short time, but it's a convivial place and he finds a vacant chair by the welcoming fire. The landlady serves a good ale. She's a large, middle aged woman with a gentle smile, but heavy eyes betraying some sadness in the past. She listens to his description of Radbourne, but shakes her head until he mentions the daughter.

"There was such a soul in here. Deeply troubled, I couldn't help him."

"Was this recent?"

"About a week ago. I've not seen him since."

As Mathew thaws out beside the fire, he's suddenly aware of the glowing coals.

"Where did you get coal?" he calls to the landlady.

She puts her fingers to her lips and comes over.

"A friend with a cart, there's not much."

"There's been no coal landed for months."

"It didn't come by sea. Truth is, I don't know where it's from. Not from Newcastle, that's for sure, been none from there since the place was occupied by the Scots."

"Curse them," a man says at a nearby table.

"They're on our side," another says.

"If they're on our side they should send the coal," the first man says.

"The Scotch soldiers won't release the coal until they've been paid," his companion says.

"Couple of days and I'll be out of it again," the landlady says ruefully, "then it'll be back to burning turf like everybody else."

"If Parliament paid the Scotch army we'd get our coal," the second man says.

"Damn this war," the first man says, "When will it end?"

"When we get rid of this serpent of a king," a third says, joining them from an adjacent table and then, turning to Matthew, "What do you say, friend, would we not be better without a king?"

"We would all be better if the king accedes to the legitimate grievances of the Parliament," Matthew says.

"England would be better without the king at all," the man persists.

"England will always have a king," Matthew says, "When we have one decisive victory he will come to his senses."

"Parliament shouldn't allow foreigners to occupy our cities," the second man grumbles.

"This king will never come to his senses," his companion persists and then eyeing Matthew forcefully, "and those that say otherwise would do well to consider their consciences."

Matthew's patience has worn thin. He leans forward, returning the man's glare with concentrated deliberation, heavily emphasising his words.

"My conscience is clear, sir and you would do well to look to yours. In these times, intemperate accusations are best avoided. I put my trust in Parliament's representatives, parleying as we speak with those of the king at Uxbridge."

Reluctant to challenge Matthew's studied stare, the man looks away. Sensing the tension, his two companions change the subject, bantering harmlessly on some local gossip and gradually drawing the third man into their conversation. Matthew watches for a few moments, but they avert their attention, unwilling to provoke his obvious irritation. He's warmed up now and having no immediate intelligence of Radbourne, rises to go.

"I bid you good evening, gentlemen," he says as he passes the three men at their table, "may God go with you."

"And with you, sir," the second man says.

"And bring us peace," the first man says.

Their companion nods, but says nothing.

"Good hunting, sir," the landlady shouts as he reaches the door, "I hope you find what you are looking for."

"Well may we all," Matthew says as he steps back into the street.

He reaches the 'Phoenix' again. Someone may have seen Radbourne, but it's so crowded with besotted revellers, he gets no sense from anyone. He squeezes his way to the bar where the waitress recognises him from earlier.

"Still looking for your friend?"

"He's not a friend, I just want..."

"I asked around, but no one's seen him."

"That's good of you. I..."

She turns to serve a customer. Another man jabs him in the ribs. Matthew glares. The man apologises. With no prospect of further progress, Matthew jostles and pushes his way to the door, where he taps a young man on the shoulder to make way. As the other turns they recognise each other. The drunken whelp from the other night stares incredulously.

"You sir " he cries, wafting his heavy ale laden breath into Matthew's face, then turning to his cronies, "Forced me into the street when I was there first!"

"Give way, if you please, sir," Matthew says.

"It does not please me, sir, I have given way to you too much!"

His two companions stare aggressively, but their eyes are glazed and one sways slightly. Matthew can't waste further

76

time and will have to act before they can muster what little threat they really pose. He slaps the whelp in the face with his left hand, forcing him against one of his friends, while elbowing the other aside with his right hand. Then, taking advantage of surprise he rushes at the door, but the friend, temporarily winded by the whelp stumbling into him, recovers enough to land a blow on Matthew's cheek. Matthew turns and hits him squarely on the jaw, forcing him down again, then runs up the street before they can catch him. He hears voices behind, but the footsteps are slow and ponderous, his adversaries' pursuit weighed down by their liquor consumption! He slips around a few corners and then, hearing no more, slows down.

He's in a narrow alley outside another tavern, the 'Dancing Bear.' It seems a quiet place. Slightly disoriented (he thinks he may have strayed back down to the river) he goes in to retrieve his bearings. Inquisitive heads turn as he enters, suspicious eyes assessing him carefully before returning to their discussions. A rumbling murmur pervades from the small groups gathered around the tables. The little light comes from the large fire. Spindly shadows dart grotesquely exaggerated figures along and up the walls. Matthew orders a drink and sits to the side of one of the tables where a debate ensues. Between puffing enormous smoke rings from his pipe, a man, plainly dressed in a dark coat, pontificates on the conduct of the war. His tall, black hat, without ornamentation, sits on the table. He is the consummate puritan, infusing every mundane word with unnecessary gravitas.

"This new army will soon be ready. General Cromwell's force will be the match of any the Royalists can throw at us."

His companions nod sagely, his words incapable of challenge.

"Let us hope you are right," Matthew says.

They all turn, then look back at tall hat as the only sure guide on how they should react to the stranger.

"I saw you come in," he says, "you have the bearing of a soldier. I noticed a slight limp. May I ask if you came by it in the war?"

His wide, inquiring eyes rest on Matthew as if the question is really an accusation.

"I did sir, Cropredy Bridge."

Tall hat signals his approval with a slight tilt of the head and then nodding to the cut on Matthew's cheek says, "Looks like you've been in battle more recently."

"Scratched on a door," Matthew says, fingering his face.

Tall hat considers this briefly, then nods silently. Picking up on his cue the others grunt their mirrored assent. Sensing sudden acceptance, Matthew asks about Radbourne.

"You are tracking down a Royalist spy?" one man says.

"Describe him," another says.

Matthew gives a few remembered details, omitting to mention he has no reason to believe Radbourne is a spy.

"They are everywhere," the first man says.

"You can't trust anybody these days," the other says.

"He's not a spy," Matthew says, trying to shift the conversation.

"We must be ever vigilant," tall hat says, ignoring him.

"Only last week," the first man says, "I heard they were at the docks, noting everything down, what comes in, what goes out, sending it all off to their Royalist friends."

The other nods deferentially to tall hat.

"Richard says, they are ready to rise up and take over the city."

"This Radbourne," tall hat says, "he could be a leader of plots."

"He's not a spy!" Matthew says, "I just want to find him."

They are taken aback for a moment. Tall hat glances sceptically at Matthew.

"You cannot be sure," the first man says, leaning over, his eyes darting conspiratorially from side to side, "about being a spy, I mean."

"They are everywhere," tall hat drones, "It's good for us Phillip Skippon is back in town."

"I take it none of you have seen him?" Matthew says.

They shake their heads in unison. Matthew asks at the other tables where similar conversations are taking place, the whole tavern obsessed with dark rumblings of Royalist conspiracies, but no one has heard of Radbourne. After exchanging a few more politely neutral comments and receiving a knowing nod from tall hat, Matthew leaves by the back door, emerging into a narrow, steep alleyway. He takes only a few steps up the hill when he hears a loud commotion from the 'Dancing Bear.' He stops to listen only long enough to hear the whining of the young whelp. They must have been scouring all the taverns. Then one of tall hat's companions shouts 'suspicious character' while another shouts 'went that way' with 'probably a Royalist' from a third. Matthew hurries up the street. The rear door is flung open as he reaches the corner. The young whelp sees him and calls out.

"Stop sir, or I call the watch!"

His two companions collide into him. Matthew stops to face them. Yong whelp runs towards him. They are too close now for Matthew to run and he feels the drag in his left leg. He draws his sword. Young whelp stops and turns to his friends, but drink has finally caught up with them. One is sliding down the door jam while the other has already reached the floor, slumped over into the stones. Matthew approaches. Young whelp's hand goes to his sword hilt, but then with a glance at his associates, puts it back. He shakes his hands in a gesture of futility at Matthew and then returns to his friends. Matthew waits a few moments. Young whelp hauls up his friend from the floor, pokes the other, then all three lurch back into the tavern.

It's getting late and Matthew is tired. After a circuit of several streets he gets his bearings and heads home. He can't get the ludicrous conversation in the 'Dancing Bear' out of his mind and wonders how many more good citizens waste their energy and peace of mind on phantom conspiracies and Royalist risings. He avoids the raucous blare from the 'Phoenix' just before reaching another tavern, 'The Rose.' He's had his fill of tavern gossip for one night, but lingers. Besides, he's unlikely now to be accosted by the pathetic trio. He can hear a fiddler and peers through the window. Many are joining in a song. Perhaps this is a place devoid of suspicious eyes and ears and alehouse bores. It'll be good to rest awhile.

He stays by the door, partly out of prudence, but also away from the revellers and asks about Radbourne. After the usual shaking heads and shrugging shoulders he settles into his seat, half closes his eyes and lets the singing surge over him. Three young women are at the next table. One keeps glancing over. There are also three young men at a nearby table and Matthew is unsure whether they are together. He wants no more trouble tonight and looks away, giving her no encouragement. Then she comes over, sits opposite and stares at him directly. She is brazenly attractive. He looks to the other table. None of the men seem to have noticed. She leans forward, her ample figure touching the table. He attempts to avert his gaze.

"I heard you asking," she says.

He looks at her quizzically. Her large eyes open wider. He feels distinctly uncomfortable as if in the presence of a forbidden temptress.

"Radbourne," she says.

He sighs with relief.

"You've seen him?"

"Not him, but I've seen her, Sarah."

"Where, when, how can I find her?"

"Steady sir, steady, you must be truly in earnest to find her!"

"No, no, it's not like that. I need to talk to her, she could be important as part of my...I just need to talk to her."

"Yes, yes," she says knowingly and then more seriously, "Not that she's that sort of girl. I hope your intentions are honourable, sir?"

"Absolutely."

Her eyes search his face discerningly and then she nods.

"She was in here a few days ago."

"Where does she live?"

"I don't know, only exchanged a few words. Not seen her since."

"Was she alone?"

"No, she was with a man. Not seen him since either."

"She must live nearby?"

She shrugs.

"Could be well gone by now. Who knows?"

Matthew scribbles his address and promises a good reward for further information. It's been a frustrating night. He's learnt almost nothing of the Radbournes, though Sarah may be tantalisingly close, but there's also the generally depressed mood. With shortages of almost everything and rife with rumours of Royalist plots it's a gloomy city. Too despondent to fight, let alone secure a decisive victory over the King and restore liberties to the country. He's filled with a heavy melancholy as he tramps wearily through the last dark streets.

The corner near the house is suddenly illuminated by the moon, creeping from the clouds and piercing the narrow divide between the houses to cast a pool of light on the stones. He looks up, but the clouds quickly flit over the moon and the brief brightness is gone. Such is hope. Brief, slight, catch it while you can. This civilian existence does not wear well on him. He longs to be back in the army, where a man's intention is clear and his role worthwhile. A last glance upward, silently wondering if it's God's will for him to take on the new role he finds so disagreeable. He goes in resolved. Tomorrow he must seek an audience with the general. The house is quiet. Elizabeth and Edmund have long since gone up. The fire only a glowing ember. He rakes and banks it for the morning before going to bed. He's soon asleep, but fitfully disturbed by recurrent dreams of the suspicious city...

...Crowds shuffle like a surging stream along the narrow streets, murmuring dolefully. A woman shrieks and a man shakes his fist at the sky.

"They are everywhere," a dark eyed hag whispers in his ear as he stands in a shop doorway.

Someone jostles him from behind and he's swept into the crowd, where faceless forms make way to absorb him in the crushed, snaking throng.

"I know you sir," says a young man, guarded on each side by an ugly companion, "Make way sir, stand aside!"

"A pox on you, sir!" Matthew replies.

The young man and his two dismal acolytes disappear. Now the crowd reaches the river, but instead of diverging, walks blindly to the quay, where people successively plunge headlong into the water.

"That's how they do it," a man says at his side, "these Royalists, they're everywhere."

Matthew reaches the edge. The man in front, straight faced, eyes closed, drops down, slipping effortlessly into the river. Matthew wants to turn aside and hesitates, but a man in a tall hat beckons him forward with a bony finger.

"They will rise up and cut our throats as we sleep."

The heaving host pushes relentlessly at his back. His foot dangles over the water. He loses his balance and feels himself falling...

...He wakes suddenly with a start and sits up, eyes wide open, but his mind still at the river, his ears still ringing with the low, persistent hum of the crowd. The half light from the window gradually fills his vision. He sts for a few moments, recovering his senses. He wipes the sweat and walks to the window, staring into the empty street, listening to the distant, intermittent sounds of the city. He shivers, though more in shock than from the chill of the night. He returns to bed, tossing and turning for a long time, before a deeper, less troubled sleep intervenes.

Next day he's up earlier than the day before, ensuring he gets his breakfast, but again misses his brother in law.

"Edmund goes to a meeting tonight," Elizabeth says, "He thought you might go with him."

"Meeting?"

"A new group, they meet in a tavern. The 'Saint George.'"

"Not sure, I've had enough of taverns."

Elizabeth glances at the cut on his cheek, which has broadened to a wide redness.

"So I see."

"It's just a scratch."

She looks doubtful.

"You'll have to curb your temper, Matthew, you're no longer in the army."

"It's not my temp...they came off worst...Anyway, that's precisely what I intend to change. It's time I was back in the army."

"Meantime you spend your time wandering from tavern to tavern, asking questions, drawing attention to yourself..."

"It's part of the task I've been set."

"Even so..."

"There's been no message from young Crittenden, I suppose?" he says, anxious to draw the conversation away from taverns.

"No."

"It is just possible, there may be a message from a young girl..."

"Young girl? Someone you met in an alehouse, Matthew what..."

He holds up his hand.

"I have left word, Elizabeth, for her to contact me. It's part of my enquiries at Harringstead."

Elizabeth goes into the yard, muttering 'girls in taverns' and 'coming in late, saying it's *enquiries*.' As she rattles and bangs Matthew finishes his breakfast and retreats upstairs, to clean his boots, brush his hat and put on his best clothes. He remembers tall hat's comment. Phillip Skippon has recently returned to the city. He has moved to new quarters and may not be here for long. Matthew will act. It's a bright, cloudless sky. Elizabeth's words return. He should not draw attention to himself.

A burly lieutenant waylays him on the first floor of Skippon's house.

"Your business, captain?"

"I am reporting on my investigations, carried out in accordance with the sergeant major general's instructions."

"You'll have to wait, there are many anxious to see him. Otherwise you could return later, it's possible that..."

"I will wait."

"I will inform the general of your arrival."

Matthew waits in an ante room with several others. A clerk scratches away in the corner. Messengers come and go, mostly on their way to or from Parliament in Westminster. The lieutenant appears a few times. Most of those waiting are civilians. After an hour the lieutenant calls Matthew. The general's room is small and sparsely furnished. His main lodgings are on the floor above. He sits at a small desk by the window, looking into the street below. He looks tired and drawn, but listens attentively as Matthew reports on the progress of the investigation. At first he omits any reference to Hugh.

"You have returned to London to follow some particular matter?" Skippon says.

Matthew is uncomfortable. Skippon assumes it's because of his leg and motions him to a chair.

"There is a servant girl, who once worked for Manning. She may have important information. I believe her to be in London."

"Is there a suspicion she has been involved in witchcraft?"

"Not that I am aware."

"Manning was particularly concerned about that aspect."

"General, do you believe witches are a serious threat in the area?"

Skippon grimaces.

"I have heard that in the eastern counties…"

"This is Middlesex."

"Even so, if this girl is not a witch and she's left the area, what of others that remain?"

"I have no knowledge."

"You have left Crittenden in Harringstead?"

"Yes, sir."

Skippon grimaces and returns his attention briefly to the street.

"Is that wise? He is inexperienced."

Skippon looks back. Under his forceful gaze Matthew feels forced to mention Hugh's disappearance.

Skippon asks a few more questions about the enquiry, then says, "You must pursue these matters wherever you think best. I trust your judgement."

It has to be now for Matthew to raise the subject.

"General, I know you are busy…"

"Indeed I am. I've been in London only two days and already besieged as you see. I shall be glad to return to the army by the end of the week. There are important developments. This may be the year when God and our rights triumph."

"General, that is what I want to talk to you about. This investigation, I know it's important for Manning and the army feels..."

"Not the army, Matthew, Parliament. Your commission is from..."

"Yes, sir, I know, but that's my point. This investigating, poking and ferreting about, it's not for me. I am a soldier. You have said how important this year's campaigning may be. It's my earnest wish to return to the army, to active service."

Skippon sighs deeply and then glances down at Matthew's left leg, pushed out from beneath the table.

"Matthew, I know you are in earnest and determined to heed the call of your heart and follow in godliness..."

"General, I want to return to the army!"

Skippon sighs again and puts his hands on the table in a gesture of openness.

"Matthew, your injury at Cropredy, you are lucky to be alive, let alone have your leg. I'm sorry, but in the field you could be a liability. This commission serves Parliament just as effectively as drawing your sword in a cavalry charge. In these troubled times, we can't tolerate lawlessness and need men we can trust implicitly. The local..."

"The infantry then. I could re-enter with you as an officer of Foot. You must have need of men."

"Matthew, in all good grace, you would be even more vulnerable on foot."

"So you are refusing my request?"

Skippon stiffens.

"Yes, captain, I am. You are dismissed."

The lieutenant is at the door with a despatch. Matthew ignores him as they pass each other. Incensed and frustrated, he lurches down the stairs, his left leg dragging as if to emphasise and broadcast his impediment. In his exasperation he catches his ankle on the banister, disproportionately increasing his normal limp as he reaches the street. He stops to adjust his hat, hammering his fist into the air, then crosses to the other side of the street, pausing briefly to gaze up at Skippon's window angrily. The general cannot be seen.

He walks away disconsolate and disappointed. His ankle aches though it's not seriously sprained. His limp is slight, but he seems to drag a huge burden, slithering along the street, watched contemptuously by everyone. Two young urchins loiter at the corner. If they mock him he'll strike them down, while any man that dares insult him will feel the tip of his blade. The boys ignore him, as does everyone else, the slightness of his injury drawing no attention. His debilitation is only in his mind. He curses his leg and kicks the ground. No immediate return to the army and all down to that accursed musket ball! Unable to settle, he goes to the riverside to clear his troubled mind, but the scene at the dockside depresses him. So much vitality, industry, scurrying activity to aid the cause, however indirectly while he's consigned to less than the commonest boy in the baggage train! He turns from the river and walks back up the hill. Is it God's will to expend his energy in this puerile digging and delving, his horse riding restricted to mundane coming and going on quiet rural tracks? Maybe the general is right. The Lord plucked him from the battle for other work. If it is so written, then he must obey, but it does not mean he must like it.

He returns to his sister's house. Elizabeth chatters and busies around him as he sits morosely in the kitchen. She asks where he's been. He answers sullenly, dismissing his visit.

"It's of no importance."

Elizabeth isn't fooled.

"Brother, if it was of no importance you would not have gone. If you were not disappointed in the outcome you would not now cast your gloom over my house."

He half smiles behind the hand he pulls across his mouth.

"Cease this unsocial dejection. I have heard and seen enough and bring some joy into your heart before my husband comes in."

"If only I could return to the army, then..."

"If only, if only, if only you would obey God's will and accept what He directs you to undertake."

"But is it His will, Elizabeth, that's what I keep asking myself for if..."

"Why there you are, Matthew! I've hardly seen you brother, since you joined us."

Blocking the doorway with his huge frame Edmund suddenly makes the room seem much smaller. Bluff and blustery, he sits opposite Matthew and banters with Elizabeth, recounting the doings of his day, the cargoes he's overseen, the mariners and merchants he's dealt with, the rogues he's seen off. He and Elizabeth joke and laugh. At first Matthew watches impassively, then smiles politely, finally easing up until he can knock back their well meant barrage of jibes aimed at his 'dark humour.' Edmund is in good spirits and blathers as much as his wife during the meal.

"Fortunes of war, which you as a soldier should know more than me," he says to Matthew's single reference to his unsuccessful appeal to Skippon, "Like the frightened complaints of my fellow townsmen, whining wails of the withered. You need to lift up your heart and your sprits. Come tonight to the 'St.George.' A new man will speak, one who throws fresh light on God's purpose."

Matthew shakes his head.

"I'm not sure, taverns are..."

"...not just for wenching and carousing, why..."

"This St. George, is it a respectable place?"

"It is," Elizabeth says emphatically, "or no God fearing man from this house would go there!"

Edmund laughs heartily, pokes Matthew gently in the chest and they set off. Edmund is in jolly mood and sets a rapid pace, but for some reason Matthew's left leg, as if to emphasise his disappointing conversation with Skippon drags and slows him.

"You must rest it more," Edmund says sympathetically as they stop on a corner.

"I am alright!" Matthew bellows angrily.

"I only..."

"No matter, Matthew says, hauling himself jerkily from the wall on which he leans, "I'm sorry. Let us go on."

They do, but intermittently, as Matthew has to stop frequently. They arrive late and the gathering has already begun. The 'St. George' is packed, but very quiet as the company strain to listen to a young man addressing them from his perch on a chair at the far end. He speaks slowly and deliberately, moving from side to side to ensure he's seen by everyone and swaying slightly forward and backward to highlight his points. Matthew and Edmund squeeze in at the door. There's much pipe smoking and a man offers one to Matthew. He politely refuses, saying he needs to keep a straight head.

"Nay sir," the man says, "why tobacco and drink are the better to get closer to God."

Matthew is doubtful, but says nothing. The young man pauses between his sideways leaning and his forward swaying to gaze round his audience, most of whom mumble assent with 'aye, aye' or 'in God's truth' or similar affirmations. Others puff even more strongly on their pipes or swill down more ale or replenish their tankards. Edmund listens intently. Matthew studies the audience. There are as many women as men, most smoking and drinking as profusely as the menfolk. The young man takes off his hat with its long, single feather, again to accentuate the moment, for he replaces it immediately back on his head and then continues.

"I tell you brothers and sisters, I see God in all things natural. God is in everything and he comes into us all with his spirit. In that spirit we are freed from the curse of the creation as recounted to us by those self styled saints. So free of that curse, we are free from the commandments and so our will is God's will!"

"What of sin, brother?" a man shouts.

"Sin? You ask of sin. Those self styled saints they lust after the wisdom, power, glory and honour of this present world. But I tell you with the restitution of all things and the liberty of the creation there can be no sin. For if there was sin it must be part of God's plan and if God is omnipotent how can he permit evil?"

He leans back expectantly, his wide eyes scanning them with anticipatory eagerness, but this time there's an awful, uncertain silence. After a few moments the young man announces a short break to 'aid the contemplation of his message' and 'afford him to piss away so much ale.' Edmund still stares at the now empty chair.

"Are you impressed?" Matthew asks him.

Edmund's eyes are slightly puzzled.

"An interesting interpretation. What do you make of it?"

Mathew clicks his teeth.

"I think I'll use this interruption to question the congregation."

Matthew moves uneasily between those silently pondering, those vigorously debating and those engaged in serious drinking and smoking, but to no avail. No one has seen or heard of the Radbournes, father or daughter. The young man resumes his perch on the chair and launches again into his harangue.

"Heaven is attainable in this life, brother and sisters, there is no Hell and there is no curse. We are all free and at one with God!"

Burbling amens pulsate respectfully, but not everyone joins in the adulation. Like Edmund some are quizzical. A few are silent. Fewer still are sceptical like Matthew. The speaker pauses again, searching his rapt audience for signs of approbation or perhaps of doubt. Matthew avoids his gaze. The searching eyes pass on. Matthew's leg aches.

"I've heard enough of this wastrel," he whispers to Edmund, "I think we should go."

"I'll hear him to the end," Edmund says.

"My leg gives me trouble. I'll leave and see you at home."

"Very well, Matthew, take care."

Matthew slips into the street, the chill night air striking him with a welcome freshness. He walks slowly and feels a little better. As the ache in his leg subsides he increases his pace. Maybe the ache is not in his limb, but in his mind and heart. All men must answer to their own consciences, but this man's message is too much. What can these fools know? This damned war must end soon. When the king is brought round honest men can return to their normal lives. He slows again. His leg drags even more, a reminder of his inability to play the part he would set himself. One great victory, it will not come easily, but it can be done. If only he could be part of it. He steps into a side alley to rest. Darkly concentrating on wider concerns, he doesn't notice the shadow on the far wall nor hear the soft footfalls behind. An arm grabs his throat, his leg is tripped and he's brought down heavily to the ground.

5

A monstrous fearful creature with huge flaming eyes, the spiky strands of its long hair flung out like spears from Hell and surrounded on all sides by dreadful companions.

"What are you doing here?" it says.

How do you answer a devilish emissary? Hugh looks into the abominable face unable to speak, unable to move.

"This is private property," another says, "Why are you here?"

Aye indeed, the property of the devil! His silence disturbs them, irritates them, angers them.

"Who are you, where are you from?" a third says.

They are indistinct and blurred. Hugh screws his eyes and gradually focuses, for the first time looking each side of the first figure and taking real notice of them. If they are devils they are *she* devils. For they are women, iniquitous, but women. Witches! The realisation breaks his stupor. Now he can speak, now he *will* speak!

"Damnable w...w...w...(even now he can't bring himself to pronounce the word)...w...wretches! Who *are* you? Who are you to question *me*?"

"I am Alice Sandon," the first of the infernal eyes and grotesquely electrified hair says, "I say again, why are you here at Prudie's cottage?"

So Prudie Westrup really is one of them. A witch! This is the coven and they come to defend their place of diabolical worship, destroying anyone in their path as they did Samuel Lexden. They cut him down as he escaped before dragging him to that hedge! Now they'll do the same to him, cut down and dragged...

How many are there, three, five, more? He looks desperately from one to the other and then at Alice as they too look to her. She moves towards him. The others follow. He looks desperately again between them. It's almost dark and he has difficulty seeing them clearly. Are there more... seven...nine...he steps back, but then stops...the cottage is no escape...they come on...he looks to the side...he must get away! No time to argue with deranged women, there are too many. No time to meddle with dark powers, their magic beyond his capacity. Matthew should not have sent him alone. Matthew would know what to do. This is the greatest threat as the minister said.

"If you do not answer us, we..."

Drenched with visions of sorcery he hears only an immediate threat. He must lose no time! If he delays they'll have him and escape will be impossible! If he can get to the side of the cottage and across the fields...he turns, but fearing he intends damage to the cottage, one of the women blocks his path. He stares frozen for a few moments, then hears the others moving behind him.

"Stop him!" Alice shouts.

He bounds forward, knocking over the woman, then sprints through the garden and leaps over the fence onto the track. He can hear the women chasing him. His first instinct is to turn and run back towards the village, but even in the dark he'll be an easy target on the open track. Ominous shadows and unknown dangers are thrust aside. He must escape from the known danger! Instead he keeps to the hedge and up towards the wood. At least there is the forbidding security and protection of the trees. In the dark it seems to take much longer before he reaches the wood. All the time the panting and pounding of his pursuers spur him to keep going. They may soon reach him, fleet footed by the devil's energy. Should he turn and confront them, but what can even a soldier do against nine women? He hammers the ground faster and faster, yet with each step the looming immensity of the wood gets no nearer.

At last he hears the crunching leaves beneath his feet, but an enveloping mouth of blackness consumes the little light, inviting him to uncertain sanctuary. He snags the bushes, but ploughs on, crashing through bracken, breaking twigs. An overhanging bough lashes his head, just missing his eye, his feet sore, his back aching, his eyes struggling to see anything. Does this mouth have teeth, but yet a tunnel of escape? He stumbles on a stone and half falls before levering against something hard and immovable. It must be a tree trunk. He has to carry on. Stopping will be fatal, but rather than a refuge the wood is a trap. What chance of finding his way out while his fiendish huntresses, guided by the devil will know every inch? He runs blindly, weaving and zigzagging haphazardly, constantly slamming into unseeable objects, hoping he'll escape serious injury. He stops, listens and hears nothing, but distrusts the silence. They too could be listening, ready to strike.

He exhausts himself trying to get out of Drensell Wood. It seems like hours, but is probably only a few minutes. He sits down, staring anxiously and hopelessly. Only the largest trees assume any shape in the blackness. They might still be close. He has to *keep* escaping, but in the darkness it'll be impossible to find any way out even if he has the energy. He must accept the inevitable. He will have to stay in the wood until morning light gives some chance. Maybe what he saw outside the cottage wasn't what it seemed. Maybe they were innocent women, looking after the home of their friend. He should have waited and talked to them, they could have vital information. That's what Matthew will say. In his panic he's exaggerated it all. He strains to remember. Maybe there weren't *nine* at all. First there are three, then five, now seven, no definitely nine or even *more*. Maybe, maybe, maybe...

He listens nervously. Nothing, but that doesn't mean they are not there. Venturing now could be more dangerous than staying still. He must make himself as inconspicuous as possible. He burrows into the undergrowth, pulling as much bracken and twigs around as he can find. In the darkness he can't be sure whether he can be seen. He'll take his chances at first light. It will be a difficult night of interrupted sleep and nervous observation.

He sleeps later than he intends. The sun is high. It must be afternoon. Valuable time has been lost and in the light he could easily have been discovered. Yet his 'den' is better than he could have hoped. Anyone without a dog would not easily find it. But what of those that don't need dogs other than infernal ones? He's stiff from a night in the confined space and stretches himself, dislodging some of the undergrowth and sending the surrounding twigs scattering to the ground. The sound echoes between the trees. He freezes, fully stretched like a cat on the hearth, waiting in increasing discomfort as his taut limbs begin to ache. He hears many things – the wood is still alive, the animals and birds busying themselves – but no other people, damnable or otherwise. He moves slowly, returning to a recumbent position. Visions of the previous night return. That villainous Alice Sandon, clearly a dangerous associate of Prudie Westrup, accosting him so aggressively, so *diabolically*? At least now he's safe.

He emerges from the den and stretches again, but has to lean down as his head swims. He sits down. Is this the effect of that damned bottle in Prudie Westrup's cottage? He listens and peers carefully around. He's sure the women are gone. He'd been right to hide. They gave up trying to find him in the wood even with fiendish aid and their powers would evaporate in the morning light. The first priority must be to get out of this damned wood! Simpler than last night, but still no easy matter. Does he make for the village or away across the fields and pursue the women? So much time lost, how far away are they now?

He takes a few faltering steps. At first his feet fall with an unnatural softness and the trees and bushes coalesce in wavering haziness. Gradually his head clears and he increases his pace, stepping out quickly in as straight a direction as he can. That way he's sure to eventually reach the last of the trees and the open fields. After an hour he realises he could not possibly have kept to one direction or the wood is much larger than he thought. In the dark everywhere is bigger, distances further, but sunlight gives it an added immensity, an unending stretch of latticed branches and thick vegetation. He stops to rest and sits down. His head lightens again, only steadying when he stands up. He walks on. Another hour and no progress, only more trees, more trees...

The sun's twinkling presence is soon lost as the evening's dolorous murk advances. By the time he reaches the last trees the dubious security of the open fields is gone and he staggers to find some indicator of his whereabouts, but this is neither Narrow Baulk field nor the hedge lined path from Prudie's cottage. As his eyes adjust to the slightly better light in the open country he feels vulnerable for this is some other shadowy emptiness. For all its confusion and mystery at least the wood gave rough sanctuary where a fugitive might find rudimentary cover, but out here there's nothing but himself between earth and sky, exposed and imperilled.

He starts to run. A moving target is less easily seen, less easy to catch, and he might quicker find the track to the village, but even if he finds such a track would he recognise it? The more he runs away from the wood, the more endangered he feels, the further he is from *any* haven or hiding place from his pursuers. The horizon shimmers dismally, his eyes contort and dissolve the night. In this crazed micro light they could deceive him into seeing anything. He stops and sits down again to gather his strength. Gradually he regains his senses. Then he sees the shape in the distance. It seems to move. He rubs his eyes and looks again. It becomes clearer. Low, squat, but definitely a building of some kind, people, help, safety. He gets up.

It starts to rain. He pulls his hat further down and runs, the raindrops splattering into his face as he gets nearer. It's a cottage, not unlike Prudie's. Escape from one danger only to be ensnared by another! Halfway he stops and looks around. They could be waiting for him. This is their new meeting place, the abode of the covern! He walks now rather than runs even as the rain increases. The cottage is without garden or hedge, gaunt and stark in the vastness of the fields. There's no light, but it is shuttered. He gets to the door and listens, but hears nothing, those inside very quiet or already abed. Drawing his sword, he stands back, looks round again, then leaning forward, knocks. No sound, no movement, nothing stirs. He knocks again, the sound echoing across the empty country back to the woods. Nothing. He pushes the door gently and it swings forward. He steps in, and turns to the side of the door, out of the meagre light, ready to parry any attack, but it doesn't come.

After a few moments he moves gingerly along the wall and scours the place. It's empty except for a rickety table and a threadbare chair. There's even little detritus on the floor to testify it was ever a habitation. It must have been abandoned for some time. He returns to the door, shuts it, pulls away one of the shutters and stares out. The siling rain swathes the night. He tries to work out where he is, forming a mental map of the village, the church, the inn, the stream, Syme House, the Collvers' house...he must have strayed so far on the other side of Drensell Wood he's within the Collver estate. This long abandoned cottage must be on Collver's land. His eyes draw heavy as he strains to make out the few dim features. He pulls over the cracked and splintered chair, easing himself down tentatively in case it sunders under his weight. It creaks, slithers and groans like a grouchy mule grumbling as it's loaded, but holds. He eases back, closes most of the shutter until only a crack remains and keeps peering out, but soon falls asleep.

He wakes with a start, almost falling from the chair. The shutter has closed completely. He shivers slightly. Gradually the blackness reveals a few shapes and he remembers where he is. The rain has stopped. The wind has dropped. Only a distant rumbling pierces the silence of the night. He listens carefully. With nothing to see, his ears are acutely receptive and he unravels the dull groaning into distinct sounds. Voices. Two or three... maybe four...no only two...a man and a woman.

"You'll have to stay away. What you know is too dangerous."

"Can't you help me?"

"Who will listen to me?"

Hugh eases open the shutter enough to put his eye to the gap. It's almost as dark outside as in the cottage and at first he sees nothing. Then he hears the voices again. There could be three this time, but he can't make out the words. Have they walked away? He opens the shutter a little more and dim shapes appear. One could be a bush, but there were no bushes or hedges outside the cottage. No not a bush, but something more solid, a lump of...could it be people? Gradually the lump separates into shadowy figures...at least two...three, four, five? He pulls the shutter open a little more to get a wider view. There could be six, but they are moving, shrouding each other. One looks his way! Has he opened the shutter too far? Surely they'll not see him in the blackness? The figure moves away, others follow. They are coming towards the cottage! He watches for a few seconds, transfixed in the hope he's wrong and they'll turn back, but they don't. He closes the shutter as he might close the stable door after the bolting horse. He lurches unsteadily across the room, crashing painfully and noisily into the table. The one wretched item of furniture and he has to stumble into it! Stradsey has probably heard him back in the church let alone the fiendish reprobates immediately outside! He finds another door and totters through the small scullery, but this is a trap. He can't get out! He fumbles along a wall, reaches another shuttered window and keeps going, hoping where there's a window there may be...yes a door!

He pushes, but it doesn't give, stuck fast, locked or bolted. He pushes again. Nothing moves. Then he hears the voices again and footsteps. He steps back and kicks into the darkness. The door swings and then falls, one of its hinges ripped from the jamb. He's out! Not bothering to look back he runs and runs with terror fuelled vigour. Behind shouting, screaming and the pounding of many feet, but he doesn't look back, intent only on getting further away. He has no way of knowing which direction he takes and doesn't care so long as it's away from his pursuers. After a time he doesn't hear them, but doesn't stop or look round. That would be inviting their devilish powers to overwhelm him. Who were they?

Witches, but one at least a man. The snatch of conversation returns. Royalist conspirators and on Collver's land? On he goes, but only further into the black bowels of the night. Escape from one diabolical fate into the grasp of another? His energy at last gives out he's forced to stop and listen. He sees nothing, hears nothing. He sits down and feels bushes close by. He gets beneath, intending to stay only a short time before moving on, but tiredness engulfs again and he sleeps. Only in the morning will he realise he's driven himself once more into the doubtful retreat of Drensell Wood.

He wakes early, stiff and cold, having spent the night almost in the open with only a thin veil of gorse to shield him from any pursuers. Either they gave up or he was too fast and lost them, but he must move on quickly. For a quarter hour he walks only a short way in gradually expanding concentric circles, anxious not to lose sight of what little landmarks he can make any sense. He must eventually reach the wood's outer rim and escape. He stops to maintain his bearings. Then he hears it again, the same rustling, creeping movement of yesterday. They are back! He crouches down as before, freezing as the rustling returns.

This terrorised timidity is not for a soldier! He half stands and turns. Between the trees, some ten yards away he sees a figure. It is still. He slowly draws his sword as silently as possible and steps a little closer. The figure moves, but still does not see him. Hugh slinks through the bushes closer still. The shabbily dressed man turns again. He has a long, pinched, pale face and large blue eyes, which gaze back fearfully as Hugh bounds across the remaining bushes and points the blade towards the baleful features.

"Do not move or I run you through!"

Frozen and horror struck, the man stares at the sword. Younger than Hugh, he's little more than a boy.

"Please...please sir, I mean no harm...please....please put that...that..."

Hugh lowers the sword slightly.

"Ned means no harm sir."

It's Ned Frattersham, the missing servant lad from the Manning household. He's not seen him before, but the voice is familiar.

"What are you doing here?" Hugh demands

"You won't tell on me, sir, you won't tell them?"

"Tell who?"

"The master, sir, Mr. Manning."

"Tell him what?"

"Tell him you've seen me."

Tall, thin, wiry, probably very strong, he stares blankly, stupidly at Hugh. He could have felled Lexden with one blow and then easily dragged him out to the field. Hugh still holds his sword at his side. Ned looks at it apprehensively. Now Hugh recognises the voice. He heard it last night.

"You won't hurt me, sir."

"Not if I have no reason," Hugh says, reluctant to put his sword away, though he lowers it almost to the ground, "Are you with those weird women?"

"Don't know no women, sir."

"Weird women, Prudie Westrup and..."

"Prudie not here, sir."

"You were with them last night. I heard your voice."

"Me, no sir, not here."

"I didn't say where it was."

"Where, sir?"

"At an abandoned cottage, not far away."

"No sir, not me sir, not with Prudie.

"What about Alice Sandon, do you know her?"

"No sir, don't know Alice. Prudie gone away."

"Gone where? Where is she?"

"Don't know, sir."

"What about Alice Sandon?"

"Alice? Not seen her."

"Did she hurt the animals?"

"Don't know, sir, don't know nothing."

"You know about these women. Speak!"

"Yes, yes, of course, sir, I know, everybody knows."

"Know what?"

"About these women, like you said sir."

"Is that why you ran away?"

"Had to sir, couldn't stay, not right there."

"What wasn't right?"

"Not right, not right!"

"Weren't you treated right?"

"Wasn't right!" Ned bellows, eyes aflame, fists clenched.

Maddened by his inability to properly express himself, the lad swells his chest menacingly as if he's about to explode. Expecting an attack or perhaps a sudden attempt to get away Hugh raises his sword, but the moment passes. Ned calms, though still fuming and spluttering like a kettle subsiding after being taken from the fire. Difficult and threatening as Ned may seem, Hugh realises it is caused by his frustrated anger and wonders whether a sensitive and observant soul lurks beneath the clumsy inarticulate skin.

"I need to talk to you, Ned..."

"You are a soldier, sir."

"Yes...I am..."

"Don't talk to me, sir, I've got nothing to say."

"It won't take long, I need to know..."

"No, no, not me sir, I won't talk!"

"I have to..." Hugh persists, but seeing Ned's simmering fury beginning to bubble again, breaks off.

"You need to go to the house and talk to them," Ned says.

"Who?"

"Them at the house, Mr. Manning, sir and Mrs, they know...they know..."

"What do they know?"

Ned shakes his head and mutters incoherently, then his whole body quivers.

"What is it, Ned, tell me what it is...?"

"Not...not...not what it seems..."

"What's not what it seems?"

"It...it...it..."

Ned's voice trails off. He shrieks, stamps his feet and flails his arms around uncontrollably.

"Do you always lose your temper, Ned, do you get excited easily?"

"Sometimes, sir, sometimes, but I tries...I tries not to."

"What do you know about Mr. Lexden, Ned?"

"Mr. Lexden sir...me sir...nothing sir."

"Were you there, what did you see, what did you do?"

"Nothing, I saw nothing, done nothing, not me, it wasn't me!"

Then he turns and runs.

"Come back, come back!" Hugh shouts, chasing him, "If I catch you Ned I cannot..."

But Hugh's threat is unspoken as he catches his breath in pursuit. Ned dives and ducks, weaving skilfully from a lifetime's knowledge of every tree and bush and within minutes disappears. Hugh keeps running in the direction of the swishing leaves, thudding ground and crackling branches, but they are soon lost and he stops, breathless and disoriented, hunter as frustrated as the hunted.

It's only when he's fully recovered and accepted his quarry really has escaped that Hugh realises he's out of the wood and facing the field wherein he entered the day before. He walks along its edge, reaches the track and turns back towards the village, mulling over all the issues the confrontation with Ned has thrown up. Two thoughts dominate – Alice Sandon and her devilish accomplices and the true nature of the Manning household. Both demand investigation, but the former is the more pressing. Delay will only benefit the infernal forces. If there is a witches' coven it will have to be revealed in the light of day before it can reassemble for another night. It will even have to take precedence over returning to the inn and reporting back to Matthew.

With the village in sight he leaves the track and skirts round the backs of the houses. He will find Alice Sandon's house, accost and interrogate her before she has time to meet up again with her confederates and hatch further diabolical mischief. From the previous day's conversation at the inn he gathered a general outline of all the houses and every villagers' whereabouts, but like the landlord's directions to Prudie's cottage, he now appreciates the limitations of his intelligence. So many of the houses look alike and can't possibly be disentangled from the landlord's obtuse descriptions...*the third house after the well before old Carter's is where Alice Sandon lives...or is it...the third house after the well...or... after old Carter's* – wherever that is? After three abortive circles of the village he retreats to meet with Matthew for breakfast and get more precise information. He cuts though the churchyard to reach the inn more quickly, turning sharply to see Reverend Stradsey bearing down on him.

"The biting cool of the sharp morning air, lieutenant, the better clarity to perceive the Lord's truth!"

"You're out early, minister."

"I assume *you* are out the earlier to waylay the forces of evil. As I told your captain, too much time has already been ineffectually expended."

Hugh says nothing, aware of Matthew's disinclination towards Stradsey's views.

"He advised me he had deputed you to interrogate these fiendish persons," Stradsey continues after a sort pause, seemingly unaware of Hugh's silence.

"I have been to Prudie Westrup's cottage."

"Excellent work, lieutenant. I knew when I spoke to your captain that…"

"Unfortunately she was not there."

Struggling to contain his disappointment, Stradsey puckers up and successively turns deeper shades of red and almost purple. Hugh even expects him to curse. Finally he begins to vent his suppressed anger on Matthew.

"I said to the captain…"

But Hugh cuts him off.

"However, I was accosted by others, including Alice Sandon."

"Aha! So you are on your way to the constable?"

"No, sir. I am on my way to see her or rather I was until…"

"But you said you had seen her?"

"Yes…well I did…and then I didn't…at least not…my interrogation of her was…interrupted."

"Indeed," Stradsey says dubiously.

"I have been trying to find her house, but…I got lost."

"I will assist you, lieutenant. Time is of the essence. There must be no procrastination in executing the Lord's work. You must hasten to her abode without further delay."

Stradsey interlaces his directions with trenchant and colourful asseverations of coming doom if this 'boil of evil is not quickly lanced.'

"Is Alice Sandon the leader?" Hugh says.

"I thought Prudie Westrup to be," Stradsey says, then warming to a pitch of sanctimonious zeal, "I have striven unstintingly in the service of the Lord against these incursions of the devil..."

"...but if she has gone?"

"...then it can be no matter for complacency. It may be part of her demonic plan. She may be away in body, but not in spirit. Even now, she may be around us. We are after all, dealing with a conspiracy of the devil!"

"You are sure there is a coven?"

"You said yourself there were others?"

Hugh nods thoughtfully as Stradsey goes on, recounting further lurid 'happenings', 'appearances' and 'testaments of the devil.'

Unfortunately none are specific and while Hugh is prepared to believe in plots and conspiracies he needs hard evidence.

"You are aware there are Royalists in Harringstead," Stradsey continues.

"I have heard rumours," Hugh says, echoing Matthew's scepticism.

"Rumours, sir? Well founded doubts in the breast of no less than Justice Manning, sir!"

"Yes, yes," Hugh mutters.

"You doubt his word?"

"No, of course not," Hugh splutters.

"The Justice is right. I fear misguided loyalty to the evil that surrounds the King is too prevalent," Stradsey says, his voice increasing in hysterical volume and pitch, "Evil manifests itself in many ways. When two heads of Satan arise they are tempted to work together. Royalism and witchcraft, lieutenant, twin heads of evil. Beware them both!"

Though readier than Matthew to accept the minister's assertions, Hugh looks around, anxious to be away. He may believe in Royalist plots and witchcraft, but associating one with misguided upper classes and the other with misguided lower classes makes it difficult to believe they act together. Of course, either could have been involved in Lexden's murder.

Stradsey carries on with his diatribe, but Hugh's mind is elsewhere.

"I also came across Ned Frattersham."

"The missing servant? Where did you see him?"

"Drensell Wood."

"Justice Manning must be informed immediately."

"Yes, I will do so...later. Tell me, whose land lies close to Drensell Wood?"

"Why, Mr. Manning."

"No, the other side."

The minister looks puzzled. As best he can Hugh describes where he came across the abandoned cottage.

"It is difficult to be precise...your exact location is difficult to pinpoint...but it could be on John Collver's estate. What were you doing there, lieutenant?"

"Oh, it doesn't matter now. I thank you for your directions, sir, but I must be on my way."

At first Stradsey seems not to hear, then gradually subsides as Hugh edges away from him.

"Ah...yes...of course...yes I see...you must be about God's work. I will walk a little way with you to the evil woman's abode."

"That really won't be necessary."

But the minister won't be rebuffed and leads him through the village. Confronting Alice Sandon with Stradsey fills Hugh with horror. He must question her alone, but Stradsey has no wish to accompany him.

"The third house beyond the stream, lieutenant. I will leave you now."

He turns and walks quickly in the opposite direction. Hugh watches him for a few moments. Despite his fire eating rhetoric, does the minister fear this woman? Lambast her from afar, inveigle someone else to prosecute her, but shy away from direct contact? Hugh crosses the stream and approaches the cottage. He passed several times earlier without realising its significance. That means she may have already seen him. He hears a loud rustling from the back and then footsteps. He runs to the rear and sees a woman scurrying through the adjacent field, leaping over a stile and disappearing into the trees. Pursuit is pointless. She already has too good a start, yet one who makes so swift a getaway advertises her guilt. An old woman is standing at the front of the cottage.

"Saw you coming, sir, you and the minister."

"That was Alice Sandon?"

"'Twas sir and this is her house."

"I must speak with her."

The old woman nods knowingly.

"Aye, aye, but she won't be back for a time yet."

There's a mischievous sparkle in her eyes. Does she revel in Hugh's discomfiture, is she one of Alice's confederates? Hugh could question her, but the damage is already done. He curses himself for allowing Stradsey to come with him. Seeing the minister would be the final signal for Alice's flight.

"You will also want to be talking to young Richard Collver?" the old woman says.

"Have you seen him?"

"I've heard those who say they saw him before he went away."

"Away where?"

She shakes her head and moves towards her door.

"Who knows?"

"When was he seen?" he persists.

"Two days...three days...or was it four?"

She shuts the door on his confusion. Suddenly overcome with tiredness from the restless night he walks desolately to the inn. The place is deserted and there's no sign of Matthew. He calls to the landlord, but getting no answer tramps wearily upstairs. He considers knocking on Matthew's door but he may be sleeping late. Hugh will see him later. He slumps on the bed and sits impassively for a few moments. The night and morning events flicker quickly through his mind before he eases off his boots. Then he lies back, intending to undress, but within seconds is asleep.

He wakes with a start and leans up. It must be mid afternoon, the sun is high and streaming through the window. There are voices below. Several men are gathered around the bench supping ale. So late and still abed, what will Matthew say? He pulls on his boots and clatters down the stairs.

"Where've you come from?" the landlord says aggressively as he reaches the bottom.

"Why, in my room," Hugh says, puzzled.

"In your room? But you didn't come in last night."

"No...this morning. I went straight up...I called...where is captain Fletcher?"

"Gone."

"Gone where?"

"London. You weren't here. He asked around. Nobody had seen you."

"But the minister...I saw..."

"Yes?"

"Never mind. Did he leave any message?"

"No. Said he was going to see squire Manning on his way, probably enquiring after you. He sent word by one of his people an hour ago also enquiring. I was to let him know immediately we heard."

"Why didn't you call me?"

"I didn't know you were here. I best send one o' the lads up to the house now..."

"No!" Hugh bellows, then more quietly, "That won't be necessary, I'll go myself."

"Then you'll be off to London too, I 'spose?"

"No...not immediately. There are other matters to detain me."

The landlord eyes him quizzically. Hugh ignores him.

"What can you tell me about Alice Sandon?"

"What do you want to know?"

"Is she a friend of Prudie Westrup?"

The landlord hesitates, then says, "Well, they know each other."

"She ran away when I tried to talk to her this morning."

The landlord remains silent, his steely eyes intently waiting for Hugh to continue.

"I saw someone else, an old woman, her neighbour. I wanted to talk to her too, but she shut her door. I think I may have seen her before on some nefarious activity with this Alice. Last night..."

The landlord erupts in laughter.

"Old Peg? You've seen old Peg, what did she say?"

"She said Alice Sandon wouldn't be back for some time yet."

"Maybe she won't."

"She also mentioned Richard Collver. She said he's been seen."

The landlord shrugs dismissively.

"I've not heard, but what old Peg's heard will be from someone close by, she never ventures far. So, this...nefarious activity..."

"It's nothing," Hugh says, turning away.

"What about last night," the landlord persists, "you were saying...?"

"I said it's nothing!"

The landlord leans away suddenly, afraid Hugh might strike him. Hugh half smiles nervously.

"I also saw that young lad from Syme House, the one who's gone missing."

"Ned Frattersham? Where did you see him?"

"Drensell Wood. He was very afraid. Why would he run away?"

"He didn't get on with Lexden, but then...not many did."

Some of the men drift in from outside and join the conversation.

"Always was a rum 'un, young Ned," one says.

"Afraid of 'is own shadow," another says.

"All strength and no brains," a third adds, anxious not be outdone by his companions.

"He said I should ask them at the house," Hugh says, "What did he mean?"

Collective shrug and shaking of heads until the landlord states the obvious, "Better do as he said and go up to the house," then adding for the men's benefit, "He's been trying to see Alice Sandon."

More shaking of heads.

"What can you tell me about her?" Hugh says.

The landlord opens his palms disdainfully and turns to the others who grimace in solidarity. Hugh stares back. This isn't going to be easy. If he comes up with the right question he might get the right answer. Nothing will be offered unsolicited.

"The cottage, it's her own place?"

"She's a tenant."

"Of whom?"

"John Collver."

Could she have gone somewhere connected to the Collvers? She might even be part of the Royalist plot, the link between that and the witchcraft scare as Stradsey said.

"Is there a *Mr.* Sandon?"

"There is. Abraham, but he went to be a soldier. Not been back these two years," one of the others says.

"He could be dead."

"Aye...or just...gone away."

Another silence, then Hugh says, "The war has disrupted so much. So many places deserted. Are there any empty properties on the Collver estate?"

"A few."

"Would Alice know of them?"

"'Course she does," the second man says, "everyone does."

"Aye and that other, Prudie Westrup, she'd know," the third adds.

"Why do you mention her?"

The shrugging is accompanied by some intakes of breath and tongue clucking.

"'Er's a rum 'un too," the first one says.

"Do you know where they are?" Hugh says, with only sight hope of a sensible reply.

No one speaks, then the third man, ever conscious of filling in the silences, begins, "There's some say that the two of 'em are..."

"Aye, aye, some say, some say," the landlord intervenes, "the officer doesn't want to hear idle gossip, Ambrose..."

"I was only..."

"Then don't," the landlord cuts him off again, then turns to Hugh, "You're going to Syme House?"

"I need to send a letter," Hugh says, ignoring the question,

"Is there anyone going to London?"

"The carter leaves this afternoon. He'll be at the market first in the morning."

"Will it get through?"

"Deliver it himself...if..."

"I'll pay him...and you...well."

"Guaranteed."

"Pen and paper then landlord."

Hugh scribbles out his message for Matthew.

"He'll be in afore he goes. I'll see he gets it."

As Hugh reaches the door the landlord takes him aside and almost whispers.

"Tread carefully, sir, the whole village is in ferment what with this evil business with Lexden and the witchcraft scare. Make haste to Syme House."

The landlord is right. He must first see Manning. He retrieves his horse from the stable and leads it through the village. He sees no one, but feels a hundred eyes concentrating on his every move. He avoids the cottages near the stream, knowing he'll not see Alice and sure Peg will do nothing to help him. The men at the inn point critical fingers at others, but never say anything meaningful. Have Stradsey's accusations ignited the whole community to fever pitch or does the minister merely reflect existing fears? The women who tried to attack him last night must be the source of the malaise. Meanwhile a dangerous Royalist insurgent is on the loose. Matthew would say it's all innuendo and malicious imagining, but Matthew is in London. If only someone would tell him where these wretched women were or provide some evidence he could work with!

He mounts his horse at the edge of the village. Though he knows the way he's reluctant to proceed too quickly, stopping at every twist in the path, hovering at the track to Narrow Baulk field, gloomily pondering on the two night's events. He moves on, but stops again, checking his directions, afraid he will lose his way and end up for a third night in that dreadful place. He shrugs it off. He's nowhere near Drensell Wood.

At Syme House he's ushered into the main room where the Justice sits alone. He looks up, hesitating for a moment as if he needs to remind himself of his visitor's identity. Then he smiles and motions Hugh to a chair.

"Do you come to bring me intelligence or to seek it?"

"Mainly to seek it," Hugh says diffidently.

"You have no progress to report?" Manning sighs, turning away.

"Not exactly progress, sir. I am trying to find and question Alice Sandon."

"I understood it was Prudie Westrup you sought?"

Manning speaks with authoritative correction. Hugh is taken aback. Matthew must have spoken to him.

"Well, yes, her too."

"You have not found her?"

"Not yet, but I have seen Alice Sandon...or at least I think I have."

"Come, come, sir, either you have questioned her or you have not?"

"I thought I saw her, but it was dark, she was some distance away."

"She has eluded you?"

"It seems so. I was wondering..."

"She has been here, but not seen by me. She spoke to some of the servants... frightened them more like."

"When was this?"

"Yesterday. She crept through the back quarters. She talked...peculiarly...about animals, then got away as quickly as she came."

"Was she not apprehended?"

"The scullery maid and another young girl were in no position to confound her. By the time cook and Cotter arrived she was gone. It was all they could do to calm the terrorised women, stricken by the witch's threats."

"Threats?"

"She cursed us, her malevolent jabberings directed at anything, animal, human, any creature associated with this house. Foul things, sir, I shudder to repeat. She has not been seen since.

"And what of Prudie Westrup, have you seen her?"

"No I have not. As I said to..."

Manning stops abruptly.

"Said what to whom, sir?"

"No matter," Manning says, waving his arms and turning towards the window.

"Then sir, I must go..."

"You will find the root cause of this abomination at Aspenfield. John Collver is behind Alice Sandon, Prudie Westrup or any other misguided wretch, just as he is the sire of Royalism in this country."

"You believe Collver has put her up to all these..."

"Indeed I do and he may be sheltering the woman now!"

Hugh remembers the abandoned cottage and its proximity to Collver's land. Manning glares accusingly as if by his lack of progress Hugh is solely responsible. Only by zealous action against the Collvers can he redeem himself.

"Captain Fletcher has returned to London," Hugh says limply.

"You must not leave the area, lieutenant until the link with Collver is established," Manning snorts disapprovingly, making no comment on Matthew's absence.

Admonished, dismissed and anxious to confront Collver, Hugh rides quickly to Aspenfield. Could Collver really be shielding, even harbouring an evil coven? Or is he misled, duped by 'gentlemanly' quarrels. Yet if their disagreements are connected to Lexden's murder or even a Royalist conspiracy which 'gentleman' does the duping? Matthew would be bound to make contact and the landlord said Matthew saw Manning before he left for London, but Manning didn't mention it. Why should the landlord lie? Why should Manning lie? He failed to mention seeing Ned Frattersham. Manning might have known more. What if Ned has returned to the house? Surely Manning would have mentioned that? Manning is obsessed with Alice. Does he know Ned is connected to her? If the conversation he overheard was part of the Royalist conspiracy that would be equally important to Manning. Ned was agitated and frightened.

Them at the house...they know...it's not what it seems... wasn't treated right...you won't tell on me...to the master.

Hugh curses. So much he should have said to Manning.

He'll have to go back. He's admitted immediately at Aspenfield. Collver is surprised to see him so late without warning, but relaxes until Alice Sandon is mentioned.

"I haven't seen her."

"You are sure of that, sir?"

"I would not forget seeing Alice Sandon."

"She has a certain...reputation I believe?"

"I do not listen to idle musings by empty headed fools. I leave that to..."

"Your neighbours?"

Collver grimaces, neither denying nor confirming.

"She is one of your tenants?"

"She was. After her husband left for the war..."

He stops, looking shiftily at Hugh before continuing.

"...I let her stay. It seemed only the Christian thing to do, but I have not seen her for some time."

"There are a number of empty properties on your land?"

"Inevitably, the war..."

"Could Alice Sandon or Prudie Westrup be inhabiting one of them?"

"It's unlikely."

Hugh looks at him doubtfully

"However, I will organise a search party."

Hugh nods approvingly, though if Collver is hiding the women he will quickly arrange for them to move on. Perhaps Hugh should ask to accompany the party, but it wouldn't be difficult for Collver to keep one step ahead of him.

"Your son Richard has been seen in the area."

Collver's reaction betrays only mild surprise.

"I have not seen him."

"You don't wish to know when and where he was seen?"

"You will tell me if it is important."

Hugh says nothing.

"Obviously you have no details, more foolish gossip."

"I do not know, but that doesn't mean that you don't."

"I have told you, I have not seen him."

Hugh leaves with the same inconclusive questioning as at Syme House. He doesn't believe John Collver hasn't seen Richard. He was too cool, too controlled, as if he expected

Hugh's abrupt statement. He slows through the village and then dismounts, intent on trying to find Alice Sandon again. It's almost dark. He leaves the horse at the church and walks the short distance, stealthily keeping to the shadows. He crosses the stream and approaches the cottages. A figure is outside. He stops. It could be her, creeping back, believing he's given up and returned to London. She could easily have found out from the inn. He edges a little closer. He can't see the face, but it is a woman and she is staring directly at him.

"Alice Sandon?" he calls softly.

"Nay, nay, not Alice."

He steps forward.

"A little late to come calling, sir," Peg says insolently.

"What are you doing out at this hour?"

"I like to take the air before..."

Hugh grabs her by the shoulders and spins her round.

"Where is she, you old hag, tell me!"

He glares threateningly, his face only inches from hers, but she's not to be intimidated.

"I don't know and even if I did..."

"You do, you do! Tell me!"

She tries to get away, but Hugh grips her even more tightly.

"You alright there, Peg?"

Hugh half turns. A neighbour stands at his door. Peg sees him too, but says nothing.

"Peg, who's that with you?"

"He, he..."

The man starts to come across. Hugh relaxes his grip, then runs back towards the church. Why does he run? It was a legitimate enquiry and he hasn't hurt the old woman. He should have stayed, interrogated all the neighbours, got to the bottom of this business once and for all. What is he afraid of – Alice, Prudie, Stradsey, Collver or the malaise that infects the whole village? He'll get away. Manning may be the local Justice of the Peace, but Hugh will take his cue from Matthew – they are responsible solely to Parliament and the army. He retrieves his horse and canters beside the fields, stopping short at a long looming shape, which must be Syme House.

He's not keen to advertise his approach. He ties the horse to a tree and walks on. He stops again nearer the house and crouches beside a bush. The lights show activity. Someone stands at the window of the main room. It's not Manning. One of the women perhaps or even a servant. He gets up, but veers to the right in a wide arc away from the house.

He slips across the rear yard, but hesitates outside the entrance to the servants' quarters. There's no sound from within. They must all be with the family or about other duties or even retired for the night. An unwholesome aura hangs over the house. He opens the door and enters the kitchen. There's only a dim light from the passage. For some moments he stares at the spot where Lexden's body briefly lay after being brought in from the fields.

There's an oppressiveness, a crushing evil in the kitchen. This was where Lexden was murdered. He cannot explain or prove it, but he knows. He was killed here and later removed to the fields as Matthew suspected. Whoever it was came as he came, unannounced, silently, purposefully. It could have been Alice Sandon or more likely the elusive Prude Westrup, abetted perhaps by John Collver or by his mysterious son. Manning's servants were right to be frightened at Alice Sandon's return.

He steps into the passage. There's no one in the hall, but he hears voices. He leans against the newel post at the bottom of the stairs, expecting to be accosted at any moment and forced to explain himself...

...Please excuse this late intrusion, there were a number of matters I wished to discuss with you earlier, sir. First, young Ned Frattersham...

He starts suddenly on hearing Manning's voice from the main room.

"Matters are bad enough. I have the army grubbing and poking in the village and now this..."

Hugh leaves the staircase and goes to the door, intending to knock and enter, but stops again.

"I've already told you. I don't know where he is."

It has to be the daughter of the house, Olivia Manning. Who is it she...?

"He has been seen."

"His father has not…"

"You have been to Collver?"

"No, no, I sent a message with…"

"Oh, Olivia, how could you?"

An older woman. The three are here – Joseph, Constance and Olivia.

"And he replied?"

"No father, he did not. He is as adamant as you in his opposition"

"Then how?"

"Jane told me. It is common knowledge at Aspenfield. Mr. Collver has not seen Richard."

"As I told the young officer earlier. This frightening of the servants by that witch Alice Sandon, Collver is behind it as he is behind everything."

"That has nothing to do with Richard, father."

"It has everything to with him. Like father, like son."

"Richard is not…"

"Richard Collver is the son of the enemy of this house! How can I hold up my head in the county and especially now with these officers…"

"You asked for them to come, father."

"Be silent, girl!"

The table is banged. Constance tries to intervene.

"Joseph, please listen…"

"No, no, Constance, I have heard enough. Olivia, this has to stop! Behind my back you have been seeing him, consorting with an enemy of Parliament!"

"I won't be stopped," Olivia screams.

Manning rebukes her again and she replies, while again Constance tries to quieten them. All their voices are raised even more. The whole house must hear them. Hugh tries to catch the words, but they are lost in the raucous interchange. He hears rustling and stamping of feet. He could go in, but that might make the situation worse. More movement beyond the door. Hugh steps away quickly, getting down behind the other side of the staircase as Olivia runs from the room, out the front door and into the night. Hugh extricates himself and follows her.

6

MATTHEW tries to turn, but a knee is pressed into his back, pinning him down. Then heavy hands fleece down his coat and light fingers move quickly through his pockets. He lifts an arm. He cannot turn, but catches his attacker's arm and gripping it tightly jerks him away enough to loosen the pressing knee in his back. He turns to his side, but his attacker is quick, rolling him onto his back and with lightning dexterity probes his front pockets too. Matthew lifts his right leg and catches the man on the side, pushing him away before slowly raising himself up as pain shoots through his left leg. His attacker is winded, but he comes on again. In the shadows Matthew cannot see his face.

Matthew's is now at his full height, but he's unsteady and his left leg isn't reliable. He moves his hand towards his sword, but it's too late. With his head down, his assailant lunges forward and hammers into him. Matthew is knocked back, but parries a blow before locking his arm round the other's shoulder. Equal in strength and resolve they shove each other around for some moments, neither able to get the better or break away. As they pant and stiffly dance in the alley, Matthew senses something oddly familiar about the other man. Then he sees his face clearly as they step into a streak of moonlight shot between two houses. It's that unmistakable smell.

"Ezra!"

The other turns to him.

"Matthew?"

They loosen their grips and pull apart.

"What are you doing here?" Matthew says.

"Trying to rob you, it seems," Ezra says and then, pulling a small purse from a pocket deep within his long coat, hands it to Matthew, "I think this is yours."

"It is you, isn't it?" Matthew says, standing back to examine more closely the unkempt stocky figure, "Ezra Stanfield, corporal, late of General Waller's...."

"No longer," Ezra says.

"So, it comes to a fine thing, your new career as a footpad!"

"Needs must."

"No needs surely. Where have you been, I looked everywhere for you?"

Voices from the main street, footsteps further down the alley. Ezra looks anxiously towards them and turns to go.

"Not now, Matthew, needs must."

"Stop, Ezra!" Matthew says, following him. Ezra breaks into a run.

Matthew quickens his step, but his left leg drags and he slows again. The footsteps get closer. At the corner Ezra stops and whispers.

"Tomorrow night, the Jackdaw."

Then he's gone. Matthew reaches the corner, but the street is empty. The footsteps die away, disappearing like Ezra into the night. Matthew waits a few moments, wondering whether they or someone else might reappear. When no one comes he trudges on. He's uneasy and nervous. The encounter with the young man the other night and again in the tavern has unsettled him. Not through any fear of him or his pathetic companions, but because it reminds him how mistrustful he's become, less able to put faith in anyone on first encounter. It's the war, fuelling suspicion, turning everyone into a potential enemy. Where are they now, those lads he knew as children, which side did they follow? What would he do if he encountered a friend on the battlefield serving the King?

Strike first or hesitate and be struck down by a more ruthless foe? Englishman fighting Englishman. It's not right, but it's necessary. Yet it won't happen, he has no friends from those days. Only those he'll never see again, forever young, forever dead. It pulls him up. If we believe in Liberty we must fight for it. Those for the King must also take their chances, so we fight together and...

He stops suddenly. He's been walking unheedingly, his musings deadening his senses. Only now he hears the soft footfalls behind. It can't be Ezra returning. In the night the city is full of rogues. He slips into an alley and waits, slowly and quietly unsheathing his sword, holding it at his side. A man passes by and then stops. Matthew peers around the corner. The man is caught in the moonlight between the houses, looking around.

"Do you look for me?" Matthew says, stepping into the street, his drawn sword before him.

"You'll have no need of that," the man says, stepping back and pointing to the sword.

Matthew recognises the voice.

"Hugh? Have you been following me?" he says, still holding his sword, though now towards the ground.

"Only for a few minutes. I had to be sure it was you. Can you put that thing away."

Matthew returns his sword.

"I went to your sister's house. She mentioned a tavern. I went to the 'St. George,' but you weren't there. I saw you as I was walking back."

"You could have waited at Elizabeth's," Matthew says suspiciously.

"I didn't know how long you'd be. I preferred to come looking."

"You're not very good at being where you're meant to be. When you didn't show up at the inn..."

"I'm sorry about that. There were...complications...didn't you get my message?"

"What message?"

"I sent word by a carrier. You've been at your sister's?"

"All the time. I've received no message."

"Strange."

"Have you seen Manning? "

"I saw him yesterday and..."

"Yesterday? Why did you not return then?"

"Well, there were things..."

"But he told you I wanted you back in London."

"He did not say."

"What? Tell me what happened."

Hugh looks around furtively

"Not here, we need to be somewhere...less conspicuous."

"We'll go to my sister's."

"No!"

Matthew is taken aback by Hugh's sudden and slightly aggressive response.

"No disrespect," Hugh says quietly, detecting Matthew's annoyance, "In the open, away from...everybody."

Hugh walks quickly down the street in the opposite direction, towards the river. Matthew doesn't move. Hugh stops and looks round.

"Not far," he whispers, "...please."

Matthew follows. After a few minutes of twisting and turning, they emerge on the waterfront close to some taverns. This is not exactly Matthew's idea of being away from people, but before he can object Hugh leads on to a quieter place beside an empty wharf.

"You surprise me," Matthew says, looking across to the south bank, "I didn't realise you were so conversant with the alleys and byways."

"I don't want to be overheard."

Matthew glances doubtfully at the nearby taverns.

"They're too busy with their own cares," Hugh says, "No one can hear us."

Matthew nods. It's a busy, noisy place, but at the river's edge they're alone with a clear space where no one can hide. Security in numbers as long as they are not too close.

"I was getting worried," Matthew says irritably, "You were meant to join me at the inn."

"I did send the message..."

"A whole night, almost a whole day..."

"Something arose I had to pursue, there wasn't time to..."

"You're here now," Matthew intervenes, "You can help track down Sarah Radbourne. Finding her is our best possibility of finding Lexden's killer."

"You believe she is the killer?"

"Not necessarily, but we need to know what she knows. If we can get this business tied up quickly, then I can return to the army."

"You've never left it, captain," Hugh says with irritating pedantry.

Matthew glares with annoyance, still wondering why Hugh insisted on coming down here.

"You know what I mean."

Hugh draws away slightly, nervous of Matthew's closeness and his habit of shifting his weight between his legs. He glances around for potential eavesdroppers though there's no one within fifty yards, then lowers his voice.

"It's not so simple. There really could be a Royalist plot."

With this last word he glances around nervously again. Matthew is irritated by his conspiratorial tone.

"Yes, yes, I heard it all from Manning myself."

"Richard Collver has been sighted in the area."

"That doesn't mean he's a Royalist. He could be hanging around hoping to see Olivia Manning."

Hugh concedes this, then tells Matthew what he saw and heard at Syme House.

"Where did Olivia go after she left?"

"Everywhere and nowhere. I followed her for a couple of hours. Then she returned to the house. I thought it best to leave and returned to the inn."

"So she didn't lead you to Richard?"

"No."

"There you are then."

"But I'm not convinced she wasn't looking for him. She may have had a prior arrangement. I tried not to be seen, but in the night... she knows the area, I don't. She may have seen me. I've had other difficulties wandering at night around Harringstead."

Matthew looks sceptically. Hugh lowers his voice even further, drawing closer again as Matthew doesn't move. He explains his encounter with Alice Sandon, her subsequent disappearance, his flights in Drensall Wood and his confrontation with Ned Frattersham.

"Quite a couple of days," Matthew says with slight amusement, "So this is what kept you from joining me. So our best approach must be with the Collvers."

"...and the witches."

Matthew raises his eyebrows and puckers his lips. Hugh continues.

"Manning told me to stay so she and Prudie Westrup could continue to be hunted down."

"I told him to tell you to return to London," Matthew says with suppressed anger.

"He said no such thing to me," Hugh replies with affronted emphasis.

"So, you're convinced this Alice Sandon is..."

"...a witch."

The word displeases Matthew and Hugh's use of it makes him edgy.

"Have a care, honest women should not be so lightly accused."

"I make no light accusation and am not easily swayed by those who do, but I'm not convinced they're honest," Hugh replies tetchily.

"Have you been speaking to Stradsey?"

"Yes, but I make my own judgements."

Matthew leans back, shifting his weight. The movement, innocent in itself, still makes Hugh nervous especially as Matthew continues to stare at him, hard and unflinching.

"I saw him before I left."

"It was him that directed me to Alice Sandon's house."

"I distrust those in search of witches and you could be in danger of becoming one of them."

Hugh steps away, annoyed and affronted.

"I do not deserve that. It is unfair."

"It was you said you made no light accusation," Matthew says, returning his weight to his good leg and leaning slightly towards him.

"As such I made no accusation," Hugh says, "I merely..."

"...used the word."

"Yes, but a word in itself..."

"Is enough in the right or wrong places. As I said, have a care."

Chastened and a little confused by his own backtracking Hugh says nothing at first, then goes on the offensive.

"How can you be confident of finding this Sarah Radbourne anyway?"

"I have made contacts and there may be more to follow."

"What sort of contacts?

"I've come across someone I knew in the army."

"Reliable?"

Matthew hesitates. Reliable is not the most obvious word he would use to describe Ezra. He opts for a neutral reply.

"A corporal, Ezra Stanfield."

The sharp intake of breath is enough for Matthew. Hugh recognises the name.

"You've been consorting with a deserter from the army."

"Not exactly consorting," Matthew says, remembering Ezra's sudden appearance from the darkness, "Besides there are many men who have left the army."

"Not all of them have killed a man."

"Many men have been killed by the army."

"You know what I mean," Hugh says, deliberately mimicking Matthew's earlier rejoinder.

"Nothing was proved."

"There was an *accusation*."

"Aye, an accusation."

"He should be reported to the authorities."

"If everything required to be reported actually was, how much time would be left for everything else?"

"When you see him again..."

"*If* I see him again."

The need for caution in his replies disturbs Matthew. He tires of their interchange and is anxious to get away. He reminds Hugh of the priority to find Sarah Radbourne and asks where he is staying.

"We shall meet again soon. I will contact you."

Their parting is stiff, official, barely that of colleagues. On the way home he goes over everything they discussed. Hugh is thorough and independent. That is good, but Matthew is uneasy with the directions he appears to follow. He may be right to pursue Alice Sandon and Prudie Westrup. They may be connected to Lexden's murder, but investigating them doesn't sit easily with the Collvers, Royalist plot or not. Most of all Matthew dislikes the growing atmosphere of fear.

The excursion to the river has lengthened the journey home and his step gets slower until it's almost a slither when he reaches the corner. As he stops to rest he sees someone quickly leaving his sister's house. In the darkness it's difficult to make out and the person's walk (the only recognisable individual feature in the dark) is not familiar though he's sure it's a woman. The door is barred and he has to rap several times.

"Who is it?"

"Me, Matthew."

Elizabeth pulls the bolt and opens it.

"Edmund is already back. He expected you home before him. It's late."

"Not too late for visitors," he says, looking around the empty room.

"Edmund's gone up," she says to his silent question, "He has an early start."

"Who was that leaving?"

"No one, I told you I bolted the door."

"Maybe, but after she left."

"There's been no one..."

"Elizabeth, I was at the corner, I saw her clearly. There was definitely someone here."

He sits at the table, his leg outstretched. She stands at the door as if unwilling to re-enter the room. Then she relaxes and bolts the door again. Is it because he didn't recognise the visitor?

"Oh...*her*...yes...that was...Katherine, my neighbour."

"But why...?" he says doubtfully.

She recovers her usual aplomb and sits down opposite him.

"You confused me, I didn't think it was important. It's...
no matter."

Matthew throws out his hands and shakes his head. He's
too tired, too low in spirits to argue and for now accepts what
she says.

"Are you going up?"

"Soon, maybe," he says.

"A lieutenant Hugh Crittenden was here."

"I saw him on my way home, we had things to discuss."

She waits, saying nothing, knowing he will speak if he
needs to.

"I should not be engaged on this work, Elizabeth. The
general was insistent, but I am not suited to listening to the
mealy mouthed thrusts of rustic reprobates and gentlemen
who should know better than say what they do."

"What lieutenant Crittenden said upset you?"

"When the heart is not in the task anything he said would
disconcert me. He is an able, determined, dutiful officer..."

He breaks off, looks at the wall. There's a noise from above
as if a chair or the leg of a bed is scraped along the floor.
Edmund stirring perhaps. He may have heard them talking
and could come down. Matthew looks up, but with no sign of
movement, looks to Elizabeth and continues.

"...but what he said concerned me..."

He tells of Hugh's pursuit of Alice Sandon and Prudie
Westrup.

"Hugh believes Alice may be connected to the death of
Manning's steward."

"And this other woman...Prudie...what does he think of
her?"

"He has been talking too long and too deep with the
minister. For a man of God he is too soon to condemn."

"Condemn?"

"Hugh believes Alice and perhaps Prudie too is a witch."

Elizabeth breathes in sharply as the word permeates the
room, repeating itself silently like a persistent fly that won't
or can't escape.

"Oh Matthew no, surely it cannot be!"

"I have heard such things, stories of..."

"I too, but this...no it cannot..."

The inflexibility of her outrage intrigues and slightly unsettles him.

"You are very adamant, Elizabeth, how can you know what happens in Harringstead?"

"Oh I don't...how can I...it's just...I just can't believe."

"Aye, it shocked me too, but since speaking to him I have wondered. What if he's right, what if I've wronged the minister...I don't know...in God's truth Elizabeth I yearn for an end to this commission, for this affair to be sorted so I can return to the real business of life."

His voice trails to a soft, anguished whisper.

"How can war be the real business of life?" she says with firm dismissal.

"It's God's work," he says, somewhat emptily, "a task to be done, without fervour, but with duty, the quicker it's done, the quicker it's ended."

"Is it God's work that sweeps up poor innocent folk? The King's cavalry swept through Birmingham and did such cruel things. They say it was Prince Rupert's men."

He has no regard for the King's nephew, but is dubious of these stories.

"How do you know?"

"It's everywhere. Edmund brought in a newspaper, *The True Informer*."

More noises from above and then footsteps on the stairs. A voice calls "Matthew, is it you?"

"Yes," Elizabeth replies, "the night cat has returned from his prowling."

Edmund appears at the bottom of the stairs, slightly bleary eyed.

"I was worried for you," he says, sitting down beside his wife and looking questioningly at Matthew, "it was late."

Matthew explains about Hugh.

"You missed the best part of the meeting."

"Perhaps," Matthew says indulgently and then glancing at Elizabeth, "but I have seen enough conflict and with more to come in this war..."

"...this war," she intones dully.

"Yes, yes," Edmund says, "but the situation opens up such debates we heard at the 'St. George,' new ideas, radical concepts, ways of getting closer to God's intent."

"Maybe, maybe," Matthew says guardedly.

"We have a duty to listen, Matthew. How else can we learn? This conflict brings us closer to the true ways of Providence. We are at the beginning of a new age, from here we can go forward."

Matthew is sceptical.

"Aye, you may be right, Edmund, but first we need to get back to normal and return the King to his senses."

"The King, the King," Edmund says, "There was a man tonight who wondered whether we needed a king any more than we need lords and all those that have been on our backs for hundreds of years."

Matthew nods politely. Edmund knows he doesn't agree, but will be unwilling to put down his brother in law.

"Well, I am settled now you are returned," Edmund says, yawning as he gets up, "I'm to my bed. I have an early start."

"Goodnight, Edmund," Matthew says, touching his arm, "You are a good man."

"And you too Matthew. God be with you in these troubled times."

"I will be up in a moment," Elizabeth says.

They hear the floorboards creak again. Elizabeth turns to Matthew.

"Is that all that happened tonight?"

"Aye, that was all."

She holds him in her eyes for a few more moments, unsure whether to question him further and then turns. She gets halfway up the stairs before Matthew speaks.

"Do you know of an alehouse called 'The Jackdaw?'"

She turns her head sceptically.

"You should have asked Edmund."

"I forgot. Besides, your knowledge of the city..."

"Hardly of alehouses."

"Is it far?"

She thinks for a moment.

"Near the Tower, Eastcheap."

"I will find it."

"I'll direct you better tomorrow. Why do you ask?"

He shrugs.

"No matter, it's not important," he says, mimicking her earlier replies about the visit of her neighbour.

It's early evening. Matthew is anxious to go out, but Elizabeth insists that first he eats. He won't be drawn on his 'appointment' and says the meal is unimportant, and she will have to prepare another for Edmund when he returns from his work.

"This *appointment* at the 'Jackdaw' must be important if it means you cannot wait," she says.

Throughout the meal she keeps glancing at him. Then when it's over and he stands at the door ready to leave she gives him yet another careful scrutiny.

"You're different, that shirt, it's a bit worn."

"It's alright."

"They are old boots. Why are you taking a different hat, it's very plain."

"Must I always wear the same clothes?"

"You always have before. There's something..."

Then he takes a coat from behind the door.

"That's Edmund's coat."

"He won't mind, will he?"

"No, but why...ah, now I have it!"

"Have what?" he says, pulling on Edmund's coat.

"The clothes...you no longer look like an officer. You don't want to be seen as an officer."

"Nonsense, it's just..."

"Don't try to fool me, Matthew," she says, adjusting his shirt, "I used to do this when you were six years old."

Then she pulls down the coat.

"It's a bit slack, but it'll do. At least I think it will, it depends what..."

"Alright, alright, I need to be...inconspicuous..."

"It's not dangerous, is it?"

"I hope not," he says, leaning back and gently touching her on the shoulder, "But who knows, when I'm crossed I can be dangerous!"

It's early enough to find 'The Jackdaw' and also allows maximum flexibility. Ezra never mentioned a time. Matthew will snout the place out in advance. Elizabeth's directions are detailed and clear, but venturing further east Matthew gets confused and loses his way several times, doubling back and retracing his steps to reach the river twice. He also has the uncanny feeling of being followed, though each time he stops or looks round he sees no one suspicious. After an hour and walking down the same street a third time, he stops and accosts a man for the 'Jackdaw.' A little older than Matthew, slighter, less fit, but probably swifter on his feet, plainly if tidily dressed, though his boots are worn.

"You're almost there, I know it well, that lane, only a short way," the man says, pointing to Matthew's right, "then left and left again."

Matthew thanks him and they part. He follows the directions, but within a few minutes reaches the river for the third time. He sits on a wall by the water's edge, then realises his search may be over when he spies a large tavern at the corner with what looks like a bird painted on its upper wall. If this is the 'Jackdaw' he must have been close to it several times earlier! It's a respectable looking place with large windows fronting to the river. There's not much movement, few people entering or leaving. A couple of men sit at tables outside. They are comfortably dressed, talk volubly and joke noisily with the serving girl. A third man comes up, salutes them both, places his large, elegant hat on the table and engages in the conversation, but doesn't at first sit down until one of the others grandly invites him, calling for more drinks. Very convivial, very correct, very polite, very normal, but not very Ezra. This is not his kind of tavern, not one where he would hang out, unless he'll meet Matthew in the street before going on somewhere else. Has he deliberately chosen it's incongruity? As an officer Matthew would not be out of place, but he hangs back. Something is not right. There's no sign of Ezra and he feels conspicuous. The three men have looked across several times. They might even invite him to join them. No, not as he is dressed now. Surely Ezra would have mentioned a specific hour?

Matthew is unsettled and irritated. It's not just the frustration of getting lost and the unnecessary loss of time. He may have been followed, though sees no one suspicious as he glances up and down the street apprehensively. He'll wait a little longer and then... at the corner a man is looking straight towards him with a puzzled, dubious expression. An ordinary, inconsequential man, not the same status as the trio at the table, not easily drawing attention to himself, the man he saw earlier who gave him directions. He's been following! If so, then he's not very good at his job for he's much too obvious as he stares across at Matthew. Experienced or otherwise his occupation is displeasing. The man sees Mathew striding over, but makes no attempt to get away, even looking towards him.

"Are you following me, sir?"

The man's open brown eyes widen further. Is it genuine surprise or alarm at being discovered?

"Follow you, why no sir, I spoke to you earlier..."

Matthew leans into him. The man pulls back. Matthew grabs his collar.

"You asked me the way..."

"Don't fool with me! I asked you for the 'Jackdaw,' you went in the opposite direction, then followed me. Why else do you loiter here and stare at me across the street?"

Matthew tightens his hold on the collar. He's so close, the man smells his breath and winces.

"On my honour sir, I had an errand to perform before..."

"So why didn't you say or even accompany me?"

"My business was concluded sooner than I expected, so I decided to come to Jack Dawe's place..."

The pitch of the man's voice has risen with his alarm until now he almost screeches.

"*Jackdaws* you say," Matthew sneers, tightening his collar so much the man can hardly breathe, "You are fooling again. I see only *one* bird above the door."

"Please sir, please let me go!"

Matthew loosens his hold slightly, then stares menacingly into his face, awaiting a reply.

"Bird? What do you mean?"

"Above the door, man, a jackdaw is it not?"

"I've no idea...this is...oh no...I see now...*Jackdaw*?"

"Yes, the 'Jackdaw' as I asked you..."

"This is Jack Dawe's tavern, sir, Jack Dawes...D...A...W...E...S... not Jackdaw."

Matthew releases his hold, but still glares.

"By Jesu sir, if you are trifling with me..."

The man brushes down his jacket, glancing nervously towards the tavern and the three men at the table. One looks across.

"I am not following you, nor was I deliberately misdirecting you. That bird above the door, it's an old painting, been there many years. I don't know its origin. This is Jack Dawe's tavern. It's been known as such for as long I can remember. The present landlord, Thomas Dawe, is his son, but we still call it by the old name. If you don't believe me we can go in and speak to him. He'll vouch for me. I am an honest man, sir, I mean you no harm."

"And you've not been following me?"

"No, I have been..."

"This place is not the 'Jackdaw' tavern?"

Recovering some composure, the man steps back slightly.

"I believe there is such a tavern though I would not have thought it was..."

"Was what?" Matthew says, jabbing his face into the other again.

"I mean...it...a man like yourself...excuse me for saying... of course... I don't know your business..."

"Stop cackling like a hen, sir, say what you're about!"

"I meant no disrespect...it's just that the tavern...the other tavern that is...it's...I mean..."

"What!"

"Something of a low establishment."

Matthew steps back and laughs. A low establishment! Frequented by Ezra? Of course it is! This man can't possibly be lying, but his eyes roll fearfully, finding Matthew's mirth even more intimidating than his aggression.

"The 'Jackdaw," Matthew says, "you know it?"

"Yes...well I know of it."

"You can direct me?"

"It's some way, Eastcheap..."

"Eastcheap?"

Suddenly Matthew realises what a fool he's been. This is nowhere near the Tower or Eastcheap.

"I'm sorry I falsely accused you," he says, "Now sir, if you will, tell me how I can find this...low establishment."

Anxious Matthew doesn't come looking for him, the man provides as detailed an itinerary as he can.

"You may have to ask again," he says nervously, "but you should be..."

"...within striking distance?"

The man shudders at the second word, not wanting any 'strike' aimed in his direction. Matthew thanks him and apologises, but the man steps quickly into the comparative security of 'Jack Dawes.' The three men at their table turn sharply before shrugging and continuing their conversation.

Matthew reaches the real 'Jackdaw' within twenty minutes. In a narrow alley a sign with a bird swings above an overhanging upper storey. The small windows are not properly aligned with each other. There's no light except for yellow cracks around the door and the shuttered windows, but there's noise inside. This has to be the right place. Lurking outside would arouse immediate suspicion and he must remain inconspicuous. Even so he hesitates. The sense of being followed has not gone. He came quickly from the river, allowing no time to look for anyone shadowing him. He checks each corner, peering into the gloom before entering the empty alley. He hears footsteps and not wanting to be caught in the open, opens the door and steps into a long narrow porch. It's very dark and he has to stagger towards an inner door.

Inside is very crowded and noisy, with a mixed odour of smoke, sweat and beer. A few people turn, but then look away. The room is much larger than it seemed from the modest exterior, an oddly crooked place, no wall exactly the same height in any two places. The laths and beams though long pressed and smoothed by many customers are still very uneven. The plaster is in need of repainting and in the half light the patches form weird shapes. Crooked windows, crooked walls and ceilings, perhaps a place for crooked people.

He walks slowly towards the counter as a performer on stage faces a hostile audience, acknowledging false acquaintances with an artificial smile as if he's been here a hundred times before. He sees neither friendliness nor aggression only a mild curiosity, but faces can deceive and enemies, spies, stalkers may lie behind them. Alone, he could be easily attacked, but in a strange, congested place chosen by Ezra should be safe. Can he trust Ezra? He glances back furtively. Anyone trailing could slip in unnoticed and signal to an accomplice. But then, if he knew he was coming here, why bother to follow?

There's no one at the door. He looks at the men sitting nearby. Were they all there when he came in? Should he have stayed at the door, but who goes to a tavern and not drink? He waits to be served at the crowded counter where ale is being dispensed in prodigious quantities. A large, middle aged, formidable woman comes over. The others defer to her. She must be the landlady. With her sharp discerning eyes she's been carefully scrutinising him. He feels like a loaf weighed and assessed by a wary customer at a cheap baker's shop.

"You're not a regular?" she says combatively.

It's an odd thing to say in a London tavern. She must be used to many strangers. He orders ale. She eyes him again as it's dispensed. He feels constrained to reply.

"No...someone..."

He's about to say he's here to meet a friend, but thinks better of it.

"...recommended it."

She takes the coins, holding him sceptically before turning to another customer. It's now even more crowded and in his haste bumps into several, glaring at them to give way. A few initially square up silently, but quickly change their minds when faced with Matthew's pugnacious glare. Since his injury, his intimidatory air of contained aggression has increased and in the crush no one notices his limp. He finds a seat close to the door. It's a good position to get away and he can observe all movements. As he sips his beer – he wants to make it last and keep a clear head – he notices an upper gallery extending around three sides. This too is crowded with folk. Many will be watching him now. He scans the rows of drinkers with an exacting thoroughness.

There's much raucous pleasure, laughing and joking, but no singing, no open revelry, no especial drunkenness. It's a shallow diversion, but all may not be what it seems. The tavern is a veil, with customers wearing masks, a place of preparation and suppressed readiness, mirroring the shifting forces and ideas sloshing in London's revolutionary waters. Is this the new age Edmund talked about where new concepts bring us closer to God's true intent? He doubts it. Elizabeth said war is not the real business of life. Abstractions are not for him, but in the London maelstrom do they move away from the conflict's origins?

His tankard is almost drained, but he doesn't get another drink. He's managed to avoid contact with his neighbours. It's getting late. Every time the door opens he looks expectantly for Ezra and apprehensively for an unknown enemy. A man at his side gets up. Matthew watches him leave, continuing to stare incongruously at the closed door.

"You should be watching the room, not the door."

Ezra has slipped into the empty chair at his side.

"How did you get there, I didn't see you come in?"

"There's another door."

"Then I'm lost. Others could have come the same way while I've been watching this door."

Ezra nods and grins. Matthew is not amused.

"Few know the back entry."

"You've kept me waiting."

"Things to do. I was delayed."

They stare at each other for a few moments, taking in the other's features, reminders of the man they've known, wondering how much has changed, how much remains the same.

"You normally attack honest men in dark streets?" Matthew says.

"Only those too slow to get out of my way. There was a time when that would not have included Captain Fletcher."

"I move slower these days."

"So I noticed tonight. Where were you injured?"

"Cropredy Bridge."

Ezra nods.

"And you," Matthew says, "what have you been doing since last we saw each other two years ago?"

Ezra shrugs.

"This and that, here and there."

"You're a wanted man, Corporal Stanfield. There are men only too willing to turn you in. You still stand accused of killing a man."

"Only an accusation as a certain officer kept reminding those who wanted to string me up without trial."

"Aye and the thanks he got was for you to immediately disappear!"

"You were one man among many, Matthew, for which I was grateful and without you…it was best not to wait around."

"Which confirmed the suspicions of the many. No one would believe me after that."

"But you still believed in me?"

"Does it matter what I believe?"

"It does to me."

Matthew says nothing

"So you are no longer with the army?" Ezra says.

"I'm still in the army, though temporarily not on any campaign – other than a special assignment."

Ezra rolls his eyes and turns his head slowly in a knowing fashion even though he has no idea what Matthew is talking about.

"You've been in London these two years?" Matthew continues.

"Mostly. It's a large place to get lost."

"And a large place to get to know?"

"I suppose it is."

"So, not encumbered by your duties in support of Parliament," Mathew says with some acidity. (Ezra starts slightly, but then smirks without taking offence. This is the captain he knows well) "you've had long enough to make many contacts – seemly and less seemly?"

"I've got myself around. I can get into the spider's web if I need to."

"A spider's web where someone may be caught maybe?"

"Perhaps," Ezra says guardedly.

"I'm looking for a young woman, name of Sarah Radbourne."

"London is packed with people who have disappeared, willingly or otherwise. Look at myself."

Ezra professes not to know Sarah Radbourne, but his reference to an 'unwilling' disappearance means he may be holding back. Matthew t explains his enquiry and direct orders from General Skippon. Ezra is impressed. Not everything and everybody about Parliament's army is repugnant to him.

"Even if I did know about her..." he says, "Those in command of intelligence cannot always be trusted."

"This is an important task. Once completed I may be able to return to normal duties."

Ezra looks at him with scepticism and disbelief, viewing Matthew's chances of returning to 'normal duties' as little better than his own.

"I know you well, Ezra. If this woman is in London you are one of the few men likely to find her and one of the even fewer I would trust to do so."

"Even so..."

"...as I said earlier, there are those very willing to advise the authorities of your whereabouts. I would not want to assist them in such a painful errand, but I have my duty..."

Ezra's expression tightens. Matthew doesn't know of Ezra's 'whereabouts,' but he's a persistent man.

"I'll do my best."

Matthew fills in the little information he's already gleaned.

"I am at my sister's."

"I know the place."

"And where can I find you?"

"I will contact you when I have more information...it will be soon."

"You won't let me down?"

"What I say I will do...to you. Now, we part. I'll go the way I came. It's better we're not seen leaving together."

This reminds Matthew of his earlier fears.

"Ezra, you were delayed. Did you follow me tonight?"

"No, but someone else did."

"How do you know?"

"Because I followed *him*."

Matthew gets agitated.

"Then why didn't you get him?"

"I wanted to find out why and who he might be working for?"

"And did you?"

"I had to be careful," Ezra says, a little apologetically, "He was a young man, I didn't see his face."

"And while you were being *careful*, I was here alone. He could have had accomplices."

"You were in no danger and not alone. Pol was watching," Ezra says, nodding to the tavern keeper, "And there are others here also watching you on my behalf."

"Aye, so this really is *your* place," Matthew says grimly, staring up into the packed throng in the gallery before turning back belligerently to Ezra, "you could still have got him."

"We tried, but they lost him. He knew what he was about."

Matthew hurries back, making more direct progress than on his outward journey and now without any sense of being followed. Elizabeth is glad to see him.

"Earlier than last night," she says, hanging up Edmund's coat.

"My business was concluded, at least for now."

"You will have to return?"

"Aye, soon...I hope."

"You are meeting someone?"

"I saw Ezra Stanfield."

"The soldier you thought falsely accused, the one who ran away? You'll surely not turn him in?"

"No."

"Is it safe for you to see him?"

"He knows a lot of people. I need to make some progress."

Elizabeth sits down opposite. He pulls off his boots.

"These women you mentioned?" she says

"Sarah Radbourne?"

"No the other, what was her name..."

"Alice Sandon?"

"No...the other..."

"Prudie Westrup?"

"Why is she so important?"

"To certain local gentlemen she seems to pose a threat."

"What sort of threat?"

"Her land lies inconveniently between the Mannings and the Collvers. They covet that strip as if the soil harvested pure gold. They've tried to get her to sell many times. It seems she's not the easiest of women to deal with. Neither are they, but they of course are *gentlemen*."

Elizabeth laughs.

"And is that all?"

"Not quite. She's rather peculiar in her habits, eccentric some might say, others even mad and it's not wise to denounce the gentry – even if you're right – as stridently as she does."

"So they're out to get her?"

"Yes, but not as much as she in turn is denounced by the local vicar."

Unwilling to go on, Matthew stops and Elizabeth has to prod him. He describes Stradsey in a few succinct sentences. Elizabeth picks up his animosity.

"You don't like the man?"

"He's a man of God," Matthew says, trying to be charitable, then adding, "in his own way."

"That's not your way?"

"Who am I to challenge those who may be better placed to come closer to the Lord."

"You don't believe that."

"Every man," he says with a half smile, then hastily adding, "...or woman...has to find their own way to God."

"You don't like him?" she repeats.

"I don't like some things he says."

He stops again. Elizabeth finds these half finished statements irritating.

"Yes...?"

"I know she's a difficult woman..."

"Was the minister the first to accuse Prudie of witchcraft?"

She utters the last word very quietly, almost inaudibly as if she's ashamed to say it. He nods.

"Always women," she says, "these men who accuse..."

He turns to her with a start. He's used to Edmund's novel questions, challenging almost anything immutable before the war, but his sister is more practical, like him less concerned with abstractions.

"What about these men?" he says.

"You said yourself...you don't like...is it right?"

Knowing each other so well, brother and sister's eyes meet as they wait and wonder. Matthew gives way first, not yet realising how she deliberately provokes and probes.

"They say women are more susceptible as they are weaker..."

"You don't believe women are weaker...do you?"

He says nothing. She stares him out.

"Matthew?"

"No...I don't...not in that way."

"So, there you are..."

"...but there are others I have heard...they say women have to guard against the devil more vigilantly. It's not that they are weaker, but more vulnerable."

"And why is that?"

He says nothing. He's uncomfortable. Such questions are testing but she won't let go and he can't break free. He struggles for an answer, his mind suddenly blank until eventually giving the one he least prefers.

"Because of the curse...the temptation they carry from the Garden..."

"The Garden of Eden?"

He nods. She knows. He needn't say more, but it's not that easy.

"Temptation...curse...?"

"Eve was tempted...so all women have the curse...of the devil!"

He raises his voice, not for emphasis, but for escape.

"That may be the belief of men like Stradsey," she says, "but what do you believe Matthew?"

"Why is it so important, why must you know these things?"

"Edmund says all things must be challenged at the dawning of a new world."

"Where is Edmund?" he says, suddenly aware of his brother in law's absence and keen to change the subject.

"He had to go out, a neighbour, someone from the dock, I forget exactly, he should be back soon."

"These things are perhaps best discussed when he..."

It might work. It sometimes did when they were children. Talk long enough of other things and big sister will give up. But that was in the fields, this is the big city.

"Matthew! Is that what you believe?"

"No it is not!"

He gets up. She should be satisfied, but she's not.

"Always women," she mutters, "always those accused of being witches are women."

He stands at the fireplace, facing the wall.

"There have been some men," he says without looking round," there have been warlocks."

"Name one?" she challenges.

He turns belligerently. She stares defiantly. His mind is a blank again. Damn! Why should it matter, it's not witchcraft he's investigating?

"There was a man...Essex I believe, I forget his name."

"Is that all?"

"There have been others, I don't recall."

"That's hardly..."

"Alright, alright!" he shouts, resuming his seat at the table, "I concede. It's nearly always women and (catching her intransigent expression) I can't explain it except..."

"So you would not rush to condemn a woman so accused?"

How does he answer? It would depend on the circumstances, on the woman, most of all on the accusers. But he knows that will not satisfy her.

"I would not rush to condemn," he says with accommodating neutrality.

She seems to accept it and is more relaxed. Her interest troubles him.

"Why is it so important? And don't tell me what Edmund says. I can't believe the two of you while away the evenings discussing such things."

"I just needed to know how you felt."

The following midday a young boy brings a message for Matthew from Ezra.

"A dishevelled creature," Elizabeth says.

"I can imagine. What did he say?"

"Tonight, the Jackdaw."

His heart leaps with expectation. Has Ezra already made contact with Sarah Radbourne? With her found the mystery will be unlocked and Skippon may agree to him returning to the army. Every man is needed if the King is to be brought to his senses this year. Did Ezra's associates frighten off whoever followed or will they catch the villain tonight? He stops several times, hiding in alleys, trying to trick anyone following, hand on his sword at the ready. He'll do the job himself if they can't or won't. But no one comes. Not even an innocent wayward traveller like the man he accosted by the river.

He's earlier than last night and it's less crowded. His arrival is more welcomed. Pol is almost cheery if that's possible from such a sour faced creature. At a table near the bar Ezra waits with a large, long haired man with a delicately trimmed moustache, which reminds Matthew of the King, though in every other respect he's utterly unlike the monarch. He gets up as Matthew nears the table and grasps his hand firmly.

"Welcome pilgrim, a friend of Ezra is a friend of mine. I am Daniel Overbridge."

Pilgrim...not a word he would normally associate with any acquaintance of Ezra. It reminds him of the gluttonous chop eater in the 'Anchor.'

"Not exactly a friend," he corrects the big man, "We were former...colleagues."

Matthew sits down as Ezra smirks. With his long hair, large bright eyes like beacons, ruddy cheeks, surprisingly soft voice and constant reference to 'pilgrim' Overbridge seems half wild.

"I understand experiences in the army best not mentioned, even here," he says quietly, leaning forward, as if Matthew rather than Ezra needs to hide aspects of his army career.

He glances at Ezra, wondering what he's said. Then Overbridge stands, lifts his voice and booms out so loudly, Matthew starts back in surprise.

"We are all free and at one with God!"

A couple of men leaning against the bar murmur polite 'amens' and return to their ale. Matthew is uncomfortable. He heard similar things from the young man at the 'St.George.' Overbridge sits down, again leaning towards Matthew, who sits back even further. He returns to his quiet tone.

"There is no Day of Judgement!"

Matthew is getting irritated and glowers at Ezra, who seems unconcerned.

"Whether there is or there is not, sir," he says sternly, "there are matters requiring my judgement and I fail to see how any of what you say has any relevance to *that!*"

Overbridge grins, his wide set of excellent teeth seeming to engulf the lower half of his face as much as his enormous eyes absorb the upper half, the whole brilliantly enclosed like the curtains of a stage by his long mop of unkempt hair, falling in ringlets from his forehead. His mouth seems to be perpetually grinning while his large wide eyes are like massive doors that never close with an unknown prospect beyond. If his eyes were to contract or his mouth close the whole roundness would be lost and his face would probably crack and implode. He speaks with the deliberation of one privy to great secrets.

"That is precisely why I tell you, freed from oppression, unfearful of being judged, that all knowledge is true knowledge, even that garnered like the scattered seed from the byways by the defiled of humanity."

"Daniel's connections reach every part of the city," Ezra intervenes with a knowing expression.

Matthew looks dubious.

"He knows everybody," Ezra says in further explanation.

"And fears no one!" Overbridge bellows, half standing again.

"Sit down, sir," Matthew says, irritated, "and restrain your voice. I'm not deaf!"

Overbridge looks at him disdainfully as if Matthew is unable to understand his simple message. Obviously there are things to be spoken discreetly, things to be broadcast and things that need not be said at all.

"Daniel will help," Ezra intervenes again, glancing hopefully at Overbridge as much as in reassurance to Matthew, "Tell him what you want."

Matthew takes the hint and briefly tells of Sarah Radbourne. The big man's expression remains rapt and attentive, his eyes unflinchingly held on Matthew, but the name seems not to mean anything to him. Matthew is disappointed. Despite the strange man's bombast and incoherence, he's been expecting a positive response.

"You don't know her?"

"If she is in London, she will be found," Overbridge says confidently, "Rest assured, pilgrim. God is in everything. That means he is in me and if He wills it then it will happen."

"Daniel will find her," Ezra interprets.

Matthew doesn't share Ezra's faith, but he has to accept it. The tavern is filling up. Overbridge calls for more beer and his pipe.

"You can stay and listen to our discussion, even join in. Another view, especially from a soldier, is always welcome."

Matthew declines. His sister will be expecting him. He has no stomach for another round of preaching, however well intentioned.

"Tomorrow I shall begin the search," Overbridge says, reading his thoughts.

Ezra comes with Matthew into the street.

"I will make contact as soon as there's news."

Matthew nods resignedly. He walks back slowly, depressed by his lack of progress. His leg starts to ache, probably psychosomatic, his limb sympathising with his heart, resolute, but tired. He could press Ezra further, ask how he found Overbridge, what success he may have had in the past, even remind him of his own vulnerable position, but he's heard enough and lacks the energy. Besides Ezra will know what he's thinking. Unspoken understandings are sometimes more powerful. Ezra swore he never killed the man and despite his rather disreputable reputation, Matthew believed him. He was a good soldier even if he did complain about everything. How many innocent men are wrongly accused, guilt too often assumed rather than proven. Just like women accused of being witches.

Deep in thought he gets to his sister's door and opens it without knocking. Elizabeth is at the table. Matthew starts at her companion.

7

SEARCHING for the firm of Ellerton and Amberley involves Matthew journeying into his own past as well as the streets of the city. He should have pursued this aspect of the investigation earlier. There have been other matters – the complications at Harringstead, Hugh's disappearance, Ezra's appearance and now this latest complication – but in truth he's put it off, afraid of the reminders it's bound to bring. As he gets closer to the merchants' building his trepidation mounts. It's the same address as the old firm, then just known as Ellertons. He came yesterday, observed the few comings and goings and made a few discreet enquiries. Old man Ellerton should be away. That should leave Amberley and the man he's come to find, the clerk, Henry Collver. The firm is not the one he knew in the past and with the changes over the years no one should know him. He will pose as the clerk of another firm if Amberley is around. A few silly enquiries might make him look foolish, but otherwise the approach should be safe and he's made himself look as much like a cloth merchant's clerk as he can. He's getting used to disguises though this is more a revival of a previous life.

He came here on an errand for Harmsworth and first caught sight of Jane. A memory best avoided. Thinking of her will lower his guard. He might even give himself away. He takes the short cut down the narrow alley, opening into a wide courtyard, where he goes to the front door of the cloth merchants. The firm's name is newly painted though on closer inspection 'Ellerton' rather than 'Amberley' is a little faded and underneath the bright lettering of 'Amberley' there is the dim word 'Collver.' Evidence of the recent change of ownership though there's no reference to Manning's involvement.

The door is unlocked and he enters the small ante room. He waits a few moments, resting his elbow on the low counter, but no one appears. He reopens the door and then pushes it closed with a loud bang. There's a faint rustling, a light step and a small man, dressed in sombre, slightly soiled clothes emerges from the back. Their eyes meet, assessing each other's station, quickly concluding they confront a clerk.

"Good day to you, sir, can I be of assistance?"

Amenable, but neutrally firm, courteous, but not deferential, the voice is slightly raised as if to emphasise the question contains an element of genuine enquiry, an acceptable address to an equal. By the man's drab appearance he might easily pass for one of the rolls of cloth in the rear room, an only slightly animated example of his own merchandise. His thick moustache is in need of trimming, the overall effect making him appear a little older than his actual years. The eyes are quick and alert, searching Matthew like one who was once in a higher position, early forties, a little younger than his brother, but unmistakably the clerk, not the proprietor.

"You are Henry Collver?"

The head turns slightly the better to appraise Matthew.

"I am the clerk of this establishment," he says with a practised rectitude.

"You are alone?" Matthew says quietly, leaning over the counter into the clerk's face.

Henry leans back, slightly intimidated, despite Matthew' attempt to put him at relative ease.

"Yes," he says after a little hesitation, unsure whether it's wise to respond at all.

"I am Captain Matthew Fletcher, on the instructions of Sergeant Major General Skippon, investigating certain events in Harringstead."

Henry's demeanour changes immediately, his eyes widening, the edge of his lips quivering, from either fear or excitement.

"I have heard of you. You've already visited my brother."

"In which case you will know that I am concerned with the sudden and unexplained death of Samuel Lexden, steward of the local Justice, Joseph Manning."

"And you believe my family to be involved," Henry says, the tremor in his voice increasing.

"I've made no such assertion," Matthew says, coldly scanning him.

Regaining some composure, Henry attempts a similar detachment, looking Matthew up and down condescendingly.

"You do not look like an investigating *officer*."

Matthew smirks grimly.

"Appearances can deceive. You do not go by the decoration of a master merchant though give yourself the airs of such a one you once were. Now sir, is there somewhere we may talk?"

Suitably rebuked and without a further word, Henry opens the counter half door and leads Matthew through the back to a corner near the yard door, separated from the rest of the storeroom by piles of cloth. He takes a chair and putting it at one side of a small table, littered with papers, offers it to Matthew before sitting in his own chair on the opposite side.

"I had nothing to do with Lexden's death," he begins, "at the time I was..."

Matthew raises his arm and pushes his open palm towards Henry's mouth. Henry stops immediately, fixing his eyes apprehensively on Matthew as he lowers his arm.

"Tell me about your family."

"We have possessed our holdings in Harringstead since..."

"No, no, your brother has advised me of the land. I want to know about the cloth business."

Henry is momentarily taken aback. Then, under Matthew's probing gaze, he launches into a discourse on the mechanics of the business, but such intricacies will not put his interrogator off the scent. Matthew intervenes, correcting various statements with succinct comments of his own.

"You know the trade?" Henry says in some alarm.

"Enough to know when my time is being wasted," Matthew says irritably, "Now begin again, this time concentrating on the personal aspects of the business."

Henry stares quizzically. Matthew sighs volubly.

"This firm was once simply known as Ellertons. Let's start from there."

Henry looks to the window and the yard and then around the walls of cloth, seeking reinforcement for his thoughts before beginning. Matthew watches him suspiciously, puts his elbows on the table, crunching several clumps of paper in the process, resting his fists against his cheeks, before turning to him again.

"And leave nothing out that's relevant."

"You knew the firm?" Henry says.

Matthew waves his hand dismissively, "I had some acquaintance a few years ago."

"And you knew it as Ellertons, that would be when?"

Matthew shifts uneasily. The conversation is almost turning on him. Henry senses his reluctance.

"If it was more than three years ago, you might not know someone else invested in the business even though there was no immediate change of name."

"When was this?"

"November 1641."

Matthew starts. He was then working for Harmsworth. He knew nothing of this and Jane certainly never mentioned it. Did she deliberately keep it from him?

Thinking aloud, he says, "That was kept very..."

"Quiet?" Henry interjects, "Yes, not many knew."

Did that perhaps include Jane?

"The investor was you or your brother?"

"How do you know it was a Collver?"

"I saw the faded lettering outside, underneath Amberley."

Henry leans back warily.

"Very observant, captain. It was actually our father, Arthur Collver."

Matthew starts again. How a sudden remark changes the preconceptions of the past.

"This investment...substantial, was it?"

"Substantial enough," Henry says ruefully.

"I understood at the time...just rumour you understand... there was a possibility Ellerton may have been considering a merger with another firm."

"From where would you hear that?"

"Idle gossip amongst tap room apprentices," Matthew shrugs, opening his palms with a smile.

Henry looks at him for a moment. He doubts Matthew places undue reliance on such sources of information.

"With my father's investment there was no need for a merger."

"When was the company name changed?"

"Two years ago. Not long after my father's involvement he and Jonathon Ellerton speculated a great deal in the market. It was one of those bubbles that invariably arise. Father would never admit it, but I suspect it was all Jonathon's idea. They did well for a time. Then Jonathon decided to pull out. Said he needed money quickly...(Matthew winces...money for what?)...they agreed to split the profits, father using his share to buy out virtually all Jonathon's share of the business. The name changed to Ellerton and Collver at that time."

"Which meant Ellerton effectively walked away with all the money they'd made from this speculation."

"Whether he was particularly wise or privy to inside information he chose not to pass on we'll never know, but shortly afterwards the bubble inevitably burst, the price crashed and father was left with enormous debts. Now he was short of cash and couldn't hang on till business improved. The shock killed him. I'd been working here for a short time before Jonathon pulled out, but father kept it all to himself. I had no idea what was happening and how dangerously extended we were. The situation was so serious, my brother and I were faced with having to sell part of the estate to wipe out the debts. That was unthinkable. The only alternative was to sell our share of the company in its entirety."

"Let me guess...back to Jonathon Ellerton at a fraction of the original value."

"Not quite. Jonathon wouldn't buy up more than a half share. That wasn't enough. We were really desperate. We pleaded with him to take more. It was unbelievably degrading."

He pauses, breathing more deeply to hold back his distress. After a few moments he continues.

"Finally Jonathon said he'd found new investors. Only later were we to learn the awful truth. Of course, to attract this new money the price of the remainder of the business had to be knocked down even further. Edward Amberley arrived and became his new partner. The firm was renamed again as Ellerton and Amberley."

"Just one new investor?"

"I'll come to that. It was a hard and bitter deal, but at least we didn't have to sell any land, which was John's life. In the meantime I'd got used to working in the city, so we thought we'd done quite well when Jonathon and Edward agreed I could stay on as their clerk."

"They probably needed your expertise," Matthew says darkly, remembering his own days in the trade.

Henry nods.

"But that wasn't all. Though his name doesn't't appear on the front door, the other new investor was Joseph Manning."

Matthew sighs and grimaces.

"That must have made you feel very angry."

"I try to be out on the few occasions he comes here. It's bad enough being a mere clerk in what was once the family firm, but to be working...*serving*...the old adversary. It's almost too much."

"Did Jonathon know you...?

"I think he deliberately kept Manning's name quiet in case we pulled back from the sale."

"But that would have meant selling your land."

"Which would have pleased Manning even more, but wasn't in Jonathon's interest. He wanted the whole business again, not providing Manning with more land."

"Something to be thankful for," Matthew says, trying to be cheerful

"Thankful for Jonathon's greed," Henry says bitterly, "so Joseph Manning can have the satisfaction of employing the family enemy."

"It must make your position extremely precarious."

"They need me too much to get rid of me. Amberley isn't conversant with the trade at all, but there's more, much more."

He pauses, then goes on, speaking as before into the distance, only occasionally glancing towards Matthew.

"I don't believe Ellerton's withdrawal from the market and his later decision to invest again was entirely fortuitous."

"Inside knowledge, as you said."

Henry smacks his lips and shakes his head.

"Not something I can prove..."

He stops suddenly, looks directly at Matthew and shrugs.

"Prove what?" Matthew says.

"No, no," Henry says, turning away, "I've already said enough."

"And you'll say more, sir!"

Matthew stands up, then leans down, his accusing eyes and grim set mouth into Henry's face.

"You can't begin and then suddenly leave off. You will assist my investigation or..."

Henry jerks back in alarm, lifting his hands as if to defend himself from attack. Matthew pulls up straight, though keeps his eyes intent on Henry.

"Or what?" Henry says, "What will you do?"

Matthew sits down and leans forward again, though not so close.

"No one is without sin..."

"But some sin more than others," Henry says defiantly, recovering some of his confidence.

"...and none are above suspicion."

"You suspect me?"

"Others do. It's my duty to investigate."

"Investigate?"

"It's been put to me that your brother John may have Royalist sympathies."

"Never!" Henry shouts, "Who would say such a damnable thing?"

Matthew half smiles wryly.

"Of course," Henry bellows, "Manning is behind this. You can't possibly believe what that man says."

"And why shouldn't I believe him?"

"Because he would say anything about us."

Matthew shakes his head and grimaces. Henry explodes.

"I tell you, it's not so, believe me."

"Naturally you defend your brother."

"It's not that."

"Not just brotherly feeling?"

"No."

"No...not if you had such leanings yourself. The city is rife with Royalist plots. It would be very convenient for you here. Why else would you continue to work in the firm part owned by your enemy, Joseph Manning?"

"I've already explained..."

"Not entirely to my satisfaction. I will need to..."

"Ellerton worked a clever fraud. I can't yet prove it, but I will...I will get to the truth...and for that I must stay."

Fraud? Jane's father involved in fraud? Does he really want to know more? Henry's afraid and has much to hide. He knows Matthew will pursue him and his brother. His only hope is to kick up so much dust Matthew won't see what's right before him, wasting his energies following other tracks. He can't believe this of Jonathon Ellerton, the father of the woman who...

"You talk of Royalist plots...I'll tell you of a link."

Matthew is bounced back to the present and stares questioningly at Henry.

"The other partner," Henry goes on, "Edward Amberley."

"Amberley is a Royalist?" Matthew mumbles.

"A link," Henry corrects, "I said a link."

"Links, plots, connections, frauds...Manning tells lies, Ellerton is a fraudster and Amberley is a Royalist. The men who took away your business or where they just better at the cloth trade? It's very convenient how all those who cross your family are lumped together."

"Don't you want to know about the fraud?" Henry says aggressively.

"Of course, but..."

"Henry! Are you there, do you skulk at the back of the shop?"

Henry leaps up, looks around pointlessly, then down at the table, finally shuffling his papers.

"Amberley," he says anxiously, "It's Amberley."

"Henry!"

Henry looks to Matthew, who nods with a wave of his hand.

"Yes, Mr. Amberley, sir, I'm here."

A few sharp footsteps and then the tall, imposing figure of Edward Amberley stands at the doorway.

"Just been updating these..." Henry begins.

"Yes, yes of course," Amberley says, waving him aside with his large hat as he looks across to Matthew, "I only wanted to...but I didn't realise...someone else was here?"

"Yes...I wasn't expecting you," Henry gibbers, "you see..."

"...and this is?"

"Matthew Fletcher," Matthew says, standing up.

"He...he..." Henry struggles.

"From Harmsworths," Matthew says, "but my business is completed now, sir, I won't trouble you any longer."

"No, that's quite alright," Amberley says, scanning Matthew carefully," Harmsworths, you say?"

"The cloth merchants."

"Yes, of course. Well if I could have a word with my clerk."

"By all means. My business with Henry is..."

"No, no, please stay. I shall not detain Henry long."

Amberley whisks the disconcerted Henry from the room. As they talk at the front of the shop Matthew quickly searches the papers on Henry's table, but they reveal nothing more than the latest prices and delivery problems. At least if Amberley returns he'll be better prepared to hold his own in any enquiries about the state of trade. From what Henry said Amberley's knowledge is no better, but he can't take the risk and prepares to leave. He passes them at the door.

"Good day to you sir," he says to Amberley and then to Henry, "Thank you for all your help, Mr. Collver. I may need to speak to you again."

Amberley nods and beams. Henry looks uncomfortable. With its mixed memories and uneasy implications Matthew gets away quickly. It's not just the past that unnerves him. With Amberley's sudden arrival he slipped into the guise of his old employment, but was that wise? He may have to question him officially, but for now it's better to have a cover for his meeting with Henry. Amberley seemed to swallow it, but beneath the veneer of reasonableness was he really so uninterested? Can Henry be trusted to keep to the story? It depends on where Henry is coming from and how much he trusts his employer. There's something worryingly familiar about Amberley and Matthew tries to recall where he's seen him before, but it eludes him.

The nearest church bell strikes two. He may be a little late for his meeting with Hugh at the 'Falcon.' The venue was Matthew's idea. In troubled times it's more secure, but there are other reasons he doesn't want Hugh at the house. Should he tell him? The tavern is quiet. Hugh sits alone at the back. He makes no mention of Matthew's lateness. Matthew apologises curtly.

"Any news of Sarah Radbourne?"

Hugh shakes his head.

"No more I suspect than you glean from Ezra Stanfield."

"Those contacts are ongoing," Matthew says stiffly.

"The only place Stanfield should be going is to the authorities."

"You've not said anything?"

"I've done nothing, but Matthew is it wise? Quite apart from Ezra's past, the connections he may have...if this was to get back to the general?"

"Are you...?" Matthew booms, banging the table loudly.

"No, not me," Hugh says quietly, nodding to the landlord who is looking over very curiously, "but such contacts... someone is bound to talk and with all the rumour mongers in this city..."

"What are you saying?"

"You have to be careful. How can you trust Stanfield?"

"You've not come up with anything better," Matthew says, though less forcefully, taking some heed of Hugh's warning.

Slightly chastened, Hugh recounts his enquiries since returning to London. Despite Matthew's remark, Hugh has assiduously followed every possible strand that might relate to the girl. Matthew should be impressed, but he is self absorbed and picks up only occasional references to 'then I saw' and 'he told me,' most of the time his mind reverting back to Henry and Ellerton.

"Very comprehensive," he mutters as Hugh completes his report, "I agree there's not much more…"

"I still think we should be investigating the Collvers."

Matthew sits up. On this at least he agrees with Hugh and recounts his meeting with Henry, though unable to fully accept Ellerton's involvement, omits anything about possible fraud. Hugh starts at the mention of Amberley.

"You know this man?" Matthew says.

"The name is familiar."

"His face seemed familiar to me too, but I couldn't place him. Where have you heard the name?"

Hugh shakes his head.

"I don't know. The business connection with Manning, I may have heard it from him."

"That's possible, something for us to follow up later."

They are silent for a few minutes. Hugh looks across enquiringly. Now is the opportunity to mention Prudie and a couple of times Matthew is ready to speak, but the stalled conversations with his sister fill his mind and the words stick in his throat.

"I won't give her up," Elizabeth said, "and I won't let you give her up either."

"How did she get here?" Matthew said.

"She is no witch," Elizabeth replied, avoiding his question.

He asked again.

"Where else could she go?" Elizabeth said.

"I should have known, that discussion about witchcraft, all those questions about her."

"Will you contact me again?" Hugh says, breaking the silence.

Matthew could tell him one suspect is safely in his sister's house, but safe from whom? His mind drifts back to Henry and the Ellertons, though reaching no more conclusions than he has about Prudie.

"Yes," he says, "when I know more. Leave a message here if you have anything."

Matthew sits for a while after Hugh leaves, troubled by recurring memories, indecisive and guilty at not being unable to tell Hugh. Is the supposed fraud relevant to finding Lexden's killer? He'll have to return and get to the bottom of Henry's allegations. Will that bring him into contact with Jonathon Ellerton? He winces at the prospect. No, he'll report his findings to the city authorities. He need only see Ellerton if he's implicated in the murder. He goes over every thing Henry may tell him. It seems unlikely Jonathon is involved. What possible motive could he have? No, he won't see Henry again. But Hugh is rightly concerned. They may be Royalists after all, though Matthew is dubious. He'll not see him. Henry is too close to the Ellertons. Which means that through him Matthew may be able to make contact with Jane Ellerton. He *will* see Henry again.

Hugh was only reminding him of his duty about Ezra. A wanted man should be turned in. He's shielding a suspect and withholding vital information from his associate. How can Hugh conduct a thorough investigation if he's not in possession of all relevant facts? He could still be pursuing Prudie, wasting valuable time when he could be getting close to finding Sarah Radbourne. If that pursuit is successful it might lead Hugh to Elizabeth's house. Hugh would then rightly go over his head to the general. Even if Matthew wriggles out of that it would finally crush any chance of returning to combat. Yet something deep within makes him wary. Hugh is young and impetuous. He may have to be protected from himself. This interest in witchcraft is unhelpful. Or is it that Matthew needs reasons to protect *himself*? They have important work to do. Getting embroiled with Prudie will be a distraction. He walks back dejectedly with the vital question still unanswered.

What is he to do about her?

At the house he has to knock. To his surprise, Edmund opens the door.

"Shortage of work?" Matthew says, stepping past him.

Edmund doesn't answer and hovers near the door. Then Matthew sees the two women at the table. Elizabeth sits near the fire, staring at him impassively. Prudie has her head slightly bowed and makes no movement. No one speaks. Edmund sits opposite Prudie.

"You're too late for dinner," Edmund says, "We've already had ours, but I'm sure..."

"I'm not hungry," Matthew says, remaining standing, his hands on the top rail of the chair, facing Elizabeth.

"Sit down brother," Edmund says.

"How long is she to stay?" Matthew says, looking towards his sister.

"She has a name," Elizabeth says.

"Aye, Prudie Westrup," Matthew says, turning to Prudie, "I wanted to speak to you in Harringstead, but when I got to your house you'd gone and left nothing behind."

"If you're going to play the soldier interrogator, you can sit down," Elizabeth says.

Prudie turns to face him. Matthew sits down.

"I had to get away," Prudie says.

"Taking everything with you?"

"There wasn't much to take."

"Are your things here?"

"Some...the rest are safe."

"I wanted to talk to you."

"To accuse me of being a witch?"

"To find out what you knew about the murder of Samuel Lexden."

"It's the same thing."

"You believe his murder was connected to witchcraft?"

"That's what Joseph Manning believes."

"And that's enough?"

She laughs and claps her hands.

"Usually. What Manning says is enough for everyone in Harringstead. It'll be enough for you."

Matthew glances at Elizabeth. She shakes her head.

"What do you believe?" he says to Prudie.

"What I believe isn't important. That's why I had to get away. If Manning says I'm a witch then...in Essex there was a woman so accused by the local Justice...no, better to get away."

"So you came to London?"

"It's easier to get lost in a big place."

"Imposing yourself on my sister?"

"Prudie is not imposing herself!" Elizabeth says, "she's welcome to stay until..."

"...you too are implicated? There are those only too quick to accuse the innocent, Elizabeth."

"Like Hugh Crittenden?"

"He's still after me," Prudie says.

"Hugh was doing what he was assigned to do, assisting me to get to the truth."

"By harassing Alice Sandon?"

"Where is she?"

"Safe."

"Like you are here."

"Prudie had nothing to do with Lexden's murder, Matthew!"

"You don't know that, Elizabeth."

"Yes I do, I know!"

No one speaks until Edmund says, "We should all keep calm."

"How did Prudie know where to come?" Matthew says, ignoring him.

"I knew you had a sister called Elizabeth and a brother in law called Edmund Culshaw," Prudie says calmly.

"How did you know that?" Edmund says.

"Your brother in law is not the only one who asks questions."

"Did you know she was coming here?" Matthew says to his sister.

Elizabeth doesn't answer.

"I came on an expectation," Prudie says.

"An expectation you would be welcomed. You were in communication."

"I was in communication with no one until I arrived."

Matthew looks to Elizabeth, who nods slowly.

"I'd been in the city two nights, avoiding the watch, trying to keep warm," Prudie says, "Then I remembered about Captain Fletcher's sister and I knew I had to come here."

"*Knew?*"

"I was drawn, I knew it would be right. I feel these things."

"She was desperate," Elizabeth says, "I couldn't leave her to wander the streets."

"*Feel* things," Matthew says, "As you felt things in Harringstead, how you made things *happen*?"

Prudie hesitates.

"Well," he persists, "I have heard that you..."

"From Manning!"

"Yes from the Justice, but also from John Collver."

"The Mannings and the Collvers will accuse me of anything to get my land."

"Running away won't help you keep it."

"What choice did I have? When a powerful person makes an accusation..."

"The minister."

"You have spoken to him?"

"The reverend Stradsey and I have exchanged views," Matthew says dryly.

Prudie laughs.

"You do not like him. That is good."

"What I like or don't like is not important!" Matthew thunders.

"Ah, but it is, captain. It's very important. For if you doubt what you hear from Stradsey, you may doubt what you hear from others. My land lies between the Mannings and the Collvers and is coveted by both, but they are bound against their will by more than my land."

"Olivia and Richard."

"They told you?"

"No. Hugh chanced upon a discussion at the Manning house. Joseph is strongly opposed to his daughter forming a liaison with Richard Collver."

"*Forming!* It's already formed and there's nothing the Justice can do to stop it."

"You're very sure."

"I know, I feel."

"Did you tell Joseph Manning?"

"I may have mentioned his daughter may not be all that she appears. Olivia flashes her eyes and flaunts herself, but it's mainly in Richard Collver's direction."

"Do you always say things people don't want to hear, people in authority, people who can do you harm?"

"I say what I feel, what must be said."

"Some would call that witchcraft!"

"Matthew, stop this," Elizabeth shouts, "Women must not be condemned for speaking their mind!"

"Not their mind, Elizabeth, but perhaps too much idle prattle, too much interference in the affairs of others!"

"Like you perhaps?"

"I am conducting an investigation."

"Then conduct it properly!"

Then Edmund says, "Matthew, perhaps..."

"Can't you control your wife!" Matthew shouts, turning on him.

"Can you not control your sister!"

"That is not the same. Your wife is your responsibility!"

"And your sister is not yours?"

"Not after she's married!"

"Then tell me..."

"Be quiet!" Elizabeth shouts, standing up, "I'll not be haggled over like a piece of meat at the butcher!"

They are silent. Elizabeth sits down.

"Save us, save us," Matthew mutters, turning with a half smile to his sister, "from the monstrous incursions of women!"

"And from men," she says.

They laugh, except for Prudie.

"I'm not a witch. People come to me and I heal them, but I'm not a witch."

"What about the notes left near the animals?"

"I don't know anything about that."

"The minister said..."

"The minister said I must have the power of the devil to make people well. It wasn't the devil's power, but of the land and the plants and the animals. I told him the spirit of God moves through the earth and the air, through the waters and the trees. He said the power of God can only come through the Church and those that say otherwise must be guided by the devil. He said I was a witch and so was Alice. It's not true, but I feel things and maybe sometimes I speak when I shouldn't. I feel things between people. That's what the Mannings don't like. They're all against me."

"Constance Manning didn't speak against you."

Prudie smiles.

"She's another one. They all have a past and hers is more like the present of her daughter."

"You speak ill of a righteous woman?"

"I speak no ill, only of what was. The workings of the past always influence the present. But I admit Constance never called me a witch."

"She defended you."

"She did not join the pack of wolves led by her husband and the minister. That was because..."

"She was afraid of you?"

Prudie laughs.

"Maybe, though more of my words, of what I might say."

"What might you say?"

She looks him at directly and nods.

"I speak what I feel between people. I feel something between you and another, captain."

Matthew starts. He looks to Elizabeth. She shakes her head.

"Not now, before," Prudie says, her eyes glistening as they stare deeply into his, "before this war, before you were a soldier, before you were...investigating...another time when you worked in the cloth trade... somewhere you've been today...yes, I feel the place...Ellertons... Jane Ellerton."

"By Jesu, this is witchcraft!" Matthew thunders and then to Elizabeth, "or else you have told her!"

"I've told her nothing."

"Then how else could she know?"

"I feel," Prudie says, "that is enough."

"This...this is..." Matthew says slowly.

What Prudie says consumes him with fear and anger, fearful of what is unknown, angry for what is known.

"It's lain dormant, but today you've determined to renew the contact."

"I have not..."

"You have determined to try to find her through this contact."

"And will I find her?"

"You will try. I can only warn you. Take this path and it can only lead to disappointment. That which was still is and will be plain to you."

"But will I...?"

"You will be unsuccessful, Matthew Fletcher. I tell you now however much you try, through these means she is lost."

"Enough!" Edmund shouts, standing up, "This is too much. I say..."

A sharp rapping at the door interrupts him. They wait. The rapping comes again.

"Who is this?" Elizabeth whispers.

Edmund shrugs.

"Matthew! Matthew Fletcher, are you there?"

It's Hugh.

"Quickly," Elizabeth says, taking Prudie's hand, leading her to the back door and hustling her out, "With me."

Then she turns to the men and shakes her head. Matthew and Edmund look to each other.

"I must speak with him," Matthew says, "Open the door, but leave the talking to me."

Edmund does as he's bidden, closing the door after Hugh steps in. Hugh glances at him nervously.

"Be seated," Matthew says, "You may speak freely before Edmund. You have news of Sarah Radbourne?"

Hugh shakes his head.

"We have lost Prudie Westrup and Alice Sandon (Matthew and Edmund exchange glances) so the Collvers have to be the most likely possibilities, but your meeting with Henry Collver concerns me."

"I will see him again," Matthew says.

There's a noise from the back of the house. Hugh looks across.

"My wife," Edmund says with unnecessary explanation.

"We may be already too late and wasting valuable time," Hugh says, "We should be pursuing Richard Collver with all vigour."

Matthew sighs loudly.

"Not this Royalist plot again."

Edmund starts.

"Yes indeed, Mr. Culshaw," Hugh turns to Edmund, "you are right to be shocked. A dangerous Royalist conspiracy is at large in Middlesex and now I believe in London. Please help me to convince Matthew of the need to proceed without delay."

"Leave Edmund out of this," Matthew says angrily, pulling Hugh away so they stand with their back to Edmund.

"Henry has probably already warned his nephew," Hugh whispers, "You said yourself how frightened he was."

"But that doesn't mean..."

"I'm sure Richard is no longer in London."

"If he ever was."

"Of course he was, he came to see Henry. We must leave London and pursue Richard."

"We have to find Sarah Radbourne," Matthew says firmly.

"Matthew, we have to..."

"We have to do as I say, lieutenant."

"But Matthew, we must pursue Richard Collver."

"No sir, we must continue to find Sarah Radbourne. Now, unless you hear from me beforehand, we will meet tomorrow night at the 'Falcon."

"It will then be too late."

"Be gone, sir!"

Hugh is ready to speak again, but Matthew's blazing eyes and firm set bottom lip convince him it's futile. He turns and goes. Elizabeth returns from the back. Edmund shuts the door and waits until Hugh's footsteps can no longer be heard.

"What is this about a Royalist plot?" he says.

"*Supposed* Royalist plot. You know how many rumours are constantly flying around the city."

"Even so, from Hugh Crittenden..."

"Hugh is a good officer, but he's young and impressionable. Sometimes he listens to more gossip than does the village crone in the chimney corner. It's the same with witchcraft. He..."

"Never mind about Hugh's interest in witchcraft. What about ours?"

"I've taken such matters into account. I've no reason..."

"I mean about Prudie!"

"Edmund," Elizabeth says, striding across the room, "Prudie is no witch!"

"Maybe not," Edmund says, "but while she's under our roof..."

"You surprise me, brother," Matthew says, "with your views."

"It's not what I believe, but those of others."

"You are afraid of others?"

"I'm afraid what they may do. Hugh Crittenden is not untypical."

"Edmund," Elizabeth says, "the woman is desperate."

"Where is she now?"

"In the back. She'll not move tonight and keep your voice down. It's not good for her to hear these things."

"Witch or no witch, her presence is dangerous, she must leave."

"Edmund!"

Elizabeth stands and glares defiantly at her husband. Edmund turns to his brother in law, but Matthew shakes his head.

"No, no, Edmund I disagree."

Husband and wife stare at Matthew in mutual disbelief.

"But Matthew, what she said about Jane Ellerton, that at least must make you wary. How could she know?"

Matthew turns to Elizabeth.

"You told her nothing?"

"Nothing."

"Then how did she know," Edmund persists, "It could mean she..."

He stops short.

"It may mean she can see into men's hearts," Matthew says, "and see there what they may not even see themselves."

"She has bewitched you!"

"No, Edmund, not her, but maybe another did a long time ago."

"Will you do as she says?" Elizabeth asks.

"I have already decided."

"Then she was right. You will try to find Jane."

"She said you would be unsuccessful," Edmund says.

"She may not be right in everything."

"But Matthew, she meddles with dark forces. This is not God's work."

"And it's God's work to burn innocent women?"

"I have not said that."

"I will give her the benefit of the doubt."

"I still think she should leave."

"And where will she go? Let loose in London and then discovered she'll be made to talk and tell where she's been. How well might that reflect on this house? It will be asked how she came here and why. Elizabeth will be questioned."

Edmund breathes in sharply, his face draining of colour.

"Aye, Edmund, think through where all this may lead."

"If Elizabeth had not..."

"This is no time for blame. I'm less concerned than you are with new novelties and forces, dark or otherwise. For good or ill the woman is here and must be protected."

"But she is part of your investigations."

"And has already provided me with useful information. Besides, what better place than this for me to question her?"

"It is dangerous."

"Yes, it is dangerous. Dangerous for her to stay and dangerous for her to leave, but her staying is the better of two evils."

"Matthew, I am not sure of this..."

"Then I appeal to your Christian conscience, brother. She is one of God's creatures. We must do what we can for her."

Edmund hesitates. Elizabeth turns to him, but says nothing, the appeal in her eyes is enough.

"Very well," he says.

"You are a strange man, Matthew Fletcher," Elizabeth says, "though you are my own brother, I'll never understand you!"

That evening Matthew speaks to Prudie again. At first she'll only talk about Harringstead and the Mannings and the Collvers, lacing her remarks with oddly cryptic comments like 'The Collvers are not the only ones who wish Joseph Manning harm.' Matthew persists, eventually getting round to Jane, but Prudie only repeats what she said before and refuses to give him better hope the Collvers will lead him to Jane. On the other hand she won't say he will never find her. That is enough, her uncanny knowledge giving hope of finding Jane. She knows. Jane has to be near and he will find her through the Collvers. For the moment he holds the investigation in abeyance, ignoring the outcome of finding her, blind to Prudie's warning.

"This woman is not free, what you pursue is not possible."

Reinforced by his faith in Prudie's 'knowledge' Mathew returns to the firm of Ellerton and Amberley the following day, determined to extract the information he feels sure Henry can give. The prospect of finding Jane invigorates him with renewed confidence. No longer just a journey into the past, but a foray into the future. If the heart is willing and the spirit released, anything is possible. Thoughts of the war and returning to combat are forgotten. Yet not so the investigation. He strides on, street by street assessing all the players, considering their involvement– Joseph Manning, John Collver, the elusive Alice Sandon, Olivia Manning and the slippery Richard Collver. Like Jane, those that are lost will be found. He will find Sarah Radbourne and she will reveal her secrets...

...and Prudie...she has a clear motive. Lexden harried her and she was in difficulty in relation to the Manning land. If she is involved in Lexden's murder could it be because she has used the terrible powers Stradsey allocates to her? He doesn't find it easy to agree with the fiery minister and prejudice must not dictate his work. From prejudice come allegations, at worst unsubstantiated, at best circumstantial and there are many able and willing to point the finger. Except Constance Manning, one of the few rational and reliable people in the entire area. Not denouncing Prudie marks her a woman to be admired. Yet Prudie was ungrateful, churlish in her criticism, resurrecting some petty gossip from the past. Why can't she graciously accept support from such a quarter? Grace is not the mark of Prudie. No wonder she's distrusted, reviled, feared even and now living under the same roof. Matthew left strict instructions she was not to leave the house.

"For how long?" Elizabeth asked.

"Until it's safe."

"When is that?"

Matthew hadn't answered. He doesn't know. With Prudie he's pulled in opposite directions as he was with Ezra. Her 'powers' disturb him as much as they do Edmund. Yet how can he dismiss someone who knows about Jane and, despite herself, gives him hope?

He reaches the courtyard. He should announce himself, demand to see Henry, but he hangs back, leaning against the wall opposite the merchant's shop. What if Amberley is here or worse still, Jonathon Ellerton? He retreats back to the alley from where he's unobserved, but can still see the front entrance. He waits a half hour, telling himself he should go in, warning himself he should not, all the time watching the movements at the firm with a wary, cautious eye.

Then, having admonished himself for the seventeenth time and determined to move forward, if only to ease the ache in his leg from remaining in one standing position for too long, Henry comes out. He carries a large bag, probably filled with cloth and makes for the alley. Matthew steps back quickly, turns the corner at the head of the lane and waits in the empty street until Henry emerges. Laden with his heavy bag he doesn't notice Matthew, who steps smartly to his side, taking him by the elbow and forcing him back into the dark alley. Henry drops his bag and leans down to retrieve it, but Matthew pulls him along, out of view of the street.

"My bag, sir," Henry says, pointing to it helplessly.

"It's not going to walk," Matthew says gruffly.

"But it'll be taken, I have important cloths."

"I'll keep you only a moment."

Henry tries to get away.

"Let me be. I told you all you needed to know yesterday. Mr Amberley was..."

"You did not divulge my true identity?" Matthew says, pulling up Henry's collar and glaring less than a breath away into his face.

"No, no," Henry splutters, "though it was difficult..."

"We did not quite conclude our business."

Henry looks forlornly towards his bag and again tries to get away.

"Have a care, sir," Matthew says, "I've no wish to harm you, but if you persist I shall not shirk from my duty."

Not knowing exactly what Matthew's 'duty' entails, Henry relaxes.

"Now, sir, yesterday you were telling me about one of your employers..."

"Mr. Amberley..."

"No, no, the other one, Ellerton..."

"I told you about his misdeeds. I am still working..."

"Yes to be sure and very commendable, but I have another interest, tangential to my enquiries, but essential just the same. He has a daughter, Jane is her name I believe."

Henry looks blank. Matthew tightens the grip on his collar. Henry glances again at the bag, lying conspicuously and vulnerable to any passing rogue. Then he looks back to Matthew.

"Er...well...yes, I have heard...Jane you say...yes, I believe Ellerton has a daughter of that name."

"She lives in London?"

"I believe she does."

"You believe?"

The collar is tightened so much Henry can hardly breathe though he still manages another anxious glance at the bag.

"Yes...yes, she does," he splutters.

"The address?"

"Yes...of course, but first...please, my bag?"

Henry's eyes widen in fearful, yet exasperated pleading.

Matthew glances back and then sighs. He relaxes his grip and releases one hand, which he places on his sword hilt.

"Don't move...or..."

He lets go his other hand and steps to the bag, kicking it into the alley towards Henry.

"Have a care, sir, please..."

Henry bends down and pulls open the bag, checking the contents are unharmed. Matthew leans over him.

"The address, you know the address."

"She lives near Cheapside, a fine place I'm told though I've not myself..."

"The address?" Matthew says, seizing his collar again.

Henry tells him the address, then gets up.

"I must go..."

"On your way," Matthew says, "but I may wish to speak to you again."

"There's just one thing...about Ellerton's daughter..."

"I have what I want, but remember our talk...it's between ourselves."

"Yes, yes of course."

Taking deep breaths as if his lungs need extra filling from sudden emptying, Henry takes his bag and hurries away on his errand. Matthew follows a short distance, then walks towards Cheapside. Those he passes seem peculiarly dull and dishevelled as if stirring from some deep sleep. Only he is fully awake and aware, confident and ready to grasp the promise of the day.

He reaches his destination, but whether from over exertion, the aching wait in the alley or stress from his confrontation with Henry his limp becomes more pronounced. He feels more conspicuous, glancing aggressively at people as if to forestall any unpleasant or mocking remark. No one says or does anything. No one notices, but his unease increases. It's not those immediately around that trouble him, but one he might soon meet. For the last time he saw her was before the battle that turned the sturdy young man into this dragging, slithering figure. He walks with only a slight limp, yet it seems long and deep, his disfigurement shouting to everyone to look, leer and condemn. If she sees him like this, what then, what will she say, what will he do?

168

Henry was right. It's a fine, elegant house just off Cheapside, a fitting residence for a fine lady. He stands close to an alley, where he might easily slip unnoticed from the embarrassed gaze, the patronising look of the beautiful and the godly. He glowers at everyone, imagining them exchanging disdainful comments. Earlier hope and confidence is replaced by fear of recognition as one whose presence is unwelcome, who should not be there. He cowers like a leper, mentally examining not just his injured leg, but every feature and contour of his body, exaggerating and imagining possible imperfections, creating a creature of unbelievable hideousness, which no one, let alone one so pure, so alluring, would wish to cast their eyes.

Then he sees her, stepping into the street in a full, blue dress, frilled and decorated to perfection, setting off her perfect form. Forgetting his stricken shape he moves forward and as the sun catches her auburn hair its sparkle transfixes him. She looks across. She may have seen him, though it seems unlikely in the crowded street and if she does, gives no indication of recognition, still less pleasurable surprise. Then she turns away. What chance he had is gone. Unless he steps out, dragging his debilitated frame, lurching through the crowd and wagons to get closer. What would he say? Can he cope with rejection, worse still the calculated cruelty if she doesn't know him? She's not alone. Another woman is at her side. Then she turns the other way. A man. She smiles. He takes her arm. Of course! The spears of recognition pierce him and the dream, if that's what it's been, is gone. This is what Henry was trying to tell him. Her husband, Daniel Harmsworth. She is Mrs. Harmsworth. *That which was still is.* Prudie's words hammer and crush. How could he be so foolish? *However much you try, through these means she is lost.* Prudie was right. He should have listened to all she said, not a mistake he will make again.

He leaves as they leave, running as best he can towards Cheapside. Then without stopping, all the way back to his sister's house, there to get into his room, wallow in the realisation of his stupidity and avoid everyone, most of all Prudie, the woman who *knew*, but unlike him knew all. Elizabeth calls from the stairs. He doesn't answer. Edmund knocks and calls quietly at the door. He doesn't answer. They will know. That is what makes it so much worse. He listens to street traders and the news cries of a ballad singer. He tries to make out what he says. It'll take his mind away and he ought to keep abreast of the war, but the horn and clapper of another ballad seller drowns out his words. Damn him! Some say there's another battle coming, a great battle, a decisive battle, but a battle in which he'll play no part whatever the outcome. His battle is closer and is one he must fight without weapons, at least not with those made of steel.

He lies helpless and desolate, constantly ploughing the same past, ignoring the present, unable to see any future. It gets darker. Elizabeth calls again. He hardly hears and doesn't answer. She calls again. Eventually he answers, feebly, just loud enough to reassure her. Then he sinks again into that withering, hopeless past, a downward spiral from which he'll not escape until he reaches the bottom. The peel of bells shatters his stupor. He lights a candle and watches the flickering shadows on the wall, mocking, challenging. Gradually the sounds of the streets intrude, clattering carts, water carriers on the cobbles, dogs howling and hundreds of people talking and shouting. A woman in the next house hurls abuse at a man in the street. He answers vociferously. Matthew strains to make it out, but it's a senseless babble. His nostrils quiver with the smell of hundreds of fires. The city is lumbering into the evening.

It's time he too stirred. He goes to the window, watching and listening to the quivering, burbling city. Some men turn the corner and the relative quiet is shattered as the noise and bustle returns. It will be like this until the curfew's imposed peace takes over, but the dawn will herald the start of another raucous day. He has to meet Hugh at the Falcon. If he's found anything important he'll come to the house and he doesn't want him here. Prudie is here. Prudie who knows, Prudie who gave the warning he chose to ignore. He should heed that warning now and return to life. Hugh may have news of Sarah Radbourne. Whatever, it'll bring him back to his own realities, his own war, fighting to bring to justice the criminals who fight Parliament behind its lines.

He says little to Elizabeth and Edmund, except to apologise for being 'unresponsive' and rejects a meal.

"I may get something at the Falcon. I may not."

The place is noisy and busy. He waits for an hour unobserved in his corner, imagining the world is watching as if he's the bear in the pit. He tries not to think of Jane and Henry and Prudie. He's ashamed. He rejected Prudie's advice and was unnecessarily harsh with Henry. He squeezes past the crush to the bar. The landlord has neither seen nor heard of Hugh.

"Will you wait for him a little longer?"

"No," Matthew says, "I've tarried long enough."

He goes to Hugh's lodgings. His landlady is alarmed by his visit.

"Another officer? You have news of the young man?"

"No, madam I have not. I was hoping he would be here or you could direct me to him."

"I've not seen him since yesterday and he didn't say where he was going."

It seems Lieutenant Crittenden has disappeared.

8

FRIENDS are always wiser in their absence. Though he's been missing for only one full day, already Hugh's words assume renewed significance. He'd talked of a Royalist conspiracy, but London is constantly rife with rumours of Royalist plots. Matthew saw no reason to take this one any more seriously than all the others and rebuked Hugh when he said they should pursue Richard Collver. He'd also been concerned at Matthew's meeting with Henry Collver. What if there really is a serious Royalist threat in the city with the Collvers at the heart of it? It may not be the only thing Hugh is right about. While Matthew can't accept Hugh's febrile anxiety with witchcraft, he may not be wrong about Prudie. Her 'extrasensory' knowledge is disturbing, though not through any infernal associations. What if she too is part of the conspiracy? Knowledge of their opposition, including personal details of potential investigators like Matthew will be vital. Was Lexden's fate sealed when he uncovered the Royalist plot and was about to reveal it? He may have seriously compromised his investigation by allowing Elizabeth to hide her. She might even be involved in Hugh's disappearance.

Matthew has returned to the 'Falcon' several times today, but Hugh has been neither seen nor heard. After a further enquiry this evening, he sits in the 'Jackdaw' waiting for Ezra. Is Hugh right about him too? He may be a useful entry to the underbelly of London, but surely a disgraced deserter, accused of murder should be handed over to the authorities? Already it could be too late. Questions would be asked – why has he waited so long to bring corporal Stanfield to book?

"Deep in thought?"

Matthew turns round sharply. The tavern is busy, but he sees no one who might have spoken.

"What is it that troubles you?"

Now he recognises the voice. He leans forward, turns to the back of the settle and grabs a hand. There's a slight gasp of pain as Matthew's grip tightens.

"Alright, alright! You have me."

Matthew slackens and releases his grip. Ezra emerges from behind the settle and settles down opposite.

"How long have you been there?"

"Long enough to spy you."

"I expected you a half hour ago."

"So might others," Ezra says, glancing around, "You can never be too careful."

"Next time you might let me in on your spying activities," Matthew says grumpily, emptying his tankard.

He pushes it over with a nod. Ezra goes to refill it, exchanging comments with a few companions on the way.

"I hope you learnt something useful," Matthew says on his return.

"A few things. Old Sam, he said..."

"Has anyone seen Hugh?"

Ezra sighs and shakes his head.

"Damn, damn, damn! Where is he?"

"London's a big place. Have you been...?"

"Yes, yes, I've been back to the Falcon."

"Perhaps he had reason..."

"He was instructed."

Ezra smiles. He doesn't share Matthew's respect for the military hierarchy.

"That might not stop him."

"He is an officer!"

"Like he was in Harringstead?"

"That was...unfortunate...this is different."

Matthew swigs deeply, draining half the tankard.

"I have other news," Ezra says.

"Sarah Radbourne?" Matthew says hopefully.

Ezra shakes his head.

"Hugh Crittenden talked about a Royalist plot."

"Not that again, don't tell me there's truth in it?"

"There's some truth in all such rumours. The city is alive with suspicions and wild agitation, but this one...you mentioned a Richard Collver?"

"He's in London?"

"He was."

Matthew throws up his hands.

"Not another false..."

"Quiet!" Ezra says, putting his hand over Matthew's mouth as several men look round, "Every place has its share of unwelcome listeners."

Matthew shrinks back on the settle, saying diffidently, almost dreamily, "It's all this looking...things half forgotten... almost totally given up."

Ezra shakes his head in half understanding and continues.

"I don't know whether he's involved in a Royalist plot or he's just mixed up, lovelorn or whatever else and I don't really care, but you seem to..."

"Get on with it!" Matthew snaps.

"Word is he's run away to join a band of clubmen. Local men who resist being drafted into the army."

"Yes, I know what they are. Frustrating Parliament's cause, supporters of the King."

"They resist the King's men too. A sort of third force, saying they are neutral in the war."

Matthew splutters into his beer.

"Anyone that's not with Parliament is against Parliament and therefore an enemy of..."

"Matthew, I'm just telling you how it is. If you don't want to know then I'll stop..."

"Where are these clubmen?"

"There are bands across the whole of southern England. They're particularly strong in the west, but Richard Collver is somewhere in west Surrey or Hampshire with a group led by a man called Nathaniel Buckden."

"And this Buckden has not been apprehended?"

"That's the whole point, Matthew, he can't be apprehended, he and his group are too powerful or at least independent."

"By Jesu, if I was there...!"

"But you're not, which is probably..."

"I shall go."

"To the clubmen?"

"Hugh has disappeared, matters in Harringstead are stalled, enquiries in London lead up blind alleys, I can't find Sarah Radbourne or...well, never mind...at least this promises some possible progress. I shall go to Surrey or Hampshire or Wiltshire or Dorset or Devon or wherever."

"Matthew, are you sure this is wise? If you stay..."

"If you don't think it's wise, why did you tell me?"

"Because I tell you everything (Matthew raises his eyebrows dubiously)...well, everything that could be useful."

"How can I find this Buckden?"

"I've not got the exact location. Clubmen are avoiding enlistment in the army, so they keep their activities as secret as possible. That makes it difficult."

"But you've got this information from a reliable source?"

"Well, I suppose..."

"And you have other contacts. Things can be found out?"

"Well, it's not always..."

"Good."

Prudie spends most of her time in the back room of the house, frequently taking her meals there even though Elizabeth constantly invites her to join her and Edmund. She's not ungrateful to her hosts. It's not their company that troubles her, but her own. 'Feelings' have been growing since she arrived in London. Unpleasant recollections of those left behind, those that frustrated her, those that angered her, those that made her fearful. When the memories can't be silenced she concentrates on her friends, Alice and the others as a mental counter weight. It works for a time. Then she remembers Constance, who never condemned her, sometimes defended her against Stradsey and helped her get away. Constance Manning is rare – honest in speech as mind. One day Prudie may have to pay back her kindness.

Elizabeth wonders if she's still wary of Matthew, but Prudie denies it. His recent defence of her was certainly surprising. In fact Prudie's 'feelings' coalesce more and more on Matthew and she can't shake them off. Unable to contain her forebodings any longer she emerges from the back room. Edmund is out and Elizabeth welcomes her. Perhaps in female company Prudie will open up. She does, but not as Elizabeth expects.

"Guard your brother well, Elizabeth, he is very vulnerable."

Elizabeth's first reaction is to laugh, but she stops at a wide smirk on seeing Prudie's earnestness.

"Matthew is a soldier," she says, "admittedly he was wounded at Cropredy Bridge, but even so..."

"It matters nothing," Prudie says dolefully, "soldiers are no more protected from the dark forces than anyone else."

Elizabeth is still ready to laugh, but stops herself.

"Matthew is in no more danger than anyone else in these troubled times. London can be treacherous, but Matthew knows his way around."

But Prudie is obdurate and isn't laughing.

"He is in immediate and considerable danger."

She folds her arms and pouts her lips with studied emphasis. Elizabeth says Prudie's misgivings are understandable, having just come up from the country and warding off false accusations of...she hesitates before whispering...witchcraft. Prudie winces, the word reprises her dark thoughts. Elizabeth talks about trivial matters. Prudie says nothing, then retreats to the back room just before Edmund returns.

"Prudie believes Matthew is in great danger," Elizabeth says.

"From what?"

"She didn't...or couldn't say. She just *knows!*"

Edmund puffs sniffily.

"She was very convinced. Sometimes it's enough just to *feel*. We must warn Matthew."

"But he's gone."

"You must go to that tavern – the 'Jackdaw' – and see Ezra."

Prudie has heard everything. When Elizabeth goes into the back room a half hour later she's gone. They search the streets, but cannot find her.

Matthew has been moving west from village to village for three days, constantly balancing between saying too much and saying too little. In the long solitary hours he ponders his position. The war at a crucial stage, while he chases a renegade wastrel in a whole company of wastrels. If survival and victory were the only things to exercise his mind, not this persistent scurrying after shadows, constantly subverted, never able to identify the subverter! Ezra's information is accurate as far as it goes –about as far as the longest reach of the clubmen. Asking, even tactfully for Nathaniel Buckden is answered by blank, suspicious looks, which may not be so blank, sending alarm signals in advance. Then near the Hampshire border a man at an inn takes him aside when Buckden's name is mentioned.

"Speak softly, sir. This is not a place yet touched by the need to resist."

The man's eyes, brown, deep, unresponsive fix him coldly, his jaw set resolutely, disturbingly firm, his beard wildly hiding any meaningful expression.

"They may not come here."

"*They?*" Matthew says.

The man says nothing.

"The King's troops?" Matthew probes.

"Either. Two sides scouring England like competing ploughboys destroying the field they intend to clear. Where did you hear of Buckden?"

"In London."

The man grimaces.

"Then the word spreads far."

"Can you tell me where...?"

The man eyes him suspiciously.

"You could be setting a trap. Are you...have you been a soldier?"

"Yes."

"Which side?"

"How should that matter, aren't they both unskilled ploughboys ripping up the same field?"

The faintest glimmer of a smile.

"What is your business with Buckden? You would not come all this way to escape enlistment."

"I am looking for somebody."

"Who?"

"That is a matter between myself and Buckden."

The faint smile disappears.

"I will trust you...a little. I will tell you where to go and whom to ask for."

"Buckden?"

"If you are to be trusted you may find him."

So the disappointment continues. He has to keep moving, asking a succession of varyingly reliable informants, always hoping he's getting that bit closer to Buckden. In one village he's rebuffed. His contact has no idea of Buckden or his group, but he does know someone who just might...At another he's sent on after fielding the same litany of ridiculous questions, false trails and obstructions. Is it a crime to be a soldier in this tangled land? Is there an unseen hand guiding these disparate irritations, the hand of Nathaniel Buckden? Patience is at it's thinnest the closer to the goal. He's now much further west, in country resisting either of the 'ploughboys.'

A man at an inn gives further vague directions including the need to 'speak to another.' He's anxious to be away, but Matthew, skilled in London alleyways, follows unobserved. The man stops to speak to two others. They exchange idle comments on absent friends and acquaintances. Matthew slides silently behind a low wall, listening for any mention of Buckden or the clubmen, but the conversation never rises above this mundane level. As they part Matthew creeps further along the wall. He glances back. The other two men are out of earshot. As the man reaches him Matthew jumps up, pulls one of his arms behind his back and grips his neck firmly, a knife at his throat. Gasping and spluttering, the man turns just slightly to recognise his assailant.

"Now sir," Matthew says quietly in his ear, "No trifling tricks. Answer me honestly and no harm will befall you. Your name, sir?"

"Caleb."

"More distractions and pettifogging hindrances, Caleb and I'll slit your throat."

"What do you want?"

"Buckden."

"I've already told you. Tomorrow..."

"I can't wait until tomorrow. You will take me to Buckden now."

"I can't do that."

Matthew tightens his grip and eases the edge of the knife on Caleb's skin.

"Then make your peace with God and take your last breath!"

"Alright, alright," Caleb moans, almost unable to speak, "If you would..."

Matthew releases the pressure on his neck and retracts the blade slightly.

"Speak then."

"It is possible in the morning..."

"Not in the morning. Tonight."

"But in the dark..."

"We will surprise them."

"But without the light...We will have to walk across the hills."

Matthew takes the knife from the man's belt and draws his own sword.

"Then lead on...and any stupidity and I'll run you through."

"You are a soldier?" Caleb says, looking nervously at the sword.

"I have used this before and I can use it again."

"But my wife, she'll not know where I am. I must..."

"No time for that. She will think you've been carousing at the inn."

"She will worry. In the morning..."

"In the morning you will return to her safely...if you take me to Buckden."

So the long trudge across the hills and through the woods begins. It seems a convoluted, circuitous course and several times Matthew queries whether this is necessary or wise.

"Lead me into a trap and you'll not long live to rue the day. I'll be quick to despatch you, if you try to trick me."

"This is no trick," Caleb says, conscious Matthew is never more than a sword's thrust behind him, "We must go where we will be least seen."

Matthew grunts disapprovingly, though he also wearies. His leg troubles him though in the darkness Caleb cannot see his limp. Just before dawn they emerge from a copse and Caleb stops.

"What's this...?" Matthew begins.

Caleb turns round nervously.

"Quiet, sir, please. We must wait for..."

A low whistle is heard. Caleb cups his hand and answers the call. Matthew stands behind, the tip of his sword at Caleb's back as he turns from side to side, looking and listening. Then he glances back into the trees. It's too dark to see anything. Suddenly Matthew feels very vulnerable. The whistle comes again. Caleb answers. Then a voice, soft, but piercing.

"Who comes?"

"Friend," Caleb replies.

"What friend?"

"One who seeks."

"What does he seek?"

"Truth."

"Come friend."

Caleb motions to Matthew and they move forward. The exchange allows them access, but Matthew remains alert. Caleb's answers might signal he's not alone. It could be a trap.

"Stay close," Matthew whispers.

They come to another copse.

"Where is he?" Matthew says suspiciously, looking to his back.

"He will..."

Then behind he hears the crunch on the grass and turns, pulling Caleb in front and raising his sword to his throat.

"Stay where you are! If you try to take me this man is dead!"

"Who is this, Caleb?" the newcomer says, a tall, heavy man with a wide brimmed hat pulled over his eyes.

Caleb opens his mouth, but Matthew speaks for himself.

"Captain Matthew Fletcher. Take me to Nathaniel Buckden."

"Is this the man we are expecting?" wide brimmed says.

Caleb nods.

"You are alone?" wide brimmed says, keeping the hat well down.

Caleb nods again.

"I am Edward Pearson. If you let Caleb go I will take you to Nathaniel."

Matthew releases his grip, but continues to hold Caleb by the shoulder, with his sword pointed at him.

"I meant let him go!" Edward bellows, "He has brought you here, that is enough, let him return to his home."

Edward is a big man. He has a long thick coat, beneath which he probably conceals a weapon. Matthew knows little of these clubmen, but to resist the forces of either armies they must be hard and ruthless. Edward comes closer, though out of Matthew's immediate reach. Reluctantly, Matthew lets Caleb go. He steps quickly away, thanks Edward and disappears into the trees.

"Come," Edward says, waving Matthew forward onto the path, then pointing to the sword, "and put that thing away."

"We'll walk together," Matthew says, replacing the sword and stepping alongside.

Edward chuckles. They walk on in silence until the sun is up and they reach more woodland. Edward stops and pulls a long scarf from one of his deep pockets.

"You will have to trust me from here on, captain. You may be a stranger in these parts, but probably have a good memory and I cannot allow you to know the way. It is only a short distance to our encampment."

He stretches the scarf tightly between his hands. Matthew hesitates. Must he continue as defenceless as a babe? Edward reads his mind.

"You can always return, but if you wish to see Nathaniel..."

"As far as your camp?"

Edward nods.

"No further."

"Very well."

Edward ties the scarf across Matthew's eyes, securing it firmly at the back of his head. Matthew keeps his hand on his sword hilt as he's led on, but blindfolded it'll give little protection. He crunches and staggers along, every yank from Edward, every bump into a tree, every lurch into a bush exacerbating his gloomy thoughts as he expects to be cut down any moment. If he's to be prodded and hoodwinked by these bumpkins he'll not make the same mistake again. As soon as he's free he'll assert himself...if he gets free again.

Twenty minutes later Edward removes the scarf. There's enough light now to make out a large clearing surrounded by several wooden huts. A half dozen men stand beside them, one in front of the others with folded arms, staring intently at the new arrival. Like Edward he has a wide brimmed hat, but unlike him doesn't use it to screen his eyes and hide his face. His lower lip protrudes slightly from the upper, giving his closed mouth a petulant sneer. He doesn't move, as if his arms are permanently fixed to his chest. This has to be Nathaniel Buckden.

"Matthew Fletcher," Edward says, "Caleb brought him"

Buckden's eyes stir slightly from Matthew to Edward.

"He was forced to bring him," Edward replies to the silent question, "I sent Caleb home."

"You've disturbed the morning, Mr. Fletcher," Buckden says gravely, "It was not intended you would be seen until tomorrow."

"You are Nathaniel Buckden?" Matthew says.

Buckden lowers his head very slightly in a single nod, otherwise remaining unmoved, arms folded, hard eyes, resolute mouth and jaw firmly set. Matthew steps forward, counting and carefully assessing the men around him, wondering if there are others unseen. This hideaway is probably unknown and the band is not used to interlopers.

With their pathetically clandestine preparations with folded scarves and passwords they will be unprepared for a professional incursion.

"Once a soldier?" Buckden says.

"Yes."

No one moves as Matthew continues walking forward.

"I cannot believe you want to join with clubmen?"

"Not join, but take away."

Matthew is very close now and belligerently returns Buckden's grim stare. Buckden emits a short, deep sound, something between a chuckle and a whine.

"Others have tried to take..."

Buckden's words are cut short as Matthew leaps onto him.

"Where is Richard Collver?"

Matthew pulls at Buckden's collar, but the man's apparent slothfulness is illusory and stepping neatly to one side he unbalances his attacker. Half falling from the rush of his own momentum Matthew only just keeps his balance before turning and drawing his sword, but he has misjudged his adversaries. Two men jump from behind Buckden, kick away his weapon and force him to the ground. Matthew unsteadies one, but a third pins his legs and arms. Eventually he stops struggling and is turned over to face Buckden.

"Who is this Richard Collver?" Buckden says, responding to Matthew's question as if nothing has happened.

Matthew gets up. The three men still hold him, but Buckden gestures them to loosen their grip.

"He is wanted for questioning."

"What is your special interest?"

"I am investigating a murder, the steward of one of his father's neighbours."

"And how is this...Collver...involved?"

"There's a history of bad relations between his family and that of the steward's employer and also young Richard and the daughter..."

Matthew steps closer. Buckden waves the men aside.

"You are impetuous and must guard your temper. Any more and I shall be less tolerant. You took a risk coming here."

"Anywhere in England is a risk. This is no more nor less risky."

"The country is caught between two armies and you are now held by a third force that owes loyalty to neither."

"I'll take my chances. I'm not caught between two armies, but loyal only to one."

"Which makes you dangerous to us."

"I think you've amply demonstrated how limited a threat I am," Matthew says, rubbing his shoulder, "Besides, you've not disarmed me."

"Do I need to?"

"I am a soldier."

"Were surely? You didn't get that leg playing skittles."

"Cropredy Bridge," Matthew mutters, stroking the side of his left leg, "and I am still a soldier, assigned to this investigation."

Buckden's lips part slightly, though his eyes like the rest of his body remain fixed.

"But not necessarily to your liking."

Matthew looks into the deep, unflinching eyes with some nervousness. He's underestimated Buckden.

"The war has altered you on the outside," Buckden continues, "It's less easy to see the changes inside."

"At least I have an inside, a conscience, principles and loyalty to..." Mathew says aggressively.

"...to the Parliament?"

"Yes."

"And where has it got you, captain?"

"It hasn't got me anywhere. If we're not prepared to fight for our freedoms we will quickly lose them."

"The freedom for marauding soldiers to rampage across our land."

"There have been oppressive impositions, gross destruction. In Brentford the Prince's troops..."

"The King's men say the same!" Buckden bellows, "Do you really believe thieving and worse is restricted to one side? Why else do you think we armed ourselves to resist?"

"We must stand up for what is right."

"So we should. Some say this is a war without an enemy. Truer to say it's a war with too many enemies."

"The only enemies are those that stand in the way of the people's freedom."

"The freedom of the Parliamentary army to encroach on our land, take our crops, our stock, press our men."

"I have already told you if true men..."

"True men, true men! How many times I have heard that. True men go to fight wars, damaged but wiser men come back. There are those that went to fight in the German wars with all the cruelties they saw there."

"This is England!"

"Oh aye, aye and we do things differently here."

"Yes we do."

Buckden's granite features ease slightly, though his hard, firm skin seems more likely to crack than relax.

"You are a passionate man, sir and I have no doubt you entered this war full of high ideals, but..."

"Do not mock me, sir," Matthew says coldly.

"I never mock," Buckden says, a little hurt, "I say what I see and what I see now is not the same man who first enlisted."

"I have not deviated in three years. When the King comes to his senses..."

"...or when Parliament come to theirs – that's how the other side see it."

"I'm not interested in the other side."

"But I am. We've had to be interested in both sides."

"Yes, yes, I am sympathetic," Matthew says angrily, "but we must all move on. Things have changed..."

"Aye, we've all changed. Some yearn for peace at any price. Some – maybe you are one – have become more... enthusiastic, while others are merely mad."

"I've told you. If the King..."

"Yes, you've told me, captain, but what you believe isn't what is. I've seen many who..."

"I've not come to be lectured by rustic adventurers, skulking in the woods!" Matthew explodes.

Buckden's grim expression turns even craggier as his voice rises higher, the lines on his face deepening and hardening.

"We do not skulk! Secrecy is our protection, but our men are spread across the country. We can have hundreds in the field in an hour."

"You make it sound like an army."

"It is an army, the clubmen's army."

"Have a care, sir. Other clubmen throughout the west have been attacked by generals Cromwell and Fairfax."

"I'm not easily threatened, captain. Cromwell and Fairfax are far from here. In the midlands I'm told on good authority."

"I say nothing *easily*, sir. If I intended a threat it would not be couched in the guise of men a hundred miles away."

"So you say, but I will not be intimidated!"

"And neither will I!"

So begins a fierce exchange, neither giving the other the chance to respond before launching into further invective. Each man attacking not what the other says, but what he believes he represents. To Matthew Buckden is the mindless neutral, prompted by narrow self interest rather than principle. To Buckden Matthew is the indiscriminate belligerent, pursuing his perverted cause whatever the consequences. Both are right and both are wrong, right about themselves and wrong about their adversary. Several times the other men draw closer, expecting the verbal onslaught to slew into real assault, though Buckden continually waves them away. Then, tiring of the futile slugging, Buckden draws back and allows two men to take up positions beside Matthew.

"You have been here long enough, captain, it is time to leave."

Matthew's hand instinctively moves to his side, but there it hovers. The men too make no further move, waiting for Buckden's orders.

"I am only interested in finding real villains," Matthew says.

"Does that involve arresting this Richard Collver?" Buckden says.

"Only if he is culpable and even then he will be entitled to a fair trial."

"You will be taken back the way you came. That means the blindfold again," Buckden says, facing Matthew again in his stiff, inscrutable way, raising his hand, but his face and eyes remain unmoved as Matthew is about to speak, "You will return to the inn. You will be contacted."

"And Richard Collver...?"

"Patience, captain."

"How long must I wait?"

"Soon. You will be alone when we meet again."

Not you *must* be alone, but you *will* be alone, not a request, not even a threat, but a prediction. For the first time Matthew is a little afraid.

Edward leads him back. It seems a shorter journey over the hills, but Matthew is less assured, more wary. In the darkness of the blindfold and the blundering collision with trees and bushes the dour clubman's grim features and unyielding determination flit across his mind. Matthew may have been lucky to get away this time. If the next meeting is unsuccessful, he'll not get another chance.

With the slightly slouching gait and the suspicious eyes darting in every direction, quickly taking in everyone, Prudie knows Ezra as soon as he comes through the door of the 'Jackdaw.' He banters with many, but is actually loading up the latest intelligence to be used for later advantage. He glances rapidly and furtively in her direction and she tries to crouch in the corner, but he notices her immediately and gradually gets closer, eventually sitting at a table opposite. After a few minutes he comes over.

"I have not seen you here before," he says, leaning over.

"Sit down, Ezra Stanfield and we can talk," she says quietly.

"You know me?" he says, sitting down and glancing uneasily around.

"We have a mutual acquaintance, Matthew Fletcher. I am Prudie Westrup, I have been staying with Matthew's sister."

"The woman from Harringstead," he says suspiciously, "You are a..."

"I need to know what Matthew has been working on in London."

This makes Ezra even more suspicious.

"And why would you need to know that?"

"Because he is in immediate and serious danger. He must be warned."

"How would I be able to help?"

"You know where he is, what he's been doing."

"I don't like being used."

"You've been used before."

"Aye, too much for comfort!" Ezra chuckles disdainfully, but keeping a wary eye on her.

"Accusations were made against you in the army."

"How did you...?"

"...I have a name...Fel...Fan...Fen...?"

"Fenwick," Ezra says with dismal incredulity, "Henry Fenwick. How did you know...only Matthew...no, he wouldn't tell you."

"He's told me nothing. I have the gift. I can see the future in men's faces. I see the past in yours."

Ezra is stupefied and not a little afraid. He leans back, looks about him. Satisfied no on has heard let alone has any interest, he regains some confidence.

"It's true then, what Mathew was told...you *are* a witch!"

Prudie snaps her fingers into Ezra's face. He jumps back instinctively. She laughs.

"What did you expect, to be turned into a toad?"

"This is no matter for jesting, woman!"

"Then stop insulting me. You of all men should desist from false accusations."

"How do I know it's false?"

She laughs again.

"If I am a witch I could do you great harm, so you better cooperate and tell me what I want to know. If I am not a witch then you have nothing to fear, but should help me anyway."

If this woman is a witch she's either very clever or very stupid, coming into a tavern where she could be arrested. If she's not a witch then her skills could be of immense value to Matthew and himself.

"Matthew was enquiring into the Collvers before he left London...(Prudie's sudden intake of breath alerts him)...you know these people?"

"They have property in Harringstead."

"He is after Richard Collver."

"He's gone back to Harringstead?"

"No, to Surrey, where he believes Richard Collver has gone."

"He must be warned. Is it possible to get word to him?"

Ezra is doubtful. Can he trust her?

"There may not be much time," she says, "If you do not act...even if you do...there will be a death...soon."

Still he hesitates.

"Ezra!" Prudie hisses.

"You will not go after him?"

"No, I must return to Harringstead."

Reassured, he says, "I have my contacts, I will pass on what you say."

Leaving London is not as easy as Prudie envisages and she has reason to regret not allowing Ezra to accompany her. A woman alone at night on the streets may invite misunderstandings, not helped by her unkempt appearance and rakish hat. She's accosted several times and just as she manages to get away from the unwanted attentions of lascivious drunks she's stopped by two men of the watch, demanding to know where's she's been, where she's going, what is her business. She evades their questioning as best she can, avoiding any mention of the 'Jackdaw,' finally asking the way to Ludgate, implying she has been going in the wrong direction. One laughs and gently turns her around, but the other is unsure.

"You would do well to ply your trade elsewhere, strumpet."

"I am no strumpet," Prudie retorts sternly, jabbing him hard in the chest.

He makes to move, but his companion stops him.

"Hold fast, Ephraim and let the woman on her way!"

Ephraim is not easily persuaded, referring to 'ungodly persons' and 'disreputable women,' but eventually relents and Prudie is allowed to go. She runs towards Ludgate, but in the darkened streets this only makes her more conspicuous, a target for any opportunist luster. She gets lost and trying to find her way is suddenly accosted at the corner of a narrow alley by a foul smelling beery reprobate. Ogling with his small, piercing eyes he lurches closer.

"Now my inviting little duck, where might you be a waddling to?"

"Get out of my way, wretch," she says, pushing him aside as she catches his breath.

"Now my pretty, that's no way to talk, you and me can..."

He grabs her round the waist and leans into her, his bristle brushing her face. She pulls back, but he holds on. She lifts her knee and kicks hard into his groin. He shrieks in pain and staggers back. She turns and runs, but hears his footsteps and looks back. Although disabled he's not as drunk as he appears and staggers behind. At the next corner she hurtles into a darkening alley and realises this may not be the best way back to the main highway. The alley is a blind one. There's no way out, while the slithering and wheezing from the blackness tell her she's not alone. Then she's assailed by his loathsome odour. He chuckles ominously and she turns back despairingly to the wall. She can see almost nothing in the darkness, so reaches up desperately and stretching her arms feels the top. He's almost upon her. She grabs the edge and pushes her feet, then slides her elbows painfully up.

"Gotcha!"

He grabs her feet and starts to pull her back, but scraping her hands painfully over the other side she hauls up further and kicks out violently. There's a sharp crack and a dull thud, then no other sound. She must have knocked him out with a fortuitous boot in the jaw! She slides down the other side, her hands and arms cut and bleeding, landing in a yard. There are sounds from within. She may have escaped one unwelcome attention only to be trapped by another. She edges along the wall until she sees a dim, narrow light from a door. She steps towards it and enters a long, cramped alleyway between the buildings.

"Who's there?" someone shouts from the house.

She picks up her feet. They scrape noisily against the inner wall.

"Someone's in the alley!"

"Who is it, who's there?"

Footsteps.

"You there, stop!"

She runs, trips, almost falls down, then reaches the street and runs even faster, splashing through the mud and filth in the gutter. She doesn't care, she's away! The footsteps recede. They've given up. Yet her troubles aren't over. A few streets further she meets two more of the watch. Her replies are evasive and they're not satisfied. The truth or even a modified version will only increase her peril. There seems no alternative. She'll have to play to the role others have already cast her.

"Haven't you men got better things to do than interfere with a woman trying to earn a living at night?" she says, leering seductively, "Unless you're looking for services yourself."

One gets closer, the other also showing interest as he stands behind. She glances quickly around. No one. Now or never. She lets him get as close as the lecher in the alley and then strikes out again in the same way. As he reels back, pushing against the other she turns and runs, faster and faster, not daring to look back. Get out of this damnable city!

It's a long cold night, but she keeps on, sleeping occasionally under bushes and stars until either real or imagined pursuers provoke her to go on again, gradually closing the miles across the county until the following day she's back in Harringstead. Reluctant to be seen, she keeps to the hedges and ditches the first day and the thicket the first night, unsure whom to contact or whether to show herself at all. Alice and the others may be watched. Constance told her not to trust anyone. That probably includes Matthew. She doesn't feel safe in the village, but there are things she must resolve. On the second night having seen smoke rising from the chimney of her own place she hides in the wood. Who is there, Manning, Collver? She scrabbles in her bag for clothes even rougher than those she's walked from London in and smears her hands and face to make it look she's been on the road even longer. The superficial disguise will have to be filled out by her behaviour and speech. People concentrate so much on what's different they can't see or hear what's the same. She walks back to the cottage, but near the door the exhaustion from days of running and hiding at last catches up and she stumbles, falling painfully on the hard stones. She cries out sharply, then lands on her face before passing out.

She comes round to see her own familiar roof. Two men and a woman stand near the fire. She turns uncomfortably to face a second woman sitting beside her, with bright blue eyes, but betraying care at their edges.

"Feeling better?"

Prudie manages only a dull groan from her parched throat. The woman assumes she's injured and calls the others. She's pulled up firmly, but gently. She levers them aside, swings her legs over the edge of the rough table on which they've lain her and rubs her eyes.

"I'm...I'm...alright."

"We found you outside, you must have fallen down," the woman says and then examining Prudie's arm, "you must have gone with a clatter, all these scratches."

"No...no," Prudie says, pulling her arm away, "they're not now, they're...another time."

"I'm Bridget," the woman says, "and this is Annie and Arthur and William."

"I'm Pru...P...P...Penny. I'm Penny."

"Been on the road long, Penny?" Bridget says, "You're worn out, anyone can see. A traveller like us, where are you from?"

Prudie is almost tempted to say who she really is and these 'travellers' are squatting in her house, but holds back.

"I've come from London."

"Then you're to be admired," Arthur says, "for it's a place of tinkling sinfulness."

"But you're a country woman," Annie says, "I can tell."

"I had...there were things I had to do in London," Prudie says, trying to disguise her 'rustic' accent, then changing the subject, "There is a fire, but I feel the walls are cold. You have not been here long."

"We've been working locally," William says, "No one was here so we thought they wouldn't mind."

"They?"

"The troubled soul or souls that left so suddenly," Annie says.

"You know...them?" Prudie says, staring inquiringly into her eyes.

"I feel," Annie says, "as you feel the walls."

"There was no lock on the door," William says.

No lock on the door! Had she left in such a hurry? She doesn't even know where the key is. Maybe with Alice. Why didn't Alice lock the door?

"Come near the fire, you need to keep warm," Bridget says.

They huddle together, silent for a time as Prudie scans their faces again. They are young, yet wearied and worn, unsure of themselves, probably more afraid than her of the locals. They talk vaguely of their origins with a woolly reference to being 'displaced.' They've been on the road for months. The war receives the blame though Arthur says 'final reckoning is coming.' From their hands Prudie can see they're used to work, but it's been intermittent and already they're ready to move on.

"Harringstead is a troubled place," Bridget says.

"Why troubled?" Prudie says, affecting total ignorance.

"The people complain of the landlords, the landlords complain of the people."

"...and both seek to oppress the other," William adds.

They recount the latest disturbances. Little has changed, yet the attacks on property have increased in the short time since she left.

"Every day I hear of fences down, crops battered on the other's fields," Arthur says.

"The other's?"

"Manning," William explains.

"You've been working for...?"

"The Collvers," Annie says, "The men in the fields, me and Bridget as milkmaids."

"You must have been lucky," Prudie says, wondering why Collver has this sudden need for more milkmaids.

"Two maids fled, frightened by the things they've seen in the fields," Annie says.

"...or their own notions and those of other foolish persons," Bridget adds scornfully.

The two women revel in repeating the local 'badinage' and 'rude talk' they've picked up from labourers and servants. It's rumoured much of the 'troubles' directed at the Manning lands have been stirred up by John Collver.

"Why would he do that?" Prudie says innocently.

"Soldiers were here. One has gone in pursuit of Collver's son Richard and they say he was put up to it by Manning saying he was a Royalist spy."

"So all these...disturbances...are instigated by Collver to get back at Manning?"

"That's the Manning version," William says doubtfully.

"You don't believe Collver has been provoking Manning's tenants?".

Edward shrugs.

"How are we to know, but people need little provocation. There are troubles all over England. It's fences and hedges behind their grievances. If Collver is stirring the pot, his own pot could boil over for people say he's been enclosing the commons just as much as Manning."

"Ranters and seekers and itinerant preachers have been in the village," Annie says, "Some went into the church on Sunday and harangued the vicar. 'Sons and daughters of Babylon' he called them, but they were not cowed, stamping their feet and calling him a 'poppycock on a stick,' challenging him to 'get down from his wooden box,' but he stayed in the pulpit."

Prudie feigns surprise and shock, suppressing her amusement at reverend Stradsey's discomfiture.

"Not just noise and ballyhoo," Bridget says, "There's real fear of witchcraft."

"Is anyone accused?" Prudie asks cautiously, trying not to appear too concerned.

"It's at fever pitch," Annie says, "We were in the eastern counties a few weeks ago. It's not yet as bad as there, but it's getting worse. It makes you so afraid to walk about, to say or do anything someone might think unusual. No woman is safe from the pointing fingers and vicious tongues. It's one reason we're moving on."

"As strangers we could be easy targets," Bridget says, "So far we may have been lucky. The razor tongued prattlers and accusers seem more concerned with those they know, but if we stay..."

"Who have they accused?"

They turn to her sharply and Prudie immediately regrets her sudden intervention. She may have blown her cover and smiles indulgently.

"I forget," Bridget says, "It's another of the complaints. Whoever they are, they've gone."

"Never a day passes without another argument and another occupation," Annie says, "Always about the land, who should graze their sheep and where, and who should not. So many coming and going, easy to find a place like this, probably left by one of those accused."

Harringstead is more dangerous than Prudie imagined. Manning and Collver have met recently after years of hostility. One of the servants accompanied John Collver to Syme House and this man heard much of their fierce confrontation. Each was the source of the other's troubles. Manning was behind the 'persecution' of Richard Collver while his father was leading the local insurgents instead of standing solidly with his fellow gentry. Now that was compounded by the soldiers having to go in pursuit of Richard, leaving Manning at the mercy of his enemies, whether high born or low. Then the row reverted to the real reason for the meeting, the stinging wound that forced a desperate Collver to approach the home of his ancestral enemy.

"He pleaded with Manning to stop his daughter seeing Collver's son," Annie says.

"But isn't Richard away?" William asks naively.

"He who leaves can return and Collver wants Manning to work with him to put an end to their relationship forever."

"So why did they argue? Surely Manning wouldn't want his daughter attached to a man he considers a Royalist?"

Annie clicks her tongue knowingly.

"Perhaps Manning hates Collver more than he hates his daughter's relationship. Perhaps he can't bring himself to agree with Collver about anything. After all, Collver said

Manning embraced fiendish antichrist and his religion was based on the An...An...Ana...Anabap...Anabaptists...or some such thing."

"Then Manning reminded him this was not the first time Richard had disappeared," Bridget continues, "He went away when the war began. There were rumours then he'd joined the King."

"Collver rushed out saying something about a mysterious death in London."

No more is said because no more is known, but it unnerves Prudie. Manning and Collver are wrong about each other, but how much trust can she put in the one sided account the Collver servants report or have been deliberately told? And what is this about a death in London? Prudie must get to people closer to Syme House. She may need to speak to Constance. She takes little interest in the rest of the conversation. She is tired and despite its discomfort sleeps soundly on the bench at the side of the fire.

The following morning the four pack their few possessions and are ready to go. William and Arthur are neutral. There's still work in the area, but Bridget and Annie are adamant. A whirlwind is coming and they have no wish to be swept up in it. They offer to take Prudie with them, but she politely declines.

"I must see what the village offers," she says mysteriously.

"It may offer more than you desire and less than is safe," Bridget says, "particularly for a woman who is...I mean..."

"...who is older?" Prudie says, smiling, "Old enough to know my limitations and young enough to keep safe."

Prudie waits until they disappear through the trees before she steps out boldly, but warily, unsure what she may find in Harringstead. She passes along the edge of Long Baulk field and sees no one. Then as she turns towards the village, someone calls out.

"Prudie Westrup! Stay where you are, witch!"

She turns to see a group of men in the distance, at their head Joseph Manning.

9

'RETURN to London. Do not delay' is Ezra's message. Would a delay of a few hours, even a day matter? Everything is prepared for Matthew's meeting with Buckden, but those words keep returning. *Do not delay.* Sending a message at all is risky enough. Ezra would only do it if was vitally necessary. Return to London for what? Something he couldn't risk divulging. Giving out details to people he couldn't possibly know would be too much. *Do not delay.* Ezra won't exaggerate danger, but neither will he understate it. If he says Matthew shouldn't delay, then that's what it means. *Any* delay is too long. He has to leave immediately.

After only five miles he gets uneasy, not about returning, but of what he's left behind and not just about the unfinished search for Richard Collver. Having gone to so much trouble to find Buckden, his failure to meet him as agreed will not go unnoticed. It preys on his mind, but he's not tempted to turn back. Ignoring what lies in London may be much worse than the danger of annoying Buckden. Besides, he knows he's being followed. He sees nothing, hears nothing, but knows one or more lurking between the trees or lying just beyond the fields. Another fifteen miles he catches his first glimpse of a possible pursuer. Stopping on a hill and looking across the valley he sees a lone rider, with a second not far behind. They stop where two tracks diverge, briefly conferring, pointing to the ground, then take the track Matthew has followed. He descends the other side of the hill, reaches a stream, dismounts and leads his horse, sloshing through the water some distance before emerging on the same bank. Then he rides up the hill, back where he's just come, close, parallel and hopefully unnoticed by those that follow. The ruse is successful and he finds another way from the hill, emerging onto an open road. After a further five miles he comes to an inn. Seeing no one suspicious, it seems a safe place to stay for the night.

After stabling his horse he returns to the front, but hangs back on seeing a slight, youngish man with a stooping gait, his hat pulled well down over his face. The man turns to him. Matthew readies himself, but keeps walking. The man watches for a few strides, noticing Matthew's limp, always more pronounced for a while after a time in the saddle and well justifying General Skippon's reluctance to let him return to service.

"Matthew Fletcher?" he calls quietly.

Matthew stops.

"Who wants to know?"

"I am Jacob Anstley. I have a message for you, passed from man to man along the road from London to those that might see you."

"How do you know me?"

"By your walk from one who knows you well. You know the name of a corporal?"

"Ezra, Ezra Stanfield."

"Then by your answer I truly know it is you, captain."

Anstley looks around anxiously.

"I must soon be gone."

"Your message?" Matthew says.

"When you return to London, do not go home."

"Why not?"

"I know no more, I only carry the message."

"How do you know Ezra?"

"I don't, but he knows others who know me."

"And so..."

But Anstley has already run away and disappeared into the trees. Matthew could go after him, but he's stiff from the ride and Anstley knows the country. *Don't go home.* Elizabeth's house is being watched, but by whom? The inn is reassuringly crowded where he can easily lose himself. Safety in numbers, too many to bother asking searching questions. He asks the landlord for a room.

"Will you go up now?" the landlord says.

Matthew declines, a meal and a drink first, a decision he will later regret. Upstairs might have been safer. He squeezes at the end of a settle next to a group of loquacious labourers, their intense discussion arousing no interest even if he could understand them. His meal arrives and he munches silently. The men ignore him until he's finished. Then, a lull in their rambling discourse on field and fur and feather (that much at least Matthew has picked up) one asks his business.

"Just passing through," Matthew says.

The man spits out "London?" as if an unwholesome lump of fat is wedged in his teeth.

Matthew shakes his head nervously.

"Tom Edridge," the man says, then grabbing Matthew's empty tankard, "let me refill you."

"No, on me," Matthew says.

The man looks at him expectantly. Matthew hesitates. Names can be dangerous. His own may have preceded him with unwelcome and exaggerated explanations.

"I am...Noah," he says, "Noah... Harvey."

The man stares. Matthew gets up for the beer. When he returns his companion is engaged in another unintelligible debate and after a few courteous exchanges Matthew draws back. It's only then he notices an older man, who's played little part in the group's ardent discussion.

"I've been a watching you," he says, drawing heavily on a long clay pipe and puffing out huge billows of smoke, "You a soldier?"

There's a hostile edge to the question. Is this place sympathetic to the clubmen?

"Was," Matthew says enigmatically.

"Thought so. Watched you come in. Got that in the war?" the man says, pointing his pipe at Matthew's leg, "Where'd you get that?"

Matthew briefly recounts his injury at Cropredy Bridge.

"Discharged?" the man says, his big eyes staring knowingly through his latest smoky discharge.

Matthew nods, then probes, "Do many here oppose the army?"

Smoke is inhaled vigorously, giving the man time to think out his response, eventually opting for a question to a question.

"Glad not to be going back?"

"I can understand why some resist to go at all," Matthew says, "the clubmen as they are called."

The man removes his pipe and exhales billowing smoke. Matthew glances around. The others do not stir from their discussion.

"With that injury you'll not need to go back," the man says sceptically.

"The army is getting so desperate, they'll take anyone."

An uncomfortable image of General Skippon comes to mind as Matthew lies, but how well do these people know what's really going on?

"Fit and able," the man says dubiously.

"Have you heard anything of the war recently," Matthew says quickly.

"The two armies are jostling for position in the midlands. The King is on the move. Could be a big battle looming."

Suddenly the others break off from their talk. Intense and encompassing, hated, but fascinating the war is always more interesting than plough and harrow, sickle and thresher. They dissect it as they've dissected it a hundred times as it's dissected by ten thousand others from the country's top to bottom, end to end. Matthew is forgotten as a bit player, hovering beside but never actually on the stage, though he can't help intervening whenever the discussion veers into military unreality. Once a soldier...

"Will Parliament prevail?" one says, looking across to Matthew.

This is no Royalist country, but if these men are sympathetic to the clubmen, how should he answer?

"The war grinds on," he says neutrally.

"But who will *win?*"

"Why should you care?"

Matthew skates on thin ice with pretended sympathy for the clubmen and non committal comments on the fortunes of King and Parliament, but the discussion moves in a wholly different and unwelcome direction.

"There are rumours of spies," someone says, "You don't know who to trust."

Fleeting, furtive glances towards Matthew

"Royalist sympathisers more like," another says.

This is not the talk of clubmen, but hardened adherents to the Parliamentary cause, maybe more out of necessity than outright conviction. Another man joins the group. His clothes are less coarse, with a smoother cut. He stands a little aside from the table, his detachment emanating authority. As he speaks his eyes frequently dart towards Matthew.

"They masquerade under various guises, listen a lot, talk little and only to ask apparently innocent questions. People who would otherwise be beyond suspicion."

"A traveller from London said one of General Skippon's men was really a spy," another says, "Right in the heart of Parliament's army!"

This produces a general 'ooing' and ahing. The man in the smoother coat smirks grimly.

"I hear a young lieutenant did his duty and exposed his fellow officer. They were working together on some enquiry in Middlesex when he became suspicious. Got back to London and went to the authorities. Now that other officer is wanted for questioning, but it's believed he's left London."

Matthew is rattled, though he relaxes a little as the talk moves on to parochial affairs. He's tempted to ask more, but that wouldn't be wise. The coincidences are too pertinent. The unnamed 'treacherous' officer must be himself. Hugh has stitched him up! He goes over their enquiries and discussions together. He has seriously underrated Hugh's concerns with witchcraft and Royalist spying activities. Clearly Hugh's loyalties lie more with his prejudices than to a thorough and measured investigation. With the young lieutenant's misplaced tenacity and rigour now dangerously aimed in his direction, Matthew feels very vulnerable, not helped by the question suddenly fired at him.

"Have you come from London?"

Fortunately one of the others gives Matthew time to think when he says, "He's *going* to London."

"But has he *come* from London?"

"No," Matthew says, "I have business there, but I'm up from... Devon."

"A long way."

"Yes...it is."

They exchange glances. Matthew waits for the inevitable question, where in that county and what is his business, but it comes in a different form.

"I hear the clubmen are strong there."

Matthew doesn't respond, hoping usual rustic obsessions will take over, but several show a keen interest in the war in the south west. He's forced to improvise, but his inventiveness carries him away as he recounts the exploits of utterly fictitious clubmen. He's talked too long and shuts up, but someone has been listening too carefully. As Matthew goes over for a drink he bumps into a rough, wild eyed character. He immediately apologises and steps aside as best he can in the crush, but the other blocks his way.

"Stand aside, sir...please," Matthew says.

The man doesn't move except to lean forward and blow a strong waft of beery air into Matthew's face. Again Matthew tries to get round him, but the man raises both arms and shoves against him. The obstruction is not accidental.

"Step aside, sir," Matthew repeats, more forcefully.

"I do not step aside to runaways from their duties."

"I do not run from anything."

"You run from the war. I heard you. A deserter from the army, consorting with clubmen and..."

"I do not consort with clubmen and I am not running from..."

"I heard you."

The man points to the group, where the conversation has stalled, everyone looking intently at the noisy interchange. Unaware of the loudness of their voices Matthew's patience snaps.

"I do not run, I do not *consort*, nor do I trifle with fools who know nothing of what they talk about. Stand aside!"

The other sways momentarily, but then straightens stiffly, lowers his arms and juts his jaw pugnaciously at Matthew.

"I'm no fool. I served the cause well and will do so again when I return to the regiment."

"A soldier?" Mathew says unbelievingly.

"Corporal Adamson, late of..."

"Hey, you could be the one that's been talked about, the Royalist spy from London," better cut of clothes shouts at Matthew as he walks over to them, "Are you sure you're not from London?"

Matthew turns to face this renewed challenge, prudently stepping away from the soldier.

"Do you know this young lieutenant?" smooth cut says.

"I know many lieutenants. As an officer..."

"So you have been in the army?" the soldier says.

"And still am."

"Then why aren't you there now, ready to engage with the King and help bring the final victory for Parliament?"

"He wouldn't be if he was really the King's man," smooth cut says.

Before Matthew can reply this is greeted with choruses of 'That's right' and 'We want no traitors here.'

"I'm no traitor," Matthew shouts over the babble, "I am a Parliamentary officer, engaged on important business..."

"Spying business," smooth cut shouts.

"It's him," another says, "He's from London, not from Devon. He goes to London to report to the Royalists. They'll be rising soon. Everybody's been talking about it for weeks."

Several men move towards Matthew and he backs towards the door, but his way is blocked.

"You're not for Parliament!" the soldier shouts, staggering as he turns towards Matthew, his voice wavering, his hand moving close to his side where a weapon is probably concealed.

Mathew turns to the door again, but stout men bar any getaway. Matthew reckons the soldier is his best hope.

"You dare insult me, sir," he bellows.

"Scurvy cur and traitor," the soldier replies, still swaying slightly, his eyes wide and empty, "Defend yourself, sir!"

"The treachery is all yours," Matthew shouts, drawing his sword, "Only someone treacherous himself dares accuse an officer who has served Parliament well!"

The soldier draws his sword and squares up with as much speed and precision as his intoxication will allow, while Matthew edges closer to the wall, his raised sword convincing those closer to the door to get out of his way.

"Come on, wretch," he shouts, while half heartedly prodding well short of the soldier.

The manoeuvres are successful, Matthew simultaneously provoking the soldier and getting nearer the door. The soldier plunges and slashes blindly. Matthew easily outsteps his impotent thrusts, while keeping up his short jabs, almost but not quite reaching him.

"Come on, man," the soldier screams in frustration, "Stop dancing like a trollop and come on!"

But that is precisely what Matthew doesn't do, at least not yet. The soldier advances, slashing a little less erratically, but still unable to secure a hit. Matthew is both more nimble and more sober, but he jumps back as if in real danger. Some of the men jeer as the soldier flings more insults along with his ineffective stabs, but Matthew ignores them. With each sneer and jibe, they move further away from the door and he gets closer. Spurred on by the stupid crowd the soldier now 'comes on,' but rather than 'retreating' Matthew stands his ground. His sword thrust is no longer delivered short and he wings the soldier, who staggers back, clutching his painful shoulder, blood oozing through his fingers. The crowd closes around him. No one is at the door. With one stride Matthew wrenches it open and runs out. If only if he can get to his horse before they come after him.

Prudie keeps running. As a little girl she wandered into Drensell Wood to follow the wayward flutterings of a butterfly, emerging seven hours later to her distraught parents, tired, hungry and knowing every tree. Since then its shrouded security has been her refuge. For others' wariness, it gives her confidence, for their caution, abandon and for their fear complete sanctuary. Nor does she fear the darkness. The trees are her friends, their latticed mantle giving her strength. If she can keep Manning's men away for ten minutes, avoid them seeing her for five, then she will be safe. She knows where the trees are closest and highest, where bush, gorse and fern are thickest. There she can hide, seeing all, but seen by no one.

Manning and some dozen men come close and then pass. They head north, hoping to drive her out towards Syme House, but she knows otherwise. They will turn and turn about, losing their way and not leave the wood for a least an hour and even then on the west side. She has seen this movement many times and knows they'll not find their way back to where she is. The more they try to capture her the more she'll have the advantage. For she needs only a few minutes, not an hour to get out the wood.

She extricates herself quickly. Even if they'd looked properly they still wouldn't have seen her. A dozen men? It's a sign of Manning's weakness rather than strength. Is he afraid of Stradsey's witchcraft stories, a force led by Collver or a rising of the tenants? According to Bridget the local people are stirred up. She shudders. Her new friends seem far away and she feels very alone. Just reward for Manning's evil tongue would be retribution by the dark powers, but it won't be by her. At least not today, though she must get to Syme House. Only there will she get answers.

She skirts the edges of the fields. No sense courting observation. Collver or a band of disaffected villagers may also be on the prowl. In the frenetic atmosphere a woman is easily labelled a witch and all too summarily despatched. She keeps a constant lookout, frequently disappearing into hedges to spy for anyone following, but sees no one. She takes a circuitous route, doubling back to approach Syme House from the most unexpected direction, slowing as she gets closer, moving sporadically, darting from one hiding place to another. She could wait for nightfall, but she's impatient and waits at the edge of Narrow Baulk Field. Manning and his troop will not yet have found their way out of Drensell Wood, but he may have sent someone back to alert others in witch hunting frenzy, determined to find not what is, but what lives in their minds. She's already been seen. She must remain alert.

Then she sees her. At the far end of the field, close to the corner. Instinctively Prudie dives into the bushes. The woman walks slowly, apparently purposefully, but glances warily from side to side, unsure which way to take, concentrating with empty intensity at the ground. She's young, pretty, not more than twenty and steps with the artless, artificial confidence of youth. She thinks she knows everything, yet knows nothing, a woman who has learnt much, but needs to know much more. Realising who she is and that she might be of help, Prudie steps from the bush and walks towards her. The young woman stops. Prudie keeps walking.

"A fine morning, my dear," Prudie calls, anxious to allay any alarm, "Am I going the right way for Harringstead?"

They're close enough now to see each other clearly. Prudie stares into the warm, disturbed eyes, unsure whether Olivia Manning will remember her. Olivia looks back inquiringly, searching for reassurance, but showing no recognition, hesitant and struggling to relocate her thoughts.

"You seem troubled," Prudie says gently.

"No, no," Olivia mumbles, "It's nothing. What was it you said?"

"I need to get to Harringstead."

"Oh yes...no I'm afraid you are going the wrong way. You need to turn back along the field."

"They told me I might find a big place this way, I thought it would lead me to Harringstead...Syme House they call it?"

"Syme House? Yes, that's right, but it's the wrong way for Harringstead."

"Would you be from the big house, you being a fine lady an'all?"

"Er...I might...I could be."

"I thought so, but... begging your pardon for my presumption... you're not happy there."

Olivia who until now has been concentrating on the ground or the distant horizon, suddenly turns to Prudie.

"How can you know that?"

"I am right then?"

Olivia nods sheepishly.

"I have the gift," Prudie says, "A wise woman traveller some call me. Show me your palm, dear."

Olivia backs away. It's a dangerous moment. Those that read palms might easily be called witch. Has Prudie has misread her? No, Olivia's desperation is greater than superstitious meddling with honest folk. Olivia is apprehensive of the 'wise woman,' but as Prudie stares back wide and open, smiling sweetly, she puts out her hand. Prudie takes it and gently rubs her finger up and down the palm.

"Your family are known and respected," Prudie says, not being too specific and alerting Olivia her knowledge is more local than other worldly, "but you are torn, something is between you and..."

"My father," Olivia interjects, "Go on, what do you see?"

"A young man, someone you have known since you were small, someone close by...or at least he was, but now..."

"He's gone! Tell me what I must do!"

Prudie lets go Olivia's hand.

"A great question, my dear and burdensome to one who is just a traveller."

"Let me be the judge of that. I choose to speak to whom I please, not dictated by..."

"Calm yourself, "Prudie says, taking her hands again, "and tell me what has happened."

Olivia's quick, jerky breathing, a mixture of anger and distress, subsides.

"I can trust you?"

"You can," Prudie reassures her, gently squeezing her hands a little tighter.

"I don't know if I can find him, he may have gone too far, but I have to try. They do not...at the house...they do not know I am out. If they knew...there have been...discussions. I have not heard all though my little brothers – they are so much better than I at hiding beneath stairs or in cupboards – they have told me. My father is Joseph Manning, the Justice..."

"A great man indeed," Prudie intones with a mild whistle of mocking respect.

Olivia doesn't notice.

"...he met with his neighbour, John Collver. There was a great disagreement. Their raised voices...the servants must have heard...I could not make out the words, but my brothers tell it was about me...or at least of me and Richard."

"Richard?" Prudie asks innocently.

"Richard Collver, our neighbour John Collver's son."

"Aha, I now understand my dear, you and this Richard, you are..."

"Close...yes. After John Collver left my father summoned me. He said he thought my relationship with Richard had ended, but after speaking to his father he knew that was not so and was furious.

'How could you defy me in this way Olivia?' he said.

How could I answer? Must I deny my heart? My silence only excited him further and he railed at me venomously.

'You have betrayed me Olivia. You have consorted with the son of my enemy.'

'He is not my enemy,' I said, 'and I will not give him up.'

My mother tried to intervene, but I would have none of it.

'You mean well mother, but this must be.'

Then my father thundered even more.

'I will cut you off, Olivia, there will be no dowry, nothing, nothing, nothing!"

Olivia starts to shake. Prudie grips her hands even more tightly.

"Peace, my dear, peace, all will be...."

"Father said Richard has been seen, but I have heard others say he has gone away. If only I knew where. Then father attacked again.

'Is it not enough that these stories could ruin your reputation, Olivia, not to mention my own standing, but then to have his father... Collver... harangue me about you and his son? I sent him away, foul Royalist that he his, but the humiliation, the shame, is that so much of what he said is right. You must not only break with this man. You must do it openly and clearly. There must be no more skulking in hedgerows, secret meetings in copses, clandestine messages. I will have none of it. None of it, do you hear?'

'But father,' I pleaded, 'Is there not a way you and John Collver can reconcile your differences?'

He exploded.

'There can never be reconciliation with an enemy of Parliament and my daughter cannot be seen with his son. You know you have been seen?'

'Oh yes and I know by whom, that foul man Lexden, your creature who spied on everybody."

"Lexden?" Prudie asks.

"Samuel Lexden, my father's former steward."

"And did he see you with Richard Collver?"

"So Lexden said, but he can't say it anymore."

"He told your father?"

"It seems so, but I didn't know that before."

"Before what?"

"Before he was killed."

They are silent. Prudie pretends ignorance and is about to ask the question to which she knows the answer when someone runs from the side of the field. He stops and seeing them looks round apprehensively as if looking for someone else. He's young, tall, thin, shabbily dressed. Olivia stares at him for a moment, then turns away in alarm.

"He has been sent for me."

Even at this distance Prudie recognises him. He could reveal her identity, but Olivia lifts her skirts and pounds quickly away from the field. The man leaps off the track, arms and legs splayed out like some wild, but clumsy insect. Prudie gives chase, diving into the hedge after him. He gets to the other side, but stumbles and she gains slightly. With his arms chopping the air and his feet thrusting awkwardly at the ground it's amazing he manages to move forward at all. He looks back towards Prudie, calls 'No, no, not you,' then runs on, but loses his balance as he turns and falls down. Prudie is quickly on him and though he gets up, she bars his way. Her dishevelled and dirty clothes, which Olivia couldn't or chose not to notice, frighten him. To Olivia her eyes seemed soft and welcoming, the kind of eyes that invited the unwary to open up. To him they are wild and threatening, grimly piercing into his terrorised soul.

"A witch, a witch!" he calls, looking from side to side for a possible means of escape.

"Don't be so stupid, Ned!" Prudie says, shaking him violently.

Ned Frattersham, a fit young man could easily knock down a smaller, middle aged woman, but he's not only dull, he lacks her alertness while her imposing presence with its whiff of magical powers frightens him. He leans back as if distance alone might give protection, his large eyes desperately trying to dismiss her from sight.

"Where are you going?"

"N...n...nowhere."

"That's a big place, Ned, nowhere means everywhere, the whole wide world."

"Don't know the w...w...wide world."

"Maybe it's more where you've come from. Why run away from Olivia Manning, what harm can she do you?"

"Manning...Miss Manning...no, no, not her...been running...running away," he mumbles, then a glint of resistance in his eyes, "somebody been after you...asking about you...wanted to know if I knew P...P...Prudie."

"Well you do know me, Ned and you know I wouldn't hurt you."

"Hurt me?"

"No, of course not. Now if I..."

"Soldier, it was a soldier asking for you."

"Where did you see a soldier?"

"Drensell Wood."

What would Matthew be doing in Drensell Wood? He never mentioned seeing Ned, but why should he alert Prudie to his designs?

"What did he ask, Ned?"

"Wanted to know about Alice Sandon. Said I'd not seen her. He said was that why I ran away. I said not."

"Why did you run away?"

"Not treated right, that's what I told the soldier."

"Who didn't treat you right?"

"Mr. Lexden. Never treated me right, always onto me, picking on me. Laughed at me, said I was slow. Shouldn't've spoken to me like that, didn't like it, made me angry."

"What did you do?"

"I ran away...after he was dead...I ran away. I saw Mr. Lexden. Had to get away. Had to get away from the house."

"Tell me everything, Ned, tell me everything you saw, everything you did."

And as he does Prudie understands.

Mathew gallops through the first miles in numbed acceptance. Escape from a hostile inn, a belligerent if drunken soldier and its crazed clientele is enough, no need at first to consider the whys and wherefores, but where now? *Don't go home.* So where *does* he go? *Return to London, do not delay.* Ezra's message can't be ignored. *Return to London...but...Don't go home.* Where else can he stay in London? Ezra will have to whisk him to some clandestine hideaway while he works out the danger. But it's clear already. A marked man, renounced and betrayed by his erstwhile assistant. What possible reason can Hugh have for falsely accusing him? A Royalist spy, the idea is farcical if the ramifications weren't so serious. If the news is important enough to be carried to this remote place, then it must be common chatter in London.

Surely General Skippon wouldn't suspect him of treachery? *The two armies are jostling for position in the midlands. There could be a big battle looming.* Skippon has probably mustered the London forces and rejoined the main army with Cromwell and Fairfax. If only he was doing his duty in the field instead of running away from these rustics like a rat in a gutter! That leaves London without Skippon's principled and restraining influence. Who then is in charge? His thoughts return to Hugh. What he put down to youthful exuberance could be a dangerous fanatic. But Hugh is not alone. The army is a growing hotbed and the war harvests a crop of extreme zealots. In the coming explosion the demands of ordinary soldiers will be nothing to the intolerant obsessions of Hugh Crittenden and his ilk.

Matthew is never comfortable with the radical elements at the wild 'meetings' so beloved of his brother in law. He can't soak up the distilled invective of Daniel Overbridge, ranters and the like to spew it undigested at the dinner table. In this war a stand has to be taken and neutrality equates with cowardice or treachery though Nathaniel Buckden seems to be neither. He has to do this job for Skippon, but mixing with people he can't trust...not even his own assistant... is too much. If he was in the army he would...but he's not in the army and any chance of return seems remoter than ever. He's been so naïve, not recognising Hugh's dangerous proclivities, not seeing how straight forward comments could be so wickedly misconstrued. How he longs for that other life...a world of a few years ago that could be another century...

...The family's life on the farm marred by successive tragedies. The two younger girls, Lucy and Anne were never strong, dying within a year of each other, aged five and four. Their mother followed soon after. They said it was the infection. Elizabeth said it was a broken heart. Old John Fletcher now left alone with his two sons, John and Matthew and Elizabeth, his remaining daughter. The elder boy took well to the farming life, but for the younger his wanderlust grew stronger. Then his brother married Agnes and with the old man passing his best they became effective heads of the family and the kitchen. Matthew and Elizabeth kept their silence, but it was not to their liking. Long hankering for a different life, at sixteen Matthew chose some minor disagreement to leave, getting to London and an apprenticeship in the cloth trade...

...There to meet Jane...will he ever see her again, talk to her and if he does, what then...

The family struggled with what remained of the farm and fell into more debt with their landlord. With Agnes pregnant the two women should have drawn closer, but pulled further apart. Elizabeth's saw herself as her mother's rightful successor and resented her sister in law's usurpation. Otherwise equable and tolerant she became as fractious as her younger brother and tension increased. Agnes' labour was long and trying resulting in a still born son. Elizabeth was attentive and comforting, but as Agnes recovered the old strains reappeared and when Matthew arrived for a brief visit she accompanied him back to London. There she met and married Edmund Culshaw in 1640. Having now completed his apprenticeship, Matthew moved in with them.

News from the old home became sparse and infrequent, though Elizabeth arranged several visits for her father's sake. The King's attempt to arrest five members of Parliament in January 1642 solidified many breaches throughout the land. Edmund was in no doubt where his loyalties lay, but Matthew made only neutral comments. When they visited in the spring the old man was unwell and the farm in further difficulties. Everybody argued about the national position. Edmund and John clashed, good natured, but heartfelt. Matthew again said little while Elizabeth was more concerned about the farm and their father. That summer the King left London and the war began. After a few days of brooding Matthew reached his decision. The King had to be 'brought to his senses,' if necessary by force. Turnham Green and Cropredy followed and then discharge...

...Everything then was clear cut, his support for Parliament and the cause is unchanged, still the raw recruit at Turnham Green making such false accusations all the more bitter and unfair. A year away from the army is a long time. Already that youthful world is long ago. Having learnt so much, changed so much, he longs to unlearn, go back...but you can't go back...The world's moved on, it's him that refuses to accept it. Maybe that other life was only as he chooses to see it, a raw youth no longer, but a disenchanted man drifting into an early middle age. But he won't give in. Freedom of conscience and thought – isn't that what this conflict is really about – if not, why do we fight?

He leaves his horse to slow to a more even pace, gallop to canter to trot, finally to a walk in keeping with its rider's mood. Then he hears hoofbeats, distant, dull, but getting louder. They are following and gaining. He spurs the horse to a gallop, but knows it's too tired and won't sustain it. The hoofbeats get louder. The track snakes left to avoid a wood. It's his only chance. The light is already fading. He dismounts and leads his horse to where the thicket is layered densest. He stops and listens. The riders are closer. There's not much time. He tethers the horse, stroking and talking to it gently to calm the animal and hoping it won't be disturbed. Then he pulls as much brushwood around it as he can before quickly scanning for a place of his own to hide.

The darkness will give him slight advantage, particularly if the horse remains quiet and unseen. He stumbles around for a few minutes, looking upward, straining his eyes in the dim light to find a tree for concealment. He staggers on, rejecting what seem too open or not easily climbable, but the subdued hammering of the approaching riders gets louder. The horse is quiet. He eases up into a tree with good branches and overgrowth, his sword bumping noisily, then finds an enclosed perch before leaning precariously against the trunk.

The riders must have reached the edge of the wood. They stop. He listens intently, his leg aching in the constrained position as he tries not to move. The stillness of the wood is pierced by the sighing of the breeze, lifting and sloughing branches, trip trapping of unseen animals, mysterious creaking of leaf and twig. Concentrated trees expand and contract sounds, tricking the ear, making it difficult to judge distances. Voices, muffled and incoherent...riders, first taking the track, then receding only to crunch the leaf crusted ground upon him! He makes himself small, willing the horse to be silent, yet still the wind heaves, the trees groan, the bats skirl and the animals scurry. The hoofbeats gradually subside again, but this time there's no sudden reprise of their advance. They really are going!

He waits to be sure, not trusting his ears any more than his eyes in the darkness. A few minutes, a half hour, longer? Eventually he stirs from his cramped perch and slips to the ground. He calls the horse and receives a soft, reassuring snort. He retraces his steps and is about to pull back the brushwood, when he hears a sharp sound at his side and feels the hard, cold pistol at his temple.

"Do not move."

Ezra has been running around madly for several days. He is in some consternation, but not despair for he never allows anything to get close enough for that. Or so he says. But he is concerned.

"Why are you bothering?" an associate says.

Ezra has many 'associates.' He knows many throughout the city and in turn many know of him. Yet few really *know* Ezra. People are not his life, what people do, what people are, above all what people *know* are important, not people themselves. People can be *useful*. If they're not, they're best avoided for even if they're useful they usually mean trouble. He's had to learn that painful lesson many times. His associate repeats his bewilderment.

"What's in it for you?"

He's right, of course. Self interest, not something Ezra easily discounts, should long ago have made him abandon Matthew's wild blunderings and save himself. Ezra agrees with his companion, but then taps his nose.

"I have my own reasons, not just those of Captain Fletcher."

Ezra doesn't expand, repeating the information he needs and reminding his informant 'you owe me one.' The man departs, leaving Ezra to ruminate on his next moves.

Nods and winks may impress casual acquaintances, but do not mirror Ezra's real intentions. He may imply he has an agenda of his own, separate from Matthew, but he hasn't. Why are you doing this, Ezra Stanfield? Joel and Arthur and Benjamin and Samuel, they're all right. Keep asking questions about Matthew Fletcher and the wrong people will start asking questions about you. In the city's feverish panic there are false rumours and ne'er do wells enough. Nothing to be gained adding to them. So he keeps moving from tavern to tavern, alley to alley, picking up bits and pieces along wharves and street corners, making contacts, seeing those he needs to see, dodging those he'd rather not. It's a long hard slog, piecing together what ordinarily should not be linked, but debts of the past cannot be ignored. It's galling going against every instinct for survival and profit, but he owes Matthew much more than the human detritus of the city owe him. What was, still is, however much it makes him mouth what he'd ordinarily never say.

"Strutting peacocks, wanting more and giving back less. They're all the same, you should know that," someone says when Ezra asks about the army.

"Not all," Ezra replies, "I *know* they're not all the same."

Some soldiers really are different. Matthew always believed in Ezra and not many have ever done that. With his day's 'work' done Ezra must prepare, with some trepidation to meet Matthew. Matthew's temper was never easily curbed and the latest troubles will have done nothing to lengthen it. He'll want to know so many things. Try as he might, Ezra cannot have all the answers. Not good for Matthew's temper and that was before he was denounced as a 'Royalist,' but he's discovered enough to get Matthew back.

There's something very odd about the firm where Henry Collver works, if only he could put his finger on...Then there's Prudie. Ezra has scouted out Elizabeth's house and observed those doing the same. Leaving too many open messages would be dangerous, but Matthew had to be warned. That meant relying on those in the country, never a very encouraging prospect. Ezra might even have to leave himself...but no, the city is his natural world. Take him away and who knows what might happen. Besides, he might be watched himself. He's safer in the city. Leaving it attracts attention, quite apart from the dangers of being alone outside.

He nears the 'Parrot,' not one of his usual haunts. It's risky, but he's taken every conceivable precaution. Maybe there's safety in a different place, stop him being complacent. He waits at the corner and slinks into the shadows, looking back, around, continuing only after he's satisfied he's not followed. A man stands opposite the tavern. Ezra slips into the shadows again, watches and waits. The man has not seen him. He keeps looking at the tavern as...then Ezra notices the unmistakable shuffle of his left leg and approaches. Matthew turns as Ezra is almost upon him, grabbing his lapel, then releasing it as he recognises him.

"You creep up like a snake," Matthew says.

"And you are too early when there are no worms to feed on. You were not meant to..."

"I couldn't wait. Does it matter?"

"Could be. Sometimes time is as important as place," Ezra says, then looking around, "Are you sure you weren't followed?"

"I couldn't stay any longer in that rathole you've put me in."

"If it wasn't for Jacob, you might now be in an even smaller one – six feet long, eighteen inches across and six feet down."

Matthew eases his weight from one leg to the other.

"He nearly killed me...with fright."

"He's the only one I could trust with the full story."

"I tried to talk to him, but he ran off."

"He was afraid. There were rumours."

"Which he didn't tell me about."

"After you went into the inn he changed his mind and hung around."

"He'd've been more useful if he'd come in with me."

"How could he, he was known, you were not. You should be grateful he stayed at all. He saw you being followed. So, figuring which way you were bound to go he cut across country. When he saw you at the river he knew what you'd do and got up to the wood. The rest you know."

"Do you know this place?" Matthew says grumpily, nodding to the 'Parrot.'

"Not been before," Ezra says, glancing around apprehensively, "We should go in."

"Not if you don't know it. I'm sick of confined spaces, dingy cellars, poky attics, backyard sheds, backs of wagons."

"We had to be careful, you're a wanted man."

"I don't feel safe out here either," Matthew says contradictorily.

Ezra sighs in frustration.

"If you don't want to go in and you won't stay out here, then..."

Matthew leans forward, checks each way, then grabbing Ezra's arm, moves off.

"We'll keep moving, down to the river."

Despite his haste, Matthew soon slows up.

"Your leg..." Ezra begins.

"I'll be alright!" Matthew hisses angrily, "It'll be stiff for only a few paces. It's probably because I've been too long in your damned nooks and crannies. It's a wonder I've got a straight head let alone two good legs!"

Matthew hobbles away, gradually getting firmer and sprightlier as they get closer to the river. Ezra follows a pace or two behind, constantly sneaking a look around and reminding Matthew to keep within the overhangs. They reach a wharf. It's that twilight hour when shadows merge, confusing the eye and tricking the brain. Many boats are tied up, some recently arrived, waiting to be unloaded, others ready for the morning tide. The air is filled with mixed smells of grain, vegetables, timber and coal. At one end of the wharf men are still unloading the last of the coal.

"A welcome arrival," Matthew says.

The wharf is busy with other folk.

"We'd better keep moving," Ezra says apprehensively pulling him away, "There's more than coal being traded."

They walk on. Ezra is tetchy and nervous. Those passing look innocent, others less so. As well as the shore, there are those that watch from the boats. Matthew tells Ezra to 'be quiet and calm,' their greatest danger is from tinkers and whores, both over eager in their selling.

"This city is a pandemonium of whispers and tattle, full of those whose tongues are too busy for their brains."

"Aye and of those fervent to listen to them," Ezra says.

"Was it because of Henry Collver you called me back?"

"Not exactly."

"Don't jest, Ezra. By the stars or I'll..."

"Not *Henry* Collver, but his brother John."

"What of him?"

"He's dead."

"What, in Harringstead? I knew when we left..."

"No, in London. He was visiting his brother and there was...an accident."

"What sort of accident?" Matthew says doubtfully.

"He fell in the river."

"Fell or pushed?"

Ezra shrugs.

"The watch questioned Henry, but got no sense from him. He was too shocked. The next day he couldn't be found, disappeared just like his nephew."

"Richard is probably with Buckden. I was about to find out when you summoned me back."

A disreputable looking character passes very close, staring at them.

"Why was John in London anyway?" Matthew says, walking away quickly.

"Whatever it was, he was killed for it," Ezra says, then on reflection, "By now Henry may have gone the same way."

Both the Collver brothers dead while Richard runs away. What did he know, could Joseph Manning be involved?

"I have to go to Harringstead."

Ezra is alarmed.

"It's too dangerous, you must stay in London."

"Safer in this infernal city?"

"More places to hide, easier to be seen as part of a crowd or confused with others. That's not to mean you should be walking about in the open at all times. Just now we should..."

"Alright, alright, you've made your point!"

Matthew plies Ezra repeatedly with questions about everything and everybody. They talk about the firm of Ellerton and Amberley.

"Something not right there," Ezra intones.

"And if I'm to be kept holed up like a frightened vixen, you'll have to find out much more. "

Ezra explains what he's found. At the side of the river in the dimming light it doesn't sound much as he lists it quickly, punctuated by Matthew's ungrateful snorts.

"You'll need to track down Jonathon Ellerton, Edward Amberley and Daniel Harmsworth."

"Who's he?"

Matthew hesitates.

"He...he...he's married to Ellerton's daughter."

Ezra looks intently at Matthew with half understanding. He suppresses a smirk.

"And William Davington."

"Never heard of him."

"He is...was...my father's landlord."

"What has he got to do with it?"

"I don't know, but you said London is full of those speaking against me."

"Which reminds me. I've heard Henry Fenwick is in town."

"Is he by Jesu? That might tell us much. What about Prudie Westrup?"

"You've not seen her?"

"Of course not, where is she?"

Ezra explains his meeting with Prudie and his subsequent enquiries, none of which have revealed her whereabouts.

"She was very concerned about you."

"Damn, damn, damn!" Matthew explodes, "Everybody we need to talk to is out of reach or has disappeared, Henry and Richard Collver, Prudie and Sarah Radbourne. We have to break this circle of silence. I have to take action!"

He stamps his good foot and turns around as if suddenly to pounce on an unseen enemy. A man on one of the boats looks across curiously. Ezra pulls at his coat

"Action?" he whispers, "Like you did at that inn in the country!"

"Ezra, remember there's somebody I can approach, someone who hasn't disappeared – Hugh Crittenden! That snake has called me a Royalist spy. I will have him now I'm back in London."

"Oh yes, that's just what to do, exactly as he wants. Matthew, are you a complete fool? That's not just walking into the trap, it's setting it yourself!"

Matthew stomps away. Carefully glancing at anyone who might be around, Ezra follows. Matthew grunts and mumbles incoherently, his rage heightening with each fuming second. Ezra is very nervous. This is when Matthew is at his most vulnerable, when his whole being is concentrated on anger.

"Trust me," Ezra says, "lay low and wait till you hear from me."

Matthew is shaking furiously, but he knows Ezra is right. He calms and stops shaking. Ezra shoves a piece of paper in his hand

"You must go to a different place tonight."

"I must go to see Elizabeth."

"No! They will take you. This is the address. Stay there until I contact you. Go straight there."

Matthew reluctantly agrees and they part. *Go straight there.* But Matthew cannot go straight to anywhere. His body too agitated in wrath, his mind too full of remembrances, he needs to extricate both. He walks beyond the boats and another wharf, then continues beside the river. He ought to be on his way as Ezra told him, but he's heading vaguely in the right direction and it's much darker now so his distinctive limp, of which he's sure Hugh has told everyone, will be less obvious.

There's a heavy stillness on the river. Matthew stops and stares across to the far bank, then hears footsteps and looking round sees dark, shadowy forms approaching. He walks on, but all around seems hazy and undefined. The dim and nebulous half light is no longer a cloak, but a menace, indistinct like the information he'd chased about Richard. Whatever his suspicions, Henry will have been totally unprepared for John's 'accident.' In shock, Ezra said. Henry may be afraid, but he's not a fool. He won't have left London. He'll want to get to the bottom of his brother's death. He'll be lying low like Matthew, but also like Matthew he'll want to sniff around. So where is he likely to be?

Matthew turns from the river. The night is coming uncomfortably alive. He needs to avoid people and not just loose women and drunken men. The watch is abroad. He tries to straighten his walk as if his betraying limp can be so easily hidden. He makes for the narrowest, darkest streets and alleys, though being accosted there will more dangerous than the open thoroughfares. Henry talked about an inn near the river. What was it called? He hears footsteps and voices ahead. He turns and retraces his steps back to the river. At the bottom of a lane he emerges once more on the bank, wracking his brain to remember the name of the inn. Then it comes to him. The 'Dancing Bear.' To go means exposure, but not to go means a dangerous trudge to the new den Ezra has found him. He'll take his chance, despite the risks, which he's sure Ezra has exaggerated. A man approaches. Holding as much of his weight as he can on his good leg Matthew asks the way.

"I know of it, sir. You have business there?"

Matthew takes this as a genuine question rather than a rebuke, but is wary.

"There is someone I need to see."

"Not a place of your own choosing then?"

"No...not really."

He's directed back along the wharf, then up a short street to where 'you'll see it crooked and crazy, staring down at you and the river together.' At the top of that street he realises the aptness of his description. The sides of the building around the main door are out of alignment, the whole place seemingly sinking into the ground as if bludgeoned by some unseen giant. He also understands the man's reluctance to associate it with Matthew, rightly recognising someone of his own worth for inside it also sinks or more properly those within have *sunk*. They hang at every wall, slink in every corner and pack over every gap between. Those that cannot stand (and there are a goodly proportion of those) lean on each other or are propped up by their companions. Others are only standing because they are so tightly packed along the counter. Over and through them ale is copiously drawn by the landlord and his waitresses, who move more like ants in an anthill than people in a tavern.

It's difficult to see beyond the crush. Matthew has to slide, gently but firmly through the mass. Once at the counter his reference to Henry Collver invites some unsavoury glances.

"It was a Collver they fished out the river?" a man says, casting his raised eyebrows at Matthew.

"His brother," Matthew says.

"Someone was in here earlier asking about him and also about that Royalist spy," the landlord says, "What's his name?"

"Mathew Fletcher," the man says, then turning to Matthew, "And who might you be?"

"Radley...John Radley."

"You a friend of this Collver?"

"Not exactly a friend...he owes me some money."

"Which one, 'im who's dead or 'im who's alive."

This produces a welter of laughter. While the mirth subsides people gather around where a man is placing a chair in the centre. Matthew recognises him immediately and tries to draw away, but the crowd is too jammed and he only manages to get back behind the first line, wedged between a heavy man and a young girl.

She turns to him and says, "Why do you really want to find Henry Collver?"

Surprised, Matthew can only repeat, "He owes me..."

Then the man gets on the chair, stretches out his arms and the room is silenced.

"Don't let the false priests fool you, brothers and sisters. God is with us in everything!"

The booming voice of Daniel Overbridge resonates across the room, silencing it seems to Matthew not just speech, but thought as well.

"If God casts you as a sinner, then where comes that sin? From God? Then it cannot be. So there can be no sinners and there can be no sin."

Matthew turns to the girl, but the overwhelming silence imposed by Overbridge transcends everyone. Even to whisper is to draw attention and what Matthew says must be between themselves. Besides, all her being is rapt on Overbridge, her eyes never deviating, every taught muscle utterly concentrated. Speaking softly will not be enough. To break through that captivation he would have to shout.

"We are fighting a war *against* sin, who are you to dispute the word of God?"

The sudden challenge comes from the back of the room. Some turn to look, but the crush is too heavy. Matthew finds it difficult to turn his head let alone see behind him. Then they turn back as Overbridge replies.

"God is in everything, brother, even in sin!"

"Blasphemy! Damned ranter! Get out!"

"Call me what you will, sir, I am no ranter, only a poor pilgrim like yourself. Listen and I will..."

It seems Overbridge has met his match as his challenger pushes through the throng, denouncing the 'ranter,' calling for his ejection and gathering supporters on the way. Now could be the time. In the distraction Matthew must ask her if she knows Henry, can she lead him there? But the crush behind gets stronger and those intent on reaching Overbridge, lever people aside.

"Come over, Daniel, come away," one of his companions says and he steps down from the chair.

Others join Overbridge and in the confusion Matthew is pulled along with them, but the girl has slipped away and stands in a small group on the opposite side.

"You're a traitor to the cause," someone shouts and this is answered by further calls of 'traitors' and 'root out the spies.'

The original religious slant to the meeting is lost. This new talk is dangerous. Matthew was safer with 'sin' even though he tried not to be seen and recognised by Overbridge. He tries to move away from the cluster and get closer to the door, but carried between the rival supporters he's thrust into the Overbridge group, the main body splitting from a 'rearguard,' which starts real fighting with their 'godly' challengers. Overbridge and a few others get to the door. Matthew looks out for the girl, but can't see her. Then someone calls "This way, Sarah" and she is pulled closer to Overbridge as he leaves.

Sarah! Matthew has to follow her. Now some of his group breaks away, anxious to get into the fight. This loosens the tightness and he slips nearer the door. The cries to apprehend 'traitors' and 'spies' get louder. He elbows and rams his way, levelling and battering anyone who can't or won't get out of his way. With one last superhuman effort he leaps at the open door and gasps at the warm, free air outside. He runs, swaying and limping down the street, the ache in his bad leg gradually increasing. Behind he can hear footsteps and shouting. There's no sign of Overbridge, Sarah or any of his supporters. At the river he stops for breath. Two men stand a short way off. They look at him suspiciously. Then a band of a dozen men come running down the hill.

"Stop him, stop him! He's a traitor, a Royalist spy!"

Matthew turns, ready to run on again, but one of the men at the river calls him.

"Hold there, in the name of the Watch, do not move!"

Matthew shuffles away.

"He limps," the other watchman calls, "It's Matthew Fletcher. Stop!"

Matthew tuns around and from side to side. One way is the watch, to his right the men from the 'Dancing Bear.' He turns right round, but behind another watchman approaches. His name is called again. He's trapped! He turns to his left. There is only the river. He steps to the edge.

"Stop!" someone shouts, "Stop!"

But Matthew turns from them all and dives into the water.

10

EDMUND leaves the house and hurries towards the river. He's late and has missed most of his breakfast. Inside his wife clears the uneaten food and takes it into the yard for the pigs. They snort appreciatively. She's already fed them this morning. She stands and watches them for a few minutes, wondering what has happened to Prudie and Matthew. Matthew is accused of being a Royalist spy and the authorities are hunting for him. She's already had several visitors. They barged in and went through the place when Edmund was out, even looking in the sty though the pigs gave them no better welcome than she did. One young man, anxious to ensure no possible hiding place was left without a thorough search, was particularly diligent. His boots got covered in muck and he slipped, covering himself up to his neck. The other officers laughed.

One said, "While you're there, make sure he's not in the trough!"

Is Mathew still in the country or returned to London? One evening someone slipped a cryptic message under her door.'

'He's safe, Ezra.'

Some reassurance, but safe where? Neither she nor Edmund dared contact Ezra even though she could guess his haunts. They could be watching him as well and being seen together would only increase speculation on this ridiculous nonsense of Matthew being a spy. If she could get her hands on that foul young cub, Hugh Crittenden...Edmund, angrier than she's ever seen him, has already threatened to kill him. This morning he'd lain too long in bed and was morose and withdrawn when he finally appeared downstairs. She'd had to hurry him out, not even scolding him for the wasted breakfast.

"Be careful," she whispered at the door, "Hold your tongue, don't be provoked. There'll be many ready to denounce you too. A brother in peril is enough. I can't have a husband in danger too."

With that she packed him off, the tears she'd been holding back finally bursting as soon as the door was shut. Now she consoles herself with the pigs. And what of Prudie? At least Matthew said where he was going, even though it was too vague to be of any use, but Prudie slipped away without warning, without farewell, without a word of thanks. Elizabeth had been angry, cursing herself for being so gullible and Prudie for her ingratitude, but it passed.

"She must have heard us," she said.

"Then she's followed Matthew," Edmund said.

Prudie would hardly wander around aimlessly in open country, though Elizabeth is sure she's left London as nowhere is safer than this house.

While Elizabeth tends her pigs at the back of her house (or in some respects they tend to her) others watch the front. At each end of the short street is a watcher, partly concealed by the corner. One arrived as Edmund left, watching the intent, weary figure hurrying away, but not following. Better to observe whoever comes to the house or follow Elizabeth if she emerges. Anxious not to be seen while ensuring he's in a position to see others, he eases uncomfortably in his cramped position. Unlike his counterpart at the opposite end of the street, he's dressed neatly and well, if a little conservatively.

The other is crouched low beside a wall, better obscured not just by his position, but by his demeanour. In his meagre, ragged clothes he's curled like a hedgehog, into the stones of the street itself. Like a hedgehog few want to get near let alone touch him for he exudes a repellent low prickliness.

Yet beneath his tattered cap nothing escapes his sharp eyes. Like his companion he watches all morning, observing every movement in the street, every flicker from the house as Elizabeth gets her provisions and throws out her rubbish. He watches not just the house, but also the other that watches. He sees, but is unseen for who notices a beggar, one of the vast army that fills the city.

When the other leaves, the beggar follows, slinking and slithering, unnoticed. Then, when he's seen and heard enough he breaks away and scampers to the river, which breathes in every vital material for the city's sustenance, where everyone who matters eventually finds their way. Invisible in wretchedness he seeking alms, wandering from street to street, tavern to wharf. But his is no purposeless journey. He knows where he wants to be and how to get there. Just after noon he takes station in a narrow crick in a wall half way up a hill between the river and a crooked building, watching all who come and go at the 'Dancing Bear.'

Two hours pass. The beggar hardly moves, unnoticed until two drunken louts accost him. It'll be good sport to harass the forlorn figure crouched in the nook. As one bends down and takes his hat an arm is thrust from the beggar's jacket with a sharp blade suddenly at the man's neck.

"Leave go my hat, sir or I'll slit your neck in an instant."

With the point of the knife impressing his skin, the youth is reluctant to move, but his friend cannot see it.

"What are you waiting for Tom, take his hat!"

"He...he...has me," the other splutters, "by the throat."

Either he doesn't hear or filled with alcoholic bravado, Tom's friend goes for the beggar's hat. A second knife in the other hand now finds its target just above the man's boot. He cries out in pain and steps back, going for his sword. Immediately the beggar is on his feet with his hand on Tom's neck while the knife is still at his throat.

"Be on your way, sir or your friend will be feeding the fish in the river!"

"Do as he says, Francis, can't you see he has me!"

"Your sword, sir," the beggar says, "Put it away and back off."

Reluctantly Francis steps away, while the beggar withdraws the knife and pushes his friend towards him. Tom rubs and strokes his neck and looks at his blood smeared fingers.

"He cut me, Francis, that rogue cut me!"

"Be glad it's only a cut," the beggar says, now standing erect.

"I should run him through," Francis says.

"Have a care, sir," the beggar says.

He squats down, withdraws a sword from his dirty bag and holds it towards them. Tom turns away. Francis stands for a few moments, staring grimly, hand at his side. The beggar moves forward.

"Be gone, sir."

Tom grabs Francis, breaks into a run and pulls him away. The beggar returns the knife to his coat and shoves the sword back in his bag before squatting down to resume his vigil. He continues to watch the tavern. After an hour his patience is rewarded. A group of men emerge, exchange brief noisy banter and then depart except for two who remain behind. One is taller, heavier with an unruly beard and wild gleaming eyes. The other, smaller, lighter talks earnestly to him. The larger man smiles politely, occasionally acknowledging by word or gesture, but most of the time seems bored or uneasy, his body twitching as if he's anxious to get away. The smaller man has his back to the beggar, but he recognises his gait and build. The beggar eases up and steadying himself against the wall waits restlessly. His interest is in the small man, but he dare not approach while the two are together. The larger man eventually tires and with a wave of his hand, walks off. The beggar watches him and mutters to himself.

"Overbridge."

The smaller man also watches him. Two pairs of eyes, locked on the same goal until Overbridge disappears at the river's edge. Then the beggar's attention reverts to the tavern as the small man walks off in the opposite direction. The beggar eases himself up, slings his bag over his shoulder and snakes his way after at a discreet distance. His quarry walks slowly, keeping to the edge of buildings, deep in thought, frequently stopping to look about him. The beggar anticipates his every move, darting to avoid those backward glances, hiding behind others, bounding from one place of concealment to another, scurrying into shadows, turning away, but always keeping him within sight. Several times when they're alone he almost gets within touching distance, but then retreats as others appear. There must be no interference, no witnesses. Above all he must not attract avoidable attention to himself. After a half hour the small man strides into a deserted alley. There's no one else in this isolated place, but it's a busy area, they may be alone for only a minute. The beggar seizes his chance, springs the few steps and leaps on him, hurling him sideways and pinning him against a wall. Jolted and cowed the small man stares, wide eyed and unbelieving into his attacker.

"You!"

"Aye, Henry, 'tis me."

"What do you want?"

"Just to talk."

"Leave me alone. I won't talk to you, Matthew Fletcher, you're a wanted man."

"All the more reason you should talk if you want to stay healthy, Henry."

Matthew tightens his grip on Henry's arm against the wall.

"Alright, alright, what do you want to know?"

"Let's start with why you're talking to Daniel Overbridge."

"You know him?"

"Not as well as you it seems."

"Just someone I met in the tavern."

"Don't trifle with me, Henry," Matthew says, pulling his knife from his coat and holding the tip in Henry's chest, "You don't just meet in the Dancing Bear, it's not that sort of place."

"He knows a lot of people."

Matthew is getting very impatient. He pushes the knife a little closer.

"Like Sarah Radbourne?"

Henry looks puzzled. Then there's a glimmer of recognition.

"The name's familiar, could be one of his followers."

"I need to see her. She was at the Dancing Bear with him."

"She's hiding."

"Why?"

"There was trouble at his last meeting."

"It was hardly a meeting."

"You were there?"

"How can I get to her?"

"Talk to Overbridge."

"No, I must approach her directly. When's his next meeting?"

Henry hesitates, then says he doesn't know, eventually relenting, after some gentle persuasion.

"What did you want with Overbridge?" Matthew says.

"I'll talk to anyone who might help me find out what happened to my brother."

"He was drowned," Matthew says, relaxing his grip silently.

"Oh yes," Henry says, "but by whom and why?"

"You believe he was murdered?"

"Mistakes can happen."

"So it was an accident?"

"Only in that they got the wrong man. John was killed by mistake. They were really after me, still are, for what I know."

"Then..."

Two men enter the alley and look suspiciously at the beggar accosting a gentleman. Matthew has to draw back, giving Henry the opportunity to slip from his grasp and run. Matthew turns to him, but the men are almost upon him. He smiles cautiously and resumes his sloping, slithering gait. Then he's away as appearances allow, but Henry is already well ahead of him.

Ezra is angry and frustrated. Keeping Matthew under cover is proving extremely difficult.

"I told you to stay put. You're lucky to be alive."

"Just a cold bath," Matthew says.

"With your leg, I couldn't be sure you'd've swam across the river."

"Neither was I."

"Lucky you did and lucky I found you."

"You'll be safe here for a couple of days," Ezra says, looking round the latest dingy garret he has found for him, "They'll take that long, assuming of course you don't go wandering around again. Then you'll have to move on."

"Henry Collver said John was deliberately drowned, but that *he* was the intended victim. I have to get to Henry and find out what he knows."

Ezra explodes.

"You can't keep roving around the city with or without a disguising uniform. (he nods to the pile of rags in the corner) It's too dangerous."

"I have to clear myself. I can only do that by finding who killed John Collver and why. It might also lead to the murderer of Joseph Manning's steward. With all other enquiries run into the sand or evaporated by treachery I have to go back to the beginning and find Sarah Radbourne."

Ezra whistles, "Not her again."

"She was in the Dancing Bear with Overbridge. Damn my eyes for letting her get away!"

"Getting *yourself* away was more important. If you go back there..."

"I have to. Before he slipped through my fingers Henry told me about Overbridge's next meeting."

"Another rowdy affair no doubt."

"Easier not to be seen."

"Yes, like last time. Matthew, it's too dangerous! My contacts in that part of the city aren't very good..."

"I thought they were good everywhere," Mathew says irritably, "I have to go to that meeting!"

"Then you'll be twice threatened. First from the ruffians that go to such meetings and..."

"Who are you to talk about ruffians," Matthew splutters, "You know every rough villain in the city!"

"Aye and there's rough and there's rough, those out for themselves and those with a *cause*."

"So long as it's the right cause. We fought for the cause, Ezra, don't forget."

"That was the army, I'm hardly likely to forget that. I'm talking about ruffians that try to bend men's minds. Bending a pocket isn't the same as bending a mind."

"I'm not afraid of Overbridge."

"Maybe not, but you should be wary of those that watch him."

"And that is the other threat?"

"You were nearly caught there."

"I've got no choice. It's my only way of getting to Sarah Radbourne and maybe Henry. With no chance of finding Richard Collver..."

"Now there I might be able to help you."

"What do you know?"

"Contacts," Ezra chuckles, "Nathaniel Buckden is not entirely a country bumpkin. He has relatives in the city."

Matthew sighs and throws up his hands.

"Not getting very far with other things," Ezra continues, "I thought it wise to try and mend some of the fences you trampled down. He distrusted you intensely when you met..."

"That was obvious and I..."

"...not helped by your usual aggression..."

"I will not be..."

"...However, he finds you a Royalist spy not only ridiculous, it inclines you more as a neutral opportunist...more like himself."

"So Richard Collver is no longer with Buckden?"

"He is...and he isn't...he has to be on the move. The two of you have much more in common now. As fugitives neither will be hampered by Buckden's clubmen."

Matthew is sceptical.

"There's too much to be done in London."

"Matthew, you wanted to find Richard, that's why you left. Now you hesitate. If you're to find him you need to leave London without delay."

Matthew gets up and stomps around the room (as best he can in the confined space) hammering his right fist into his left palm.

"So long getting nowhere, now I could be in striking distance of Sarah Radbourne, you want me to run around the countryside again. You said yourself it's not safe out there!"

Ezra is disappointed. His plan seems to be backfiring.

"I can't keep this up for much longer. Sooner or later you're going to be seen or discovered. I hear Hugh Crittenden's been very active."

"That snake!"

"Calling him names doesn't make him any less effective."

His head almost bent under the eaves, Matthew sits in the corner, quiet and thoughtful, but not subdued. He rubs his leg and curses under his breath. At last he gets up, smacks his hands together and sits beside Ezra.

"It's not impossible to accomplish both. I will leave London to find Richard, but first I'll go to Overbridge's meeting."

"You're decided?"

"I'm decided."

"In that case I will come with you."

'The Ship' lies away from the river.

Mathew says little on the way, other than to wonder why Overbridge has moved the meeting from the 'Dancing Bear.'

"He must sense trouble," Ezra says gloomily.

Ezra talks incessantly except when he's trying to see round corners and looking out for anyone who might be watching. The constant prattling is annoying, but Matthew's silence is the best antidote to Ezra's intense nervousness. He's no longer rigged as a beggar. Ezra said its relative tidiness 'would never have fooled those in the know.' That said he's dressed too shabbily for an officer even one 'slumming on other duties.' Ezra is dressed as always, dull without being dissolute, inconspicuous enough to distract attention from sharp eyed informants. The last stages of their journey seem interminable. Matthew is sure they've passed the same corners and alleys several times and suspects the circuitous wanderings are part of Ezra's precautions. When they see the tavern Ezra stops at the end of the street. Matthew is happy to rest his leg. After a few minutes of close observation Ezra scurries ahead, stopping at the tavern door and ducking under the windows before returning.

"Overbridge is sitting quietly. Are you sure there's to be a meeting?"

"That's what Henry said."

Ezra smacks his lips doubtfully.

"Matthew, if you don't find him or the girl tonight then..."

"We'll see it through. Anyone else you know?"

"There are so many, I'm bound to know somebody."

"I don't know whether that's good or bad. Come on."

Matthew lurches towards the rowdy tumult. Ezra scampers behind, looking nervously over his shoulder and curling up as he skips along, an exasperated spider disturbed from his dark cosy corner. They take up position just inside the front door, Matthew looking for Henry or Sarah, Ezra looking at anyone looking at them. Overbridge is at a nearby table with a few companions, self absorbed, not noticing their arrival. Ezra recognises a few faces, but there's no immediate threat. A man gets up and starts singing a bawdy song to a gradually increasing accompaniment of catcalls and raucous embellishments.

Matthew scans every table for either Henry or Sarah. The singer finishes to loud applause and further renditions of his last few verses. Someone else starts another, slightly less ribald song. He has a better voice and is joined by others. As the whole group sways together in time a relative calm settles though it's short lived, the cacophony erupting again as soon as they finish. Overbridge gets up and raises a hand, simultaneously turning around to grab attention from all sides. Immediately the noise subsides. Despite their rowdiness this is the man they have come to see and hear. As at the 'Dancing Bear' there's an involuntary clearance around him while those at the back crowd closer. One man catches Matthew's eye. He's seen him weeks before in another tavern, a man who was looking for his daughter. Overbridge begins.

"Though we fight with princes and powers, the greater struggle is with the demons concocted by false prelates who raise them from their own foul minds to infect our souls! Therefore, take heart brothers and sisters, in the sure and certain knowledge that..."

Overbridge booms on, his audience goggle eyed in his new world of 'undisciplined faith in everything.' Matthew and Ezra are unconvinced as is a third man who has edged even closer to the fiery preacher. Then Matthew sees Sarah Radbourne, sitting at the table just behind Overbridge. She stares up at him, ready to receive his message, any message, yet unable to do so, her eyes empty like an undisturbed pool in which many pebbles have fallen, but whose ripples have left no permanent impression. She has not seen her father, nor as he seen her, but he soon will. Matthew must get closer and speak to her. With his usual sensitivity Ezra has detected a slight change in mood. The three sceptics are no longer alone. Not everyone listens to Overbridge and some are getting restive. To Ezra's consternation Matthew pushes closer to the centre of the disquiet, then realises it's not Overbridge, but the girl he is trying to reach. He tries to stop him, but another man is already between them and not wanting to risk drawing further attention Ezra has to stand helplessly, willing Matthew to be careful. Then Sarah sees him and seems relieved. She will talk and not shout out in fear. Now Matthew might learn why she ran away, why she's here and...then, as Overbridge reaches the feverish climax of his harangue, her father interrupts with a long accusing finger.

"Enough of this ungodliness! A man who steals away the innocence of another man's daughter has no right to direct others in ways that are the sole preserve of the Almighty!"

Cries of 'What daughter?' as Overbridge turns to his accuser.

"You charge unjustly. Women are as free as men. Therefore..."

"An innocent girl with no experience of the city, cajoled into a noxious sect, delivered into the hands of blasphemers and devil worshippers!"

"You go too far, sir, "Overbridge thunders, "I will not be spoken to...who is this woman of whom you speak?"

Only now does Thomas see Sarah and she him. Her eyes lose some of their emptiness. Here is a pebble from the past, whose impression has been lost, but can be regained.

"There she is!" Thomas shouts, pointing to his daughter.

"Sarah? Sarah is your daughter?"

Several of Overbridge's men push their way through the throng and surround Thomas, but he is undaunted.

"You will release her immediately!"

Thomas breaks free and jumps at Overbridge. Two try to restrain him, but he elbows them aside. A third intervenes and receives a sharp backhander across his mouth followed by a heavy punch in the stomach. He reels back in pain. A fourth tries to grab Thomas as he lunges towards Sarah. Another man snatches her away as Thomas pulls Overbridge from his chair and hammers him repeatedly. Overbridge stumbles and falls to the ground. Thomas is ready to attack again, but three of the men stop him. The crowd splits into rival 'supporters' of Overbridge and Thomas and blows are exchanged.

Overbridge is unabashed by the mounting bedlam and keen to resume his address, but others are less sure and he and Sarah are steered from the chaos as Matthew and Thomas get within grasping distance. The uproar spills into the street, the noise attracting passing watchmen. Hearing this, Ezra pulls Matthew from behind. Matthew resists and swipes at Ezra, but he drops down, grabbing Matthew's ankles, yanking him to the ground. The watchmen enter as they disappear beneath the feet of the nearest grappling opponents. Oblivious to the mayhem, Thomas Radbourne pursues Sarah, now shielded by Overbridge and his supporters.

"Get out of the way, infernal rabble," he shouts, pulling the nearest man by his coat and levering him aside.

"That's him, he started it!" the landlord shouts, pointing to Thomas.

The watchmen plunge towards Thomas. Matthew is furious. Ezra has stopped him when Sarah was so easily within his grasp. Ducking and diving between the antagonists, he crawls between their legs, ignoring Ezra's pleas to 'make for the street.' His disappointment turns to rage when he gets on his knees and sees Sarah and Overbridge at the back door, but then drops down again when he sees the watchmen heading towards them. Ezra wriggles down further and slips like a snake, part crouching, part sliding, striking out a path of escape. Men stagger and stumble as Ezra drags Matthew behind. One man challenges Ezra.

"Out of my way, worm!" he snaps and kicks Ezra in the chest sending him reeling on his back.

He pulls out a knife, but can't use it fast enough in the split second Ezra remains vulnerable. Ezra arches his legs, springs back on his ankles, butts the man in the face and squats down out of reach. Then he fells his companions, punching at their legs before leaping at the door. Matthew gets up to follow and glares at the one man who remains standing, his hand at his side, but Ezra wrenches him away.

"There's no time for that, Matthew!"

Ezra reaches the door, jostles and prods those in his way and jumps into the street. Matthew follows, turning back momentarily to see Thomas Radbourne arrested by the watchmen.

Next day Matthew is disconsolate as he prepares to leave London. Last night Ezra arranged his hurried and 'definitely last' move.

"I shall be able to write a guidebook on all the garrets of London," Matthew complains grumpily.

He didn't sleep well. The room was hot and stuffy, but the real reason was his unsettled mind. The closer he gets to the nub of the enquiry the further away it is. Ezra has confirmed what he suspected. Buckden knew about Richard Collver. Buckden might have cooperated, but the opportunity was lost when he returned to London in pursuit of the Collvers and a trap for himself. Now he's close enough to get to Sarah Radbourne and Henry Collver. One or both must lead to the truth, but he's lost one while the other is out of reach. Ezra interrupts his thoughts.

"There's no time to lose. Getting you into the city was a lot easier than it's going to be getting you out."

"And once I'm out – if I get out – will I ever get back in?"

"Thomas Radbourne's been held for disturbing the peace, but that's as far as it's gone. Overbridge is in hiding."

"What about Sarah, have you...?"

"No."

"What about us, what have you heard?"

"There's a lot of talk," Ezra chuckles, "most of it about Overbridge and Thomas. There are a hundred versions of the ruckus that followed. You can take your pick."

"I don't have to, I was there."

"But the authorities weren't."

"The watch was."

"They were too busy going after Thomas and placating the landlord though someone noticed a man with a limp and his companion fighting their way out."

"What! They're on to us!"

Matthew leaps up and bangs his head painfully on one of the low beams. Ezra pushes him back down.

"I told you, one of many stories."

"Then...I'm safe... for a time..."

"Don't get complacent. They know you're in the city and will probably guess you'll make a break for it. They're stopping traffic at the gates and on the bridge, but I have a plan..."

"If only I could get a message to Phillip Skippon."

"...if I can get hold of a cart..."

"...even if he's on his way north..."

"...and somebody reliable as a driver..."

"...he won't let me down, he'll make sure..."

"...now, what should we put in the cart...?"

"Cart, what cart?"

"The cart that's going to take you over the bridge to Southwark."

"I have to make contact with the army, then..."

"No, Matthew, it's too risky. You don't know what lies Hugh Crittenden has fed to the general and now with Fenwick involved, (Matthew hisses through his teeth) would he believe you?"

"Crittenden and Fenwick, two snakes entwined together, poisoning the air with foul accusations!"

"Matthew, we have other concerns..."

"Ezra, there can be no relaxation in the struggle with the faithless. You above all should know, when Fenwick..."

"Matthew!" Ezra shrieks indignantly, "I need no reminding about that man."

"Yes, of course," Matthew says quietly, putting his hand on Ezra's arm, "One day...one day there will be justice."

"Maybe," Ezra says, placing his own hand over Matthew's, "But first, you have to get away."

Matthew has calmed and sits back quietly as Ezra busies around the room, muttering names of contacts and what he needs, interspersed with little chuckles as if ticking off some unseen list.

"Where are sending me?" Matthew says.

"To Buckden."

"What!"

"I told you. He no longer distrusts you and he knows where Richard is."

"You said young Collver is on the move."

"He is, but Buckden knows the movements of everybody in his area."

"*His* area, *his* area? It's Parliament's area, it's Parliament's country, the people's country!"

Ezra says nothing. He waits for Matthew to subside again.

"Is there no way I can get to Richard without Buckden?"

"Not unless you make the right contact. These people keep moving. Put the right name with the right place and you might find him, but..."

"Then that's what I must do. You must give me names and places."

Ezra is reluctant.

"It'll take too long. Without Buckden..."

"Give me the names and places."

"Alright, but it will be better for you to work through Buckden."

"If I'm out of London it's vital you keep watch for Overbridge."

"I'm not interested in Overbridge."

"Neither am I, but I am interested in Sarah Radbourne and she's with him."

"Once he's released her father will get to him."

"Then watch him too."

"I've got a lot of watching to do."

"It's what you're good at."

"Then we must prepare. With luck I will have the cart within the hour."

"First I must see my sister."

"What! Are you mad? Elizabeth's house is watched."

Matthew stamps his foot and hammers his hand angrily at the beam. It's the same one he just hammered with his head.

"I have to see her!"

Ezra sighs and whistles through his teeth. Matthew is unmoved.

"Alright, but it will have to be tonight," Ezra says, throwing up his arms, "We can't risk it in daylight. It means a delay..." he stops to consider, then with a resigned shrug, "You must be away first thing in the morning. We must pray God will preserve you for another day. After this I'm done."

Ezra wants to accompany him to Elizabeth's house, but Matthew insists on going alone, promising to take every precaution. Ezra is still anxious, but he can't be in two places at once.

Matthew crouches in the shadows for a half hour before daring to approach his sister's door. He's sure no one is watching, but even then first raps twice, then three times on the window. It's a game they played as children and he hopes she remembers. She does and immediately opens the door. Tears of surprise and tears of relief are soon followed by tears of fear for Elizabeth knows too well the extreme danger of Matthew's position.

"You give me nothing, but heartache brother, just as you did as a little boy," she says as they embrace, gently drubbing a feeble fist on his shoulder before breaking away and drying her eyes with her apron, "You were not followed?"

Matthew shakes his head.

"They've been here," she says, "turning everything over, how dare they come into my house and all because of that vile pup Crittenden. If I get my hands on him..."

"You told me not to lay my hands on him," Edmund says.

"That's different, you're a man. Men go too far."

"And you wouldn't?"

241

"Hah! He would feel...something he'd not easily forget."

"You've not seen him?" Matthew says.

"No. Now, what of you, where have been, what have been doing?"

Mathew quickly tells of his attempts to find Richard and Henry Collver and Sarah Radbourne and his encounter with Buckden

"Where have you been staying?" Elizabeth asks.

"Ezra has been very busy."

"That won't please him," she laughs and then more seriously, "I suppose he has no news of Prudie?"

Matthew is surprised.

"Why should he have knowledge of Prudie?"

"She's gone. At first we believed in pursuit of you because she overheard us talking bout you, but she fled to Harringstead. I don't know her exact intentions, but things have turned out very differently. Olivia Manning ran away and Prudie found her. Then Olivia was accused of being involved in the murder of her father's steward, Samuel Lexden. Prudie intervened and now they are both in great danger."

He promises to find Prudie after he's got hold of Richard Collver though he doesn't believe that'll take long. Elizabeth isn't convinced, but he says he'll have to return to Harringstead in any event. Elizabeth is sure of Prudie's innocence. If she's right and with Prudie defending her Olivia could not be involved in Lexden's murder, but Matthew isn't so sure. Rumour and her flawed reputation should not colour his judgement, but he has even more doubts about Olivia Manning. If Samuel Lexden saw her with Richard Collver she'd have a strong motive to silence him, but what if it goes further than that? If Richard is a Royalist, could she be one too? If Lexden surmised their relationship was more than personal he would pose a greater threat than merely snitching to her irate father. He would be informing the Justice of a Royalist conspiracy led by her lover.

He gets back from Elizabeth's without incident, slipping in through the back door of the house next door as directed and then climbing up to the roof. It's later than he promised so when he drops through the garret window with a great

242

thud Ezra jumps back in alarm. He's been finalising his preparations – and not just the material ones – for Matthew's journey. Reports from recent 'contacts' have updated him on Buckden's movements. Nothing conclusive, nor comprehensive, but as he keeps reminding Matthew every time he grumbles about 'more wild goose chasing' it's 'as good as they're likely to get.'

"George can get you so far, then he has to finish his business."

"You mean all this furniture and planking is a real delivery?" Matthew says incredulously.

"Well, it wasn't, but it is now. Turn every threat into an opportunity, isn't that what you used to say, Matthew? It doesn't make the arrangements for you any less effective and we've still had to go to a lot of trouble."

"You mean it wasn't part of the original plan to put somebody under a pile of timber and furniture?" Matthew quips.

"There was no *original plan*. It's a matter of making best use of resources as they arise."

"Ezra, just exactly where do all these tables and chairs come from...and this planking, it wouldn't have anything to do with one of those boats at the wharf?"

Ezra squirms.

"In these enquiries of yours, there are many questions to which you need answers. That question is not one of them."

"The only question I really need an answer is how do I get to Richard."

"Through Buckden."

Matthew is dubious. Buckden isn't necessarily the only one who knows Richard's movements. The few names and fewer places Ezra supplies might suffice if he can get to the right place and the right name, bit it's risky. If he's betrayed to Buckden all contacts and support will be gone. Buckden no longer distrusts him, so why incite opposition? Time is short with none to spare playing blind man's buff across the fields. The clubmen ways are not his ways and he'll not wait on Buckden's patronage.

Early next morning they split up.

"You will remember what I said about Sarah Radbourne," Matthew says, gripping Ezra arm.

"I will be diligent."

Matthew smiles.

"I don't doubt it."

"Now, no more delay. Get in and get down."

Matthew climbs into the back of the cart and eases under the assorted planking and furniture, which has been stacked high, leaving a small and concealed space within. The story is that this is intended for a Londoner's daughter, recently married in the country. The planking is a contribution to her joiner husband so he can build a small extension to their modest home. It covers the bottom of the cart, leaving no gaps through which Matthew can be observed. The heavy furniture, packed tight, almost locked together and difficult to lift should frustrate any prying inspections. It took Ezra and George, the 'driver' nearly two hours to assemble last night while Matthew was visiting Elizabeth.

"You'll have to be patient, you'll be slow moving," Ezra says.

Too long cramped in the constricted belly of the bouncing cart, Matthew's leg aches and his back is stiff. He can stretch his leg very slightly, wriggle his toes, ease his shoulders and his elbows, but anything more means moving his whole body, which is impossible. He'll have to be content. It may be some time before they reach their destination. Matthew's patience barely lasts until they reach Southwark, never before appreciating how long London Bridge is. Like the cart's rumbling wheels, it seems to go on and on. In his narrow enclosure, every sound is exaggerated. Dogs roar rather than bark, peddlers whoop and screech as if it's a bridge leading to Hell rather than the south bank. The grinding of other wheels, the shouting of a hundred voices, each trying to out-yell each other and the tramping of many feet grating and gnashing as if some horrible monster gouges through the cart's flimsy rails. With everyone trying to clear his or her path there's a constant jostling and scraping, cursing and arguing. Despite this, George the driver is quiet. He's under Ezra's strict instructions.

"Curb your tongue on that bridge no matter how much you're provoked. Don't draw attention to the cart. Just keep moving."

So he does, if a snail's pace qualifies as movement. Then they are stopped and Matthew's every muscle freezes, consonant with the intense cold permeating his whole body. Are they at the far end or still in the middle of the bridge? A disgruntled interchange between George and two other voices followed by a prodding and poking, clattering the furniture and a dull, fortunately heavy tapping to the planking. It's not too close. Matthew's neck is very stiff. Dare he move it? More grumbled words, then the wheels move. They're off! But it doesn't last and they're stopped again. By now they must be near the end of the bridge.

Someone asks where they go. Guildford, George lies. Long way to take furniture, comes a suspicious voice. More explanation is demanded and given. Matthew only hears some reference to a special place and a special daughter. A long, worrying silence follows. Then more prodding, poking and tapping, this time accompanied by a rocking of the cart. The furniture pile creaks and Matthew curls up (as much as he's able) expecting the tangled edifice to crash down, revealing its hunted human heart, but it remains firm and the rocking ceases. A few more unclear, but bellicose words exchanged with a disgruntled 'on your way' followed later by an aggressive 'and to you' from George. Over the bridge they speed up, but progress is still painfully slow with the same disjointed and confusing noises. Then it's quieter. They must be in the country by now and Matthew wonders why the charade continues. Surely he can emerge from the depths and join George at the front of the cart? Secreted in the congested cart, jangled and thrown around on the stony, pot holed road his thoughts return to his quest. Buckden commands more than a rustic rabble, so somewhere amidst those names and places he'll find Richard Collver.

The cart stops. George gets down, taps the side several times and calls. Then a scraping and sliding above. It's like a jigsaw that's been put together and taken apart dozens of times, taking only a couple of minutes for enough furniture to be slid aside before George is working on the planking. The sunlight streams through and Matthew forces away the last timber himself and rises up, though he's still stiff. George helps him down. They are in open country. A small clump of trees gives some cover, though the track is empty. Matthew strides around, swings his arms and twists his neck to get feeling back into his numbed limbs and constricted torso. George watches him grimly. As usual, Matthew limps badly for the first few paces.

"It'll pass," he says as he's said so many times before.

George nods, half convinced though he notices how quickly the limp becomes less pronounced.

"Now," Matthew says, "Are we there?"

"It's safe for you to be seen."

"Meaning nobody knows me here?"

"Ezra told me to let you out near Cravenhurst," George says with a non committal nod, "close to the church. It is just over the rise."

"Will Buckden be there?"

"Before sunset."

The sun is low in the sky, but still some way above the horizon. It could be a long wait.

"I must be away," George says, getting back on the cart, which he turns in a wide circle to face the way they have come.

"Aren't you going to take me?" Matthew says.

"As I said, just over the rise," George says, already getting the horse to move on, "It's better you're not seen with me and the cart...a man travelling alone, it's better."

He flicks the reins and the cart gathers speed.

"God be with you," he shouts, waving as the cart reaches the corner before disappearing behind the trees.

"And with you," Matthew mumbles, "though I fear I'll have more need of Him than you."

He trudges towards Cravenhurst, reaching the village in a quarter hour. He stops at the church and surveys the gravestones and the green. All is quiet, no one around. He could wait here, but remembers Ezra's information. *Richard has been seen at an inn at Cravenhurst*. There's only one inn and he soon finds it. Ezra told George it was safe to be seen at Cravenhurst. He's tired and thirsty, but first he must have a story. He's on the tramp looking for work. Where? Basingstoke, that can't be too far away. If he's on the wrong road they'll direct him. It'll have to be the cloth trade. Where's he come from? Not London, that only leads to trouble. Guildford will do. He doesn't speak with a Surrey accent, but does it matter? He's been on the tramp a long time and with the war and...He gets to the inn, a small, modest, quiet place. He pushes on the door. It's dark inside. A couple of men in the corner and another at the counter with the landlord all turn as he goes over. He orders ale. It takes a few moments for his eyes to adjust to the dimness. He'll take the initiative.

"Am I on the right road for Basingstoke?"

"If you want to go the long way round," the landlord says.

He doesn't smile. The others look askance. A man in the corner titters into his drink. Being on the wrong road in these parts is more than negligent, but an indication of idiocy.

"You'll not make Basingstoke today unless you've got wings," the man at the counter says with undisguised delight at Matthew's lack of foresight.

"You can always stay here," the landlord grunts, going over to the men in the corner, leaving Matthew left alone with the man at the counter.

They stare at each other for a few moments over their drinks, each assessing if they can be trusted. Cravenhurst is on Ezra's list of places. What of the names?

"Do you know a Ben Anderton?" Matthew says.

"Why would you want to know?"

"You know him?"

The man nods. Matthew takes a further chance.

"I have a friend who has another friend who has a son..." the man's face contorts as he grapples with Matthew's convoluted detachment, "...he may be in the area."

"He has a name...this son of a friend of a friend?"

Mathew has to be sure.

"You are Ben Anderton?"

Ben nods.

"Richard Collver."

"He has been here with the clubmen."

"Could you get a message to him?"

"I might."

"Tell him I have news of Olivia Manning. It's important. He'll understand."

Ben makes no promises, but asks if Matthew will be at the inn. It's a commitment Matthew would rather not make, but he has no choice. No mention is made of Buckden and after Ben leaves Matthew wonders whether he should keep the appointment. This contact may be more productive than Buckden's questions and evasions, empty assurances and irritating disappointments. If Ben is reliable Matthew will soon get to Richard without Buckden's help, but if Ben is a clubman he'll report back to Buckden and they'll find Matthew at the inn. But if he's unreliable, why didn't he mention Buckden?

It's almost sunset. Matthew walks to the church and through the yard. Harringstead and reverend Stradsey cross his mind. It seems a long time ago. He hurries into the fields, losing sight of the church. It's a warm, tranquil evening. He feels relaxed even if only for a brief hour the peace of the land calls him and there's no enquiry, no flight from his accusers, no clubmen, no danger, no war. It's alluring, but transitory like a dream for in his real awaking the threats remain and the war remains. He walks in a wide circle, sees no one and returns to the church. It's dark. Cravenhurst sleeps. He skirts around, keeping as unobtrusive as he can. If Buckden came he has gone and Matthew is beset with doubts. He may never see Ben Anderton again. What if Richard doesn't come? He walks back, suddenly very tired, his leg aching, though this could be as much from his troubled thoughts as from the walk. The night encloses. Sleep beckons and it's the worst time for judgements and decisions. The inn is crowded. Matthew checks with the landlord. As he turns to go to his room, Ben approaches, leans very close and speaks quietly amidst the hubbub.

"Tomorrow, at the church, eleven."

"Collver?"

Ben nods, returns to his seat, then ignores him. Matthew goes up and is soon asleep. Next day he waits behind the large headstone in the churchyard. He's already been into the empty church. He doesn't have to wait long. A man, around twenty, approaches from the fields and looks round apprehensively. He looks tall, but only because he's so thin, his pallor almost white as if he's been shut up for a long time. If this is a Royalist conspirator Matthew is unimpressed. Then he notices the same firm determination of the mouth and the languid eyes of his father and uncle. He stops and turns nervously. Matthew approaches him.

"Richard Collver?"

"Yes," Richard says almost inaudibly, "You are Matthew Fletcher?"

"You are alone?" Matthew says, nodding.

"You have news of Olivia?"

Matthew takes his arm.

"Let's go into the church where we can't be observed."

They sit in a pew about half way down, Matthew at the aisle end, turned towards Richard, who is about three places along. Richard speaks rapidly, spitting out short sentences in stabbing thrusts like a series of counts in an indictment.

"She is in danger. I've known it for some time. I must go back. It was a mistake to leave. As soon as I left I knew, but what could I do? It was not possible. Even so I despise myself. I will return. Tell me!"

"She is accused of Samuel Lexden's murder."

"He is murdered then."

"You do not seem surprised."

"Olivia had nothing to do with it."

"The steward saw you together and informed her father."

"That doesn't mean she killed him."

"It gave you both good reason and you ran away."

Richard looks down, but speaks with a determined passion, lifting his head towards Matthew only for the last few words, his eyes in a wide seeming innocent pleading.

"To protect Olivia. If I was not around, Manning might not pressure her. He will never agree to us being together. I am not good enough."

"You protect her by being away from her."

"When everybody is against you with only detestation in their eyes and your presence draws their enmity."

As Richard recounts the highs of their meetings, the lows of their absences, how they couldn't 'curb their feelings' and how being apart was 'pure pain' Matthew's concentration drifts. For if Richard feels what he felt for Jane Ellerton, then Matthew understands more than Richard can ever know. He watches Richard, but he's not listening, nor as he loses himself in remembrances does he look around the church. He doesn't notice, he doesn't see.

"...which is also why I couldn't immediately go back, could I?"

Richard waits

"Could I?"

"What...couldn't go back...why?" Matthew mumbles, surfacing at last from his reverie.

"When I realised the real reason why this war had to be won."

"The war, the real reason, but aren't you with the clubmen?"

"Was...I was glad to escape the bondage of convention, but in their company I realised how this was much more than a struggle between King and Parliament."

"I can well imagine," Matthew says knowingly.

"It's about the rights of the people, all the people and how they must be involved, how they must rule."

With a fiery passion only slightly less than his feelings for Olivia, Richard launches into a burning exhortation. The 'gentlemen' of the Commons as well as the Lords and the King must give way to a Parliament translated into one that represents the rights and free will of all the people. Matthew can hardly believe what he's hearing. Far from being a Royalist or even a 'neutral' clubman, Richard has been heavily influenced by radical ideas.

"You're a Leveller," he mutters, "You've even less chance now of being accepted by Olivia's father."

"Or even by my own father."

"Perhaps not," Matthew says gravely, "I have other news."

There's no immediate response to his father's death and his uncle's apparent disappearance, just the same intense concentration on the floor. Then he turns to Matthew and repeats what he's just been told.

"...drowned...in the river?"

"Could your father swim?"

"Yes."

Then the anger rises, as it must.

"It was no accident."

"No."

"And uncle Henry has gone too?"

"It seems so."

"Manning killed him."

"You can't be sure of that."

"You mean I can't prove it."

"I mean you can't *know* it."

"Oh but I do and I know why. My father was killed by mistake. Manning intended to kill my uncle."

"That's what Henry said, but why?"

"Because of what he knows about Ellerton and Amberley, especially Edward Amberley, you need to talk to him."

"Maybe I will, but you must come back to London so we can clear up your father's death and that of Samuel Lexden."

Richard shakes his head.

"I'm having nothing to do with that."

"Where were you when Lexden was killed?"

"I've told you enough."

"I'm not satisfied. You must come back with me to London."

"No."

"Then I shall have to take you by force."

"On what authority?"

"The authority of Parliament."

Matthew stands.

"Leave him alone!"

The voice comes from the back of the church. Nathaniel Buckden and another man are striding towards them.

"It would have been better if you had been here yesterday evening, captain."

"You cannot stop me in the execution of my duty!"

Matthew steps into the aisle to face Buckden and protect his 'prisoner,' but Richard slips along the pew towards the north aisle.

"You will not take him," Buckden says, stopping just before Matthew, "He comes with me!"

Matthew's hand goes to his sword, but then he hears footsteps behind him.

"You will be taking no one today, Matthew Fletcher!"

Matthew twists round to see several soldiers and an officer. Now he knows the voice and stares into the hard eyes of Henry Fenwick.

"You're under arrest," Fenwick says with a satisfied leer and then barks to the soldiers, "Take him!"

As the soldiers accost and disarm Matthew, Buckden, his companion and Richard Collver run, unchallenged and escape from the back of the church.

11

OLIVIA doesn't run far from Prudie. She knows the village offers little chance of escape. Her absence from Syme House will soon be noticed and her father's servants will be sent to forestall her. The village is dangerous, plenty of people with a grudge against the Mannings who will relish intervening when the family is fighting amongst itself. Then she remembers the mysterious woman, who seemed to know so much. Hasn't she seen her before? If she is local, she hadn't betrayed her, so perhaps can be trusted. Olivia turns back and gets to the field where Prudie is speaking to Ned Frattersham.

"I'm so afraid, what am I to do? Please help me!" she says, cartching Prudie's hand.

It's too much for Ned. Prudie tries to grab him, but he's too quick and Olivia pulls too strongly the other way.

"You have to help me. I know you can. You are from here."

Prudie looks at her angrily and Olivia notices Ned's disappearing figure.

"That's Ned Frattersham. What was he telling you?"

"Enough. Come, we need to get somewhere safe."

Olivia runs with Prudie through places she never knew existed, arriving by a roundabout route at Alice's cottage. Manning's men see them coming. Alice escapes, but Olivia and Prudie are taken. Putting Prudie in the village lock up, which hasn't been used for over a year inflames the latent conflict between Manning and the villagers.

"What's good for one is good for both," many say, "The poor woman in the lock up, the daughter of the Justice in her own house, yet both accused the same. It's not right."

That said, Prudie might not necessarily be the worse off. Doing his duty without especial fervour, the constable keeps her secure, but spares her Stradsey's 'spiritual' guidance while the landlord of the inn and others maintain her material needs, even if her immediate friends have gone into hiding. Olivia may be held in more congenial surroundings, but she's still held, locked most of the day in her room and subject to the admonitions of the minister. While Manning can't contemplate Olivia imprisoned in the village with a common woman of dubious reputation, that might have served both him and Olivia better. For reverend Jeremiah Stradsey sees his duty as stiffening the Justice's questioning.

Prudie isn't even sure of what she's accused other than 'disturbances in horses and cattle.' Alone with her thoughts she shudders. A formal accusation might soon follow. Witchcraft frenzy is gripping the eastern counties and Stradsey has referred to someone called Matthew Hopkins, who purports to 'find witches.' She can guess the methods such a person will use on innocent women. She's safer for a time out of the grasp of crazed villagers, but for how long? There's a noise outside. She turns nervously. Its the landlord's girl with her food, let in by the constable, who watches the whole time she's there. She's a sullen, silent creature. Is she afraid of Prudie or contemptuous of her? Either way she offers no comfort, but the food is good and she's hungry.

"We're very busy. I have to get back to the inn," she says, then to the constable, "Can I come back for the dishes?"

"Can't you wait?" he says impatiently.

The girl shakes her head.

"I'll let you back in a half hour," he says.

The girl is glum even edgy, though as she leaves Prudie detects the hint of a smirk. It's only when they've both gone she realises why. Concealed under the plate is a note. The girl must have been afraid Prudie would pull it out while the constable was there.

Have news. Don't despair. The girl will be back. Leave a message. Ezra Stanfield.

She scribbles a reply on the paper. If Ezra is half the man she believes him to be he'll play his part well. He's her only hope. A half hour later the constable and the girl return. They are greeted by noises, the howling of a wolf, the mewing shriek of a fox.

"I told you," the girl says, "I saw something earlier."

Yet she's surprisingly unconcerned and steps ahead lively, but the constable holds back, already afraid to get close to the door. Prudie has been waiting. Inside they find her alternately squawking like a bird as she points to the window and then bawling as she retreats to the corner.

"See, see, he is here!"

"Make sure his familiars are not around," Fenwick shrieks as Matthew is held, "Witches make themselves innocuous, then when your guard is down they let loose their devils."

"Even you don't believe that ludicrous nonsense," Matthew shouts.

"Always made excuses, didn't you Fletcher? Charged with rooting out witchcraft, but fell down on your duties, not carrying out a proper investigation."

"The only one falling down on his duties was you," Matthew says icily, jerking forward and wriggling to try and break free, "Treacherous viper, I'll slice your bowels and throw them to the crows!"

The soldiers have to grip him firmly.

"Aye, this is no devil worshipper," Fenwick says coldly, "but an enemy of the state."

Matthew gets no more opportunity to challenge his accusers as he and Fenwick exchange trenchant and bitter comments about their acrimonious past and harangue each other's 'lack of authority.' With his prisoner secure, Fenwick gets bored and hurries back to London, leaving a sergeant in charge of Matthew's escort.

The return journey is much quicker than the outward and despite being in custody, more comfortable. The custody is quite 'loose.' Some of the soldiers are from Matthew's old regiment and they remember well his kindnesses. They will do their duty, (Matthew expects nothing less) but with no enthusiasm and little respect for Major Henry Fenwick.

"It's a mistake, captain," one soldier says, out of the sergeant's earshot, "In London, you'll easily explain yourself. When General Skippon returns..."

"Quiet!" the sergeant shouts, drawing closer, "No talking with the prisoner. Ride on and keep a sharp lookout!"

"Yes, sergeant."

Sergeant Phillips rides silently beside Matthew for a while until the soldiers are some way ahead. When he speaks, his tone is surprisingly forbearing and sensitive.

"I hope they've not been annoying you, captain. They mean well. We are all on heightened alert. The King is close to Leicester. There are fears for the security of London. Royalist spies could be everywhere."

Matthew notices the reference to Royalist spies doesn't include him.

"General Skippon is not in London?"

"Not at the moment."

"Major Fenwick is the most senior officer?"

"The most senior in charge of security," the sergeant replies carefully and then with studied correctness, "He has friends in Parliament."

Then they are silent until they reach London, the sergeant intent on the road, alert for any possible interruptions, Matthew's thoughts dominated by the forty eight hours immediately before his capture. Ben Anderton's communication to Richard Collver, however and wherever that was delivered, included more than Matthew's words. He must have said something about Matthew himself for Richard knew his name. Yet Matthew hadn't told Ben either, so how did *he* know? Because Matthew was expected or through Buckden or both? For Buckden was there. *You should have kept your appointment, captain.* Maybe, but if he had would Matthew have been any safer? How could Buckden betray him alone? What about the London end? *This time I'm done*, Ezra said. Was Ezra behind this, talking to this one, getting messages from that one, finding a cart, where did all that furniture and planking come from? George didn't come in to the village. Where is Ezra now? This time I'm done.... *this time*...not anytime, *this* time...I've had enough. Enough of running and hiding, helping Matthew, his investigation interfering with more lucrative activities?

Matthew is led to a forbidding building close to the river. It looks around two hundred years old. With grim resignation his escort leaves him at the door, from which he's conducted by two other soldiers to an upper room. It has only one window, but the curtains are drawn. He stands in front of the single small table, facing the empty chair on the other side. No one speaks. The soldiers shuffle uneasily. Someone enters, shuts the door, but then doesn't move. Matthew doesn't turn. He knows by the breathing it's Fenwick. Ignoring his accuser his only weapon and he intends to use it to greatest effect. No one moves for a couple of minutes. Eventually, Fenwick steps behind the desk and sits. He's in his late twenties, a little older than Matthew with a long sallow face, high eyebrows and a wide, close trimmed moustache. He spends some time adjusting his coat, stretching his legs, lighting his long clay pipe and pulling papers from his pocket, which he smoothes out on the table. All the time Matthew stares dispassionately, his eyes boring into the top of Fenwick's head. At first Fenwick doesn't face him, looking left and right to the soldiers on either side of Matthew.

"Hold him fast. Fletcher is a dangerous and ruthless man."

The soldiers take hold of Matthew's arms. An hour ago Matthew would be tempted to lunge at Fenwick, but he's calmer now and thinking more carefully. There are bound to be more soldiers Fenwick can summon and assaulting an officer in his present predicament would only make his position even more precarious.

"Why did you leave Harringstead before your enquiries were completed in direct contravention of your orders?" Fenwick says without looking up.

"I contravened no order. My enquiries in Harringstead were temporarily halted."

"That is not what Lieutenant Crittenden says."

Fenwick looks up. Matthew doesn't flinch, ignoring both the statement and Hugh.

"I repeat, Lieutenant Crittenden..."

"I heard what you said."

"You deliberately abandoned a fellow officer, leaving him surrounded by hostile persons, in particular two dangerous witches."

"Lieutenant Crittenden undertook his own investigations."

"He was working under your instructions."

"He was in no specific danger."

"You deliberately left him alone with your devilish confederates..."

"Don't be ridiculous."

"...so you could return, unhindered, to London because you knew Prince Rupert's offensive in the midlands was imminent, preparatory to an attack on the city and Parliament. For this the Royalists needed up to date information on the state of our defences. That's why you left Harringstead, unencumbered with another officer, loyal to Parliament."

"That's preposterous."

"It would have been impossible for you to reconnoitre our dispositions with lieutenant Crittenden at your side. He would naturally want to know why you were spending so much time in so many different parts of the city."

"Ludicrous."

"You have been seen in various places, including the river."

"I was undertaking my enquiries."

"The better to meet up with your Royalist contacts in various taverns."

Matthew shakes his head.

"Your guilt is clear, Fletcher, all we need are the names of your associates."

"I have no *associates* at least not Royalist ones. I am a loyal officer of the Parliament."

"Don't trifle with me, Fletcher, you forget I have experience of your lies."

"*My* lies! It was you, *major* Fenwick, or rather lieutenant Fenwick as you then were, who was responsible for an unnecessary and disastrous charge at..."

"You led that charge, Fletcher, not I!"

"You passed on the orders from the colonel, except they were false orders, they never existed, it was your incompetence that was responsible for..."

"Lies! There was no proof of that."

"There wouldn't be, the colonel was killed if you remember. That left only a certain corporal who accompanied you, the only one to contradict you!"

"You were the only one who believed that reprobate Stanfield, later shown in his true colours as the criminal he is."

"It was his word against yours."

"Exactly. Strange how it was you that helped him to get away."

"He was innocent of the charge."

"So you say," Fenwick laughs, gradually subsiding to a mischievous chuckle as he looks intently at Matthew, "Stanfield will do anything to redeem himself."

"What do you mean by that, foul mouthed villain?"

"Names, Fletcher, names, give me the names!"

"Go to Hell!"

"Hold him, you men. We'll waste no more time. By God, we'll have it out of him!"

Fenwick jumps up, casts the chair aside and leaps on Matthew, landing two heavy punches in his stomach. Matthew reels back in pain.

"Who are your associates? What information have you passed to your Royalist masters?"

Winded and tottering, Matthew crumples up, but then regains his strength and tries to break free.

"Damn you, Fenwick, damn you to perdition. You're the same evil and stupid villain you always were. I'm no spy, you cretinous dog!"

"Want some more, do you, Fletcher? You'll tell me, you'll have to."

Fenwick hits Matthew hard in the mouth and punches him again in the kidneys. As Matthew staggers back, one of the soldiers loosens his hold.

"No, sir, no, this is enough."

"What, defy my orders?" Fenwick shouts, pushing the soldier aside and grabbing Matthew's arm.

He tries to hit him, but the other soldier pulls Matthew towards the door shouting, "No, no, leave him, leave him."

Mathew struggles, but he's weakened. Both soldiers now take hold of him again.

"No, sir," the first says, "We will hold him."

"But you will not touch him again," the second says.

Fenwick glares angrily at them before retiring behind the table to slump into the chair.

"I demand to see General Skippon," Matthew says defiantly.

"General Skippon is out of London," Fenwick replies.

"Then another officer with legitimate authority."

"I am that authority," Fenwick says coldly, "I'll get some other men up here with stiffer backs and more than water in their veins so we can properly resume this interrogation."

Reluctantly the constable edges into the narrow room as Prudie claws her arms, licking the blood from them, then lifting them high over her head.

"He comes, he comes! See, see!"

She points at the window and slides menacingly along the wall. Fearfully the constable moves closer, unsure how to restrain the deranged woman. She shrieks again, pointing to the door. The constable freezes against the opposite wall and stares horrified, but refuses to follow her finger. Prudie is closer to the door now, next to the girl.

"He's here," the girl says with bleak, quiet deliberation.

Then the room is filled with a terrifying whoop followed by a high pitched wail. Prudie takes the last two steps to the door where an awful, shapeless blackness stands next to the girl.

"I have my power now," Prudie shouts excitedly, sidling up to the creature, then turning to the constable, "Now, for you!"

"Stay where you are, constable," the girl shouts, "or she will set him on you!"

Open mouthed, wide eyed and flattened against the wall, the constable knows he should protect the girl, but is petrified and dumbstruck. He braces himself, pathetically pushing his back into the wall. The creature sways, then with an ear splitting bawl its black skin suddenly expands its form into a grotesque bulge like some eyeless monster insect. Still it grows. The constable closes his eyes. Then he hears a scuttling sound. When he reopens his eyes the creature has enveloped Prudie and the girl, for they are now through the door and it bars the way between them and the constable. Then it's gone, through the door and away as if it flies. The constable, stunned, bewildered, but oddly relieved, waits a few moments and then approaches the door. He goes through the outer passage and into the empty street, looks up and down, but there's no one. He goes to the inn and raises the alarm. The 'witch' Prudie Westrup has got away, aided by her 'familiar,' a peculiar black apparition.

"Your girl saw it," he says to the landlord.

But the girl is away on an errand and over the next few days, despite constant reminders, will recall nothing of any 'presence,' remembering only the unlocked door that the constable left, through which the prisoner escaped. She'll not mention the large black coat in the shed at the bottom of the yard and the stranger from London, to whom she'd lent it after receiving the note.

Prudie and Ezra slip silently and unseen through the undergrowth and trees on Harringstead's eastern side, skirting by Prudie's lone cottage, but do not linger. It's too dangerous. On the way, Ezra tells what he's found out, that Olivia is being held against her will at Syme House, accused of involvement in Samuel Lexden's murder. Prudie doesn't respond.

"Did she do it?" he says.

"Is that what they believe at Syme House?"

"Not her mother. She'll not think ill of her daughter."

"Lady Constance is hardier than her husband. He's too influenced by that villainous minister."

261

"But *did* she do it?"

"She was desperate to find Richard Collver and still will be," Prudie says, conspicuously avoiding his question, then light-heartedly, "You played your part well."

"Not one I'd want to do again. It was a dangerous one for you."

"If they brand you a witch, it makes sense to act the part. If the constable is stupid enough to believe such nonsense, then it's easy to make him believe a little more."

She laughs.

"You are not yet accused of witchcraft," he says solemnly.

"Only a matter of time if that sanctimonious scoundrel Stradsey has anything to do with it."

"But you will be accused with Olivia, because you were with her at your friend's cottage."

Still she avoids the issue of Olivia's guilt. It makes him uneasy.

"Why did you come here?" she says.

"Matthew is taken, accused of being a Royalist spy."

He explains Matthew's arrest by Fenwick.

"You can do nothing?" she says.

"I need some answers."

She stops. Their eyes meet in mutual scepticism, yet also a drawing together of two people recognising themselves in the other.

"Then we must hurry without delay to Syme House," she says.

They pass Narrow Baulk Field and run through the open country even though there's virtually no light until Syme House comes into sight.

"You know where Olivia is held?" she whispers as they crouch behind the wall close to the house.

He points to a window on the first floor.

"How do you find out so much in such a short time?" she says.

"The same way I got the message to you in that stinking hole. By keeping to my own kind and making contact with those I know will help me. We are survivors, Prudie. For those at the bottom of the heap it's the only way."

"You got that young girl to play *her* part so well."

"Only because she believed in you."

"Can you get Olivia out?"

"With you help and another contact."

"Let me guess, the scullery maid."

Ezra has made his arrangements with Martha. On a prearranged signal, she gives the reply. The house is quiet. Everyone is in bed. They enter through the kitchen.

"You'll not need me no more," Martha says nervously, "I can go up?"

"Yes, Martha," Ezra says, "and thank you."

As soon as she leaves, he lets in Prudie.

"Better she thinks I'm alone," he chuckles, "That girl may not like Stradsey, but she's even more frightened of witches."

They steal softly through the main hall and pausing only to make sure there's no lingering late night conversation before going upstairs. It's very dark and they have no light, yet Ezra picks his way with the sight and sureness of a cat, learnt from many late night wanderings along the alleys and courts of London. He's never been in the house before, but has remembered every detail, every room, door, stair and corner, all from a pithy, hurried description by Martha. Ezra knows where Olivia is held and by whom.

"You're sure he has the key?" Prudie whispers as they get to the door of Stradsey's room.

"Oh yes, he trusts nobody this one."

"What if the door is locked?"

Ezra pulls a short, thin knife from his pocket and grins. He twists it gently in the lock, but the door is unlocked. The open curtains allow a little light to peter through the window. They stand for a moment for their eyes to adjust and hear a soft, dull wheezing – Stradsey is asleep. They move to their positions, stopping only when Prudie inadvertently steps on a creaky board. Stradsey moves, breathes more heavily, turns and then is silent. Ezra leans down beside the pillow. Prudie moves to the bottom of the bed, silhouetted against the light from the window and raises her arms as Ezra gives the sleeper a forceful prod. Stradsey jumps up suddenly and seeing the dark, fearful form is about to cry out, but Ezra shoves a hand over his mouth and presses a knife at his throat.

"Quiet, reverend, very quiet or you'll be meeting your maker afore you've prepared yourself!"

Stradsey continues to stare unbelievingly at Prudie.

"Out of bed, reverend," Ezra says, easing the knife from his throat, "and get your keys."

Stradsey keeps looking at Prudie. She moves away from the bed and Ezra digs him sharply in the side with a sharp 'Up!' and 'Get the key to Olivia's room.'

"This is a grave offence to my calling," Stradsey says as he goes to the cabinet.

"Aye, maybe," Ezra says, "So is locking up innocent young women."

"She's not innocent!"

"Shut up and get the key."

Prudie has moved to the door. Stradsey glances at her nervously as he opens a drawer. Ezra grabs the key and pushes him towards Prudie. Stradsey hesitates. Ezra shoves him further.

"Come along, reverend, no hanging back."

With mixed outrage and terror, Stradsey reluctantly goes to the next room and unlocks the door. Prudie runs to the bed, wakes Olivia and gets her up quickly. Only now does Stradsey recognise Prudie, rather than see her as some devilish apparition.

"You'll never get away with this."

"Sit," Ezra says, pointing to a chair.

Stradsey hovers, glancing between Olivia and Prudie. Ezra pushes him down, stuffs a scarf in his mouth, which he ties tightly before binding his ankles and arms to the chair.

"We'll be leaving you now, reverend."

They lock the door, then creep to the stairs with the still only half awake Olivia. The house is quiet. No one stirs as they descend softly, though every creak of the stairs, every sighing of the roof, every croak from the walls, denounce and inveigh, threatening to rouse and rally the household. Even Ezra wonders if someone has heard Stradsey and how long before he's found. They reach the main hall. Only a few steps now to the door and escape. Then a figure emerges from the shadows.

"Would you go without saying goodbye?"

"Mother!" Olivia calls.

"Quick," Ezra calls, grabbing Olivia and Prudie by the hands, "we are done for!"

But Prudie pulls away and holds him back.

"No, no, discovery by this lady will not be our undoing."

Constance Manning embraces Olivia, then turns to Prudie.

"You are right, Prudie Westrup, I will not betray you."

"You saw us?" Ezra says.

"No, nor heard you until now. I couldn't sleep. I came down to await the dawn," she says abstractedly, then turns to Ezra, "If you are to rescue my daughter you should not delay."

"Before they come from the village," Prudie says dolefully, "I deceived the constable and escaped from the lock up."

"And if he had organised a hue and cry, they would already be here. The radical contagion has already reached these parts. You are seen as an opponent of this family, so few will join in your recapture. Thomas Radbourne has been seen again though my husband will say the Collvers are behind it," then she adds with a hint of amused satisfaction, "Of course, the constable might have found it more difficult with the minister not in the village. Now, you must be away before the house is up. You have a plan?"

"Yes..." Prudie begins.

"No," Constance says, putting up her hand, "I have no more heard you than I have seen you. I am back to my bed."

She mounts the stairs without a backward glance. Grateful for the extra time they've gained, they run to Drensell Wood. Prudie leads the way, twisting and turning through impenetrable undergrowth and trees, hardly pausing until they arrive at a small clearing, deep in the heart of the wood where Alice is waiting with Richard Collver.

"It seems I'm not the only one with contacts," Ezra says incredulously when Richard reveals his identity, "How long have you been here?"

"Since last night," Richard says as Olivia runs across to him.

"Let me guess...Buckden...is he...?"

"He led me here, but he's gone."

"Back home?"

"To London."

"Why there?"

"He has a debt to repay."

"Matthew! He's gone after Matthew," Ezra shouts, "Prudie you've got to get me out of this place."

"But we've only just arrived."

"I have to get back to London. I have to get to Matthew."

12

FAMILIARITY encourages acceptance. The routines of imprisonment can be accommodated when there seems no hope. Coming to terms with bare walls, a stout door, the tiniest window, a cold, dank, acrid floor and a dark impenetrable ceiling, imagining the worst and acceding to it...

...Last night Matthew was moved to this deserted place in the east of the city. Too battered and bruised to walk properly, the gaoler dragged him down the steps and into the meagre, fetid cell where he was thrown onto the bare and uncomfortable bunk. Yet he rested and was undisturbed throughout the night. He woke to see the dawn light fingering the edge of the window, but exhaustion swept over him again and he fell into a final fitful sleep. Now he remembers little of the journey, hardly able to open his eyes, let alone take in what could be seen from the back of the rumbling cart. He turns over on his back, winces with a sudden ache and lies, staring at the grim, brown stained ceiling. It smells damp and probably leaks when it rains. He hears a soft though distant light scurrying. A sure sign there's at least one four legged fellow inmate. But Matthew will not give up. What is right is immovable. He moves again and rubs his side.

After the soldiers intervened and refused to assist his heavy handed tactics Fenwick completely lost control, shouting hysterically at Matthew, saying he'd 'brought the wrath of the

Lord upon himself.' Matthew said 'The Lord has no hand in this, only the wrath of Henry Fenwick.' Hurling incoherent curses at Matthew, Fenwick rushed out and returned with soldiers more amenable to his inclinations. Then began the second stage of Matthew's 'interrogation.' From an investigating officer, commissioned by one of Parliament's most senior generals, he's now a common criminal, charged as a spy. Such is the dust thrown up by the wild forces of revolution. Who had betrayed him? He tries not to think of Ezra, though there's a disturbing logic behind Fenwick's despicable assertions.

"When you associate with the dregs of London you embrace their standards and will be treated as one of them."

This time I'm done. Ezra's parting words. Discharging his debt to Matthew by getting him out of London and afterwards free to betray him? It's a bitter thought. Matthew shivers as if an icy draught suddenly passes through the room. He crosses his arms and rubs his shoulders. Can anyone be trusted? He feels more alone than ever, more than before Cropredy Bridge, before he faced the prospect of death. It's an abyss he'd rather ignore. Like the lone traveller on a country road at night. What you don't see can't hurt you. Buckden ran off with Richard Collver. It was his contacts that enticed Matthew out of London and what of his local contact, Ben Anderton? He fell into the trap and now languishes in this stinking hole at the mercy of his worst enemy. Better to believe Buckden also duped Ezra. How can the London authorities have allowed Fenwick to have control of security? With the country facing the greatest crisis of the war, Skippon and other senior officers away, who knows what 'gentlemanly' dregs have been left to fill the shoes of more honourable men?

There's a noise outside the door, someone shuffling along the stones. Probably the old man with the keys he saw last night. He stops, deep, sonorous intakes as he catches his breath. Will the door swing open with Matthew dragged off for another 'discussion' with Fenwick? More footsteps, dying away until another door is closed. Maybe he's forgotten or thought better of his task. Matthew sits up. His back is less painful. It's lighter now. He gazes forlornly around his tiny room. How long will he be here? What if Parliament is defeated and Prince Rupert's 'gallant' horsemen sweep into the city? What chance has he then? His throat cut without demur or burnt alive as the building is destroyed in the sack of the city? Then, as his sweep reaches the door he notices something on the floor. He gets up and picks a small, dirty piece of paper. He unfolds it, sits back on the bunk and reads the short, scrawled message.

Prudie and Ezra in Harringstead. Now in London looking for Sarah. The barn door sticks. Await a tinker – Elizabeth.

It's not written in Elizabeth's hand, but it's from her. The barn door sticks is from their childhood. Only she would know. He's filled with mixed feelings of regret, relief, apprehension and expectancy. Await a tinker.

Less than a mile away one man leaves and another arrives at the house of his sister. It's the first time Edmund and Ezra have met. They examine each other in the doorway, like two travellers from opposite directions, surprised to find they journey to the same place.

"You will be careful," Edmund says to Elizabeth, his eyes darting to Ezra, "I'm not sure..."

"I'll be safe enough," she says, nudging him gently, "With your information and Ezra's help, what have I to fear?"

Edmund is still doubtful. He can be sure of the information, gleaned from his trampings around the city taverns and meeting rooms, but is less sure of 'Matthew's unusual, but trusted confederate' as Elizabeth calls him. He goes reluctantly. They discussed the situation at length last night. Edmund reminded her Ezra was a deserter from the army, a man accused of murdering a fellow soldier, but it only stiffened her resolve.

"You did not say those things before."

"He was not then responsible for my wife's safety."

"I can look after myself and if Matthew believed in him, so must we. He's one of the few men prepared to risk his neck for my brother."

"Even so, you should not be alone. I will come..."

But Elizabeth was adamant. They had gone over it a hundred times. Edmund's unrivalled knowledge of radical movements was the key to finding Sarah Radbourne, but because of that he was known throughout the city.

"I don't adhere to any one of them."

"It doesn't matter," she said, "You must go and be seen so we are unseen."

So it was agreed and this morning he leaves to tramp the city and be seen. Ezra has travelled from Harringstead through the night. He's ravenous, but there's a price for his meal. Between gargantuan mouthfuls he must give Elizabeth every detail of what has happened. He tells of Prudie's arrest and escape and how they rescued Olivia.

"You did well," Elizabeth says.

"We had some help. Thomas Radbourne was also in Drensell Wood. He has a following in Harringstead. He and Prudie's friend Alice Sandon stirred up many in the the village against the landlords, especially Manning."

"Does this mean Richard Collver and Olivia had nothing to do with Lexden's death?"

Ezra shrugs.

"Richard Collver has been hiding in the wood with Alice. He will stay there with Olivia. They'll be safe for a while. Like Prudie Alice knows the wood. If need be they can keep on the move and never be found. At least until we can return."

"How did Richard get to Harringstead?"

"Buckden arranged it."

"So it wasn't him that got my message to Matthew?"

"I don't know about that," Ezra says, slightly puzzled, "I have to speak to Buckden. He'll know how to find Matthew. He left after seeing Thomas Radbourne. Thomas was arrested at 'The Ship' and briefly questioned by that slug Fenwick."

"Oh no, how did he get away?"

"Fenwick is so obsessed with Royalist spies, he's questioning virtually everybody. Thomas managed to get off with a day in the pillory for disturbing the peace, but he learnt more about Fenwick than Fenwick learnt about him. Fenwick has been watching Daniel Overbridge and he also saw a man called John Walter..."

Ezra pauses and clears his throat as if pronouncing the name is physically repugnant, then continues.

"...who talked about me. Thomas delved and Walter boasted of another man he knew called Seddon, he was my contact and without realising it passed on all he knew to Walter who then told Fenwick."

"And that was how they knew where Matthew was going in the cart?"

"Yes, all because of JohnWalter."

Elizabeth asks of Prudie.

"She has what she needs. Alice told her everything."

"But we were to search for Sarah Radbourne."

"Prudie will be here soon. She will help you. I must away after breakfast. I have to see Matthew."

He takes another mouthful, but Elizabeth pulls the plate away.

"What are you...doing?" he splutters, spitting some food from his mouth.

"First you will tell me the whole story about yourself and how Matthew helped you."

Ezra looks forlornly at the plate and the inviting three quarters of unconsumed breakfast. If he doesn't tell he'll miss his breakfast. Ezra is forever practical. Breakfast inevitably wins. He grips the edge of the plate. Elizabeth holds the opposite edge. He looks at her. She looks at him. He nods. She lets go. He pulls back the plate and scoops a huge mouthful.

"Now," she says, before it reaches his lips.

He puts it down.

"It was in the army. Two men were fighting outside the camp. I went to stop them. As I approached one man was stabbed and fell down. The other soldier ran off. When I came up I saw the knife on the ground and picked it up. Then others came and I was caught with the knife."

"But surely you explained?"

"Of course, but lieutenant Fenwick wouldn't listen. The dead man was very popular. The camp was in uproar. Fenwick said I'd get a fair trial, but we were due to move out the next day and I didn't trust him. Several men slipped away that night and some more the next. I reckon the guilty man was one of them, but I didn't know his name, I'd not even seen him properly. I'd already crossed with Fenwick when we gave different versions of orders we received. I told the truth, but Fenwick's version was accepted. Matthew believed me and didn't trust Fenwick. That night an unknown soldier overpowered my guard and I got away."

"That soldier being Matthew."

"Nothing could be proved, but Fenwick knew it was him. I've been sought for the murder ever since."

"This man John Walter, do you know him?"

"No, but I intend to find out."

"All in good time," Elizabeth says, grabbing the plate and pulling it away again.

Ezra looks longingly at the now half remaining breakfast.

"You say Prudie is coming, but you wouldn't leave her to travel alone," Elizabeth says, "She's come to London with you. Where is she?"

Ezra's eyes remain on the plate.

"Ezra?"

He nods.

"I couldn't bring her here. She's somewhere safe."

"I want to see her."

"But I have to see John Walter and Matthew and..."

"Later. First you will take me to Prudie."

"She's with Thomas Radbourne."

"All the better. I also want to know what he has to say."

"Alright," Ezra agrees, "but I must speak to Buckden."

"You have an hour," she says, "No longer."

At last Ezra is able to finish his breakfast. They agree to meet up later. It'll look less suspicious if they leave separately. Ezra goes first to find Buckden. As Elizabeth makes her way to the house where Thomas Radbourne is staying, she senses the ferment in the city. People are snappy, wearied by the war as the final settling between King and Parliament approaches. She passes through the market. People are arguing with stallholders, the usual scarcities inflaming tempers, but there's added tenseness, a fear for tomorrow, yet a yearning for resolution, a determination for victory and freedom. She takes some precautions against being followed, at last reaching the small, inconspicuous alley and the upstairs rooms on the west side of the city, close to the great defensive ditch they'd all worked so hard to build. She has a momentary shuddering thought. Surely these defences will not need to be used?

She is admitted after knocking the appropriate times and answering the relevant words to certain questions, all as Ezra directed. She thought this a little ridiculous and typical of Ezra's clandestine approach, but then remembers her and Matthew's own secret messages from their childhood. Thomas is out. Prudie is in the back room, staring over the rooftops. Her eyes are heavy and drawn, her face sallow. Elizabeth puts it down to tiredness from the journey. She's glad to see Elizabeth and they exchange experiences since Prudie left London.

"Why did Thomas return to Harringstead?"

"Finding his daughter determines everything," Prudie says.

"He thought Sarah had returned to Harringstead?"

Prudie waves her hands up and down and sways.

"Not really. He knows she's in London, but can't get to her. Ezra told you of his arrest. While recovering from his day in the pillory he saw someone he'd seen before in Harringstead and followed him. He thinks this man, Edward Amberley had something to do with Sarah's disappearance."

"Has he?"

Prudie waves her hands again and shakes her head.

"It seems not."

"Who is Edward Amberley?"

"He's the Amberley of Ellerton and Amberley."

Elizabeth starts.

"You know him?"

"No...no, but I know the name Ellerton."

Prudie waits, but Elizabeth says no more. Prudie continues.

"Ned Frattersham, a young servant of Joseph Manning has been on the run from Syme House. He was around when Samuel Lexden was killed. He's a bit simple and gets very confused, but he tells the truth. He won't say anything in front of Olivia, but I have his trust."

"Did this Ned Frattersham see the murderer?"

"He saw the body...in the house..."

"As Matthew believed."

"The body was moved. Ned has been out in the woods and he's seen Edward Amberley several times in the area."

"Did he murder Samuel Lexden?"

Prudie doesn't answer. There are footsteps on the stairs.

"It will be Thomas," she says, "He followed Amberley back to London. He's out most of the time looking for Sarah. He nearly found her at 'The Ship,' but she's disappeared again."

"We will find her," Elizabeth says, "There's a ferret on the loose in the city."

"Ezra?"

"He'll be here within the hour."

London is not Nathaniel Buckden's natural habitat. It's too big, too noisy, too smelly and too dangerous. He longs to get away, but there's business to be done, scores to be settled which can't be left to others. Dealing with the army is unpredictable enough, but with Fenwick loosed on the country no one is safe. For a man used to woods and fields the city lacks natural hiding places, but he's quickly acclimatised and is now so well hidden the best observer of all that moves would almost find it too difficult to find him. *Almost*. Ezra's exhaustive, even *exhausting* knowledge and perfectly tuned ear to the slightest wheeze in the sprawl of gutter and smoke, alley and river, has not deserted him. Now he stands before Buckden and they stare at each other with mixed awe and surprise.

"You're smaller than I expected," Buckden says gruffly.

"And you bigger," Ezra says, "though I've never put much store by stature as a reliable measure of a man."

"I've waited as you asked," Buckden says, as if Ezra has disrupted his whole day, "If you are ready, I don't want to waste any more time."

"You know where he is?"

Buckden puts on his coat and goes to the door.

"Do we need others?" Ezra says, following him.

"He's not expecting us, only someone sent by Fenwick."

For Buckden time is precious. He wastes none talking without moving or moving without talking when he can do both. He steps lively and Ezra has to step not only quickly, but erect so that he can hear Buckden. Neither come naturally. He's used to shadows and a bent frame, one to make himself smaller, the other to be less easily seen. Striding in the open with the big man makes him very nervous.

"I've been digging through Fenwick's lies. Your contact Seddon is innocent of any treachery, but John Walter is Fenwick's creature. He has crossed both you and captain Fletcher before."

"He was there the night the man was stabbed?"

"He was the soldier you saw running away. He killed the man with the knife."

His eyes gleaming with hatred, Ezra thumps his fist in his hand and shouts, "I'll have..."

Buckden grabs his arm.

"Silence! There is more. He ran, but returned to join a scouting party, busy stealing from a farm. Walter is one of the scoundrels we've been fighting against."

"Then you'll want to settle with him too?"

"Aye, maybe, but there's been some settling already. He was caught by captain Fletcher and disciplined severely. Walter never forgot and was only too pleased when the opportunity arose to betray both you and him to Fenwick."

They reach the house close by Ludgate. John Walter is a stiff, gaunt man with deep set cunning eyes behind high eyebrows. He has a large mouth, oddly clothed by thick protruding lips that threaten to gobble up the objects of his penetrating eyes, yet hardly move even when he speaks. He wears a bright and very distinctive green jacket, his only obvious aspiration to higher status. He opens the door without question, then tries to close it as quickly on seeing his two unexpected visitors, but Buckden's boot stops him, while Ezra forces him inside.

"John Walter?" Ezra says, grabbing the fancy gaudy lapels as he pins him against the wall.

Buckden closes the door, then pulls Ezra off him.

"Easy, easy, I want this sprat pulled out alive so I can relish him with pleasure."

"You know me?" Ezra says, pulling back just enough to let Walter speak.

"You're Ezra Stanfield."

"The one you betrayed, you bony faced, long slick of dripping and shit..."

"Ezra!" Buckden cautions as Ezra tightens his grip on Walter.

"You work for Fenwick?" Ezra continues.

"Yes."

"You've been watching Daniel Overbridge?"

"Yes."

"You'll tell us where he can be found and how we can get to him undisturbed."

Walter splurts out the information, all the while held in Ezra's steely grip, face thrust into his with wild, violent eyes.

"Now leave me alone." Walter says.

"What, so you can run away like you did that night in Hampshire? Not until I've rid the garden of this particular worm..."

"Not here, Ezra," Buckden says, pulling him off, then to Walter as he thrusts a sharp blade at his neck, "When does Fenwick expect you?"

"Two hours."

"Does he come here or do you go to him?"

"I go to him."

"And you have documents? Search him, Ezra."

Ezra rifles Walter's pockets roughly, prodding him viciously.

"What do we want with these trifles?" he says.

Buckden throws most things on the floor, but keeps a few papers.

"Now," he says to Walter, "take off your clothes."

Bemused and fearful what will happen, Walter strips off.

"Not a fatty crow, are you?" Buckden says, staring at his lank nakedness, "Now you Ezra."

"Me?"

"Yes and then take his clothes."

"I can't be seen in that…"

"Not as Ezra Stanfield…but as John Walter…you understand."

Ezra and Walter exchange clothes.

"Keep these safe, you may need them." Buckden says, handing the papers to Ezra.

"What now?" Walter says.

"You stay here with me until my cousins arrive."

"Then?" Walter says apprehensively.

Buckden doesn't reply, his eyes remaining firmly set on him, only the edge of his mouth quivering faintly in what could be the beginning of a smile as he turns to Ezra.

"Now be gone, you have other work to do. Leave this cur to me."

"I am indebted to you, Nathaniel."

Buckden moves his head very slightly, the side of his mouth even less.

"My greetings and God speed to captain Fletcher."

He nods to the door, then gives Ezra curt instructions to his cousins' house. Ezra delivers Buckden's message, then goes back to the house where Elizabeth and Prudie are waiting. All the way he tries to keep himself or rather the distinctive green jacket out of sight.

"Where did you get *that*?" Prudie says.

Before he can reply Thomas Radbourne arrives. He's tetchy, almost despairing, having scoured every inn, tavern, meeting place and lodging house in London. They go over again all possible places where Sarah might be. Thomas suspected Amberley, but now regrets his brief foray to Harringstead, having only achieved a lot of wasted time.

Ezra listens impatiently, at last saying, "She is with Overbridge?"

"I have no doubt," Thomas says, "but Overbridge has gone to ground or rather the ground itself has consumed him."

"Aye, under a certain house," Ezra says.

"You know where he is, where I can find Sarah. We must go now!"

"In good time," Ezra says, sitting down and stretching his legs.

"Time, time! I've had enough of time. It's trifled with me in London, in Harringstead, everywhere. I'm a man in a hurry, Mr. Stanfield, I'll brook no more delay."

"So I heard in Harringstead. Thomas, I'll take you to your daughter, but getting her away won't be as easy as you think. Her head is turned. Overbridge has an influence over her and in these..."

"The villain, you mean he has...?"

"No, nothing like that, but she's frightened. She ran away, but has found no real safety. She needs to be with someone she trusts. She has seen new things, met new people. If she goes back to Harringstead..."

"She cannot stay in London..."

"...it will have to be with someone who understands these things and understands her."

He glances to Prudie. Thomas follows his eyes.

"I believe I can help your daughter," Prudie says, "but we may need her help."

"How can she help you?"

"By helping us," Ezra says, "...helping captain Fletcher that is...to unravel the knots tied up in Harringstead. You know where Amberley is?"

"But how does that...?"

"I will explain later. Will you give Prudie free rein to talk to Sarah?"

"Alright, alright. Then we can go?"

Thomas hovers at the door, ready to hustle the others. Elizabeth and Prudie move, but Ezra raises his hand.

"One more thing. To help captain Fletcher, we must first free him."

Ezra outlines his plan. At first Thomas refuses to cooperate, but Ezra is equally adamant. If Thomas doesn't help, then Ezra won't help Thomas. Prudie and Elizabeth get restive and are anxious to get going, but Ezra won't budge. It's all or nothing. Sarah for Matthew, whatever it takes. Time for Thomas is running out and eventually he gives way. He needs Ezra and Ezra could wait. It's only a short way. They soon reach the house in Cripplegate. Ezra spies the front while Thomas goes round the back.

"Buckden's information was reliable," he whispers to Ezra when he returns, "Just Overbridge and one other in the back room."

"Sarah is alone in the front?"

Thomas lurches forward, but Ezra stops him.

"Don't be a fool. Remember what I said and what we agreed. We'll deal with them in the back. Leave Sarah to the women."

Thomas sighs and then nods. Ezra motions to Prudie and waves towards the front door, then he and Thomas slip away. Prudie knocks softly on the door. No one stirs within. She knocks again.

"Sarah," she calls softly, "Open the door. Don't be afraid, I am Prudie Westrup from Harringstead and no friend of Joseph Manning."

There's a scuffle from the back of the house, then some cries and further scuffling. Sarah edges away, closer to the front door. Prudie calls again.

"We've come to help you, please let us in."

"Mr. Overbridge," Sarah calls, "William? Is anybody there?"

No one answers. She opens the door slightly and looks through the narrow gap, unsure what frightens her most, the two women facing her or the ominous silence from the back of the house.

"There's nothing to be afraid of," Prudie says.

"Prudie," Sarah says, recognising her, "the woman of the woods. They say you see things, know things."

"I see things about you."

Sarah opens the door a little more, but looks apprehensively at Elizabeth.

"Elizabeth is a friend in London," Prudie says, "She is here to help you too."

The door opens widely and they step in as Overbridge and another man are pushed into the room from the back by Ezra and Thomas.

"Sit down and be quiet," Ezra says pointing to chairs in the corner, "We'll have no preaching today."

The men do as they are bidden.

"You know me, Ezra," Overbridge says, staring bewilderingly at Ezra.

"And I thought I knew you, Daniel," Ezra says, "but you..."

"Father!" Sarah calls.

Thomas goes to her, but stops as she looks to Prudie.

"Why did you run away? What has happened?"

"I was so afraid," she says, still looking at Prudie rather than him.

"But why, what for..." he says, then turns to Overbridge, "What has he done?"

"Nothing, nothing father," she says, turning to him at last, "Nothing except take me in when I had nowhere to go. I went to one of his meetings. It was the first time I'd felt safe..."

"Safe in low places like 'The Ship!"

"Father, why do you always see the worst of people and get so angry. It was the same in Harringstead."

"I had reason to be angry in Harringstead, dealing with Manning and..."

Sarah shudders and looks away again. Thomas stops and turns questioningly to Prudie, who says, "I...we...know."

"Then you can tell me..." Thomas begins.

"Leave it," Ezra says, taking his arm and forcing him to sit, "Leave it to Prudie...as we agreed."

"Don't take me back," Sarah pleads to Prudie, her voice rising with fear, "I can't go back."

"What you fear in Harringstead," Prudie says, "is no more."

"But I won't go back."

Prudie takes Sarah's hands and strokes them gently.

"You have to face your fear and defeat it, Sarah."

"But not there, not there."

"The man you feared is no more."

Sarah stares at Prudie incredulously.

"I am right, aren't I?"

Sarah nods.

"So you can go back."

"But would I be safe?"

"We will make sure you are."

"No one will touch you, Sarah. Not like before," Thomas says, "I will see to it."

She doesn't look at him, but only to Prudie for reassurance.

"He...he tried...you know?"

"Yes, I know, but he's gone now."

"But they will think I did it."

Almost at bursting point with suppressed anger, Thomas shakes, his mouth quivering to speak, but Ezra holds his arm firmly and he subsides.

"We will protect you," Prudie says, "but you must help us."

"By going back?"

"With us."

Sarah looks from Prudie to Elizabeth, then to Ezra, finally to her father.

"All of you?" she says.

"All of us," Prudie says.

"And one other," Ezra says, "We need him and for that we need your help."

The soldiers and the old gaoler resent the intrusion. It's too late for visitors and they look up from their card game at the man in the distinctive green jacket and the woman with the large hat and scarf covering most of her face.

"I am John Walter," the man says, "here with this lady to see the prisoner, captain Matthew Fletcher."

One soldier looks intently, frowning questioningly. There's something vaguely familiar about this man.

"John Walter?" he repeats.

"Sent by major Fenwick," the man says, thrusting papers into the soldier's hand.

The soldier flicks through before handing them to his companion. The other studies them more slowly, at least able to read if somewhat slowly.

"See," the visitor says, pointing to Fenwick's signature.

The soldier turns to the gaoler, who grunts assentingly, waving to the green jacket without looking closely at the man's face.

"Been before," he grunts.

The soldier hands back the papers, glancing briefly at the 'lady.' She averts her face and he notices only the flour white complexion. His companion stares again at the man.

"We have met before."

"Perhaps," green jacket says hesitantly, "when I came before."

"Perhaps," the soldier says doubtfully.

"Come along," the gaoler says and leads the way, shouting "Fletcher, Fletcher, wake up Fletcher! Visitors!"

When Phillip Skippon assigned him as roving constable Matthew kicked against it to the last grain of principle, but that is now an age away. There are many fights and many fighters. A world is not just turned by musket, sword and pike. He is now the tenacious investigator and he has an uncrushable ferret and an instinctive interpreter of feelings. Ezra and Prudie will not desert him and he must also trust himself to complete the task. *Look for a tinker*, Elizabeth said in her note. In their childhood games a tinker meant an unexpected, but welcome surprise.

The gaoler slithers outside. There's another...no two other footfalls. One heavy, but not too heavy...a man, but a smallish man. That step, careful, but impatient, could it be...and the other, soft, lighter, hesitant...a woman, a young woman, not yet wholly exposed to the wiles of her world. Yet for her youth, maybe she has already experienced too much...like many other young girls and young men, grown old too soon in this war...

The keys slide and jangle in the lock. Matthew looks up, seeing only the green jacket and the woman, shrouded by her hat and scarf, neither familiar to him.

"Knock when you've finished," the gaoler says and closes the door.

Then Matthew's eyes widen in recognition as Ezra puts a finger over his mouth.

"How did you...?" Matthew says as the gaoler's footsteps recede.

"I am John Walter," Ezra says, "the man behind your betrayal to Fenwick."

"Anything would be possible for someone in that abominable jacket."

"It is...was...his."

"I guessed as such. How did you...?"

"I'll tell you later."

"And this...?" Matthew says, turning to the woman.

"You've been striving so hard to find her. This is Sarah Radbourne."

"Then we have the final piece. Now I understand everything. Ezra, you must get back to the country and to Amberley...you know where he is (Ezra nods)...you have to get to him, then you can..."

Matthew breaks off and looks again at Sarah. She's been concentrating, a little in awe, a little in fear, a great deal in bewilderment. Matthew turns to Ezra, talking as if she's not there.

"I'm glad you've found her, but to bring her here? Ezra, sometimes I question your unorthodox methods, but to bring her here, is it really wise? She had to be found and (he turns to Sarah with the trace of an almost imperceptible smile) what she can tell us will be of great value, but in this place..."

"There is a reason for..." Ezra says.

"Easy to get her in, with you posing as this John Walter, perhaps you can get her out, but why bring her here?"

"There is a reason..."

"If she's to stay, then..."

"She stays and she doesn't stay."

"...she may as well give us the information we need. Now..."

Matthew turns to Sarah again. His kindly, determined eyes contrast with hers, sorrowful and apprehensive, his face full of vigour and energy, hers worn and sorrowful as if she is the prisoner.

"...just a few questions, it won't take long, but..."

"No," Ezra says, "Don't mess things up Matthew. Prudie has already talked to her. Getting you out of here is the main priority."

"Don't waste time on that. If Prudie's done a good job there's not a moment to lose. If you follow up everything you have and what I can tell you about Amberley, then it will get me released anyway."

"Oh yes, I'm sure it will, the day after you're hanged!"

Matthew puffs and blows contemptuously, then glances at Sarah again with irritation.

"If Prudie already has the information and I'm not to question her, what is the point of taking the risk of bringing her here at all?"

"To get you out," Ezra says and then to Sarah, "Now, disrobe."

"Disrobe?" Matthew says in alarm, "What is this, Ezra? I'll have no part in your lewd tricks. Is this why you brought this young woman here? I'd rather rot in Fenwick's gaol."

Ezra ignores Matthew's protests and helps Sarah pull off her long dress. Matthew gets up, but Ezra waves him back.

"Shut up, Matthew and get your things off."

"What?"

"How else do you think we're going to get you out? John Walter and a woman came in, John Walter and a woman will go out with a wide hat and scarf and long dress that hides his boots!"

At last Matthew understands.

"It won't work."

"Get changed," Ezra says, pulling off Matthew's jacket, "Now your hose. Matthew, she has to look like you."

"Ridiculous. Nobody looks like me."

"Nobody with a choice would want to look like you," Ezra mutters, "Now get this dress on."

"We can't leave her here."

"She will say we forced her. She came in under the impression there were other intentions."

"Disgraceful! The woman's reputation, she will lose..."

"Better that than you lose your neck. In any case, her father is ready. After a discreet time, he will demand the release of his daughter. He'll say he's been in pursuit of a notorious rogue."

"That at least will be true."

After Matthew and Sarah have exchanged outer garments, Ezra stands back approvingly.

"Under that hat and scarf and the dress, no one will know you. Why Matthew, I might..."

"Don't even think about it!"

Matthew is still unsure.

"It's the coat," Ezra says, "They'll only look at the coat, just as you did. The coat makes the man. I *am* John Walter."

"Maybe," Matthew says dubiously, looking at the female shape within his clothes, "but Sarah will be in danger when they discover my escape."

"My father will come for me," she says with quiet resolution, "You have to be free to help us, captain Fletcher. I will follow with my father. Thank you for your concerns, but I'm not afraid anymore."

"Then God be with you. You are a brave woman. I will send your father to you as soon as it is safe."

Ezra hammers on the door. The gaoler returns his call and starts his slow, withering tramp.

"Do not linger," Ezra says to Matthew, "We must be away quickly. Do not look back at Sarah. It will invite suspicion."

The door is flung open. The gaoler suspects nothing, not even glancing at 'captain Fletcher,' who stands by the window at the rear of the room. They pass by the two soldiers. Ezra opens the outer door. Outside, Prudie and Elizabeth are waiting in the shadows.

"Wait," one soldier calls.

It's the same one who seemed to recognise Ezra earlier.

"Go to them quickly," Ezra whispers, pushing Matthew through the doorway.

Matthew goes out and joins the others.

"I know you," the soldier says to Ezra, "From the army. You're not John Walter. You're a wanted man. You are wanted for murder."

13

BEFORE she was six Prudie's mother and aunt had taught her every byway and track in Drensell Wood. By seven only the birds and insects could find their way better. The tighter the trees, the denser the undergrowth the safer she felt. In the stillness the compacted habitat, shadowy imminence of every growing, crawling, scurrying, flying thing enhances the spirit and magnifies her receptivity. A day and a night and now another day. She is patient and unafraid. She knows the hiding places that will withstand even a forest fire and if she waits long enough all will be revealed as it always has been since she was young.

"That girl sees and feels in her head," her aunt said to her mother, "It's a gift she'll need to foster."

"And keep secret," her mother replied, "A gift to use, not talk about."

So the two elder women guided the growing girl. Guided, but not instructed, for as they admitted 'the gift was not with them.' With the years Prudie's skills increased, but she was not always discreet, sometimes crowing about her achievements and rebuking those that challenged them. Care came with experience but those youthful outbursts were unwelcome and there were those who remembered long after the madcap splutterings. Her peculiar 'gifts' could be hidden within her marriage, her husband affording not only protection, but steadying restraint. Then Ben was carried off by one of those sudden fevers that ravaged the country, disappearing as rapidly as they appeared, leaving behind a trail of misery and death. She became reclusive, keeping her own company except for a few reliable and trusted friends like Alice Sandon and reverting to childhood habits, tramping the woods, communing with the plants and birds. If these excursions coincided with natural disasters it proved she was either mad or consorting with 'dark forces.'

Isolation from all but her own quirky circle and her stubborn behaviour only intensified the wild stories. She was called 'the woman of the woods' and credited with making trees walk, birds talk and turning spiders into a malignant army, wreaking vengeance on any that crossed her. She was wise enough not to stoke the fires of these crazy tales, but did nothing to put them out. Frightened enemies are more compliant. Choosing to believe she had supernatural powers made them less likely to bother her – at least until the reverend Jeremiah Stradsey arrived. He had none of his predecessor's common sense and lethargic uninterest in the villagers more absurd prattling. Stradsey's faith was of the newer, intenser sort and he took *everything* seriously. The enclosure of the fields and commons brought troubles on the land and struggles between the landlords and their tenants. Suddenly the eccentricities of middle aged women became less innocuous as the war sharpened conflicts and heightened trivial setbacks. Normal reversals in crops and misfortunes of animals now had to be explained. For isn't everything else being explained – King and Parliament, lord and tenant, peace and war, rights and privileges, those that have and those that have not? So it must be with nature. *Somebody* is responsible, *somebody* is to blame and it must be that crazy creature in the lone cottage, the woman of the woods, who 'sees' and 'makes things happen.'

Prudie's 'gift' is as strong as ever. Sitting beneath the trees day and night she sees and understands what must be and it frightens her. She and Alice have met many times in this lonely and secluded part of the wood. It's difficult to find and known only to them, but by the second evening she longs for Alice to come. Then a slight, almost imperceptible rustle against a tree, unheard by ears less attuned is the only signal.

"I trust your absence has not been fruitless," she says as Alice emerges from the undergrowth.

Bedraggled, bruised, her dress torn at the hem, her face smeared from overhanging branches, Alice is even more unkempt and dirtier than when Prudie last saw her. She moves slowly, says nothing and sits down, her head bowed in her lap.

"They sought you, found you, imprisoned you, then you escaped and left. They know you're back and look for you and for me. Manning's men are everywhere," she mutters, then looks up with a sly grin, "though not all of them are the best in his service."

"Too many discontented villagers," Prudie says, squatting down beside her, "Half Harringstead must be against the Justice."

"More like three quarters."

"You've had to keep on the run?"

Alice nods.

"Is Ned safe?"

"As safe as any rabbit in a burrow, but the fox moves, I can't keep him..."

"Soon," Prudie says, taking her shoulder and lifting her head up, "Now, tell me, is Ned's recollection reliable?"

Alice hesitates.

"He wavers, sometimes he talks, sometimes it's as if he's struck dumb."

"But when he speaks....?"

"He has to be reminded of what he's said before."

"But what he says, does it vary?"

"Prudie, he is a simple soul, bullying him won't work."

"I won't bully him, but we have to know what he says he'll also say to others."

Alice shakes her head.

"He's been telling you the same as he told me?" Prudie persists.

"Yes, he still says..."

288

"Good, then you must keep him safe."

"But Manning's men get closer. I can't keep moving with him. I must soon go back."

"We can't afford to lose him!"

"That's what I'm afraid of."

"Soon, Alice, soon. Not much longer and the others will be with us. Before you return to Ned I have another errand for you."

Prudie pulls a scrap of paper from within the large pockets beneath her dress and writes a brief message.

I know now. Will meet you at the usual place.

"Be sure to give it to her alone. There must be no one else around," she says, pushing the paper into Alice's hand.

"What if I cannot get to her alone?"

"I've told you where she walks. But you must be away as soon as she has it. There must be no discussion. You know nothing. You will say nothing."

Ezra has had little sleep, constantly interrupted by persistent questioning. Fenwick's need for rest gave some respite, but Ezra's been regularly woken by one of the soldiers. The one who accosted him last night said something about having 'seen him in the army.' For some reason Fenwick didn't like it and the soldier disappeared. Ezra doesn't remember him. Fenwick's been particularly interested in John Walter

"You must know where he is, you've been wearing his clothes," Fenwick sneers malevolently.

Ezra gets a good beating for denying any knowledge of his whereabouts. Buckden must have done a good job. Fenwick won't find him, not alive at any rate. He might turn up one morning white and bloated on the Thames shore or picked over by the dogs in the filth of the Fleet. Not wanting to give the vicious jackass even more ammunition Ezra keeps silent. Like the Ranters from the taverns when they're up before the justices, he denies everything. Nobody believes them and nobody will believe him, but at least there'll be no confession for the 'godly' to throw at him. Even so he can't resist some foolhardy challenges to Fenwick.

"Still watching Overbridge?"

It wipes the almost perpetual smirk from Fenwick's lips.

"No?" Ezra continues, "It wasn't just Matthew your slug Walter betrayed. Nathaniel Buckden is not the sort of man to be crossed."

"That so called clubman has Walter?"

"I wouldn't know whether he has him *now*."

For a few minutes Fenwick looks uncomfortable. Matthew knows he's here, but he has important work in the country and should take his own advice. If matters are resolved they will both be freed, though Matthew said that when *he* was the prisoner. Now his impetuous temper will take over and he'll come for him. He mustn't. No, Elizabeth's good sense will prevail. He'll not come. But he'll tell Thomas and *he* will come. For Thomas is a man who works with the people, working in the country as Ezra works in the city. He has to come for Sarah. He won't forget him.

"What is Fletcher planning?" Fenwick says.

Does he accept Ezra doesn't know about Walter?

"When is the rising?"

The edges of Ezra's mouth move, into not quite a smile, nor even a smirk, more a slight twitch, but definitely wry. *The Rising*. It's so ludicrous. Fenwick notices the twitch and with a sharp slap from the back of his hand brings blood to those same edges.

"You can't fool with me, Stanfield. I know there's a conspiracy and Fletcher is at the heart of it. You are his accomplice, his runner."

This is too much of an insult even for Ezra.

"I don't work for nobody. Nobody gives me orders."

"No? Not even the King?"

"Especially the King."

"You would do well to remember the fragility of your position, Stanfield."

"There's no need to keep reminding me. I never consider any position other than my own."

"Then consider this. Fletcher has only given you trouble, Stanfield. He tried to help you before. It didn't work."

It *did* work. Matthew got him away from Fenwick. But that was before. Now Fenwick has him.

"You could replace John Walter."

"You clear slugs, not replace them."

"I could forget your former association with a Royalist spy. Work for me, be my eyes and ears in the city. Do a good job and it will go well, prove you are trustworthy. Then that night in the army might be *reinterpreted*. How there was a terrible misunderstanding..."

"The misunderstanding was all yours."

"...that you just happened to come along..."

"That's exactly what happened."

"...your subsequent *cooperation* would show your good intent. The charges would be dropped...if...you cooperate. Otherwise..."

Fenwick nods to the soldiers nearby.

The old gaoler keeps Thomas waiting. It's been a quiet night. The prisoners, mellowed perhaps to their fates have given no trouble and no visitors have disturbed his sleep. After a good pork chop and a full flagon of ale he slept soundly to the dawn. Now this cove appears, demanding to see his daughter.

"Ain't got no daughters. No women in 'ere."

"She was brought in against her will."

"They're all brought in against their will."

"I mean unofficially."

"Oh *unofficially* is it?" the gaoler laughs, "You mean someone who sort of *asked* to come in?"

"I mean someone who was forced," Thomas booms aggressively.

The gaoler looks him up and down, carefully and contemptuously, then leans back for a final lingering scrutiny.

"How am I to know...?"

"You have a prisoner, Matthew Fletcher...except it's not Fletcher, it's my daughter, Sarah."

"I'm not in the habit of having female prisoners and even if I was I wouldn't be a giving 'em men's names, would I?"

"I want to see your prisoner, Matthew Fletcher."

"It'll cost yer."

Thomas is reluctant and grimaces disgustedly. Then one

of the soldiers emerges from a rear room. Realising he may have no choice he reluctantly engages with the gaoler and coins are quickly exchanged.

"You're from the country," the gaoler says as he leads Thomas along the dim corridor.

"Is that a problem?" Thomas says aggressively.

"No, no, your honour," the gaoler says in a peculiarly merged bleat, half mocking, half fearful, "The city is full of folk from all places. Your...er...daughter...she's from the country?"

"Of course."

They reach 'Matthew's' cell. The gaoler thumps the door, calls 'Fletcher, visitor,' unlocks and swings it open. The prisoner stands by the window with her back to them.

"You can call me," the gaoler says.

"No," Thomas says, "I want you to stay."

Sarah turns at the sound of his voice though she bows her head with the hat pulled over her face.

"Take off your hat, Sarah," Thomas says, "I have come to take you from this place."

Sarah lifts her head, releasing her long hair, which falls first onto her neck and then to her shoulders. The gaoler gasps.

"Come Sarah," Thomas says and then as she goes to him, turns to the gaoler, "You see, sir, no officer, but a young woman as I said."

"Indeed, sir," the gaoler says, leaning against the door, hand at his mouth, keys jangling in his nervous hand as he tries to take it in and wonders what to do.

"Then....this is not captain Fletcher," he says, staring stupidly at Sarah and then to Thomas, "Where is Matthew Fletcher?"

"Gone last night."

"But there was a woman, she left..."

"Someone dressed as my daughter."

"Matthew Fletcher, but how...?"

"You were forced weren't you Sarah," Thomas says, pulling his daughter slightly away from him and staring meaningfully into her eyes, "Fletcher and the other..."

"Ye...yes...I was forced," she says anxiously as he nods reassuringly.

"I followed his associate here, the one who escaped with Fletcher. My daughter came here because...she's an innocent girl in the city..."

"But we have the other man"

"He's here?" Thomas says in alarm.

"Yes, he's..."

"Ezra Stanfield!" the soldier from the night before says as he stands in the doorway.

"You're late, Ernest Appleton," the gaoler grumbles.

"Never mind that now," Appleton says, "Where is Ezra Stanfield?"

"He's not important."

"Where is he?" Appleton persists.

"Upstairs with major Fenwick, but he's not important."

"I need to see him."

"You were desperate we held him last night. If it wasn't for that we might not have let Fletcher go. While you were arguing with that Stanfield, he swapped places and dressed up as this young woman, then slipped out."

"She was forced," Thomas intervenes.

"Yes, yes," the gaoler says, irritated and recovering some of his self possession, "But Fletcher's gone. We have to deal with that. Stanfield can rot, perhaps he'll feel like rotting after Fenwick has finished with him."

"He can't stay here," Appleton says, "That's what I was trying to say last night before Fenwick sent me away. I'm sure it's the same man I saw in the army."

"Yes, Fenwick recognised him, Ezra Stanfield, wanted for murder as you said. He's questioning him now."

"But he's not."

"Not what?"

"Not a..."

"Hallo there, gaoler, is anybody about?"

The gaoler freezes, edgily glancing from Thomas to Appleton, to Sarah, back to Thomas and so on, his eyes darting more frequently with each successive circulation.

"The lieutenant," he mutters anxiously, "What do I do, what do I say?"

"Gaoler, are you there?"

The gaoler fiddles with his keys, but still doesn't reply.

Hugh Crittenden is at the end of the corridor. Realising their opportunity Appleton and Thomas try to speak together, only succeeding in overriding the other with incoherent eruptions.

"What..." the gaoler begins, turning nervously towards Hugh's advancing footsteps.

"Tell him the truth," Appleton says.

"It's your only chance," Thomas agrees.

Appleton and Thomas push and prod the shuffling gaoler while trembling Sarah comes up at the rear. The gaoler coughs noisily as they meet Hugh half way along the corridor.

"Ah, lieutenant. I wasn't expecting you so early. Though of course, you've every right...it's just...so early..."

"Who are these people?" Hugh says, rigidly eyeing the others,

"Ah yes...indeed sir, yes indeed, these people, yes...this is..."

"I am Thomas Radbourne and this is my daughter, Sarah."

"Radbourne?" Hugh repeats, recalling the name, then more purposefully, "The prisoner, captain Fletcher..."

The agitated gaoler interrupts nervously.

"Yes, yes, lieutenant, the prisoner, yes indeed, captain Fletcher, indeed *Mister* Fletcher, Matthew Fletcher he is... was...he is...here...no, that is he's not...it was difficult with... and then there was the other one and so he..."

"What are you talking about, man?" Hugh bellows.

The gaoler swallows hard, holding his hands together in a futile attempt to stop them shaking.

"He's not here, sir...that is...he's gone."

"Captain Fletcher has been released?"

"Well, not exactly released...more...gone, sir...It wasn't me sir...it was the other prisoner, he that came and was taken, that is he..."

"His name is Ezra Stanfield," Appleton intervenes

"Stanfield is here?" Hugh says.

"Upstairs with the major," the gaoler says, adding as if it

might explain everything, "He's a wanted man, a murderer and an associate of..."

"That's just it, sir," Appleton says, "I knew Stanfield in the army and last night I recognised him, not knowing he and this so called murderer were one and the same man. We were...we parted...one night, many of us left."

"You deserted, but you re-enlisted?" Hugh says.

"Yes sir, but I saw him the night of the murder before I... before I left...Stanfield didn't do it...I saw him come up after the fight. He didn't kill that man in the army. Ezra Stanfield is innocent. The major shouldn't be questioning him. He should be released."

"He called himself John Walter last night," the gaoler says, desperate to turn the discussion away from himself, "How was I to know? Because of him the other prisoner escaped."

"I don't know John Walter," Appleton says.

"If you did you might recognise him too," Thomas says, "For he's the real murderer of the soldier."

"John Walter is a trusted man. He assists major Fenwick," Hugh says.

"A murderer nevertheless."

"You are sure Matthew Fletcher escaped?" Hugh says to the gaoler.

"Well, as I say...he's gone," the old man jibbers almost incoherently, "The major..."

Hugh ignores him and turns to Thomas.

"Do you know where Matthew Fletcher is now?"

Thomas looks at him suspiciously. Isn't he the man who has made the allegations against Matthew? Thomas's first priority is to get Sarah away. He daren't be delayed, but neither can he betray Matthew.

"Matthew Fletcher, the man who was the prisoner here...?" he begins, desperately playing for time, fortunately saved by another outburst from the gaoler.

"It wasn't me. How was I to know? When they came in..."

"Sometimes things are said which are best not said," Hugh says, drawing him aside, "In the last few days I have had my doubts," then nervously, "When I see the major..."

He stops suddenly, interrupted by the loud clatter of boots on the stairs and Fenwick rudely pushes past Thomas.

"Ah, Crittenden. Good, you're here. I have to go. Make sure these fools (he glances haughtily at Thomas and then with a resigned sigh at the gaoler and Appleton) keep a close eye on Stanfield. I shall be back shortly."

"Major, unfortunately there's something..." Hugh begins.

"Not now, lieutenant. Events are pressing. I'll talk to Stanfield again when I return. I don't believe he'll say anything in the meantime, though you're welcome to try. I leave him to your discretion."

Fenwick pulls up his coat collar ostentatiously, casts a final withering glance at them all and sweeps out. Thomas follows him to the front door, ensuring he's safely across the street before turning back to Hugh, who stands beside Appleton and the gaoler, the three in a line, he as much a part of them rather than their superior.

"*I leave him to your discretion,*" Thomas says, "Ezra Stanfield is in your care, lieutenant. Fenwick may not be long gone. This is your opportunity, from which you must not falter."

"Is major Fenwick aware of captain Fletcher's... disappearance?" Hugh says to the gaoler.

"Well, as I said lieutenant, last night, it was all very quick," the old man begins again, "And this morning, there's not been time until you..."

"He doesn't know?" Hugh roars.

"N...n...no sir."

"This man has proof of Stanfield's innocence," Thomas says, waving to Appleton.

"You want me to release Stanfield?" Hugh says.

"No sir," the gaoler shouts, "I can't lose two prisoners. When the major returns..."

"He will believe they escaped this morning while he was out," Hugh says grimly, then to Thomas, "You are sure captain Fletcher is...safe?"

"He is away," Thomas says.

Hugh muses for a moment, then says, "Very well, I will give you Ezra Stanfield on one condition."

"Which is?"

"You will tell me where Matthew Fletcher is."

"He won't be there," Matthew says to Elizabeth, "He'll either ignore it or run."

"He'll be there," she says, "He'll be intrigued."

"Did you see him?"

"I sent a boy with the message."

The message from Elizabeth was clear.

Matthew Fletcher needs to see you. It's important. He will contact you soon.

"You're sure he got it?"

"Oh yes, I've used the lad before. He came back for the rest of his money. He gave the note to Amberley as instructed."

"Then Amberley will have him followed."

Elizabeth shakes her head at Edmund, who smiles benignly'

"Not this boy. He's so good, he might even have been trained by..."

She stops short.

"Ezra," Matthew says softly, then with sudden deliberation, "I'll go, but first, about Ezra..."

"Thomas has already gone."

Edward Amberley's house near Cheapside is easy to find, but its proximity to where Matthew last saw Jane Ellerton slows him as old memories flood his mind uncontrollably. He's late, but Amberley has been waiting patiently and ushers him in. It's a surprisingly small house, the few rooms barely furnished. It reminds Matthew of the ante-room where he waited for General Skippon. Yet barer still for except for the different smell and lack of dirt, it might even be that cell.

"How did you find me?" Amberley says.

"I was told."

"Yes, but who..."

"Someone saw you in Harringstead and followed you here."

"This person..."

"It doesn't matter."

"When you came before to the office, you weren't on trade business were you?"

"I came to see Henry Collver."

"That was before the death of his brother or was that connected?"

"It could be. I may not have been on trade business, but I did want to talk to him about the firm."

"I was sure you weren't who you said you were. You had... you have...a military bearing, *Mister* Fletcher..."

"Even despite my..."

"Your limp? Oh, I would say if anything because of it. I've since heard your name in connection with Royalist conspiracy."

"You seem unconcerned."

"The city is always rife with incredible rumours. However, I could have you arrested."

"But you won't."

Amberley grimaces, shrugs, says nothing, turns away and then looks back.

"Henry Collver has disappeared."

"We both need to talk to him. He may have returned to Harringstead to make contact with his nephew, Richard and Olivia Manning."

"You are warning me?"

"You could say that. Will you cooperate?"

"Yes."

Neither Matthew nor Amberley want to continue the conversation. They both need to get to Harringstead. Matthew's only concern is Ezra and Sarah, but Elizabeth reassures him on both when he returns.

"They've already left. Trust in Thomas."

Next day he waits in the field close to Syme House as Elizabeth directed, trusting his sister to be right. She said Ezra would come. He'd better bring help. This is more than two can handle. The warm afternoon turns into a cold evening. He shivers and pulls up his coat. No one has left the house these past two hours and only a few retainers have arrived. Joseph Manning is within, collecting the latest news. He probably has most of his resources in and around

Drensell Wood, vainly hoping to recapture Prudie and find Alice Sandon. They'll be able to hold out almost indefinitely, certainly until help arrives, but by now will be scurrying through the country, keeping a few vital steps ahead of their pursuers. Matthew hopes the women are also not alone. If others can help them they might also help him.

Manning's resources are dwindling. The people have their own struggle and like the war it comes to its climax. This war, this cursed war, it must soon end. Then the Joseph Mannings will find their world has changed forever. He'd not wanted to investigate the fears of a country Justice and the obsessions of a country parson, but all that has changed. It began with witches and uncovering the murderer of a steward, but that was before he was accused of being a Royalist spy, before he'd become entangled with Henry Fenwick, before...

The faintest depression of the grass, the sound so slight it's almost unheard. By the time Matthew turns the perpetrator has a hand at his mouth, then, reassured it is released.

"Are you alone?" Matthew whispers.

Ezra shakes his head and nods to several bobbing heads in the grass, "Thomas's men."

"They are reliable?"

"Reliable enough to take on anyone Manning has left. Thomas vouched for them."

"Thomas is not with you?"

"Coming later, with a reluctant constable – and Sarah."

"Then she's safe. Thomas got you away?"

"With a little help from a friend."

"What friend?"

"Hugh Crittenden."

"How come, he...?"

"I'll tell you later."

"What about Fenwick?"

"Probably now chasing Hugh as well as us," Ezra chuckles.

"But how did...?"

"Is he there?" Ezra says, pointing to the house.

"Oh yes, we have our Justice in his lair," Matthew says, "What about Prudie and the others?"

Ezra hesitates.

"Alice Sandon is with Richard Collver and Olivia."

"And Prudie?"

"Prudie is...Thomas looked...but can't find her."

"Then our plan..."

"She knows. She'll be here."

"I wish I had your confidence," Matthew says, shaking his head and kicking the ground, then standing and turning towards Syme House, "Then we pursue the bird we have."

He walks towards the house and Ezra beckons the others, four stout lads and two older men.

"Keep them in the yard," Matthew says as they near the house, "We don't want any avoidable trouble, besides it could alert Manning."

"He could have men in the house. We ought to take a couple with us."

Matthew stops as the others catch up, studying them carefully.

"One of the older men and that big fellow, just in case, the other four can deal with any problems outside."

These precautions are unnecessary. Only the immediate servants are in or around the house. Every available man has been sent out to find Prudie. They get to the front of the house without hindrance or challenge. Matthew hovers to make sure no one is about before rapping heavily on the door. Cotter is surprised to see him.

"Captain Fletcher, I thought..."

"Your master is at home?"

"Yes, sir."

Matthew barges past, closely followed by Ezra, but Cotter tries to stop the other two.

"You men, what are you...?".

"They stay with me," Matthew barks.

Cotter is ready to argue, but then seeing the doorway totally hidden by the huge frame of the young man, he pulls back.

"You best let us by," the older man says.

Ezra leads the way, remembering every detail from his recent visit. Joseph and Constance Manning are alone in the main room. Joseph leaps up from his chair as Ezra wrenches open the door and marches in.

"What is the meaning of this?" he says, staring at Ezra, who stands grimly without saying a word, then, "Who are...?" breaking off as he sees Matthew sidle in beside Ezra.

"The meaning of this is Samuel Lexden," Matthew says.

The two other men enter, taking position silently at the door, behind Matthew and Ezra. Cotter sheepishly enters beside them.

"Cotter," Manning bellows, "Why did you let these men into the house?"

"It was difficult, sir," Cotter says as the huge young man glares down at him, "They sort of got by me."

"You have no right," Manning starts to Matthew.

"Our right will be vindicated in due course," Matthew says, "You knew about Lexden and the young girl, your servant, the one who ran away."

Manning says nothing.

"Didn't you?" Matthew thunders, "You knew!"

"Yes, I knew," Manning says very quietly.

"But you did nothing. Your steward, abusing his position to harass a young innocent girl, forcing his unwanted attentions on her and you did nothing."

"She was only a maid," Manning says.

"Aye sir," Matthew says, stepping forward, "*Only* a maid, but even a maid..."

"I meant she was a common girl. She would understand these things, not like..."

"Not like a lady, not like your daughter?"

"If you say so."

"Oh I do say so, but then your daughter only ran off with the son of your family's enemy, not caught in the corner under the stairs or pinned to the wall in the kitchen by the steward."

"There's no need..."

"There's every need, sir, every need when a young girl in such a position is driven beyond her wits!"

"You mean she killed him?"

"I mean she ran away in sheer desperation, forcing her father to search every pot swilling dive in London to find her."

"She could have done it."

"So she could and maybe that's what you preferred to believe, but you chose not to tell me. Was that because you were afraid I might dig deeper than a mere servant girl and consider the involvement of your own daughter? After all, she too had a reason to wish ill of your steward. He had seen her with..."

"It was because I believed you would unearth the foul events."

"Unearth the witches?"

"If necessary."

"If only it was that simple, but there were other things you preferred me not to know about."

"I would have preferred if you'd not ran away to London and deserted your assistant when your duty lay here."

"So you denounced me?" Matthew thunders.

"I may have drawn certain conclusions and exchanged them with certain gentlemen."

"Aye, I've been in the company of one of them."

"I would have preferred if you had not got mixed up with..."

"Royalists?"

"With tapsters, rebels against the Parliament and other politicos, rabble leaders, junkheads, savage women and (glancing at Ezra) those that aid them."

"And what of those you are mixed up with? What of Jonathon Ellerton and Edward Amberley? They swindled Arthur Collver out of his business and you were only too willing to pick up the pieces at a knockdown price."

"All of this conveniently put together by my enemies and then regurgitated by a Royalist spy."

"Joseph, please, captain Fletcher did not say that!" Constance suddenly intervenes.

"Keep out if this, Constance. If the cap fits..."

The door is thrust open and the two men stumble into Ezra as the reverend Jeremiah Stradsey suddenly forces his way through.

"You!" he shouts, seeing Ezra, "Foul fiend of the night. Manning, arrest this reprobate. He is the man who imprisoned me and meanwhile I'm being pursued..."

Then, hearing further footsteps in the hall Stradsey suddenly bounds across the room, skirting around Matthew to stand nervously, half beside and half behind Manning. Henry Collver appears in the doorway, elbows Cotter aside and joins Ezra and Matthew.

"This man has pursued me from the village," Stradsey screeches, "You sir, captain Fletcher, it's your duty to stop this insurrection immediately!"

"The only insurrection, sir is that which emanates from this house," Matthew says solemnly.

"You must apprehend this ruffian," Stradsey says, pointing to Ezra and then addressing Henry, "And you sir, why do you chase me?"

"I do not chase you," Henry says.

"Then who are those ruffians that accompanied you across the fields."

"I bring no one, but myself, they come for their own reasons, not for mine."

The front door is flung open, more footsteps are heard and more men enter, but most are in the hall. Then they turn and are heard running quickly out of the house.

"See you have brought them," Stradsey squawks, his voice rising anxiously, "You come for me!"

"I come for only one man in this room," Henry says, "and it is not you."

"You disturb the peace, sir."

Thomas Radbourne arrives with Sarah and strides across the room. Now the four, Mathew, Ezra, Henry and Thomas stand defiantly together facing Manning and Stradsey.

"It's not me that disturbs the peace, but him," Henry says, angrily pointing to Manning and leaning forward aggressively across the table, "when he killed my brother!"

"That is a foul accusation, Collver," Stradsey intones, "Withdraw it immediately! You speak of our Justice of the Peace. Hc is here to uphold the law, not break it!"

"Murder is not his only crime," Thomas says furiously, adding viciously, "Your brother is just another landowner. We have greater matters to resolve here."

This angers Henry, destroying any chance of he and Thomas working together and sows confusion among the men. Manning looks uncomfortably at Sarah, who with the two men has edged away from the door and stands a little way behind her father.

"Lost your tongue, Manning?" Thomas shouts, "Afraid to face up to your crimes. It was you that molested..."

"No, no father," Sarah says.

"Quiet, Sarah, leave this to me."

"Have you no shame, sir?" Stradsey says, "addressing your better in this tone? Whatever your complaints are, there are ways and means..."

"Complaints, complaints?" Thomas explodes, "This is more than a complaint!"

"No," Matthew says, trying to restrain Thomas, "It is not Manning..."

"Enough of these trifles," Henry shouts, "This man is a murderer!"

"It is not a trifle!" Thomas says, turning suddenly on Henry.

Constance stands beside her husband, the dutiful wife, the gentler yet loyal face of local authority, but that face is now drawn and ashen white. Manning too is shocked, but some colour returns to his face. He is the Justice, one of the pillars on which society rests. He is for the Parliament, but not for disorder or surrender to the rabble. Without men like him there would be no order, no structure, no harmony, no one would know their place and position. The man glaring before him represents everything he is against. Stradsey is right. He must not be permitted to get a hearing, let alone dominate this precarious moment.

"Your presence here is an abomination," he shouts at Thomas, pulling himself back and lifting his toes, trying to give strength and command as much to his appearance as his words, "Villainously inciting peaceful men to foul acts, infesting the country with your wicked creed of hatred, you..."

"Never mind that, murderer," Henry says, "We won't be deflected from our purpose with clever words and empty protests. For years we heard enough of those from the King!"

"You know better than most the words of the King," Manning shouts back, "You and your nephew...where is my daughter?"

"Safe with my nephew," Henry says.

"Your hand is in this foul business, Collver, you and that damned brother of yours."

"The brother you killed, Manning."

"Who abducted her from my house!"

"You lying scoundrel!"

Henry lunges at Manning, but he's pushed aside.

"Out of my way!" Thomas says, elbowing into Henry, "I'll have this dog put down!"

But Henry is now in his way and won't be moved. They bump together, each desperate to be first at Manning.

"No!" Matthew shouts, coming between them.

The three jostle for a few moments until Matthew disentangles himself. Thomas and Henry shout and curse in their frustration, some directed at Manning, but mostly insulting each other. Then Henry makes a further accusation.

"You killed Samuel Lexden too!"

"That's right," Thomas shouts, not to be outdone by his rival.

"...because he saw Richard and Olivia," Henry continues.

"...because he saw you with Sarah," Thomas thunders.

Sarah tries to correct her father, but he won't listen and waves her to be quiet. There's further commotion outside as the men from the house spill into the yard.

"Prudie must be here," Ezra says to Matthew.

Manning overhears him and suddenly shouts, "That witch Prudie Westrup killed Lexden!"

More men arrive outside, including some of Manning's own servants, returned from fruitless searches for Prudie. They shout at the group inside and some get round to the front door and enter. Among them Manning sees the village constable, confused and bewildered as ever and turns to him and the others in desperation.

"I say Prudie Westrup killed Samuel Lexden. These men (he nods to Matthew, Ezra and Thomas) are in league with her. They are all part of her coven. The minister was right all along. She's outside with more of her foul company. She must be arrested without further delay. You must do your duty, constable. The fate of us all and of our immortal souls is at stake!"

A flurry of perplexed crosstalk erupts between the men. Seeing the danger, Thomas shouts at them.

"Don't listen to him. He and his like have fooled you for centuries. The Parliament did not take up arms so he could continue his petty tyranny here as the King wielded his bigger one over the country!"

"Get the witch!" Manning shouts back.

"That's him," the constable says, recognising Ezra, "He duped me and let the dangerous prisoner go!"

"No, no, constable," Matthew shouts futilely.

"It proves what I say," Manning says, "This wretch duped the constable and is one of her confederates. You men who came with Thomas Radbourne have also been duped. You should be obeying the lawful commands of me as your Justice!"

The men are now split into two groups. Those still capable of being swayed by the ancient power of the lord of the manor and those adamantly sceptical of anything he says. As they stand ready to tear each other apart Matthew despairs. The absurd diversion can only impede the arrest, but he's unable to get to them and too late realises Sarah is perilously cut off from him and her father. Having waited to try and make her father accept it was Lexden's attentions, not Manning's that forced her to run away, she stands alone. But Thomas is obsessed with Manning. All the pent up frustrations and grievances of many years suddenly released.

"Still he fools you as well as oppresses you!" he shouts.

"He," Manning replies, "with his godless message, he is the troublemaker!"

The noise outside is deafening. Almost everyone jostles around the windows, the better to see and hear the tumult. While Thomas and Henry are fully absorbed, pushing each other to get at him, Manning moves towards the door and pulls a knife from his jacket.

"Follow me and it'll not go well for her," he says, grabbing Sarah.

She screams.

"Stay back, Radbourne and you men. Keep back!"

Manning pushes the knife closer to her throat as he drags the whimpering Sarah to the door.

"Be quiet, girl, it'll go better for you if you keep quiet."

"You won't take her," Thomas shrieks with impotent fury.

"No, Joseph," Constance says, "This is not the way. Leave the girl. I can't believe you've done these dreadful things."

"I have done nothing, Constance, I have not touched this girl, you must believe me."

"Then leave her and come back!"

Matthew and Henry move towards him, but Thomas holds them back.

"He means it. You'll only make it worse for Sarah."

Manning and Sarah disappear through the doorway.

"Damn, damn, damn!" Thomas cries, hammering his fist into his hand.

"Get to the window," Ezra shouts.

He tries to push through the throng. Thomas joins him and they ram into the men, ruthlessly ejecting those that refuse to move. They get to the window and try to lever it open, but it's stiff and won't budge.

"Step aside," Thomas says, gently easing Ezra from the window.

He thumps his elbow against the glass, smashing the window and pulling away part of the casement. Ezra and Thomas climb out and drop onto the long terrace, breaking their falls on the balustrade. Dozens of men are running, shouting and waving sticks, clubs and knives. Thomas turns in the opposite direction towards the far end of the terrace where several figures are gathered. Sarah emerges from the kitchen door, closely followed by Manning. Thomas sprints along, followed by Ezra. Two men and two women stand in Manning's path where the terrace merges with the garden. One man approaches Manning. He stands back and draws Sarah closer to him, threatening her again with the knife. One woman shouts, but they can't make out what she says. Manning shouts back, but at the other woman. Ezra is anxious to get to Alice and Olivia before Manning lashes out, while Thomas is determined to free Sarah. Hearing them coming, Manning turns to the garden, but his way is blocked by the two men, one short, stocky, the other tall with a peculiar lilting gait. The younger is shouting and flailing his arms about. As Thomas and Ezra come up, Manning turns Sarah to face them, standing behind her with the knife still at her throat, continually turning between the men and the women, Alice and Olivia and Richard Collver and the young man.

"Who's he?" Ezra says, pointing to the second man.

"Ned Frattersham," Thomas says, then to Manning, "You can't escape, let Sarah go."

"I seen 'im," Ned shouts, waving his arms again, "I seen 'im and I seen them."

"Shut up, Ned," Manning says, "You shouldn't have run away. You had nothing to fear. There's still a job for you at the house."

"I seen…"

"Shut up!"

"Why shut him up?" Alice says, what are you afraid of?"

"I am afraid of the danger this young tongue tied idiot will do to himself and others."

"By telling the truth?"

"You are more afraid of that than me. You did it with that witch Prudie!"

"Where is Prudie?" Ezra shouts.

"Give her up!" Thomas repeats.

Manning backs to the edge of the terrace. Sarah stares at her father, terrified, her eyes pleading for him not to do anything rash. Ned raves again, but his noise is swallowed by a louder commotion. Men are approaching from both directions. Those from the house clattering at Manning's back, those in the yard running along the terrace.

"You're trapped, Manning," Thomas says, getting even closer.

Manning steps onto the grass and looks around anxiously. Richard steps closer, but is distracted as Ned suddenly swings round with another 'I seen 'im,' allowing Manning to sidle past. The men from the house and those from the yard, led by Matthew, skipping painfully to keep up, are almost upon them.

"Circle around," Matthew shouts to the men from the house, "Don't let him get away," but his words are lost as the two groups converge.

"Take her, take the witch!" Manning shouts.

There is still a small vociferous group loyal to Manning with Stradsey screaming from the rear.

"Take the righteous path my children, scourge the land of evil!"

Men from the house and the yard collide. Matthew pleads for them to 'work together and catch the villain,' but to no avail. A fierce fight erupts, the greater conflict subsumed in more personal, long held squabbles.

"Smite down those that protect the instruments of the devil!" Stradsey shouts.

"Be silent, pernicious preacher!" Matthew shouts in his frustrated anger, pushing the minister and sending him to the ground, "It's God's work we do here."

In the thrashing arms and bobbing heads it's difficult to keep a close eye on any individual and Manning is soon lost in the melee. Then he screams as Sarah bites his arm and as he staggers in pain, stout arms from the battering pile wrench Sarah away. Matthew tries to get through, but the brawl is too intense and ferocious. He calls, but his voice is lost in the beating and bludgeoning. He looks for Ezra and Thomas, but cannot follow them in the mass. Then they appear at his side with Sarah. Thomas is pleased to have rescued his daughter, but Ezra is disturbed.

"Where is Prudie?" he calls to Alice, "I thought she was with you and these two," he says, pointing to Olivia and Richard.

"She...she had to go," Alice says.

"Never mind Prudie, look to Manning, don't let him get away," Matthew thunders and then generally to the battling crowd, "You're letting him get away, Joseph Manning must be apprehended."

"He murdered my brother," Henry calls.

"Stop," Matthew shouts again, "You fight for the whim of your ancient oppressor while your fellow countrymen fight the true battle for freedom. Shame on you, men, stop now!"

To his amazement, Matthew's words are heeded as men pull back, arms lowered and faces turned to him, momentarily jolting him into silence until he sees a figure fleeing through the garden and into the trees.

"After him," Matthew calls, "Get after Manning."

A few turn and give chase, then more until most are in pursuit. Matthew is about to follow when New Frattersham steps away from where he has been hiding behind Alice and calls out once more.

"I seen 'im, I seen 'im."

"Seen what?" Ezra says, "You keep saying it, what is it you've seen?"

"I seen 'im, I seen Mr. Lexden. I seen him in the house and then he was gone."

"Gone where?" Matthew says.

"Gone out to the field. He was took, carried he was. I seen 'em, they took Mr. Lexden out the house and into the field."

Then they see Olivia Manning and Richard Collver also running away.

14

FROM the depths of the rumour ridden capital Matthew escaped to the unpredictable land of Nathaniel Buckden's clubmen only to be brought back and incarcerated in Fenwick's London prison. Now he's escaped again to the dubious sanctuary of the feverish village, fractured alike by the warring landowners and their struggles with the maddened villagers. He should have had it – Prudie with the proof, Thomas Radbourne with the local people energised to forestall any counter moves by Manning and Stradsey, Ezra with Olivia and Richard out of the woods. All close confined in Manning's house, but Prudie wasn't there, the local people had fought amongst themselves and Olivia and Richard ran away.

Manning too has escaped and Matthew leads a motley band of 'helpers,' who only an hour ago were preparing to tear each other apart. He's also 'assisted' by the remaining leadership of the contending families, Constance Manning and Henry Collver, pounding him with advice when they're not snapping at each other. He's not sure which he prefers – the treacherous alleys of the plot infested city or the obscure wildness and concealed danger of this open land. He no more trusts each hedge and tree than the hidden threats in men's eyes or the suppressed perils in women's smiles. Even Ezra is quiet, as if he too is overwhelmed by the immensity of their task. When Matthew says they'll need to cover an ever expanding area and how easily it will be for their quarry to get away, Ezra says resignedly, "Thomas knows the country." When Matthew asks about Prudie, rather than the expected "She'll be here," he only gets, "That's what she said."

An hour has passed since Thomas sent a contingent with Ezra to track down Olivia and Richard. Henry continues to berate Constance about her husband with dozens of "He killed John" and "Joseph Manning is a murderer."

"Shut up, Henry," Matthew says angrily, "There are more pressing matters. You'd be better advising where Manning might be or your nephew for that matter."

Henry mumbles he's 'been away a long time' before subsiding into a sullen silence. They reach the river. Matthew stops as Thomas fans the men out along the bank.

"He's either crossed the river or is hiding in the grass," Thomas says.

Mathew grunts morosely. Thomas waves to the men and points towards the river, muttering "we'll find him." He wanders to the water's edge, kicks the ground and stabs the grass with a long stick. Alice sits on a clump of higher ground with Sarah and Ned.

"We have to find him," Henry says, glaring at Constance, "He is the killer."

Matthew moves towards him, forming two fists aggressively. Henry shrinks back. Matthew stops, shakes his head, then walks over to Alice and the others. Constance follows and grabs his arm.

"Answer him, captain. Is he is right?"

She continues to grip his arm, her eyes demanding a judgement on her husband's guilt. Matthew shakes his head with the same annoyance he shook it at Henry.

"We have to find Mr. Manning."

"But you must tell me..."

He grimaces. She's asked for it.

"I believe he killed John Collver."

"I knew it," she says, releasing his arm, "And all because of your questions. Without you John Collver would still be alive."

"Doing what the Mannings have always done!" Henry screams, "Shifting the blame for generations, grabbing property, fooling the people, plundering the land. No longer able to fool yourself of your husband's guilt you shift the blame to the man who reveals that guilt. Joseph Manning's murder of my brother had nothing to do with captain Fletcher and everything to do with me!"

"Yes," Constance says, "because he mistook John for you."

"You see," he shrieks, "That's what I said, even she..."

"I seen him, I seen him!"

Ned is standing on the tuft of grass, pointing out across the river.

"We heard you," Matthew says, "You saw him being moved..."

"But it wasn't me," Ned shouts, still looking across the river and pointing, "I only saw it, I never touched Mr. Lexden. It wasn't me. I wanted to, I shoulda done...maybe I shoulda done...but I didn't...I didn't do it. I never touched him."

"We know, Ned," Alice says, pulling him gently back to the ground, "We know it wasn't you."

"He was always a mocking me, said I was a fool, called me a sim...simple...simpleton, said I didn't know, but I didn't touch him. I wanted to, but I knew it wasn't right so I didn't touch him."

"We know you didn't touch him."

"It wasn't me that knocked him, I never touched him, it wasn't me, I never knocked him down."

"Then who did?" Henry shouts.

"Leave him alone," Alice says, glaring at Henry as she tries to quieten and calm Ned, who gibbers on, incoherently between more 'it wasn't me' and 'I didn't do it.'

Then Sarah speaks.

"It was me, I did it."

"You?" Henry says.

"Leave her alone," Alice says.

"No," Sarah says, "I did it."

"Did what?" Matthew says.

"I knocked him down. I knocked down Samuel Lexden.

I couldn't take it anymore. He was always around me, never letting me alone. I was behind the kitchen door. I saw him coming. He saw me. He grinned and wagged his finger."

She shakes her hand with an outstretched, curled forefinger, then whimpers noisily, almost crying.

"Enough," Alice shouts.

"No," Sarah says, shaking her away, "I have to tell. He came closer. I had a hand behind my back. I could feel something and picked it up. It was the big frying pan. As he got near me I leaned back, then swung it over my head. He looked up and tried to dodge it, but he was too late. I brought it down, hard, fast, so hard, so fast and hit him full on the head."

"*You* killed him?" Henry says.

"No, no!" Alice cries.

"He fell down so hard with such a clatter. Just the once I hit him, but it was hard, so very hard. He was lying crumpled on the floor, not moving. I dropped the frying pan. I thought by then he would move, get up, but he didn't move, didn't stir. He was dead and I had killed him. I was going to get down, but I was so frightened. What if someone found me with him? I was shaking. I couldn't stop shaking and I was so frightened. Then I turned and ran. I had to get away. I just ran and ran. I kept running and running. I never knew I could run so far and so fast. Towards the village, on and on, then away from the village, anywhere so long as I got away. Then it got dark. I kept running all night without stopping except for short rests. I was afraid of what I might find on the road, but more afraid of what I'd left behind."

"You saw this?" Henry says, turning to Ned.

"Yes, I seen him," Ned says, still staring towards the river, "I seen him."

"You saw her kill Lexden?" Henry says, though he wants not to believe his own words.

"Yes I seen him."

"Shut up," Alice shouts, enclosing her arms around both Sarah and Ned, "You're confusing him."

"What did you see, Ned?" Matthew says.

"I seen him in the kitchen."

"Did you see Mr. Lexden being struck down?"

"Of course he didn't," Alice says, "He only saw..."

"Let him answer! Ned, did you see Mr. Lexden being struck down?"

Ned mumbles incoherently for a few moments. Matthew goes over to him. Alice protests, but he ignores her, spinning Ned around and staring him full in the face.

"No one will hurt you Ned if you tell the truth. Now, did you see Mr. Lexden being struck down?"

Ned hesitates, then starts shaking his head forcefully.

"No, no, sir, it wasn't me."

"I know that, Ned. I know it wasn't you that struck him, but did you see it, did you see Mr. Lexden being hit by someone?"

"No, no, sir, but I did seen him in the kitchen."

"Was he moving?"

"No, no, sir, He was...he was still."

"Did Sarah move him?"

"No, no, sir, not Sarah, it was..."

"Oh Joseph, what a terrible thing you have done!" Constance cries as she gently takes Sarah's hand, "I understand my dear. You were so badly treated. I suspected it. I told Joseph, but he wouldn't hear anything against Lexden. I can see the pressure you were under, how you were driven to act, but you must not blame yourself. You could not have killed Samuel Lexden."

"You're very sure of that," Matthew says.

"But of course. You've heard Ned. Sarah didn't move Lexden. Why would anyone else move him if he was already dead? No, no, captain, Sarah did not kill Samuel Lexden. She may have incapacitated him, but that was all. She ran away, poor girl, terrorised by Lexden and frightened she had killed him. But she didn't."

"Then, who...?" Henry says.

"Oh Joseph, Joseph, how could you?" Constance shouts, wringing her hands, "How could you allow this young girl to take the blame? He must have seen Sarah strike down Lexden. He should have acted earlier. Questions would now be asked. Especially by her father and it would reflect badly on him. He had to get Lexden out of the house. Then he would report him

315

missing, the body would be discovered and this poor young abused and oppressed girl would take the blame because she had run away."

"So Manning finished off Lexden after Sarah knocked him down?" Henry says.

"I seen him, I seen him," Ned splutters, again pointing across the river, "There, there, look, I seen him, I seen him! I told you, I seen him!"

At last Ned's frustrated pleadings are answered as Matthew follows his waving arm, pointing to a figure running down the hill on the far side of the river.

"See, see, it's him," Ned shouts, pulling away from Alice and slithering down the bank.

Matthew follows him. Thomas has also seen the running man and calls to the men who are searching the reeds along the bank, waving and directing them.

"Cut him off, don't let him get away!"

Matthew reaches the bank, where Ned is jumping up and down and continually shouting.

"It's him, I seen him, he's there, I seen him!"

As they come up he paddles into the river, shouting, "I told you I seen him, up there on the hill, I told you I seen him."

He waves both his arms and jabs his fingers towards the far bank.

"Come back," Alice calls, "It's not safe."

Ned stops, suddenly aware of his precarious position and turns back towards Alice and Matthew.

"Don't let him take me, don't let him get me."

The water is almost up to his knees and is rising. The man on the far bank has stopped running and looks across. Ned glances over his shoulder, then turns back. He tries to lift his leg, but it doesn't move. He tries again, struggles and only manages to shake it. The water level rises further.

"He's sinking in the mud," Alice says, then to Ned, "Lift your leg, get it up!"

"He'll get me!" Ned shouts, trying to lift his leg, but only succeeding in sloshing his feet deeper into the mud.

Matthew wades out. The man on the far side starts to walk towards the riverbank.

"He'll get me!" Ned shouts.

Matthew treads warily, searching the firmness of the stones on the bottom, not wanting to repeat Ned's foolhardy rush into the mud. Thomas's men are strung out along the bank. On the far side another group has appeared on the higher ground above the solitary figure. They are the men Thomas sent out earlier, Richard Collver and Olivia Manning in their midst. At least that part of the pursuit is over. Then one man breaks away from the main group and runs towards the figure on the bank.

"Stay where you are, Manning, we have you!"

Ned turns nervously as Ezra shouts, loses his balance and falls to the side, his legs giving way as his feet slide further into the mud. He splashes uncontrollably, his arms flapping like the wings of a duck, except instead of taking flight he drops down to the water. Joseph Manning reaches the river edge and runs along the bank where there are fewer of Thomas's men. Matthew reaches Ned and grabs him under the arms, hauling him to the surface as Ezra pounds down and reaches the bank. Manning looks back and seeing his retreat cut off, jumps into the river.

"Take him, Matthew!" Ezra shouts.

Mathew drags the floundering Ned towards the near bank, but in his terror Ned pushes and strikes against him, continually sliding into the water and threatening to take Matthew down with him. Seeing the danger, some of Thomas's men run along the bank and enter the water, leaving an open, unguarded stretch, opposite the fleeing Manning.

"No, no!" Matthew calls, "Don't let him get away."

As he struggles with Ned, Matthew is joined by at least four others, while Manning gets towards the empty space. Ezra wades in behind, trying to keep up with him in the deeper water. Then something jabs into Matthew's side.

"Take this!"

Alice pushes a long stick she's prised from the shallows. Ned catches it and she's able to haul him to safety as the other men close in. Matthew dives beneath the surface and swims towards Manning, who has almost reached the near bank. It takes a few seconds to adjust as his leg feels frighteningly stiff and at first he panics, fearing his lack of thrust will force him down. Then he regains some buoyancy, but as he closes in and grabs Manning's leg, he's kicked violently away. As Matthew grabs him again, Manning thumps his shoulder and pushes him down, trying to hold him under the water. He almost succeeds, but the delay is enough for Ezra to catch up and disable him with a punch in the back of the neck. As Manning goes down, Ezra and Matthew seize his arms and, stomping through the water, land him on the near bank. More men run up and Manning is quickly surrounded. Meanwhile the men on the far bank find some shallows and cross over with Richard and Olivia.

"Not very gentlemanly behaviour, your honour," Ezra says as he turns over the spluttering Manning with his foot.

"Is he alright?" Matthew says, nursing his shoulder where Manning jabbed it.

"He'll live," Ezra says, kneading Manning's back to expel the last water out of his mouth.

"Not for long," Henry says as he comes up, "He'll soon hang."

He pushes Ezra aside, grasps Manning by both arms and pulls him painfully over the stony bank.

"You should have left the murderous swine to drown. No matter, we'll not wait for the hangman, I'll finish him off here."

He presses his thumbs behind Manning's neck, then squeezes his hands around his front. Matthew reaches down to push Henry away, but the exertions in the water have weakened his leg and he stumbles. Henry only releases his grip on Manning's neck as Ezra leans up and hits him sharply with his elbow.

"Not that way," Ezra says, "Let him breathe first."

Henry glares and then relaxes.

"Aye," he says, lifting Manning from the ground and pulling his arm sharply up his back, "We *will* save him for the hangman."

Manning cries in pain as Henry twists his arm further, saying "Or I might just break him now."

"Stop him, Ezra!" Matthew shouts.

Ezra gets up, but makes no move to restrain Henry, waving his arm disdainfully.

"He's been so long passing sentences with his kind of justice, maybe it's time he tasted our quicker version."

"Ezra!" Matthew shouts, trying to get closer, but his leg fails him once more, "There has to be a trial, fair and open."

"So there should be," Ezra says, but avoiding eye contact with Matthew, "Let's do that, let's give him the kind of trial his sort gave me in the army!"

"We only need a confession!" Henry shouts into Manning's face, pulling his arm so far up his back the bones crack, "Confess you went to London, cornered my brother, murdered him and..."

Regaining his strength at last, Matthew lurches across, hammers Henry and wrenches Manning from his grip.

"There'll be no arbitrary judgement," he says as Henry tries to grab Manning again, "That's what we are fighting against!"

With only slightly more strength than his charge, Matthew holds Manning loosely. Henry reaches out, ready to overpower him, but he's blocked by Ezra.

"Matthew's right, Henry. If he's guilty, he'll be punished in good time."

"Is the constable with you?" Matthew calls to Thomas, "Send him here with some men to hold this prisoner."

"There'll be no need for that," Manning says, his arms at his side like some grotesque exhausted ape. "I will come quietly. There will be no struggle."

Then he slumps further, his shoulders hunching witheringly as if he'll wrench his arms from their sockets.

"You are right. I killed John Collver," he says, then turning to Henry, "And *you* are right. At night in unfamiliar surroundings, two brothers inevitably look alike. Besides, I expected to find you in London. I did not expect to find your brother."

"And it was the company, the fraud?" Matthew says.

Manning nods.

"You were discovering much more than you realised, captain. It was only a matter of time before all the pieces would become clear. I knew you would track down Henry and connect me to his family's troubles. But knowing is one thing, proving it is another and I had position and reputation on my side. Whereas you...a discharged soldier with a rough edge. Reverend Stradsey," he smiles briefly, mimicking the minister, "found you only a 'slight cut above the rabble you must have led," he glances quickly at Ezra and then away, "Dismissing you as coarse and ineffectual, but I knew rough edges in a man can be deceptive. Rough can also be sharp and a coarse cloth picks up on everything it touches."

"And you killed Lexden too?" Ezra says.

"No, I had nothing to do with that. What possible reason would I have for killing my own steward?"

"He seemed a very knowledgeable man," Ezra says sarcastically, "or at least an observant one. He knew about your daughter and Henry's nephew. He might have known other things."

Manning looks towards Olivia and Richard expectantly, but is not acknowledged.

"No," he says quietly, "Whatever Samuel may have known, I did not kill him."

"Take him away," Matthew says.

The constable looks at his erstwhile superior with regret and disgust, then takes the arm of his prisoner. Thomas and Henry also take a hand on Manning, but their firm grips are unnecessary. He offers no resistance, his eyes fixed on Matthew, but as limp as his arms, reflecting utter weariness and defeat. He looks again to Olivia, but she turns from him, half hiding at Richard's side. He also looks for Constance. She has stepped back and stands with the group that came with the constable.

"They have broken me, Constance."

"How could you, Joseph, how could you?" she says.

"It had to be. This man knew too much," he says, turning to Henry and then to Matthew, "and that man would get me as he's got me now," then back to Henry, "It couldn't come out. He had to go down, into the water, down, down, so he couldn't come up again. It had to be, but it was so dark. I didn't know, I couldn't see. Now, they've broken me."

"No, Joseph, you've broken yourself."

"But it's not yet the end of this business," he says.

Shock and disgust crease her face. She's about to speak, but Ned breaks away from Alice and slithers down at Manning's feet.

"They took him away, a man and a woman, they took away Mr. Lexden, took him out the kitchen...they...they did it."

Manning starts back as Ned keeps mumbling, almost inaudibly into the ground.

"Took him away, took him away to the falling stones."

Manning tries to step over him and stumbles, almost falling onto Ned.

"Aye, aye, the stones in the field, that's where they went," Ezra says, taking Ned and pulling him clear.

Manning steps aside again and tries to walk away from Ned and Ezra, but Henry grips his arm, pressing his thumbs hard into his shoulders.

"It was you moved the body, after you killed him, you and..."

"Not me! A man and a woman? Not me, but her!" Manning shouts, pointing accusingly at Alice.

"Aye, with you!" Henry barks.

"Me consort with a witch? Not me, but that reprobate nephew of yours, he did it with the witch!"

He momentarily pulls free of Henry and the constable, but makes no attempt to escape, forlornly trying to regain his lost dignity. For an instant his eyes dance with the fiery authority of the Justice again, his mouth holding firm, but it doesn't last. His lips quiver and his eyes dart nervously. From Henry to the constable, to Matthew, to Ezra, finally settling with desperate hatred on Alice.

"Stay where you are, Manning," Thomas shouts, pushing two men to hold him again.

"I'm no witch, Joseph Manning and you know it," Alice fumes.

"You and that other witch, Prudie Westrup," Manning continues.

"Watch your tongue, confessed murderer," Thomas says.

"Two women?" Henry says.

"Two witches," Manning says defiantly, "carrying their victim to the field."

"Falling stones," Ned intones quietly.

"A man and a woman according to the boy," Henry says, "Not two women. Isn't that right?"

He turns to Ned, who keeps repeating 'falling stones.'

"That's what he said," Ezra intervenes, shielding Ned from both Henry and Manning, "We all heard, no need for him to repeat it."

"You can't rely on a poor simpleton, bewitched by two she devils!" Manning says, "They made him say anything to suit their devilish purposes."

Alice laughs, but it's strained and quickly cracks into a forced chuckle. Even from a confessed murderer it's a dangerous accusation and she looks nervously between the men. They stare silently. No one rebuts Manning's charge. However much they may have embraced the new freedoms, it's still too easy to label an eccentric, argumentative woman, blaming her as a witch for everything that can't be explained. Her eyes rest on Matthew. Stubborn, independent, sometimes obtuse, he revels in going out of his way to be different. A man not easily swayed except by the facts. He will listen.

"Ned is no more bewitched by me than you are by evil delusions. A man and a woman, he said and a simple boy does not lie or change his story however much he's bullied and cajoled."

She stamps her feet and turns a half circle to concentrate on Manning and Henry.

"Those that pranced and postured over us for generations with their fancy ways and fancy clothes, fooling us with their fancy tongues and fancy lawyers."

Thomas claps vigorously.

"Don't be afraid. We're not listening to false clamours from desperate men. Idle words come cheap. We'll know who to believe and it won't be those who've lied and cheated their way to riches. Go on, answer him!"

Alice looks to Matthew again, but he remains impassive. He'll need something definite, no more influenced by the bluster of Thomas Radbourne than that of Joseph Manning.

"There's your man and woman!" she says, pointing to Richard and Olivia, "Secret lovers threatening both families, discovered and condemned by Samuel Lexden and determined to silence him. Everything they did was deceitful, skulking in corners, hiding in bushes, creeping behind backs, denying each other, fleeing from..."

"It wasn't like that," Richard shouts, "we were..."

"Waiting your chance to strike back. Poor Sarah, the common servant, lower than you in everything except decency and true living. Knocked down Lexden, then ran away, the only way she could be free. Lexden wasn't dead, but you seized your chance and made sure he was. Then you carried him to the fields, dumped him in the hedge to make it look like he'd been struck down there. Poor foolish Sarah would get the blame. Sneaking and sliding, just as you'd lived, but you'd reckoned without another common soul, poor simple Ned who saw it all."

"But we weren't there," Richard shouts, turning to the others.

"You were, you were seen."

"It wasn't us," Olivia says, "and how can you believe Ned Frattersham, he ran away?"

"Another who ran away? Frightened out of his wits, he was running away from you. You killed Lexden and carried his body out the house."

"No, no," Manning shouts, "Olivia would never kill anyone."

"Why not, because she's a lady? And anyway, *he* could do it," Alice says, pointing to Richard.

"No," Henry says, "Richard's innocent, he's no murderer."

"You all oppress common folk like Ned, Sarah and myself while our betters like Olivia and Richard are capable of much greater villainy!"

Manning and Henry respond with equal invective.

"Shut them up," Matthew shouts above the uproar, but it's impossible and no one tries to curb Alice.

"Not just her, but Prudie Westrup, that damnable harridan," Manning screams.

"Shut your foul tongue before I cut it out," Ezra says, smacking him across the mouth.

Manning falls back and Ezra is ready to strike again, but Thomas stops him. Ezra quivers furiously in the sudden silence, then turns again to Manning.

"What have you done with Prudie?"

Manning shakes his head. Ezra turns to Matthew and mouths a silent 'where is she?' Matthew grimaces and looks around, only then noticing Constance is no longer with them.

Strangers walking along the bank might hardly notice where the river bends almost completely around itself. Even if they step onto the narrow spur that projects into the bend they will see only the middle of the river. The nearside edge is out of sight. For a quarter mile the banks rise abruptly as if shovelled by the boot of some passing giant or a clod dropped from his cart. The water swirls noisily making the stones in the riverbed appear to be falling. Many believe the 'falling stones' to be a waterfall, unknown in the whole county of Middlesex. Enclosed by the unyielding banks, accessible only by the narrowest crick of land on one side and completely impenetrable through the dense, barbed overgrowth of brambles and hawthorn on the other, the real 'falling stones' are known only to a few. In recent months its sinister mystery has been inflated as the meeting place for a coven of witches. They find their way down to the river by diabolical flight, free to carry out their foul practices undisturbed.

But the real and only way to the river is through a narrow, steep defile, passable with difficulty by one person at a time, its entrance almost completely hidden by bushes on top of the narrow spur. The wary intruder who ignores the 'false hole' and squirms down the cramped, slippery and perilous fissure emerges onto a wider, sandy but firm stretch, overhung by the bank above. At one end, cut off by the almost sheer side of the bank, the sandy floor extends a couple of feet inside, resulting in a small 'cave' of soil and roots.

With her back to this soily wall, Prudie has been waiting patiently for an hour, undetectable even from the far bank.

The water ripples noisily, but she listens for sounds in that narrow cranny through which any encroacher must come. The long wait has given her time to reflect on the wisdom of coming at all. Few may know this place, but those that do may bring others. She may be safely concealed under the bank, but the hideaway may be a trap rather than a refuge. The crack in the ground is not just the only way in, but also the only way out except for the river itself. She looks tentatively into the water and up the far bank with its bristling lattice of impervious stalk and stick. Could she get over the slippery stones and scramble up the bank? Could she penetrate the solid barrier at the top? She'd be bound to fall, crashing to the truly *falling* stones. No, the only possible escape is the river, but how far would she have to scramble and slither before reaching a secure bank? It's too late now. She didn't come for safety, but to resolve and confront. Those that meddle with forces beyond normal powers...

There's movement above. Someone is sliding, wriggling through the narrow gap. Someone careful, but not without confidence, who knows the hazards because they've been here before. Someone she's been expecting.

Manning is captured. Most of Thomas's men have returned with the constable and his prisoner. Olivia and Richard are also returning to the village under escort, despite their continual protestations of innocence.

"There are others," Matthew says darkly.

"Let them run," Thomas says, reluctant to believe Matthew when he says Manning did not murder Lexden.

"We haven't finished the job," Ezra says, "We need your help to find Prudie."

Thomas will recommence the search, though only a couple of men will join him and he's doubtful where to look.

"Ned keeps talking about the falling stones." Matthew says.

"Fanciful nonsense there's no such place."

"I have heard of the falling stones," Alice says, "and I always believe Ned."

Since Constance left she's been oddly silent, not even encouraging them to arrest Oliva and Richard despite her earlier accusations.

"So Prudie may be there?" Matthew says.

"It's possible," she says ambivalently, "She gave me a note to deliver to Constance Manning. She told me where Constance always walked at certain times of the day away from the house. I was to approach her when she was alone and give her the note. I was so afraid of being seen, I just thrust it into her hand and ran away."

"What did the note say?"

"*I know now. Will meet you at the usual place.*"

"So it could be the *falling stones*?"

"It's possible."

"But why would Prudie be meeting Constance?"

Alice puckers her lips and shakes her head.

Matthew considers for a moment, then says, "We have to find the *falling stones*."

"There's no such place," Thomas says, "It's just a silly tale picked up by fools like Ned."

"There *is* such a place," Alice says, "Ned wouldn't lie."

Matthew turns to Ned.

"Be careful with him," Alice says.

"Get it out of him," Ezra says, "We can't delay, we have to find Prudie."

Matthew tries to be gentle, as much as frustration allows.

"I seen 'em there." Ned repeats to every question.

"Who, who did you see?" Matthew says.

"Seen 'em there at the falling stones."

"Even if he did, he doesn't know where the place is," Thomas says.

Matthew persists. It's hard work, but eventually Ned concentrates on finding the place rather than what he 'seen there.' It starts to rain as they start out. They make slow progress, but it's not just the wet. Their only guide is erratic and easily confused. Thomas remains doubtful and Henry distrusts Ned and both keep complaining.

Constance stands in the middle of the sandy level, catching her breath after slipping painfully down the crevice.

"It's hard to get a grip after it's rained. I caught my hands trying not to fall."

Prudie is silent.

"You know I will always protect you," Constance says, "We need to protect each other."

"Assuming we both need protection," Prudie says, sitting in the half darkness of the concealed corner and studying Constance in the full light.

"Isn't that why you asked me here?"

Prudie doesn't reply. Constance continues.

"Joseph has confessed to drowning John Collver in London."

Prudie raises an eyebrow.

"So the long cold feud now burns."

"He mistook him for Henry, afraid of what Henry knows."

Prudie is perplexed. Constance explains about the firm, the fraud, the Collvers financial disaster.

"Such knowledge is worth killing for " Prudie says, "Yet it is nothing compared to knowledge of secret passions. Who knows them may have even more to fear."

"Samuel Lexden," Constance intones quietly as if she speaks of some vile insect, then with increasing volume, "He was a vicious man, taking delight in humiliating any weakness, whether in the body of a crippled old woman in the village or in the mind like Ned or...(not directly at Prudie)... someone who was different..."

"I was just myself."

"Ah yes," Constance sighs, looking wistfully towards the water, "being yourself...how difficult that is...has been...for some of us."

She stops for a moment, reconnecting her thoughts and then turns back to Prudie.

"They tried to hound you out of your house."

"Your family has always wanted my land."

"As have the Collvers," Constance adds defensively, then with a nervous smile at Prudie, "Lexden led that particular pack of hounds, but to his eternal shame he was encouraged and abetted by my husband."

"He didn't succeed."

"Because I protected you, curbed the worst excesses especially when you were accused of being a witch. I warned you to get away to the woods and when to return."

"I always wondered why."

Constance expects thanks rather than a further question. She doesn't respond, but steps along the small stretch, touches the walls of the bank and looks at the emptiness above the surface of the river, her eyes focusing on a thought or recollection rather than any physical presence.

"A safe, special place, to be one's self," she says, then turning back to Prudie, "We could always meet here, so few know it."

"Some think the 'falling stones' are only an old tale," Prudie says, "not a real place at all."

Constance turns back to the water, her eyes intent on the stones, her ears tuned to the rippling water. A brief instant of remembered intensity, a sudden cut and respite from present troubles into another almost forgotten reality. It soon passes.

"It's not the place you see, but the place you imagine, apart, untouched, where you can do different things, live a different life no one knows, no one can find out."

"But they always find out, don't they?"

Constance turns suddenly, her wide eyed intensity homing on Prudie.

"I can forgive what you've done. We've both learned to keep silent, we must continue to do so."

"Some say the 'falling stones' is the place of witches," Prudie says.

Constance laughs, then scowls, noticing Prudie's firm expression and unsure of her seriousness.

"The powers I used then I can use again," Prudie says, moving towards Constance, who steps back reflexively to the opening to the top of the bank.

"If you were involved in Lexden's murder, you would do well to..."

"Keep quiet about my special powers?"

Then they both start to a sound from the cranny. Someone is coming down.

Ezra complains. They have tramped the same track for twenty minutes. Matthew stops, spins Ned around and tries again to break through his vague directions.

"I know you're trying, but you do want us to find Prudie, don't you?"

"Oh yes, sir, yes, I know Mrs. Westrup she's lost and we need to..."

"We rely on you, Ned. You're a very important person because we believe she's at the 'falling stones' and only you know where that is."

"You *do* know, don't you?" Ezra says, emulating Matthew.

Matthew glares at him, shaking his head. Ezra shrugs and rolls his eyes in response.

"We're too far from the river," Thomas says, "If...*if* this place is at the river, then we need to get..."

"Alright, alright," Matthew says, waving him back as Ned shrinks away, "Now, Ned, I want you to think very carefully. Do you know the way to the river?"

Ned looks bewildered.

"River, the river...yes, yes, that's where the 'falling stones' are."

"Of course they are, Ned, good lad, you understand. Now, if we go towards the river. Do you understand? Which way is the river?"

Ned looks puzzled, then with a gleam of understanding he points away from the track.

"The river, yes sir, the river, over there."

"Good, good, show us the way."

Ned bounds at right angles and the others follow.

"Bloody kid hasn't got a clue," Thomas mumbles.

"Be quiet," Alice rebukes him, "He'll hear you. He'll get us there."

Ned now strides with renewed confidence.

"Not long," Mathew says, sensing Ezra's mounting impatience.

"We've lost a lot of time," Ezra says, "Too many messages to too many people. I'm not even sure Prudie will be at the 'falling stones."

"She'll be there, but who will she be with?"

Edward Amberley is a little dishevelled, but the speed of his descent from the top of the bank shows he's been here before.

"Is this her?" he says wagging his arm and staring truculently at Prudie, "The one they call a witch, what do they call her?"

Constance shivers. Still musing edgily on her 'powers,' she's reluctant even to mention Prudie's name.

"There's much to do," he says, "The King is on the march. I have what I need and must go north. London is a dangerous place now for a King's man. So many rumours, the truth may soon come out. I might already have been betrayed."

"You are a Royalist!" Prudie says in alarm and then to Constance, "Did you know this?"

"I do not understand these things, Prudie, politics is not my concern."

"But to follow the King when your husband is a Justice of the Peace. It is treachery."

"Be silent, witch! Since when have you been concerned for Joseph Manning's fortune?" Amberley shouts.

"I had no way to get a message through," Constance says, laying her hand on his arm, "I wasn't sure where you were."

"I've had to keep moving in the city."

"How did you know to come?"

"The wily captain Fletcher asked me help clear up the mystery," he says with a chuckle, "little realising he was inadvertently giving me the nod to escape. If a Parliamentary officer needs my help then it has to be time to move on, but I couldn't leave without you."

"They've taken Joseph."

"That makes things easier."

"He's confessed to killing John Collver."

He looks puzzled.

"He mistook him for Henry."

His smirk recedes.

"So, they're onto the firm."

"There's been so much conflict. Joseph against the Collvers, Olivia and Richard, both families against the tenants stirred up by Thomas Radbourne. You remember Sarah, his daughter?"

"Has he found her?"

"Yes...she's returned and..."

"She's been speaking?"

"Even worse Ned Frattersham has returned."

"Surely no one will listen to a dunderhead like him?"

"I got away in the confusion as they were taking Joseph."

"Then we are safe."

"I fear captain Fletcher *will* listen to Ned."

"No one knows this place."

"Except...her," Constance says, nodding to Prudie, "She sent me a note, asking to meet her here."

"How much does she know?"

"Enough."

"Then we can take no chances. No one knows she is here. We can silence her for good, then throw her in the river just as Joseph did with Collver. They call her a witch, even when she's found they'll assume she's perished from one of her own foul deeds. No one will question."

"Matthew Fletcher will, stories of witchcraft have never impressed him and he's very persistent."

"Then we must be away and after we've dealt with her."

"Oh, Edward, must it be?"

Amberley goes towards Prudie. She turns to the river, but Constance bars her way. She steps back until she feels the earth behind and cringes in the corner. Amberley pulls a knife from his coat and raises it, stepping closer to Prudie. Then he cries in pain. A stout, but short club is flung at his hand, knocking the knife away. He staggers and almost falls. Beyond him Prudie sees Ezra, his hand still high from the lob of the club. She leaps past Amberley and joins him. The small space fills with others, emerging from the crevice. Matthew, his leg somewhat stiff from his laborious descent, limps across to Amberley, prone on the ground, while Alice holds Constance. At the back, guarding the remote possibility of escape is Thomas.

"You are my prisoner," Matthew says, his boot locked on Amberley's arm, then he turns to Prudie, "Are you alright?"

She nods.

"You didn't tell us, we didn't know..."

"I had to be sure, it was the only way."

"We never heard you," Amberley says.

"That's 'cause we came down nice and easy," Ezra says, "quiet and careful, just like in town. What d'you take us for, country bumpkins?"

"How did you find us?" Constance says.

"Ned." Alice says.

Ezra turns angrily to Amberley.

"Trying to get rid of an inconvenience like you did with Lexden?"

"I don't know what you're talking about," Amberley says.

"You were going to put Prudie in the river," Matthew says, "Making it look like someone else was responsible. Just as you did with Lexden, taking his body out of the house to the fields."

"I don't know what..."

"Ned saw you both."

Amberley raises to a sitting position.

"You'd take the word of a simpleton?"

"I'll take the word of anybody who tells the truth."

"Exactly, as I said a simpleton."

"How many times have I heard that? He may be simple, he may be confused, but he doesn't lie. I believe him and so will twelve good men and true."

Still Amberley tries to dismiss both Ned and Matthew.

"I am only here today because you told me to come. I have no other connection with the area.

"Then why this particular place?"

"I was looking for you and then heard this lady in distress, threatened by this...witch."

Mathew almost laughs. Prudie and Alice make to move towards Amberley, but Matthew waves them back.

"Hold the *lady*," he says, then looks down again at Amberley, "I'm tired of that accusation. It won't do, Amberley. You knew this place, you've been here many times to meet Constance."

"I've told you, today..."

"You've been seen and not just by Ned Frattersham. He kept telling us he'd seen *them* at the falling stones. At last we took notice of what he said."

"You can't rely on him. Who else saw us?" Amberley says arrogantly.

"By me!" Thomas shouts.

"Sightings of you wandering around the village made me suspicious," Matthew says, "You appeared in London when I went to see Henry and I had to find out more. I had a head start with my contacts in the cloth trade, but there were many gaps. For a time I gave up. There were other matters to concentrate on. Then John Collver was killed and I had the same feeling I'd had about Lexden's murder. Nothing was what it seemed. John had to have been killed by mistake. Henry had to be the intended victim. That led me back to Joseph Manning and though all the pieces didn't yet fit, it reminded me of the fraud, the firm...you. Who was it you came to see in Harringstead? Then without realising it Prudie sent me off the track. Recognising another woman who'd also been desperate, she had every faith in you, Constance."

"You *knew*?" Constance says directly at Prudie.

"It drew me close. I'd always *felt* Joseph was not Olivia's father."

Constance whimpers softly. Prudie goes on.

"I told Matthew Lexden had nothing to do with you. You were a victim, like me."

"So I put my suspicions aside," Matthew continues, "but Ezra had been ferreting around, coming back with snippets of information from all over the city. Most were of no use, but one day he mentioned something about you, Amberley. Two separate pieces provided by Prudie and Ezra, each unknown to the other, but which suddenly fitted so well together. In earlier days you'd been a soldier. Like many a young man looking for adventure and glory, you went abroad to the

German war. You'd not come back for many a year and at home you were assumed dead. I got Ezra to get more precise dates and that clinched it. You went away around the time Olivia was born. It could be a coincidence, but it was worth pursuing."

"Oh no," Constance says, bowing down and clutching her stomach as if some awful pain has suddenly gripped her, "What could I do when no news came? I thought Edward was dead. Then Joseph approached me. I was desperate. He was so in earnest..."

"Did he know about Olivia?" Prudie says.

"He never asked and I never said, but deep down I believe he knew."

"The tension between Olivia and her father troubled me," Matthew says, "even allowing for her relationship with Richard. He would be angry. The pride of his family was at stake, but there was something more, a deeper, more personal pride, a wound from the past that was opening up again."

"Then Edward returned like a ghost," Constance says, "Out of that terrible war. If only I'd waited, if only I'd been patient."

"So you started seeing each other again?"

"Infrequently at first and of course in secret."

"Then you saw him more often and were less careful."

"We became more desperate...it was difficult...until we found this place."

"And that's when Lexden saw you?"

"Out one day spying on Olivia and Richard. Instead, he found us."

"He was an evil, despicable man," Amberley says.

"So much so that he deserved to die?" Matthew says.

"He wasn't content to make Olivia's life a misery," Constance replies angrily, "After Lexden saw us he threatened to tell Joseph unless..."

"He wanted money?"

"Not money...favours."

"God in heaven," Amberley cries, "You never told me this, Constance. You said...was he not content with the serving maid?"

334

"Evidently not," Matthew says.

"Lower than a rat in the ditch."

"So you saw him knocked down by Sarah and took your chance."

"I didn't kill Lexden," Amberley protests.

"No. You moved the body, but you didn't kill him," Matthew says, then turning to Constance, "You did!"

"No, no! It was...an accident..." Amberley cries, but Constance cuts him off.

"No, Edward. It's no use. I heard the scuffle in the kitchen. When I came in, Sarah had gone and I guessed what had happened. The worm was lying there, unconscious, but alive. What else could I do? Surely injured vermin should be quickly dispatched? Then Edward came and we moved his body."

A week later Matthew, Ezra and Prudie are sitting in his sister's house with Elizabeth and Edmund.

"The King's army was totally routed at a place called Naseby," Edmund says, "A great victory. Justice and order will soon be restored, a newer brighter, freer time."

"Aye, but where is the King?" Ezra says doubtfully.

"Our soldiers discovered incriminating papers in the King's baggage," Edmund goes on, "It shows he's been intriguing with foreign powers for years. It's all in a pamphlet called *The King's Cabinet Opened.*"

Ezra grunts an insulting expletive.

"He will come to his senses," Matthew says, "and this damnable war will end."

"Henry Fenwick has disappeared," Edmund says, "He ran out of town quicker than Prince Rupert's cavalry from Naseby!"

"But what of Hugh Crittenden?" Matthew says.

"Not seen since he released Ezra."

"If only we could help," Matthew says.

They fall silent for a time, then Elizabeth says, "I have others news. William Harmsworth has died."

"Jane's husband?" Matthew says, "What will she do?"

"The house in Cheapside is boarded up. I don't even know if she's still there."

335

"Jane, a widow," he says quietly and then with new expectation in his voice, "I should try to see her."

Elizabeth lays a hand on his arm.

"Caution, Matthew, give her time. You don't know how much has changed."

Then she turns to Prudie.

"What news from Harringstead?"

"Henry Collver has left Richard at Aspenfield. He and Olivia are to live there. Henry has already returned to London and wants no part of affairs at Harringstead though he's instructed Richard to reach agreement with the tenants. Thomas is already involved. There may be peace in the village now."

"What of Syme House?"

"Some of the servants remain, but for how much longer I don't know. They say the two estates are to be amalgamated."

"Just leaving your own land between them?"

"No, I am selling up to Henry."

"This is a sudden decision. You're not returning to Harringstead?"

"It's not a place for me anymore."

Ezra snorts dismissively.

"Don't give up too easily. Within a few weeks the place will be as nothing happened with Manning and the rest. In months it'll be as if there's not even been a war. That's folk for you, they forget those that helped them as they take profit from their new life."

"I'll not give up easily. I have new friends now. You're probably right about the place, but as for people...I'm for a new life. If Matthew is right, there'll be opportunities after the war. I shall take to the road for a while, selling whatever I can or dispensing relief to the afflicted with my *special powers*."

They all laugh.

"What about you, Ezra?" Elizabeth says.

He lights his pipe, takes a long deep pull then, handing it to Prudie says, "Like I said, everything changes and everything stays the same. I'll do what I've always done, a bit of this, a bit of that."

They laugh again, interrupted by three sharp raps on the door. Edmund looks to Elizabeth.

"I'm expecting no one," she says.

Edmund opens the door and a dishevelled young man steps in.

"Hugh!" Matthew cries.

"I have nowhere else to go," Hugh says, twisting his hat in his hand, "I wondered if I might stay a few days?"

"Was it you that arranged for my message to reach Matthew?" Elizabeth says.

"Yes, it was me."

"Then come in. You are welcome to stay as long as you need!"

"Is Fenwick after you?" Ezra says.

"He was, that's why I had to leave London. He followed me, but now *he* is hunted."

"And rightly so. I never had a chance to..."

Hugh waves Ezra's thanks aside.

"It was my duty."

"But what happened? When I left you in Harringstead..."

"I said foolish things and they were misinterpreted. I became an unwitting creature of Fenwick."

"I cursed you lieutenant. I have misjudged you."

"No, Matthew. It is I that misjudged you and if you are asked again to undertake an investigation, I would be honoured to serve you, if you will have me."

"With pleasure, though I'm not immediately seeking an assignment like the last! Now, this calls for another cask of ale!"

Elizabeth goes out and Matthew helps her, but stays in the yard when she returns to the house saying he'll join her soon. He looks out across the myriad of roofs, chimneys and spires, happy to be alive with everyone he holds dear, the group now complete with Hugh. The day is almost over and the city's last clamouring cries die down with the setting sun. For a few moments the sky flames with the last fiery orange streaks and then is gone. He wonders about the new day and those that follow and whether this land will at last find some peace.

Cross Cut

ISBN 978-0-9557928-0-9

"All darkness now. Silence, then the sounds again, scratching, voices. Someone is close, very close as if they're breaking through to him..."

Where is Bernard Weston? Is he dead or alive? How is his disappearance connected to the campaign to reopen the brooding and abandoned Cross Cut canal?

For Detective Chief Inspector Jenner a routine missing person enquiry quickly turns into something more sinister with the present dislocated against the turbulent background of 1840s Nottingham. Trusting his instincts as much to reason and logic and teaming up with Ettie Rodway with her psychic insight, he's forced to adopt unconventional methods. Combining their skills of intuition and deduction produces a powerful partnership, but this is stretched to breaking point as they try to avert disaster.

Looming ominously throughout this tense thriller is the foreboding atmosphere of the canal with its shrouded secrets and the fearful power of its tunnel to reach across time.

Can Jenner trust his gut feelings and take a path he's reluctant to go down? How much can Ettie risk her own safety to help him? Can they unravel the crime only in the present or must they step into the past?

Cross Cut is historical novel meets thriller, ricocheting through time, keeping the reader guessing to the end with its dark alleys, riots, foreboding tunnels and caves, gaslit docksides, terrifying train journeys and nerve racing pursuits across town and country, vividly recreating the desperate world of the past.

Out of Time

ISBN 978-0-9557928-1-6

"...a tall angular figure appears, dressed all in black with sharp penetrating eyes, a long nose and short black hair ... she flies around the whole circle, accompanied by the ear splitting clamour of the birds and the whoosh of her black cloak, pointing her finger in menacing jabs..."

International financier Sarah Layman wants to discuss a 'mystery' with freelance journalist Carla Diemer, which has nothing to do with finance. Carla arrives to find Sarah dead and is immediately embroiled in a murder investigation led by the dogged Chief Inspector Jenner.

Carla links up with psychic investigator Ettie Rodway, who has also been approached by Sarah. Joining them is a maverick historian, obsessed with a lost Anglo Saxon Chronicle and Carla's dubiously motivated father. Their perilous search of revenge, discovery and intrigue spans 1200 years, from the perilous wetlands of eastern England to the shrouded hills of the west and even to America, pitting them against forces of power, greed and deception.

From the 9th century they must find a ring, a sword, a brooch and a belt, which can solve the mystery, but also unlock immense unpredictable powers, sweeping them into the swirling currents of a distant age where fearsome warriors fight out their bloody inter family feud. Confronted by ruthless adversaries intent on the same discovery further deaths follow, the hunters become the hunted and they realise the Chronicle is much more than an obscure historical document.

A riveting quest, combining mystery, thriller, detection, historical drama and the interplay of past and present, Out of Time unravels against this tense atmosphere, penetrating to the heart of origins and identities in which friend and foe are difficult to disentangle. Once the past's magical powers are invoked, all the pieces have to be fitted together against a frightful deadline in which Time could itself be the ultimate victim.

...only those that dream can return from the far journey...